Praise for Kathryne Kennedy's fantasy romance:

"Fast-paced, elegantly written romance."

—*Fresh Fiction*

"Quality writing full of heart, adventure, and a world that will astound a reader with its vivid imagery."

—*The Long and the Short of It Reviews*

"Incredible, amazing, fantastic world building… I can't wait to see more from this incredibly talented author."

—*RomFan Reviews*

"You get it all when you read Kathryne Kennedy. It's magic at its best."

—*The Good, the Bad, and the Unread*

"With dazzling descriptions, nonstop action, and searing romance, Kathryne Kennedy thrusts you headlong into an extraordinary world brimming with wonders and treachery."

—*Linda Banche Romance Author*

"A delightfully entertaining blend of fast-paced action and tender emotion, interspersed with plenty of humor and breathtaking intrigue… All of the elements I've come to expect from Kathryne Kennedy."

—*CK2S Kwips and Kritiques*

"Kathryne Kennedy brings amazing depictions and unique characters to any reader's world."

—*Coffee Time Romance*

THE LADY OF THE STORM

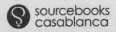

Published by Sourcebooks Casablanca, an imprint of Sourcebooks, Inc.
P.O. Box 4410, Naperville, Illinois 60567-4410
(630) 961-3900
FAX: (630) 961-2168
www.sourcebooks.com

Printed and bound in the United States of America
QW 10 9 8 7 6 5 4 3 2 1

◦◦◦

The link between the world of man and Elfhame had sundered long ago, the elven people and their magic fading to legend. Tall beings of extraordinary beauty, the fae preferred a world of peace. But seven elves—considered mad by their own people—longed for power and war. They stole sacred magical scepters, created their dragon-steeds, and opened the gate to the realm of man again and flew through.

Each elf carved a sovereign land within England, replacing the baronies that had so recently been formed by William the Conqueror. They acquired willing and unwilling slaves to serve in their palaces and till their lands. And fight their wars. Like mythical gods they set armies of humans against each other, battling for the right to win the king, who'd become nothing more than a trophy. They bred with their human slaves, producing children to become champions of their war games.

The elven lords maintained a unified pact, using the scepters in a united will to place a barrier around England, with only a few guarded borders open to commerce. Elven magic provided unique goods and the world turned a blind eye to the plight of the people, persuaded by greed to leave England to its own, as long as the elven did not seek to expand their rule into neighboring lands.

But many of the English people formed a secret rebellion to fight their oppressors. Some of the elven's children considered themselves human despite their foreign blood and joined the cause. And over the centuries these half-breeds became their only hope.

One

GILES BEAUMONT HEARD THE SOUND OF BATTLE COMING from beyond the rocks in the direction of the village at the same moment Cecily emerged from the waves of the English Channel. His magically cursed sword flew from its scabbard, smacked the palm of his hand, and it took every ounce of Giles's considerable strength to shove it back into the leather sheath. As much as his blade longed to be finally used, the years of training to protect the young woman held firm and he ran away from the village to the beach.

He'd removed his stockings and half jackboots after the first hour of waiting for Cecily, and now his toes dug through the hot sand while broken seashells stabbed his heels. But the elven blood that ran through his veins allowed him to reach the tide line soon enough, his feet now slapping on wet sand, the spray of the crashing waves cooling his face, the ocean breeze billowing open his half-buttoned shirt with even more welcome relief.

He kept his gaze fixed on naught but her.

Cecily Sutton, half-breed daughter of the Imperial Lord Breden, elven lord of the sovereignty of Dewhame, did not look like a direct descendant of the elven royal line. At least, not at the moment. She had one arm wrapped around the fin of a dolphin, the creature propelling her through the water at wicked speed. Her black hair gleamed in the sunlight, her luscious mouth hung wide open with laughter, and she'd half-closed her eyes against the spray of flight.

A wild magical woman, indeed. A mysterious creature whom he'd been assigned to protect since she was nine years old—and Giles himself only fifteen—in hopes that she would be of use to the Rebellion some day. But a daughter of those cold, reserved elven lords? No, she did not fit that mold.

She swam by herself the rest of the way to the shore, with a wave and a last caress for her dolphin-steed. Her magical affinity for the water made her look one with it, her swimming near effortless as she crossed the final distance to the beach. Giles waited for her, waves lapping about his ankles, watching as her eyes grew round with surprise when she recognized him. With her large inhuman eyes, he could not deny her birthright to the elven lord. They glittered in the sunshine, twin jewels of blue, with a crystalline depth that bespoke the enormous power the young woman could summon.

Although she'd managed to keep that power well hidden through the years.

"What are you doing here?" she said, her gaze flicking away from him to stare at her abandoned clothing on the beach. Cecily kept her body hidden in the water, but the motion of the waves occasionally revealed the swell of her breasts. Giles made sure his gaze stayed fixed on her face, but despite his efforts to appear unaffected by her nudity, the warmth of a flush crept over his cheeks.

For he'd been ordered to protect her but keep his distance. Thomas had warned him that the girl was destined to marry a great lord. And in more subtle terms, that Giles would never be good enough for her. So by necessity he had spied upon her from a distance for years. Many times he had damned her for her magical affinity to water, for scarcely a day went by without her sneaking off to this private cove where she stripped and flung herself into the ocean. Perforce he'd watched her body develop from skinny youth into the full curvature of womanhood.

Now her curves rivaled those of any woman he'd bedded; indeed, once she'd matured, he would often dream of those perfect features while he made love to one girl after another.

Many times he had fancied himself in love with one of the village maidens. For a time he would feel relieved that he had been able to put the forbidden girl from his thoughts. But thoughts of Cecily would always intrude yet again. He would find himself comparing those vivid blue eyes, that heart-shaped brow, the lilt of her laughter, with every girl he met. And would find himself dreaming of her once again, chiding himself for a fool.

"There's something wrong in the village," he managed to say. "I want you to stay hidden in the water until I return."

As usual, she avoided looking into his eyes, her gaze fixed somewhere around his nose. "How did you know I'd be here? How did you manage to climb the rocks? No one knows about my secret place—" A more urgent question suddenly halted her flow of indignation. "Has Thomas returned?"

He shook his head. "No, but I fear that your father may have something to do with it."

"With what? What is happening?"

"I'm not sure, and I don't have time for this. Just stay here!"

Giles spun, raced back to his hiding place, struggling damp skin into woolen hose, sandy cloth into leather boots. He pulled his sword from the scabbard, the greedy thing ringing with delight, eager for the taste of the blood Giles had denied it for so many years.

A thrill went through him from hilt to hand and he fought it with a clench of his muscles. "You devil," he murmured. "If I could have gotten rid of you, I would have. Father's gift or no."

The sword answered him with a tug in the direction of the village, where the sounds of battle had grown louder. Giles took one last glance over his shoulder...

The little hoyden had ignored him. Cecily stood next to her clothing, her net with her day's catch abandoned in shallow water, flopping fish and scuttling crabs quickly making their way back to ocean. Giles would have cursed if he'd had the wits to, but the sight of her bending over to pick up her chemise near knocked the power of speech completely from his head.

He sprinted back to the water, his sword resisting him all the way. Giles should have known she wouldn't listen to him. She treated him like all the villagers did, as if he had nothing between his muscled shoulders but his fine elven features. He had carefully cultivated that impression of course, assuming the quiet manner of a humble blacksmith, in spite of how much he despised the role. But Cecily's attitude had surpassed his assumed disguise. After the night she offered herself to him and he gallantly refused her, she'd avoided him with a disdain that bordered on contempt.

By the time he reached her side Cecily had pulled on her chemise, struggled into her stays. Her fingers fastened up the front-lacing stays most working women wore, and she pulled on her jacket and skirt without benefit of her quilted petticoat.

Giles found it easier to speak once she'd covered that glorious body. "I told you to stay in the water."

She did not answer, pulling on stockings and shoes.

Not for the first time, he mentally cursed the task of having to protect this young woman. "I cannot keep you safe while fighting."

She straightened, her eyes widening at that. "Why would you care—what in heaven's name is wrong with your sword?"

The damned blade kept twisting his arm around, pointing at the village like a dog scenting a hare. Giles's boots began to slide across the sand, little furrows left in his wake. "It smells blood—"

She flew past him in a blur of black hair and linsey-woolsey skirts. Giles blinked then followed. He'd forgotten she shared the speed elven blood could provide; indeed, it ran even stronger through her veins than his. But his eager sword aided his flight and he managed to catch up with her at the top of the rise. He threw an arm about her waist, managed to drag her and his sword behind an outcropping of rock.

Despite years of watching over her, he had never dared touch her before and the shock of it took him by surprise. A thrill ran through him and for a moment he could only stare speechlessly at her.

Before he lost himself completely in the crystal blue of her eyes, she lowered her gaze. "Let me go."

"Not until you promise me you'll stay here."

The sound of gunfire drifted up to their perch and Giles fought against more than just his sword arm to seek out the source.

"I do not know why you have this sudden concern for me, sir, but I assure you—"

"How many more will die while you argue with me?"

Her mouth snapped shut, those eyes sparkling with uncanny brilliance. "I will stay."

"This time you will promise."

"I promise. Now go!"

Giles leaped to his feet, racing down the other side of the rise toward the village. He kept his attention on the scene before him, praying he judged her rightly, that the lady would keep her word, for he knew her life held more value than a village of peasants, and leaving her alone to fend for herself went against everything he'd been sworn to do. But the villagers had become his friends, and in good conscience he could not forsake them.

Smoke curled up from beyond the trees. The sound of steel ringing against steel grew louder until the way opened up before him, revealing the village clearing.

Soldiers wearing the blue livery of the Imperial Lord fought against peasants in their coarse wool clothing. But Giles had made sure every man had a blade from his forge, and despite their ragged appearance, the villagers' weapons had a quality that surpassed the common soldiers'. They held their own.

The devil-blade sang in his hand and plunged him into the fray.

For the next few moments Giles could do naught but concentrate on keeping the hilt in his fist. One blue uniform went down, then another, warm blood splattering his face, gore dripping down the front of his chest. Giles had always longed for battle but he did not relish death like his sword did. It thirstily sought out one enemy after another until nothing but dead bodies surrounded him.

Fortunately, the villagers stayed clear of his blade.

It appeared that most of the soldiers had discharged their muskets and probably hadn't the time to reload them before the villagers fell upon them, because no shots rang out as they had earlier. But the back of his neck suddenly itched. Giles turned to meet the furious glare of a uniformed man across the clearing. The soldier raised his gun and took aim at Giles—the village blacksmith who had taken down so many of his fellows.

He heard Old Man Hugh cry out a warning, saw the fisherman lunge for the soldier, but the shot rang out before his friend could reach the musket. And time slowed. With a curse Giles wrested control of his sword, which had now drunk enough blood to allow such impudence, and thrust the weapon in front of him, catching the edge of the bullet with the slightly wider bottom of the blade, diverting it away from him.

If Giles had ever doubted the enchantment of his sword, the lack of any nick in the steel now confirmed it. He did not credit his blade for saving his life—his elven blood gave him more than a handsome face and pointed ears. His strength and speed rivaled that of a mere projectile.

Hugh plunged his blade into the soldier who had fired his musket. The officer didn't even appear to notice at first, his ruddy face frozen in sheer incredulity at Giles.

But fall he did, joining the rest of his fellows. Giles regained his breath while he wiped his blade on the uniform of the last enemy, and returned Hugh's sad smile of victory.

A sudden quiet descended on the once-pretty little village, broken only by the crackling of burning thatch, the sobs of grieving women. Dead bodies defiled the town fountain, had turned the water a sickly pinkish hue. Giles winced at the number of villagers who lay alongside the soldiers that littered the clearing, but many more of them still stood. They had won. Blood-spattered and weary, the fighters gathered together around Giles, slapping each other's backs. Celebrating the fact that they still lived.

But Giles suddenly hushed them, his pointed ears cocked toward a faint rumble of sound. Soon the few other villagers who possessed a bit of elven blood— and therefore a keener sense of hearing—joined him in quieting the rest.

Up the road that led inland came a cloud of dust,

the pounding of hooves. Giles did not need to see their uniforms to know more soldiers were coming. Hugh gave him a look of surprise while several of the younger men cursed in dismay. He knew what they were thinking. For years upon years Imperial Lord Breden of Dewhame had left this village alone. While other towns had lost their young men to the raising of Breden's new army, they had been left in peace to farm, raise families, and grow old.

"Why have they suddenly come for us?" asked William the shepherd.

Giles already knew the answer to that. Thomas had been gone too long. The Rebellion's most skilled spy had crafted a spell about the village to hide it, and the enchantment must have faded in his prolonged absence. Although the villagers had benefited from it, Thomas had cast it to protect his adopted daughter, to hide her from her true father, Breden, the Imperial Lord of Dewhame. And Giles could not speak of it. "What started this skirmish? You know what happens to villages that refuse the draft—have you become so arrogant, then?"

"Damn it, Giles!" sputtered William, his freckled face near purple. "Ye know I've been longing to join the wars, as stupid as they be! 'Tis the only way a lad can gain some glory, leastways." Several of the younger men grunted in agreement. "We woulda' gone with 'em with nary a fuss, but they took it upon their brutish hides to feel up the skirts of our women. Are ye thinking we shoulda' let them?"

"No, you did right," replied Giles, knowing the soldiers had gotten much more than they'd bargained for. Most villages had already been stripped of their fighting men for the wars; only children or old men were usually left to protect their families. "But I'm thinking that when the rest of the troops get here, we allow Old Hugh to explain what happened to avoid more bloodshed—"

The fountain suddenly erupted, pink arcs of water splashing against the still smoldering thatch of the roofs and the timbers of the cottages.

Cecily.

She walked toward them, her blue eyes gazing about the ruined village with a fury Giles had never seen the likes of before. The men surrounding him muttered a prayer under their breath at the power she so casually wielded, her fingers but flicking at the water to divert it until the fires were completely extinguished. Even the few villagers who had enough elven blood to possess a bit of magic crossed themselves. For they had only a little, since the elven lords destroyed all half-breeds who might possess enough power to be a threat to their rule.

Like Giles's younger brother, John, who commanded enough magic at the age of six to help their father craft the devil-sword, a weapon more powerful than the sovereignty of Bladehame had produced in centuries.

And like Cecily.

She had never displayed such power before; indeed, Giles had thought Thomas might have found a way to suppress it in her. To better hide her. But he had never seen her this furious before, either. She'd never had a reason to be, in the idyllic little village life they'd led, safe from the horrors of the rest of their enslaved England.

And the full import of what had happened struck Giles. The soldiers could find her now.

When Giles had been assigned the task of protecting the girl he'd been naught but a headstrong lad determined to join the Rebellion that would free England of the elven lords who had invaded their land... and killed his father and brother. But after years of working the forge and feeling like nothing more than a glorified bodyguard—even if he enjoyed watching Cecily more than he should—when he longed to *fight* for freedom...

Ah, but Thomas had insisted Cecily could be the Rebellion's greatest weapon, that Giles's task held more importance than he knew. That Thomas himself could not leave the girl and do his important work for the Rebellion without knowing someone would protect her in his absence.

Giles had pleaded with Thomas to be assigned another mission. A small task even, just so he would be able to shed this disguise of a thickheaded village blacksmith, if only for a few days. But Thomas denied him, and each time Giles grew more restless and frustrated, suppressing his feelings as surely as Cecily hid her magic. For Thomas insisted that one day Giles would be needed to protect his adopted daughter. That Giles was the only man Thomas would trust in that task.

This must have been the moment Thomas feared. When he would be unable to return to watch over Cecily.

Thomas must be dead, or he would have come home. And now, Giles had full responsibility for the Rebellion's treasured weapon. And a part of him did not regret that the day for action had finally come.

"I did not break my promise," said Cecily. "I did not come until the fighting stopped."

Giles nodded. He thought she would keep her word—that's why he'd forced her to give it. Fie, he probably knew more about the lady than she knew about herself, after constantly keeping her in his sight for the past nine years.

He prided himself on the fact that she hadn't been aware of his scrutiny.

"There are more soldiers coming." Giles glanced over his shoulder at the rapidly approaching dust cloud. "Go back to the water and stay beneath it until I come for you."

Her raven brows rose at that. "Your sudden concern for me is… mystifying, but there are others here—"

He grabbed her arm. The second time he'd touched her. And that same shock of excitement went through him. "No one is more important than you are; do you understand?"

Old Man Hugh made a choking sound and William, who'd been sweet on Cecily since they were children, took a step forward. "Now see here, Giles, if anyone be protecting Cecily, it'll be me. Don't think the number of men ye killed here today gives ye any rights to be bossing around—"

Giles grabbed the smaller man by his dirty collar and lifted him off his feet. In addition to his elven strength, he'd been pumping bellows for years to work off his frustration and had the muscles to prove it. "She's not meant for the likes of you, William, so let it be."

The younger man's face paled until his freckles stood out in stark relief. Giles carefully set him back on his feet. He'd watched William moon after Cecily for years and for some reason it had irritated the hell out of him. With the aftermath of battle and the threat of another, Giles had allowed his hidden feelings to surface. He needed to rein in his control.

Cecily stood there, with eyes wide and mouth hanging open, staring at Giles as if she'd never seen him before, rather than almost every day of her young life. For a change, she looked straight into his eyes.

The world suddenly appeared to come to a stop, and Giles could no more tear his gaze away from hers than he could tear out his heart. Cecily appeared equally transfixed. They might have stood there enthralled with each other, if not for Eleanor Sutton.

The frail woman staggered into the clearing, clutching at her chest, her face black with soot. "Cecily!"

She wrenched her gaze away from Giles and turned. "Mother!" Cecily ran to the older woman's side, clasping the thin hands in hers. "Are you all right?"

Eleanor coughed, an affliction she'd had for years, but which seemed to have worsened since her husband's disappearance. "The smoke—the fire destroyed half of our little cottage, Cecily. The one Thomas built with his own two hands."

"Mother, I'm so sorry." Cecily turned back to Giles, the expression on her face now completely altered. "You shouldn't have made me promise! She needed my help."

The older woman collapsed at her daughter's feet. Giles took a step toward them, but Hugh spat and said, "Stand firm, boys."

Giles spun back around to face Breden of Dewhame's

soldiers. Hundreds of them. He wondered what had brought them out in such force. Thomas had been his only source of information from the outside world, and he'd been gone for nearly a year. But he'd gone on assignments for months before, and Giles had expected him to return any day.

It suddenly occurred to Giles that he might be wrong about the failure of the spell surrounding the village. Perhaps Thomas had been found out. Interrogated with elven magic. Perhaps he'd given away Cecily's location to Breden of Dewhame. And his army had been sent here to capture her.

To hell with Hugh trying to reason with the soldiers. Giles couldn't risk it.

With a roar he leaped forward, sword aloft and singing with glee, decapitating the mounted officer before the man's body realized it, swinging around to kill another while the first slowly slid off his horse. The rest of the villagers had apparently forgotten his suggestion as well, for without hesitation they joined the melee, destroying the mounted officers before the soldiers on foot behind them could even get a shot off.

But the enemy rallied soon enough, firing at the villagers with abandon.

Giles took a bullet in the shoulder. He barely noticed. He had complete control of his devil-sword this time, and it flew in dizzying arcs, slicing through anyone foolish enough to get close enough.

They kept coming anyway.

Until he walked on bodies to reach the next group of fighters, saving his fellow villagers time and again.

But it would not be enough.

There were too many soldiers this time.

Screams of fury and agony surrounded him. The sharp scent of blood filled his nostrils. Betimes a red haze covered his eyes until he could barely see. Battle was not all he had dreamed of. The reality of it twisted his gut, brought a bitter taste to his mouth. Giles's blade hummed with happiness while he regretted the death of each man he killed, trying not to think of the widows he created today.

Magic bit at him more than once—a pool of water threatening to trip him up, a liquid flail that sliced across his chest like a knife, ripping through linen and skin.

There must have been a few soldiers from other sovereignties as well, for fire magic from Firehame licked at his breeches. Giles fought an illusory Cyclops created from Dreamhame, and he even met the steel of another enchanted sword crafted in Bladehame. But none of the paltry spells could overcome his devil of a sword. It dissolved the flail, quenched the fire, cut through the illusion, and shattered the other blade.

Through it all, Giles knew he fought a losing battle. But he would not allow despair or regret to make him falter, for not once did he forget the reason he fought. And after nine years of his life revolving around one slip of a woman, he did not allow his awareness of her to waver.

And so. When she approached the circle of fighting he felt her. He cursed, took one dangerous glance behind him, cursed again. That quick glance revealed Eleanor's lifeless body behind her, Cecily's furious blue eyes sparkling like sentient jewels as she strode toward the fray. Giles gathered all the elven strength he possessed and jumped, landing lithely in front of her, effectively stopping her advance. His sword danced a pattern around her, warning anyone foolish enough to approach the woman to stay clear.

"Get out of my way," she growled.

"The hell I will."

"You cannot defeat them all. I can."

She could. Giles could hear it in her voice. She might even be the villagers' only hope of surviving this battle. But then what? For the past nine years she'd hidden the true strength of her magic. And Giles had to consider every possibility. If he was wrong about Thomas being captured, and the elven lord *didn't* know about Cecily's existence… word of this battle would spread quickly to Dewhame Palace. Breden would know one of his elven bastards had enough magic to threaten his rule.

They would hunt her down like a rabid fox. He wouldn't be able to keep her safe.

"No," he finally said. "When I say the word, you will run. Find a horse. Ride away from here as fast as you can. Go to Firehame Palace—ask for the Prime Minister, Sir Robert Walpole—tell him you are Thomas's daughter."

"The hell I will."

She'd thrown his words right back at him. Damn if he could not stop the smile that cracked his face.

"If you don't get out of my way," she continued, "I shall have to go through you."

And she would.

He'd admired her growing beauty for years, but this was the first time he admired her strength of character.

Giles stepped out of her path but stayed near, protecting her back. For even the most powerful sorceress could be felled by a bullet or a blade.

A pile of bodies lay between them and the remaining fighters. Cecily's uncannily brilliant eyes narrowed at the sight, her lips tightening with resolve. Giles could feel her call to the magic in her blood, could hear the distant sound of the waves which constantly crashed against the shore grow more furious by the second, could sense the multitude of ponds and lakes that surrounded the village rise up into pillars of whirling dervishes.

Giles had known of Cecily's command of water but he'd never felt the complete force of it until now. Thomas had once told him she also commanded the more dangerous elements of the sky, that he'd seen her use a storm to defend them long ago. But the consequences of her actions had made Cecily turn her back on most of her magic, and Thomas had allowed it for his own reasons. If she called down her sky magic now, Breden of Dewhame would know that he dealt with more than an ordinary half-breed. That the daughter he'd let slip through his grasp still survived.

For only Breden could command the power of sky. Even his general, Owen Fletcher, reputed for his magical abilities—and more quietly—his perversions of that power, could not summon the tiniest of rainstorms.

Giles glanced up at the sky, still blue and soft with clouds, and breathed a sigh of relief. Perhaps Cecily's aversion to using that gift still ruled her.

But the power she commanded from earthbound water was impressive enough. The young woman

who stood next to him radiated enough magical resonance to make the hair on the back of his neck stand
up. And her head barely topped his shoulders.

Spears of liquid raced from ocean and pond,
swirling in columns of water to create a density strong
enough to wrap around the soldiers of Breden's
army. Saltwater tangled about their boots; pond water
circled their arms and muskets. At first it soaked their
clothing, the bloody dirt beneath them, but more
water arced toward them until it surrounded them in
a cyclone that had the strength to lift them off their
feet. Their screams were muffled behind the silvery
sheen of liquid.

Two of the officers possessed magical abilities and
they managed to break free of their watery traps. Five
other soldiers wielded swords that must have been
crafted in Bladehame, for they sliced through their
cyclones, trying to cut the tendrils that led to their
fellows. But they did not wield a devil-blade like Giles's,
and Cecily's power overwhelmed such puny strength.
Soon they were trapped like most of their fellows.

The villagers gaped at the maelstrom around them
for a few moments but soon began a retreat toward
Cecily. The officers who remained free followed them
with a yell of defiance. Giles resisted the impulse to
leap forward and engage them in combat, his mission
to protect Cecily keeping him by the half-breed's side.

Her hands moved in a pattern that followed the
swirling motion of the water. Those jewel-like elven
eyes barely blinked, the blue irises glazed with some
emotion Giles could only guess at. What would it feel
like to wield such power?

His devil of a sword thrummed in his hand, reminding him that he did indeed possess a similar gift, although not one he would have chosen. Unlike the inferior swords of the officers, Giles's blade could withstand almost any magical spell. Cecily would find it nearly impossible to entrap him with her powers. Giles suspected his sword might even surprise an elven lord bereft of a scepter.

The villagers ran past Cecily. Giles cursed. They had brought the officers right to them. He swung his blade in a warning pass and the closest soldier came to an abrupt stop. Seemingly unaware of the danger, Cecily continued to weave her magic with her hands. She lifted her palms to the sky, raised them above her head. The cyclones surrounding the trapped officers rose in unison, drifted toward the ocean. Cecily turned to watch her creations, and as each one reached a point that Giles judged to be over deep water, she made a fist then quickly splayed her fingers. The cyclone disintegrated into thousands of droplets, releasing the man trapped inside to plunge downward with a scream of terror that Giles heard even from this distance.

He could not determine if they would survive the fall.

The officer who had halted a few paces beyond where they stood narrowed his eyes at Cecily's hands, suddenly threw back his head and screamed, "To me, men! To me!"

Giles did not wait for anyone to answer that cry. He lunged forward, forcing the other man to raise his sword in defense, and with a spin of his wrist and a twist, he quickly disarmed the officer and ran him through. Giles risked a brief glance around as the man fell to his knees, but none of his troops remained to answer his call.

Old Man Hugh stood over the other officer's body, one bare foot of gnarly toes placed firmly on the back of the blue uniform. He gave Giles a crooked grin as Giles yanked his sword free of the fallen man and half-turned toward Cecily. But Hugh's eyes widened and Giles turned back just in time to see a pistol pointed at her. He had no time to consider if it had already been discharged or gotten water-soaked. He removed the arm from the soldier who pointed the barrel at the Rebellion's coveted treasure.

Despite the horrors Cecily had witnessed already, or perhaps because of it, a sob of dismay ripped from her throat as the severed appendage flew through the air. Giles turned, his chest contracting for a moment at the expression on Cecily's face. The dreamy haze had faded from those blue eyes and now each individual facet sparkled with hypnotizing flashes.

"How could you do that?" she demanded.

"I had to." Giles bent down and cleaned his hands on a blue coat. "He would have shot you."

Cecily waved her hands wildly about her. "I cannot believe this is happening." With a sudden slash of her arms, a curve of water arced over their heads to crash onto the bloody battle site, washing it clean before curling upwards and returning to wherever it had come from. The surviving villagers released a gasp of terror despite the cyclones she'd already conjured, and as one, they backed away from her.

Giles stood, shoved his sword back into his scabbard. Or at least, he tried to. The damn blade resisted and nudged the tip away from the opening, causing Giles to nearly impale his own boot. Faith, not only did he have to endure the hysterics of the battle-scarred young woman, but he couldn't even manage to sheath his own weapon.

"Get in there, you bastard, or I swear I'll melt you down for horseshoes," muttered Giles as he slammed the blade into the scabbard again. This time it settled into the leather with a satisfied hum.

If he had not vowed to avenge the deaths of his father and brother, Giles would have abandoned the magical sword long ago. But the enchanted blade had the power to aid him in his revenge against the elven lords, in his goal to one day become an important leader in the Rebellion. He hated the necessity of its thirst for blood—and needed it, all at the same time.

"You talk to it—you are mad," hissed Cecily.

"Me? Aren't you the one who just dropped a troop of Breden's soldiers into the ocean?"

"They killed my mother."

Giles wiped his bloody palm down his breeches, took a deep breath of patience and strode forward, placing his fingers on her cheek, as if now that he'd touched her, he could not stop from doing so again. "I'm sorry. Many more would have died if you had not called your magic to defend us, and I am grateful. But we have no time for your fit of vapors. If any soldiers survive, they will tell the story of what happened here and the elven lord will come with an even larger army. You must leave the village."

"Now I know you're demented," she said. But she did not pull away from his touch. "I do not understand your sudden concern for me. You… you do not know that I am alive. And I… I despise you. That's the way it has always been."

"Has it?" Giles found this revelation of her inner thoughts startling, but he didn't have time to dwell upon it. "Listen. I promised your father I would look out for you while he was gone, and since he has not returned, that makes you my responsibility."

"You? You would be the last person I would ever want to watch over me."

"Apparently Thomas did not care what you thought." Giles noticed the women had emerged from their hiding places, had started to tend to the wounds of the injured. His own bullet wound suddenly began to ache, and his vision swam for a moment as his hand dropped to Cecily's shoulder to steady himself. He didn't have the patience to reason with her, but he would have to try. "You are no longer safe here. Even if word of this scuffle does not reach Breden of Dewhame's ears, more soldiers will come. Thomas has been gone too long and the spell that has hidden this village has faded. The Rebellion cannot let you fall into enemy hands."

Cecily's enormous eyes glittered. "Now I understand. You aren't just a friend of my father's. You are part of this Rebellion—how long have you been spying on me? No, no, don't answer. I'm sure it will be a lie. Fie, you almost had me believing… never mind. Your concern is for me as a tool, not a person."

She stepped away from him, dislodging his hand. Giles swayed.

"I'm not going anywhere with you, Giles Beaumont… if that's even your real name."

His vision developed odd black specks and he blinked to try to clear it. "I assure you, lady, that *is* my name. And after nine years of protecting you I think you could at least trust me for the next few…" The ground suddenly flew up to meet his face, but before he felt the impact the black specks exploded and the world disappeared.

Two

AT FIRST CECILY COULD DO NOTHING MORE THAN STARE down in confusion at the large man. Indeed, she'd felt nothing but confusion since she'd emerged from the ocean to find the blacksmith waiting for her. His concern for her safety had astonished her and her foolish heart had thought...

Fie, she'd found out the truth of it soon enough.

Perhaps she should take the opportunity to get as far away from him as she could. He seemed awfully determined to take control of her life. And she had tried so hard, for so long, to plan her future the way she wanted it.

And certainly not as some weapon for the Rebellion.

Cecily raised her trembling hands, stared at them in dawning horror. What had she done? Years of hiding the true strength of her power—all destroyed in one day. How could she have allowed this to happen? And yet, how could she stand by and do nothing while her friends and neighbors were being slaughtered?

Her entire world had suddenly changed and Cecily couldn't quite grasp the full extent of it yet. Especially the revelation that the man at her feet had been spying on her for years.

She huffed and bent down, rolled Giles over. So much blood covered his chest that she couldn't determine how much of it was his. She unbuttoned his shirt with shaking fingers, trying not to look at his beautiful face. He had too much of the elven's beautiful features for her not to be affected by them.

She spread open the blood-soaked cloth, pushing it over his muscular shoulders. The wound did not look very large but it still bled prodigiously. Cecily tore off a strip from her chemise and balled it up, pushing it against the hole in that otherwise perfect skin.

"Somebody help me," she cried.

"I'm here, Cecily."

She looked up into Will's warm brown gaze and suddenly the horrible things she'd seen and done today caught up with her. She didn't fight the tears that stung her eyes, trailed down her cheeks. "He needs a healer."

"Aye, that he does. But it's not a mortal wound, me girl, so he can wait a bit. I daresay that elven blood of his will have him healed before any of the others."

Cecily gave him a wondering look. He'd said "elven blood" with a touch of scorn in his voice, and she could not forget she carried even more than the blacksmith. Indeed, she'd tried very hard to keep her odd eyes lowered to hide that damning trait, for despite Giles's pointed ears and pale blond hair, he still had the ordinary eyes of a human.

"He does look very elven, Will. Is that why you don't like him?"

William hunched down and laid his arm about Cecily's shoulders. "Nay. I don't like him because he's a strange man, with strange ways. He's been here nigh on nine years and we still don't know nuthin' about him." He gave her a slight squeeze. "Ye know yer blood has never bothered me, Cecily. Nor yer swimming with all manner of creatures. But ye should have told me about this magic of yers. 'Tis enough to make a man shake in his very boots."

"I'm sorry, Will. I just hoped that if I ignored it, it would go away."

Will laughed at that. "No more'n the crystal in yer eyes would fade, me girl. But ye have managed it well, and I don't see why ye can't continue to do so."

Cecily hoped she understood the meaning behind his words. She'd had every intention of marrying Will, had waited only for him to gather the courage to ask her. For the past few years she'd dreamt of a little cottage of her own, filled with freckled babies and Will's gentle contented sort of love.

It did not concern her that her dreams did not include passion. She had experienced the madness of infatuation once, and never wanted to have her heart crushed like that again.

"Does that mean," whispered Cecily, "that you still care for me?"

"Ach, me dear girl, I would never let a bit of magic come between us."

Giles moaned. Cecily focused her attention back on him. She peeked under the cloth and reduced the pressure when she saw that the bleeding had slowed. "That bullet needs to be removed before his skin heals over it."

Will scratched his head. "Do ye reckon he can heal that fast?"

"I can, Will."

"And ye have proved to carry more elven blood than even this sword-gifted fiend. Ach, now don't look at me that way. I told ye it doesn't change the way I feel."

But Cecily noticed none of the other villagers had come near them, and realized Will might be the only one of them who felt that way. The few who had the gift of healing had chosen others to care for, the women tending to their own men. Yet if it hadn't been for Giles, none of them would have survived. He had fought so valiantly for them, yet they now seemed to fear him.

Or perhaps they avoided *her*.

When Giles's current lover hurried by with nary a glance at the fallen man, Cecily wanted to scream at the young woman to help him. She wished the black-smith would wake up and see what a self-centered chit he'd chosen to bed when he could have had—

No, best not follow that thought.

"I once pulled a splinter from little Ralph's finger with my magic," she told Will. "Do you think it would work with a bullet?"

"I dunno. But I don't see the harm in tryin'." Will glanced up and frowned. "It seems it may be awhile before someone else can tend to him."

Cecily gathered the power to her again, her blood thrumming in response until it felt as if her very skin shivered with the force of it. Will jerked his arm from about her shoulders. Perhaps it truly did.

Several healers had already started pots of water to boil, and she called thin streams of it to her, the air cooling it by the time it reached her. Cecily guided it with her fingers, washing off Giles's chest, noting a thin wound across that perfect skin, but otherwise no injuries except for the bullet hole. She angled the liquid into a point and swirled it to make it strong enough to penetrate that opening, then allowed it to trickle back out with red, then a tint of pink. She continued to force the water into the wound until the musket ball popped out.

Cecily heaved a sigh of relief.

"Well done," whispered Will.

She nodded at his words, ignoring the awe that had crept into his voice. She tore more cloth from her chemise and bound the blacksmith's shoulder.

"What shall we do with him?"

Will rose to his feet, grabbed Giles's ankles, attempting to drag him. "I'll take him over with the rest of the injured—damn, the man must weigh a hundred stone."

"Do stop, Will. You're likely to hurt him." Cecily curled her arms beneath the blacksmith's back and knees, lifting him with a grunt. Despite her elven strength, all that muscle of his made him heavy. And her smaller height allowed his head to nearly touch the ground, his feet to drag through the mud. But it was better than Will tugging him about like one of his sheep. "Where?"

Will just gaped at her.

Cecily inwardly groaned. For years she'd hidden her elven strength just as much as she'd hidden her magic, longing to fit in with her fellow villagers. Well, except for the time that beam had fallen on Gregory—but she'd been careful that no one had seen her move it. And once, when Becca's little sister had wandered near the cliffs, Cecily had used her elven speed to catch the girl before she tumbled over the edge. Isolated incidences with few witnesses. Quickly forgotten because for most of the time she appeared entirely human. But today…

Today's events had destroyed all of her diligent subterfuge.

"Where do I take him, Will? He's heavy."

He snapped his mouth shut and led her to Old Man Hugh's cottage, which already held several other wounded men. Cecily laid the blacksmith down on a clean pallet just beyond the doorway, her muscles trembling with relief as she settled him. Despite everything, she felt hesitant to leave him. What if he'd lost so much blood he'd never manage to wake up?

She broke another habit she'd developed to protect herself. She looked into his face.

Merciful heavens. Cecily stroked his thick white hair off his brow. The pale strands lacked the sparkle of silver that marked the elven lords, but it only made him appear more human. Made his beauty more real. The sculpted cheekbones, the perfectly formed nose and chin. His skin also lacked the paleness attributed to the pure elven—a light golden color that, along with his ordinary-shaped eyes, betrayed his more human blood.

But he'd inherited entirely too much of the elven beauty for any woman to be unaffected by the mere sight of him.

Cecily had been but nine years old when Giles had come to apprentice to the old blacksmith. At the age of fifteen, Giles had already reached his manhood, while she had been nothing but a scrawny child. Within a few years Giles had taken over the forge and seduced half the maidens in the village.

And like all the rest, Cecily had imagined herself in love with him.

She could not look into his eyes without feeling as if she'd swoon, so she had avoided his gaze. His mere presence left her breathless, heart hammering and palms sweating, so she could not gather the nerve to speak to him. But she took to hanging out about the smithy with all the rest of the young girls, until Giles lost patience and shooed them away.

She'd fought with her best friend, Becca, over who loved him the most. The stupid girl thought she did, and that argument had strained their friendship.

Cecily might have continued to moon after him in quiet adoration if she hadn't accidentally stumbled across him on the beach one night.

She'd managed to hide most of her peculiar elven traits. She felt grateful she hadn't inherited the pale locks that were a telltale sign of the blood. Indeed, her black hair helped, and she took to wearing it long over her forehead to hide her freakishly large eyes. She had even managed to suppress her magic until she almost forgot she had it.

All in the attempt to erase the memory of the knowledge that her magic could kill.

But she could not fight the attraction for the ocean. She longed for it like a flower longs for the sun. So she took to the water at night, to swim with the dolphins and become one with the waves. And she'd stumbled across Giles and his lover, their bodies entwined at the edge of the tide, the moonlight highlighting the muscles in Giles's back and shoulders... in his shapely legs... in his firm buttocks... as he moved atop the woman beneath him. Cecily stared in wonder at the beauty of his face when he arched his back and moaned, his eyes closed in some sort of bliss.

Even the mere thought of how she'd reacted years ago made her face heat with shame now.

For she should have been frightened, or appalled, or even disgusted. She'd never seen such a sight before. She had only a girlish inkling of what went on between a man and a woman when they were alone together, much of it involving kissing.

She had not believed Will when he'd told her it was much like what sheep did.

So witnessing the act should have sent her running in the other direction. Instead, she watched. And studied. And tingled in places she'd never thought of before.

And longed to be that woman beneath him.

Cecily had gone to bed that night, touching herself in those new places of interest, imagining his hands upon her body.

And her determination had grown beyond her shyness.

When her body had finally developed enough curves that she felt the admiring glances of the village boys and a sense of the power she could wield with just a sway of her hips, she had snuck into his private rooms behind the smithy and waited for him.

She could still remember the way he looked when

he entered his bedroom. The way he smelled. He must have just come from his bath—another habit of his that marked him as an oddity in the village—for he smelled of spring water and soap, and his naked chest gleamed from scrubbing. His pale hair still dripped sparkling droplets of water about his shoulders and down his back. He wore nothing but his drawers, wet and plastered to his body.

Cecily stared in fascination at what they revealed, forgetting for the moment her rehearsed seduction.

But she must have made some noise, for he swung round toward the bed, his eyes narrowed, and he groaned, "Not again."

The firelight played across the smooth planes of his chest, the ridged curves in his stomach. He had little body hair marring that expanse, just a bit in the center of his chest, creating a light line straight down into his drawers.

"Lud, woman. Are you married?"

Cecily blinked. Of course, in the dim light he hadn't recognized her. "No."

A sigh. "Widowed, perhaps?"

"Um, no."

"Known for offering your favors freely?"

"Certainly not!"

He strode toward the bed and ripped the covers off her. "Then, my dear, I'm afraid I have to ask you to leave."

Cecily squeaked and tried to cover herself with her hands. She had disrobed, hoping the sight of her new curves would be more than he could resist. But, fie, he hadn't even given her a chance to appear… tempting.

Something flickered in his eyes as they traveled over

her body, but his face froze into a sort of dispassionate boredom. "Get dressed. Before I do something we shall both regret."

"But... but..." Cecily tried to gather her wits. He didn't understand. He thought she was some foolish girl who didn't know what she was about. Who wanted to use him for his good looks, and nothing more. "But I love you," she managed to whisper. There, she'd done it. Confessed her secret longings, let him know that she desired him beyond what his other lovers surely did.

He dropped the bedcovering, took a step backward. His voice, when he spoke, sounded oddly breathless. "Yes, yes. I'm sure you do. Now, be a good girl and get dressed."

Cecily rose to her knees. He just didn't understand and this might be her one and only chance to tell him. She had to explain, and then surely he would fall into her arms as she had dreamed. Unlike Becca, Cecily would have the boldness to take what she wanted. And she had never wanted anything more than she wanted Giles Beaumont.

So despite the heat in her face, she confessed her heart. "You think I'm like all the other girls, don't you? But, Giles, I'm not. None of them are worthy of you. Not a one of them will cherish you the way I do. I am your soul mate, and ours will be a greater love than you can possibly imagine. You just don't know it yet. You just need..."

He'd stepped closer again, his hand reaching out to her face as if her words had somehow cast a spell over him, and he couldn't stop himself. His handsome features had softened; his eyes glazed with some emotion Cecily couldn't identify, yet somehow understood.

She suppressed a grin of victory.

But his fingers halted mere inches from her face, and he snatched them back as if the thought of touching her might burn him as easily as molten metal. He shook his head, water droplets spraying her skin like tiny spears of ice. And then he laughed. "Who the hell *are* you?"

"Why, I'm…" She could not say her name, for the meaning of his words slowly drifted past the intensity of her feelings. How could he not know her? She loitered in the forge every day. She knew his every habit. What he liked to eat, how the corners of his eyes crinkled when he smiled, the way he would grow silent when angered.

And he couldn't even recall her name?

He hadn't noticed her among the bevy of his admirers. She hadn't been worthy of his notice.

A humiliation unlike anything she had ever known before suffused her. She had confessed an infatuation that was entirely one-sided. Hers. She gathered up her clothing and backed out of the room, her passion turning into a rage that threatened to overwhelm her. She ran before the control over her magic slipped beyond redemption.

And learned that love could fool. That passion could blind. And that…

Will cleared his throat from the doorway of Old Man Hugh's cottage. Cecily untangled her fingers from the blacksmith's hair. How long had she been sitting here staring at him? Revisiting memories she'd thought she had managed to bury years ago?

She attempted to rise but Giles's eyelids suddenly flew open and he grasped her hand. "Must leave... keep you safe."

His big hand felt so warm, her fingers dwarfed in his. Something ran through her, a frisson of feeling similar to what she had felt all those years ago. She should never have allowed that old memory to resurface with such excruciating detail.

And yet, she now realized he had lied to her. That night, he had known who she was. He had used those words to hurt her, to discourage the childish infatuation she'd felt for him. But his laughter had been genuine, of that she could be sure. For he had been assigned to protect the Rebellion's tool, had never truly seen her as a person. And what a lark the tool had turned out to be!

Cecily twisted her hand from his and near growled her next words. "I told you, I'm not going anywhere with you."

But his eyes had already rolled back into his head.

Will stood frozen in the doorway, his brown gaze flicking from her to Giles. "What is going on between the two of ye?"

"Nothing." Cecily stepped over to his side and took his hand, so much smaller in comparison to the blacksmith's. "Father asked him to watch over me while he was away; that's all. Although why he would choose such an oaf is beyond my ability to comprehend."

Will bristled. "Thomas should have asked *me*. He knows how I feel about ye."

Cecily could not explain to him about the Rebellion. About who her true father was. For then she would have to explain about the night she'd escaped the clutches of an elven lord. And how even as a child, she had killed more than a hundred men in the process. Today had been bad enough.

"I don't need anyone to watch over me, Will."

"Aye," he replied as he led her across the village square. "Ye've proven that, well enough."

She caught some inflection in his voice, perhaps a bit of the betrayal he'd mentioned, but chose to ignore it. She would just have to work twice as hard to make the villagers forget what she'd done here today. It would take a bit longer for them to forget this incident. But she had every confidence they would. She would not give up her life here so easily. She had worked too hard for it.

"Do ye wish me to help bury her?" whispered Will.

Cecily realized she'd stopped beside her mother's body. What was she doing here lying in the dirt? Mother hated to get dirty.

"Yes," she replied. "Let me fetch a blanket, Will."

Before he could respond, Cecily dropped his hand and ran to their little cottage on the outskirts of the village. Thomas had built it close to the ocean, for he knew his daughter couldn't bear to be far from the waves. The thatch had been burned along with most of the south wall, and it reeked of smoke when she entered it.

Cecily opened the cedar trunk that sat at the foot of her mother's bed. She pulled out the quilt she had so painstakingly sewed many a night, dreaming of when it would be spread on her marriage bed, the beam of

Will's smile as she proudly displayed the work she had done for him. She had pieced the blue-and-green cloth in a pattern of waves, with dolphins leaping from between the curls, and then overlaid the entire piece with tiny stitches of even more waves.

Mother had professed it to be the most beautiful quilt she'd ever seen.

Her poor mother could not sew. Indeed, it appeared she had no skills whatsoever, and Cecily often wondered what grand house she had lived in that she couldn't manage to do anything for herself. But feared to ask about their life before they'd come to the village.

Cecily took to domestic life like she took to the sea. She had but to watch a quilting circle once to learn to sew. She cooked all of their meals, inventing her own dishes to tempt her mother's delicate appetite. She tended the finest garden in the village, her vegetables and herbs always growing large and fine. She spun her own thread, wove her own cloth, and made her dresses from hand-drawn designs that Father would bring from London.

Cecily glanced around their little cottage, her gaze picking out the many things she'd created to make it a home. From the curtains at the windows to the seashells filled with flowers, the room spoke more of her tastes than her parents'. Mother professed time and again that she didn't understand where Cecily had acquired such a gift for peasant life. Father only smiled and patted her hand in sympathy. And then winked at Cecily.

Father. What would he do when he came home? He adored Mother.

Cecily curled the blanket under her arm and ran back down to the village clearing, hopping over the small streams and rivulets that laced the land. Will stood patiently where she had left him.

Cecily laid out the blanket, and Will helped her place Mother in the middle of it. She brushed the dirt from her mother's hair and dress, then carefully folded the quilt around her. "There now. This will protect her."

Will nodded, as if what she said made any sense at all, and picked up Mother, following the line of villagers out to the small cemetery. Too many of their own would be buried today.

The plot stood on a small knoll, the driest place near the village. The elven lord of Dewhame had changed the land with his magic: springs spouted from meadow and wood, ponds softened any lowland, rivers and streams flowed in a wild profusion across the landscape.

Cecily knew that although the sovereignty of Dewhame had always been green, it had lacked the wealth of water the Imperial Lord Breden of Dewhame had created with his magic. Since the liquid nourished her very soul, she could not regret the change in the landscape, despite her adopted father mourning about how England had looked before the invasion.

Cecily dug the grave herself, until it grew too deep for her to get out of, and then Will helped her up and took over the task. Other than the weeping of the women, the villagers went about the burying of their dead with quiet grief.

Although many offered their sympathy to one another, not a one spoke a word of comfort to Cecily.

She tried not to be hurt. Hadn't she lived among them for years? Hadn't she tended their families when one of them grew ill? Hadn't she brought them gifts from the ocean to sell at market to help them through the winter? Surely her display of magic had not made them forget she was still one of them.

She had frightened them. Their fear would lessen when they realized she hadn't changed. That she was the same girl, despite carrying too much of the elven blood.

Cecily sat at her mother's side, watching the hole growing ever deeper, her chest tightening until she could scarcely breathe. If she allowed Will to place her mother in the grave, it would all become real. Oh, her head knew very well that her mother had died, but her heart had not acknowledged it yet. She could not allow it, or surely she would splinter into a thousand pieces, never to be whole again.

"Cecily?"

She stared up through the branches of the old elm tree, watching the sunlight filter through the leaves. If she didn't answer Will, he might go away. She could not put her mother into the ground. She could not. Then it would be final. And she would never hear her mother's laugh again, or feel the softness of her arms enfold her, or know the joy of her words of praise when she thought Cecily had done something particularly clever.

She couldn't do this.

Will tried to take up the blanket. Cecily frowned at him, picked up her mother herself. She felt so slight. So frail.

Will jumped down into the hole and lifted up his arms. Cecily carefully handed Mother to him, and when Will crawled back out and made to cover her with dirt, Cecily grabbed his arm.

"Wait."

And she flew down the small rise, into the meadow, gathering as many flowers as her arms could hold, and then took them back to shower down around her mother.

"This will make it bearable for her, Will."

He only nodded, and followed her on her next trip, this time partway into the woods, gathering violets and wild roses and buttercups. Then he followed her back toward the ocean, and they gathered knotgrass and sea holly and the small yellow flowers that grew along the cliffs.

By the time they returned, most of the villagers had finished their burials and left. The few who remained kept their eyes averted from Cecily's.

Will began to shovel the dirt onto their mound of flowers.

"Wait," she panted, and raced back home, stripping her garden bare of any plants that had managed to flower, gathering the honeysuckle she'd cultivated near the front of the cottage, until she could barely see past the blooms in her arms.

When she'd dropped them down into the hole, the combined perfume of the blooms made her head spin. But she nodded at Will, who had waited with infinite patience for her to return. The sun started to set while he shoveled, and this time she joined him, until they laid the last clump of earth atop the grave.

"She will like being surrounded by the flowers."

"Aye. Ye did right, Cecily."

He took her hand, and they stood for a moment without saying a word. Mother knew what lay in her heart, without her having to say it over her... place of rest.

Will escorted her back to her empty cottage, placing his cheek against hers in farewell. "Are ye sure ye will be all right by yerself?"

Cecily nodded. "I can't stay at your place, Will. It wouldn't be proper."

He flushed. "I was thinking of Becca. Surely ye can stay with her a time?"

She should have known Will would never suggest anything improper. But even if Becca would welcome her, Cecily knew her friend's family would not. They had always stared at her odd eyes with suspicion, despite everything she'd done to endear them to her.

"No, Will. This is my home. I just hope it doesn't rain tonight."

He nodded, red hair falling about his forehead. "I'll see about fixing the roof in the morning."

Cecily smiled with gratitude. She knew she could count on Will. Despite everything he saw her do today, he still cared for her.

Night had fallen and shadowed the familiar interior of the cottage, and Cecily shivered as she closed the door, grateful that at least the smoke had finally cleared. She lit a rush light, the meager illumination doing little to vanquish the shadows. But she hesitated to light a fire. The early summer night was too warm, and their pile of wood too meager. Mother kept saying that as soon as Thomas returned she would set him to chopping wood.

But Father had not returned. And now Cecily wondered if he ever would.

While she ate a cold meal of bread and dried fish, she wondered if the blacksmith had been right. Thomas had never been gone this long before. He often went away for months at a time, never telling them where he was going, or what task the Rebellion had set for him. Cecily had reassured her mother that Thomas could take care of himself. Hadn't he shown her the way he could make himself almost disappear? Hadn't he regaled them with stories of his escapes from danger time and again?

And it hadn't occurred to Cecily that something bad could *really* happen to him. But today's events had shown her that the evils of the world could come upon one suddenly, when they least expected it.

Cecily could bear her thoughts no longer. She pushed them from her mind, climbed into her parents' bed, and allowed herself to cry until she fell asleep.

When she woke the next morning, it took a moment for the events of yesterday to filter into her mind.

"Mother?"

Of course, she didn't answer. But Cecily tried to keep up her usual routine.

"I'm going out to tend to the garden." She glanced down at her wrinkled clothing, grimaced at the stains upon it, and changed into her second-best set of clothes. "And to the beach. I left my favorite quilted petticoat there."

The small house near vibrated with silence.

In her garden, the plants had a layer of soot covering them, and she washed them all down with her bucket several times. A stream ran not too far from her garden patch, and walking back and forth soon grew tedious. It would take but a flick of her hand to call the water from stream to garden, but she had never used her magic so casually. Nor would she do so today. Indeed, she would have to work even harder to fit in now.

"Cecily?"

She glanced up into Will's rather haggard-looking face, pushing the hair away from her eyes and wondering if she looked as bad. Probably worse. "Good morn, Will. My plants are doing well this year. I will make dinner for you this eve—what's wrong?"

He spread out his hands. "How can ye ask me that? Everything's wrong; everything's changed."

"But not you and I."

"Not the way I feel about ye, no. And yet—the men have been talking. We don't know why the elven lord suddenly decided to raid our village for his army. 'Tis said that he's determined to win back the king from Firehame. Our king who is naught but a trophy to them! Ach, we should be a united England, conquering the world. But because of the elven we are nothing but squabbling sovereignties, pitting our own men against one another."

Cecily dropped her bucket, the water sloshing over the sides, wetting the hem of her skirt. "I've never heard you talk like this before. What has gotten into you?"

"Ye can ask me that, after yesterday?" He shook his head. "Ye cannot keep things the way they were, Cecily, no matter how hard ye try."

"Don't say that. We can repair the village. We can go back to our peaceful lives. The elven lord will forget about us."

"Nay, he will not! He will send more soldiers… or just destroy us with one of his storms. We are doing what's best."

A shaft of ice ran through her body. "What do you mean?"

Will took a breath. "The men and I are going to Dewhame to join Breden's army. They will attack the village again if we do not, and we will not sit and wait for them to come to us."

"You can't leave."

Will stepped forward, lifted her hands in his. "Don't ye see it's the only way to protect ye?"

Cecily had her fill of men trying to protect her. "Liar. You've always wanted to join the army. You long for glory. This is naught but an excuse."

He flinched as if she'd slapped him and quickly withdrew his hands from hers and stepped back warily. For a moment, she saw a hint of fear in his eyes. Dear, sweet Will, despite what he had said, feared her. Or rather, her magic.

"Do not be this way," he whispered. "Ye cannot change what has happened. Ye cannot hide from it."

Will couldn't go. She might never see him again. All of her plans for a quiet comfortable life would go with him. "When are you leaving?"

"This morn. Old Man Hugh will take care of my flock until I return. I know I don't have the right to ask, but if ye could wait for me…"

Cecily shook her head. "It doesn't matter. You know

what I am now, Will. Even if you manage to come home, you'll never be able to forget that, will you?"

He dropped his gaze, studied the toes of his boots. He wore his best pair, the leather only slightly scuffed. "Ye cannot help what ye are. Many others have more elven blood than they'd like."

He didn't deny her words. Cecily sucked in a breath. "You had best go."

Will wouldn't leave her like this. He would take her hand and tell her he could never be parted from her, for any reason.

But he turned and walked away.

Thomas had always told her she had too much romanticism in her heart for her own good. She knew it to be true the day she had snuck into the blacksmith's bedroom and humiliated herself beyond redemption. She now knew it to be true with Will. She had thought she could always count on his love. But it was just as tenuous as the life she'd made for herself in the village.

Cecily spun and ran to the one place that always offered her comfort. That always soothed her whenever Thomas tried to shake the romanticism out of her.

She flew through the scraggly woods, over the steep rocks and across the sun-warmed sand, not stopping until she reached her private cove. The sharp tang of salt nipped her nose and tickled her tongue. She stripped off her clothing, dropping it atop her discarded petticoat from yesterday, and plunged into the waves.

Thomas had always told her that one day she would become a tool of the Rebellion. The magic in her blood had chosen her destiny, and she could not fight it. She had firmly denied it, telling him she didn't want such power.

For she remembered the night Thomas and the lady Cassandra had rescued Mother and her from the prison of Firehame Palace. The night she'd called up a storm to stop the troops that pursued them. Cecily's magic had killed hundreds of men, and she could still see their deaths limned by the fury of lightning, shadowed by the deluge of the storm.

And she'd sworn to renounce her magic. Had done such a jolly good job of it that Thomas had quit trying to teach her the ways of deception that made for a good spy. Indeed, as she grew to love Thomas as a father, he'd grown to love her as a daughter, and eventually put her needs before those of the Rebellion.

He no longer saw her as just a tool for the Rebellion. Had found ways to protect her, not only from her blood father, Breden of Dewhame, but from his own Rebellion.

Cecily swam ever deeper, leaving behind the sun-dappled water until she moved in a world of twilight. Luminous fish spotted the water with bright color; anemone and coral swayed like a garden of flowers beneath her. Two dolphins swam up to greet her, brushing their smooth cool skin against hers, inviting her to play.

But Cecily did not have the heart for it, and instead pushed herself to swim farther out to sea, to leave behind the world of man once and for all.

Although her lungs seemed capable of supporting her for hours within the water, she knew she could not stay below forever. Nor could she go back to that empty house and pretend her life would go on as it had before. She had nothing, now. No one.

A fury of movement to her right made Cecily slow her sharp kicks, float in weightlessness for a moment. A school of sharks circled, a multitude of other sea creatures below, feeding off the bits that floated from the shark's feast. She felt the agitation of the dolphins at her side, smoothed their hides with the palms of her hands.

She should swim away, but her eye caught something wrong about the scene beside her. The sharks did not feast on the carcass of another fish.

Cecily tried to swim around them and abruptly hit an invisible wall. She placed her hands against the barrier, knowing she could not pass through it. Neither could she go under or over it. For it was the magical barrier that the elven lords had crafted to surround England. To cut them off from the rest of the world—to contain their magic or keep the English people prisoner, she could not be sure. But Thomas said it allowed the elven lords to monitor trade and hide their evil from the rest of the world.

But Mother said the rest of the world could care less about the plight of the English people.

And Father said they would have to help themselves. And he would go off on another mission for the Rebellion.

Cecily drifted up to the surface, her hands trailing against the invisible wall, watching the school of sharks circling again and again, until finally a gap opened between the sharp-finned bodies, and she caught sight of their feast.

And why it had seemed so very wrong.

They fed on soldiers. The soldiers that she had plunged into the ocean. Arms, legs, shredded torsos and a head with glazed, staring eyes…

Cecily clutched at her dolphins, kicking her legs away from the carnage. And her friends responded by swiftly pulling her back to shore, her arms slung about their backs, her head lowered against the spray. She normally took such delight in their swift passage, but the horror of what she'd seen robbed her of any enjoyment.

She had done that. But she'd dropped the men in the water because she assumed they would swim to shore, too worn out to fight the villagers, their weapons lost. Surely some had made it to shore…

She hadn't meant to kill them. If her world was no longer the safe, contented harbor she'd worked so hard to create, she was no longer the harmless girl she'd tried to fool herself into being.

Thomas had been right about everything. She pictured his smiling face, with his golden hair gone slightly gray at the temples, his pale eyes surrounded by a network of laugh lines. How could he have stayed so kind in the world in which he lived?

How could he have allowed Cecily to hide for so long?

Perhaps his home in the village was the only place he knew peace. Perhaps he wanted to keep a little part of his world as a safe haven to return to.

If Giles was right, Thomas had even found a spell to place around the village, keeping them all safe.

But Thomas had not come home to renew it. Wouldn't he have known how long it would last? What if something truly horrible had happened to him? What if he lay imprisoned by some elven lord at this very moment, in pain and crying out for help?

Her toes dragged against the sand and she dropped her arms from about the dolphins, giving them a petting in their favorite places, while the waves bobbed her up and down.

Will had been right. She could not hide from the world anymore.

But she need not become a tool, either.

She walked to the shore, ignoring the waves that battered her, the plaintive cries of her friends begging her to stay and play. Her eyes narrowed as she studied the far rise, looking for a hint of movement.

Ah, he was good. Had she not been looking, she never would have spied him. But a brief flash of pale hair told her Giles had resumed his post of spying upon her, wounded or no.

Cecily did not bother to hurry into her clothing. He had watched her for years, so it hardly mattered now that he saw her naked body. Besides, it obviously held little appeal for him. She'd offered it and he had easily rejected her.

She felt that familiar rise of humiliation turn into something harder. Something cold and brilliant which formed from the events of the last four-and-twenty hours. It served to strengthen her resolve.

Cecily surreptitiously used her magic to shed her skin of water and pulled her chemise over her head. She had always just struggled her damp skin into her clothing. But now that she'd made her decision, there was no reason to hide her magic, even for the little things.

But she had no magic that would assist her into her stays, and she could only be thankful that working women had laces in front and back. She wouldn't have a servant to aid her on the journey ahead.

She pulled on both of her petticoats, then her serviceable brown dress, and carried her shoes in her hand as she made her way up the rocks.

The spy did not attempt to hide. Why would he, now that his secret was revealed? Giles stood as she approached, looking as pale as an elven lord, favoring his shoulder as he brushed the hair from his eyes with his other hand.

He stood too tall. Cecily could meet Will's eyes, but her head barely topped Giles's massive shoulders.

Despite that new, hard little knot inside of her, she could not stop the racing of her heart, the flutter in her stomach, at his nearness.

Nor could she stare into his face. So she spoke to his chin. "I need a horse."

Three

GILES COULD ONLY STARE AT HER IN STUNNED AMAZEMENT.

"You're a blacksmith, aren't you? You have horses in your stables, don't you?"

He nodded, feeling like the rather slow oaf that he'd pretended to be since he'd come to the village. Cecily looked... different, somehow. Oh, she was still beautiful. With the elven blood that ran through her veins, she could never be otherwise. Her enormous blue eyes glittered like crystal jewels, her black hair shone in the sunlight, and her skin looked like translucent parchment.

But her soft mouth had hardened, her posture rigidly alert like a soldier about to face battle.

Giles regretted the change in her.

"I am in need of one," she said.

"Of a horse."

"Yes, quite. Has your injury addled your brain?"

He cocked a grin. His brain always seemed to get addled when she neared within a few feet of him. Another good reason that had kept him at a distance from her for so many years. "I'm just astonished you've managed to find your good sense. You understand that you must leave this… place."

He hadn't meant his words to sound so derisive. But the thought of finally leaving this little village, of relinquishing his task of watching over Cecily so he could serve the Rebellion in a way more suited to his character, had made him speak more harshly than he intended.

He longed for adventure. He ached for the chance to deliver a blow to the elven lords that would ease the suffering in his heart for the death of his father and brother. And he had felt stifled in this little village. An entire world waited for him, and now he had the chance to experience it.

Her gaze finally left his chin to glance up into his eyes. He resisted the urge to take a step backward, to escape the feeling that she delved into his very soul.

"It must have been dreadful for you," she said, "having to watch over some foolish little chit, while my father went off on his grand missions."

She had struck too close to home. For the first time, it occurred to him that the girl might know him just as well as he knew her. She had watched him often enough. With the other young women of the village. Until that night she had… fie, she'd almost destroyed his entire mission when she had climbed into his bed and offered herself to him.

If she had not been so innocent, he wouldn't have been able to resist bedding her. And Thomas would have killed him.

"My feelings in this matter are not significant." This time he willed himself to speak harshly. He felt sure any infatuation for him that she'd suffered from as a child had faded on her maturity. Indeed, he should have felt relieved by the coldness she had treated him to since that night. The fact that it rankled still confused him. "We will leave at once."

"I beg your pardon," she replied, in a tone that suggested she offered no such thing. "I do not recall asking for your company."

"You will have it, whether you wish it or no. Until I deliver you into someone else's safekeeping, you are my responsibility."

"Indeed. You still seem to suffer under the delusion that I need protection. Did you not witness what I did yesterday? Do you not realize how many bodies litter the waters of my ocean?"

She raised her hands, her fingers playing some invisible melody in the air. He knew how deadly a mere gesture from her could be, although he had not truly understood the extent of her power until he'd witnessed it. But behind the anger in her eyes, he saw a deep sadness, and her breath had hitched when she spoke of her waters.

Perhaps another would not have noticed. But he'd studied her interactions with others often enough to see past the shield of her public face.

"You did what you had to," he said, closing the distance between them. She smelled like lavender and deep ocean. A heady scent no other woman could ever match. "Just as I did what I needed to do."

"I do not like killing."

"Nor do I."

She waved her fingers again. "I do not like *you*."

Giles laughed. "Do not think you frighten me, little girl. You shan't be rid of me so easily."

Her mouth dropped open, and he fought the urge to kiss her. Heaven help him on their journey to Firehame. His only defense against her appeal had been distance, and he would not be able to keep it. And now that she knew the truth about him, it seemed it had broken some sort of barrier between them, for they spoke to each other now more than they had in the past nine years. Which meant he would have to be even more vigilant against his affection for her.

At the thought, he raised his hand and touched her cheek, that thrill of anticipation running through him again. Indeed, he did have an affection for her. How astonishing.

She stepped away from his touch. "Do not think to use your wiles upon me. I am no longer a child. And do not think I am going with you to become some pawn for your Rebellion. I will not be used—by you or anyone else. I am going to see this Sir Robert of yours only to find my father. He will know of Thomas's last mission... unless... did Father tell you?"

Giles shook his head. Even if he did know, he wouldn't likely tell her, nor did he think Sir Robert would, either. But if he wished the young woman off his hands and the end of this task so he could be given another, he wouldn't admit this. "No. And please refrain from bandying the man's name about. I confessed it to you only in the dire need of your circumstances."

"I'm surprised you were given his name."

"The Rebellion will risk much to protect you."

She grimaced. He could not help but grin at such a look.

"Come," he said, bending down to pull on his boots. "We should leave at once." A bit of sand had stuck to his stockings and prickled his feet as he walked up the rise. He did not wait for her, knowing she would follow. For he'd heard about the men leaving, had known that Will would go with them.

The village held nothing for her now.

Indeed, as they made their way to his smithy it felt as though they walked through an empty village. The young men must have already left, and perhaps many of their families as well. It would be foolish to stay and wait for the soldiers to come.

Cecily tried to walk away, and he stayed her with a raised hand. "It's best if we do not part."

She gave him an indignant look. "I need to pack some items for the journey. I will meet you back here in a few hours."

Giles entered the stable next to the smithy, his mind already racing with plans for the journey. It would take at least six days to reach London, perhaps more since they needed to travel in secret. He had but one horse, Apollo, a brute big enough to bear his weight, but Thomas kept extra mounts stabled, and he thought the small brown mare would suit Cecily. "I think it's better if you stay with me. I have already packed the supplies and need only to prepare the horses. Does this little mare meet with your approval?"

Giles turned around and realized he spoke to air.

He frowned and patted the mare's neck. "Ah, Belle. It would seem that this is going to be a most difficult journey, eh? With that young lady hating me—and me wanting her—all at the same time." The horse nickered, nosing into his pockets in hopes of a treat. Giles fetched out a bit of wilted carrot and saddled her while she crunched. "The hatred doesn't worry me. It's the wanting that could get me into trouble."

When he'd finished with the mare he saddled up Apollo, who stamped his feet until he'd been given a carrot as well.

It took Giles only a few moments to arrange the bags on the mounts. When he'd awoken this morning, he had decided to take Cecily to Firehame whether the woman would come willingly or no, so he'd packed the bags and dressed in his buckskins. He supposed he should be grateful she had changed her mind. He'd never had to force a woman to do anything.

"Although," he muttered as he led the horses from the stables, "Cecily is not a woman who can be forced to do anything. And that, my beasties, will have her and I knocking our heads together before we travel far."

Belle nickered and Apollo snorted. Fie, how he loved the beasts. They listened to everything he said and never talked back.

Giles didn't spare a glance for the smithy he left behind. He had always known that it had been but a temporary arrangement for him, despite having lived here for years. And although it had become his home, and he'd made a few friends in the village, his heart felt light as he left it behind for good. He did not lock the doors, and welcome to any man who wished to take up where he'd left off. He didn't suppose it would be any time soon, but after a while the village would become populated again.

The fishing hereabouts made for a comfortable livelihood.

As if on cue, Old Man Hugh popped his head out the door of his cottage as Giles passed.

"Ye be taking her away then?"

Giles nodded.

The old man spat. "Can't say as I'm sad to see her go. Nor ye, for that matter."

Giles turned to him in surprise. One of the men he'd thought he had made friends with was Hugh.

"Ach, now, don't be looking that aways. It's not that I don't like either of ye. It's just… ye two are not for the likes of our little village. Ye belong in the world that made ye." He stepped out of the doorway of his cottage, holding out a hand knobby with age and hard work. "I'll miss ye, though, Mister Giles Beaumont."

Giles shook the dry hand.

Hugh let out a cackle. "Lud, don't ye think I know that blade of yers is destined to protect more than this humble village?"

The devil-sword shivered in its scabbard, as if it knew it was the object of discussion.

"You see more than most, Old Man. More than I had thought."

"That I do." Hugh stepped closer and lowered his gravelly voice. "I'm naught but a worn-out fisherman, son, but sometimes I see things—there's a bit of elven blood in me own line. So heed the advice of this old man, for I'm given it to ye in good faith. Ye may not get what ye want, but it will be more'n ye ever thought to have. So be patient. With yer ambition, and the girl."

One of the injured cried out from within the dark recesses of the cottage and Hugh turned to answer.

"Wait," said Giles, his fear for the old man over-riding his confusion about the advice he'd been given. "Come with us. When the soldiers return, they may not feel like talking. It's dangerous to stay."

"And who will take care of the injured?" asked Hugh. "Besides, I no more belong in yer world than ye do in mine. Naw, get on with ye, boy. And use the elven blood in yer veins to help the human part of ye. For freedom is worth any cost." He scrambled back into his cottage, throwing his parting words over one strong, bony shoulder. "Good luck to ye, Beaumont, and may the Good Lord bless ye."

With that parting benediction, Giles left the village for the last time, following the small pathway that led to Thomas's cottage. The honeysuckle that usually surrounded the front of the little house had been torn away, straggles of blossoms releasing a strong aroma as he tread upon them to knock at the door.

She answered it within a heartbeat, her gaze quickly skimming past him to the waiting horses. "I'm more at home in the water than on the back of a beast."

"I know. But Belle is a docile mount."

"It's the sidesaddle," she continued, stepping back from the doorway and allowing him in.

"I know," he said again.

She huffed. "I suppose you know a great many things about me, after spying on me all these years.

And I suppose I will have to become adjusted to who you really are… and not who I thought you were."

Giles shrugged, surveying the homey cottage. "I'm the same person and so are you. Only our circumstances have changed."

"Perhaps." She hefted a rather large valise.

He shook his head. "We travel light."

She sighed but didn't argue, setting the bag on the bedstead and sorting through it. "I shall have only one change of clothes, and no hoops. The prime minister will think I'm a country bumpkin… ah, faith, that's what I am. I just hope he takes me seriously."

Giles purposely looked away from her smallclothes and examined a shelf laden with an assortment of seashells, coral, and some items he could not identify. Cecily's ocean finds often traded for large sums, and more than once, had fed the village through a lean winter. They should have been grateful for her contributions, but instead it had served only to set her even further apart from them.

Indeed, in the same way his gift with steel had made the young men only more distant from him.

"You've only to twiddle your fingers at water," he finally replied, "and I'm sure Sir Robert will take you seriously."

"And I will nick my finger, and your sword's hunger for blood will make him take *you* seriously when he realizes the power of the magic it holds."

He turned with a smile. "Well met. It seems we are a pair of magical aberrations, does it not?"

"I was perfectly ordinary until yesterday."

"You, my dear lady, were never ordinary."

She gave him an odd look, but didn't reply, only handed him a much-smaller bundle of tightly rolled clothing. He accepted it this time, striding out to her horse and stuffing it into the empty bag he'd left for her things. He checked the horses' shoes again, the straps of the saddles, and when she didn't appear he went back into the cottage.

She stood in the middle of the room, her magnificent eyes bright with tears. "I will just fetch Father and return. I will sit at this loom again, and spin my cloth. I will swim in my ocean with my friends. I will cook at that fire and embroider Father's shirts. I will not so easily give up this life I've worked so hard for."

Giles had a feeling she would never return to this little cottage but he said nothing. If it comforted her to believe she would one day return, he wouldn't take that from her.

Such an odd young woman. He constantly sought change, yearned for excitement. If it hadn't been for the distraction spying on Cecily had provided, he might have gone mad with boredom these past nine years.

It was time to start a new life. His heart jumped at the thought, and he could not keep the eagerness from his voice. "Come. It's dangerous to tarry."

She followed him out this time, turned and closed the door firmly behind her, latching it with a murmur of a promise. Belle nickered and Cecily smiled at the small mare, pulling an apple from within the folds of her skirts.

Giles studied her beneath lowered lids. Cecily wore a riding habit, the coat similar to his own, but with pearl buttons instead of his dull brass. Her skirts lacked a hoop, which made mounting and riding easier, and the wool cloth would be sturdy enough for their journey. She'd placed a straw hat over her mobcap and wore her hair in a single plait down her back.

An odd mixture of dress that spoke of a working-class woman with the elegance of a lady. But he knew she'd acquired the pearls using her magical abilities and not through trade, and that the fine weave of the cloth came from her own efforts.

A remarkable young woman. But not for the likes of him.

She scrambled into the saddle without his assistance, scowling as she wrapped her leg about the saddle's support, but too much of a lady to suggest she ride astride. She smoothed down her skirts and patted Belle's neck.

"Clever of you," said Giles as he mounted his gelding.

"What do you mean?"

"The apple."

She shrugged. "Father taught me about bribery."

And apparently that should have explained everything, for she said no more, just watched him with an expectant look on her lovely face.

Giles nodded and tapped Apollo with his heels, the beast starting out at a brisk pace. Despite his success with the village girls, Cecily often made him feel like an untried youth, clumsy and flustered in her presence. Fortunately his natural elven grace hid most of his human failings, so he didn't think he betrayed his uneasiness around her.

To make it all worse, he began to suspect that he might have been wrong about Cecily's feelings for him. She used her disdain for him like a shield, as if she sought to hide her true sensibilities.

And he had never quite managed to erase the vision of her in his bed.

Fie! Perhaps it was only wishful thinking. He could not have the one woman he truly wanted. Whether she knew it or not, they came from entirely different social classes, and as soon as they reached Firehame this would become very clear to her.

He would rather not face the humiliation of her rejection once she realized her true status, so he would just have to ignore this attraction... and never allow her to guess he felt it.

Giles started to get warm and stripped off his jacket then his neck cloth and finally opened the topmost buttons of his shirt. Then realized his discomfort came not from the sun overhead, but from the feel of her gaze upon his back. He slowed Apollo so that he rode by her side, which kept her scrutiny firmly directed away from him.

His body ceased to burn.

Giles stayed on a path that paralleled the channel, knowing Cecily would feel more comfortable if they kept close to the ocean, but eventually they would have to head inland...

"How many days will it take to reach London?"

It seemed her thoughts ran similarly to his own. "Five or six days, depending."

"On what?"

Giles glanced over and down at her on the smaller horse. "You weren't born in the village. Do you have no memory of how you came there?"

She smoothed the hair away from her face, the ocean breeze having loosened black tendrils from the plaiting. "I have worked very hard to forget everything that happened before Thomas rescued me and my mother."

"I see." Giles knew that when Thomas had rescued her from the Imperial Lord of Firehame, Cecily had called down a storm that had destroyed their pursuers. And that she could not forgive herself for killing so many. Yet it seemed a simple matter to Giles. They would have brought her back to Firehame to die a horrible death, so why should she feel remorse that she had stopped them?

"Tell me what our journey will be like," she asked. "For I would feel better knowing what to expect."

"I'm not sure if we shall reach Dorset today, but when we do, we will have to head inland. It will dry out as we leave Dewhame and enter the sovereignty of Firehame, but until then we avoid the lowlands, for Breden of Dewhame's water magic has turned them into marshes. Most of Dewhame is littered with streams and fountains similar to the land about our village. It is said the land was quite different before the arrival of the elven lords, but that their magic has changed it… surely you know of the seven sovereignties and the elven lords who rule each of them?"

She glanced at him with a look of annoyance. "Firehame in south central England ruled by the black scepter of Mor'ded. Verdanthame to the east ruled by the green scepter of Mi'cal. Terrahame to the northeast with the brown of Annanor; Bladehame next to that, then Stonehame, Dreamhame… yes, Giles, I know my geography and the powers that have shaped each land. I am not ignorant of the outside world. My question referred to the actual court of Firehame. Thomas had hinted of changes there."

And if Thomas hadn't seen fit to reveal all of the Rebellion's secrets to his daughter, Giles most assuredly would not. "You needn't worry about it. We shan't be going to the palace, but to Sir Robert's townhouse, and I haven't been past the front entry, so I couldn't tell you what to expect. It's a grand home though, almost as large as our village."

She raised a brow at that, but he ignored it. She would soon see for herself. "Perhaps if you allow yourself to remember, the memories of your earlier life will return."

Her head shook emphatically. "I was imprisoned in a rickety old tower the entire time I was in Firehame, and before that..." Cecily frowned, watching the gulls and cormorants gliding above the ocean waves. "I recall only running and hiding, dark places and whispered conversations."

The path they rode upon curved away from the ocean again, but they had been steadily climbing and so this time the poplar trees did not block their view, and they had a fine prospect of the land of Dewhame.

A wild moor spread out below them, heather blooming in a lavender blanket that rippled in the breeze and made a sort of shushing sound. A river sparkled on the far horizon, small streams flowing from it to weave through the heather like some giant spider web. Fountains of water erupted from several of the streams, glittering in the sunshine and overlaying the land with a sheen of mist. Giles resisted the urge to spread out his arms as the open land filled him with a feeling of freedom.

But Cecily showed no such restraint. "How glorious," she murmured, opening her arms wide. The water responded to her call, forming shimmering columns in the air and snaking their way toward her. Apollo came to an abrupt halt and snorted as the beams of water curled around them to reach Cecily. Giles felt the cool glide of a tendril caress his face, curve about his neck, leaving behind a soothing dampness.

For a moment, Cecily sat surrounded by shimmering columns, her eyes closed and a rapturous smile on her lovely mouth. She looked ethereal and beautiful and entirely dangerous.

"You make the water look almost alive," said Giles.

She turned and looked at him, light gleaming from within the facets of her eyes. "It is. Can't you feel it?"

"I come from Bladehame, lady. The elven blood that runs through my veins is attuned to dry metal."

He patted Apollo's rump, but the gelding did not need any urging from him, and picked up a quick trot.

Cecily dropped her arms as the little mare followed, a loud splash and a new puddle behind her on the trail. But Giles noticed that translucent wisps of vapor still clung to the young woman's cheeks and hair.

The trail curved back toward the ocean and they rode atop jagged cliffs that ended in smooth rocks below, the view to their left now hidden by bush and tree.

"You do not resist your magic now."

She brushed a rather damp tendril of hair away from her cheek. "It's odd, but it feels stronger than it ever has before. It's as if I unleashed a dam when I used it to save the village, and now the fallen stones resist my attempts to block it back up... Oh, it's hard to explain."

"I think I understand." Giles glanced down at the hilt of his sword. "We humans were not meant for elven blood and magic."

"Besides," she continued, as if he hadn't spoken, "I see no reason to hide what I am anymore. My attempts at a normal life have failed miserably."

"Normal is boring."

"It is safe."

He did not reply. Safe was boring too, but the lady would probably argue about it for the next several hours if he told her so. They rode for a time in silence, twilight falling gently about them, until it grew cool enough that Giles pulled his coat back on. Just over the rise ahead they should be able to spy the small town that boasted an inn. He had stayed there many a time to barter his trade. The rooms were tiny and damp, but the innkeeper's wife served up a delicious fish stew.

Giles pulled back on the reins. He narrowed his eyes at the town below them and muttered a curse.

Cecily pulled the mare a bit ahead of him, craning her head to see down the rise. "What is it?"

"Bluecoats. Everywhere." But it must be a somewhat peaceful occupation, for his sword did not try to fly into his hand, only hummed a bit in the scabbard. "Just keep the horses walking."

When trees blocked their view again, Giles urged Apollo to a trot, until they'd left enough distance behind them for comfort.

"Why this sudden interest in our small villages?" asked Cecily.

"There have been rumors that Breden of Dewhame is building up his army again, that he intends to win back the king from Mor'ded of Firehame."

Cecily wrinkled her rather pert little nose. "I don't see why they care whether the king resides in Firehame or Dewhame. It's not like the king has any true power anymore."

"It's part of the game, my lady. Whoever wins the king has beaten the other elven lord in skill and battle... although it's humans who suffer the true losses. For the Imperial Lords, it's just a matter of pride and love of chaos."

"I wish they had never opened the door to our world," she said with a shiver.

"Then you never would have been born."

"Point taken. Then I wish they would open it back up and leave."

"Not very likely. They consider their home world of Elfhame... boring."

"Peace is not boring."

Giles shrugged. He would not debate this subject with her either, so he switched to the subject he'd been meaning to discuss all day. "There could be another reason for the soldiers' presence, Cecily. They could have heard about the magic you performed in our village."

"So soon?"

Giles knew the elven lords had a magical means of communication, but again, if Thomas had not seen fit to tell her... "Anything's possible. So to be safe

I suggest you do not use your full powers. I think we can escape them if we move in secret, but if you use that magic of yours, they will know where to look for you."

The trail brought them closer to the channel again, and the wind picked up with a vengeance. She buttoned her coat while Giles did the same.

Cecily raised her voice over the crash of the waves. "I'm back where I started—running and hiding. I won't do it again."

Giles studied her face, looking for the determination behind her words, but unable to stop himself from noticing how lovely she looked in the wind, with pink cheeks and curls of midnight hair playing about her face. Her lips were a dark red, like the finest claret, and so damn kissable that he wondered where he'd found the force of will all those years ago to deny them when she'd offered. Of course, she was a woman now and not a young girl and that made a difference… although he knew he had done the right thing, the only thing he could have under the circumstances…

Alas, what had she been saying? Oh, yes. "Do not think to give yourself up to Breden of Dewhame. The elven lord does not understand mercy. And despite your impressive magic, you would not stand a chance against him."

"Must he hate me so?"

Her voice trembled and he brought Apollo to a stop, the mare placidly halting alongside. He reached down and touched her shoulder in sympathy, a flare of tenderness running through him. "Do not allow yourself to think that the elven lords have feelings like we do. It is not in their nature. Indeed, their own people consider them mad, or so says Thomas."

Her eyes flashed. "Thomas is my true father."

"Indeed. So think of him. You cannot find him if you give yourself up to Breden of Dewhame."

She nodded, and Giles breathed a mental sigh of relief. The young woman could be stubborn and unpredictable, but she would listen to reason.

Giles urged Apollo forward, allowing the gelding to pick his way carefully in the near darkness. The jagged cliffs had softened to a smoother slope down to the ocean, and he took a trail that he remembered from his visits here. Once in Dorset, however, he would be in unfamiliar territory, and would have enjoyed the adventure of it if he didn't have the young woman to protect.

"Where are we going?" she asked from behind him.

Giles did not answer, for she would see quickly enough. Sand softened Apollo's hoofbeats. Giles guided him to the right, behind a fall of rock that looked solid, but held a gap just barely wide enough for the beast to pass through. The ocean breeze no longer pummeled them, the crash of the waves now muffled. When Giles felt the chamber open, he dismounted and set about gathering driftwood by feel, and making a fire.

The flames lit the cavern and Cecily still sat atop her horse, staring about with joy.

"I knew you'd like it," he said. Faith, every time he came here he had thought of her, and how he would like to show her this place. He just never thought he'd actually have the opportunity to do so.

Magic had crafted this cave, he knew. But how or why, he couldn't fathom. Seashells had been imbedded into the walls to form pictures of sharks and dolphins, and seals near the bottom. A layer of blue shells separated water and sky, with a myriad of birds crafted above. Some of the birds he could put a name to: puffins, razorbills, and kittiwakes. Some he could not identify, and wondered if they were native to England… or perhaps that fabled land of Elfhame. For dragons had also been crafted on the ceiling above, with wings spread wide and claws outstretched. And although he'd only seen them from a distance, he knew the dragons had been brought with the elven lords when they'd opened that door between the worlds.

"It… moves," breathed Cecily as she continued to stare about her. "Look, Giles, the dolphin is jumping through the waves. And, ho, that seal is evading that shark and making him angry." Her eyes widened as she tilted her head farther back and stared at the ceiling. "Those dragons are battling one another… the black one is breathing fire, and the blue… that is Breden's dragon-steed, Kalah. I'd heard that he belches lightning…" She shuddered, quickly pulling her gaze down from the scene above.

Giles rose and approached her horse. Her face had gone white. "What is it?"

She shook her head, her lower lip trembling. "I wielded lightning once. It's deadly. And so powerful."

"When you escaped from Firehame?"

She nodded.

"And that is why you have turned your back on your magic?"

"No one should be able to hold that much power. It makes you feel…"

"Frightened?"

She smiled at that, too sadly for his liking. "No, Giles Beaumont. It makes you long for more. It makes you want to destroy, just because you can."

He did not know what to say. Perhaps he knew the young lady's habits from watching her all these years, but he suddenly realized he really didn't know her at all.

Giles held up his arms to her and she allowed him to help her off the horse. Her legs wobbled beneath her, so his hands lingered on her shoulders to keep her from falling. Or so he told himself. In truth, he enjoyed the feeling that touching her always seemed to excite in him.

"You are not used to riding so long in the saddle." His voice surprised him. Low, husky, as if he spoke to one of his lovers.

She looked up at him and damn if he didn't think he'd drown in her eyes.

She licked her lips.

He would not kiss her. Thomas had forbidden any familiarity with his daughter. Giles's own ambition of working for the Rebellion made the act disastrous. Pretty girls had always gotten him into trouble, but not this time. The stakes were too high.

Giles dropped his arms and broke whatever spell had fallen between them. He turned and saw to the mounts, removing their saddles and spreading the blankets on the sandy floor near the fire. He frowned, and then set the blankets on opposite sides of the fire. 'Twas a sad thing when he couldn't trust himself to sleep next to the minx.

Cecily didn't comment on his actions, just settled herself atop one of the blankets when he finished arranging them. From his pouch he withdrew some dried fish and journey cakes lumpy with nuts and berries, and handed them to her while he fetched water from a small spring near the back of the cave. By the time he'd finished watering the horses, Cecily had finished her meal, removed her hat, and unplaited her hair.

Giles settled himself on his blanket and surreptitiously watched her while he ate his meal. She drew a comb through her hair, and although the black strands lacked the white color of the elven, it appeared to sparkle with a silver luster at her every movement. He wanted to fill his hands with the silken stuff and bury his face in it.

Damn it.

He brushed the crumbs from his lap and drank greedily from his flask.

Another glance across the fire, and he saw the tips of her slightly pointed ears as she combed her hair back from her face. Cecily always kept her ears covered with her hair by means of tightly binding it down in the back. The rare sight of them made him feel as if he'd glimpsed some forbidden flesh.

He shifted where he sat.

Lud, he'd seen her naked more times than he could count. A bit of softly spiked ear should not have bothered him. Perhaps it was due to their new understanding of each other, or perhaps to their circumstances… but now that he pondered it… hadn't he dreamed of the sight of her body every night? Hadn't he been disappointed by one lover after another, when they lacked the long length of Cecily's legs, or the dark pink of her nipples, or the small beauty mark on her left hip?

Perhaps the sight of her nude body *had* bothered him more than he allowed himself to admit.

When he glanced up again, she'd braided her hair and covered those ears. He couldn't decide if he felt relieved or annoyed.

"Are you well?" she asked.

"Why?"

"You made an odd sort of noise."

"Did I?"

"Mmm."

They sat companionably for a time, with the distant sound of the surf and the snuffling of the horses to dispel the quiet. Despite the summer evening, a chill emanated from the walls of the cave and Giles unrolled his cloak.

"Did you bring a wrap, Cecily?"

"No. You told me to pack lightly, and I needed my petticoats."

"Yes, of course. Here." Giles stood and walked around the fire, feeling as if he breached some intimate barrier. He took a breath and ignored the feeling, crouching and laying his cloak lightly about Cecily's slight body. He allowed his hands to rest on her small shoulders for a moment, relishing the contact, breathing in the scent of her hair. Lavender. Soft and sweet.

"Thank you," she said a bit stiffly, and he noticed how she'd stilled, like a doe in sight of an arrow.

He flinched away from her. Just because she'd offered herself to him all those years ago did not mean she desired him now. Indeed, with all the upheaval in her life, and his sense that she blamed him for most of it, the young woman had every right to regret being forced upon this journey with him.

As he settled himself back on his blanket, he told himself it was probably for the best. If he couldn't manage to control himself around her, at least she did not suffer from the same weakness.

Giles removed his sword belt, but left it near to hand. He felt safe enough within the cavern not to stand watch, but that would probably not be true for the rest of their journey, so he'd best get some sleep while he could. Besides, his devil-blade always alerted him to danger.

In anticipation of a fight, no doubt.

His shoulder still ached a bit from his wound, and he groaned and shifted as he lay down. His eyes tried to make out the dragons above, but the smoke from their fire obscured the mosaic. After a time he heard Cecily lie down as well, but he refused to look at her again.

Apollo snorted and the wind moaned. Except for their small ring of light, the black of night surrounded them like a shroud.

"I cannot sleep."

Cecily's words drifted over the banked flames. He'd never noticed how smooth her voice sounded, like water flowing over stone.

"Tell me about your sword."

Giles glanced at his devilish blade. It lay quietly within his scabbard, looking for all the world like any other ordinary weapon. Perhaps an even less-than-ordinary blade, unless someone looked closely. The stone that had once been imbedded in the pommel had long ago fallen out, leaving behind a small depression. The leather on the hilt had been worn down to shiny smoothness, only the wire encasing it allowing a firm grip. The quillon was nothing more than two plain crosspieces of metal, lacking any sort of engraving or design.

But the blade itself looked newly forged, without dent or scratch, and never needed sharpening. "My sword?"

"Up until yesterday, I thought it but an ordinary weapon."

"Up until yesterday, we had no battles within the village."

She shifted, and he caught the gleam of a soft cheek, the sheen of midnight hair. "I vow, Giles, it *pulled* you into battle. How did you come by it?"

He threw an arm over his eyes. "'Twas my father's blade, and the making of it, my younger brother, John's. From somewhere far down our family line came a strong influx of elven blood, and although I inherited the looks and grace, John inherited the magic of the Imperial Lord of Bladehame."

The thought of his brother made his chest constrict. Time should have dulled the memory of his young face, but he could see it just as clearly as if he had but seen John yesterday. So small and plain, but those silver eyes of his glittering with the enormous elven power he could wield. As the eldest, Giles had felt John to be his responsibility, and perhaps that was why his father had not told him of the testing, until after John had been taken. Giles had been furious with his father, and they had exchanged harsh words before he had died. Words that Giles now regretted.

His mother had died long ago, so he had been left with no one. For a long time, Giles had felt lost and alone. Until he had discovered the Rebellion. And had filled the emptiness inside of him with a lust for vengeance.

For some reason, Giles wanted to tell Cecily about John. And perhaps, a bit about himself. Giles could not imagine what opinions she had formed about him, and he found that it mattered. More than it should. "When my brother and father died, the sword came to me with a promise. A promise to avenge their deaths."

The wood in the fire crackled and popped.

"I suppose," she said, "that the Imperial Lord of Bladehame… Lan'dor, is that his name?"

"Aye."

"I suppose he discovered your brother's talent for magic and sent John to Elfhame after his testing. But the chosen ones aren't sent to Elfhame, are they, Giles?" He heard the shift of her skirts. "It is true what Thomas says, then. That those gifted with enough magic to threaten the elven lords' rule are murdered. And your father must have known this. But what of your father? How did he die?"

It became harder and harder to speak. Giles swallowed against his dry throat. "At the hand of Lan'dor of Bladehame. This devilish sword had been crafted to murder the elven lord."

Cecily gasped, and Giles dropped the arm from his face, met her gaze across the fire. "John forged it with his own blood. To withstand not only any blade of steel, but magical assaults as well. When they hauled John away after his testing, my father challenged

Lan'dor. But the devil-blade could not withstand the power of an Imperial Lord *and* his scepter."

Shadows played across her lovely face, and he saw but flashes of the sad curve to her lips, the welling of tears in her eyes. "And so you joined the Rebellion."

"Aye. It will take the might of many to defeat an elven lord. Or…"

She finished the thought for him. "Or perhaps the powerful daughter of but one."

Four

CECILY WOKE THE NEXT MORNING SURROUNDED BY THE spicy scent of the blacksmith's skin. Her eyelids flew open with a start. She took in a deep breath before she realized the scent came from the cloak around her, then hastily threw off the covering.

He still slept, with one arm thrown over his eyes and the other resting upon his sword. His broad chest rose and fell with his heavy breathing, his mouth slightly parted and his white-blond hair spread about him like a halo. His face looked a bit pale and Cecily wondered if his injury still pained him.

She frowned at the thought, and quickly scurried out of the cavern, avoiding the mosaics on the wall. Beautiful, yes, but their movement made her dizzy.

The crisp morning air erased any lingering drowsiness. Seabirds swooped above the waves and scolded each other with harsh cries. She skirted clumps of green and purple seaweed and scuttling crabs. A boulder with a slight overhang provided an outdoor dressing room for her to strip, a protrusion of stone a dry shelf to store her clothing.

What use had she for fine palaces when her beach provided her with all she needed?

The thought made her think of Mother, and the way she had always seemed to be a great lady, even in their humble cottage, and tears burned Cecily's eyes. How she wished she could talk to Mother about her confused feelings for Giles.

Cecily ran into the waves, sucking in a breath when they reached past her hips, but she soon became accustomed to the coldness of the water and dove into the next high wave. It didn't take her long to find what she sought.

Lobster. Giles loved it.

With a skill from many years of capturing them, Cecily avoided the snapping claws and managed to carry several of the large shellfish back to dry sand. She set them in a small tide pool while she dressed, humming a tune beneath her breath. And caught herself.

She bowed her head, staring down at her hands, the skin only slightly puckered from her long swim. How could she feel so content after all that had happened?

Because she had been thinking only of Giles, and the look on his face when she brought his morning meal.

She carried her shoes in one hand and lobster in the other, the fine sand softly padding her footsteps as she returned to the cave.

No, 'twas more than Giles. Despite losing the life she'd worked so hard to achieve, she was no longer hiding. She'd made a decision, and would confront the Rebellion on her own terms. She would find her father. She had to believe she hadn't lost everything.

She did believe it.

Her footsteps felt light as she walked along the tunnel-like rock that led to the hidden cavern. Belle nickered at the sight of her, Apollo deigning to give her a snort, and suddenly Giles flew to his feet with sword in hand.

Cecily froze.

"I overslept," he said with a scowl.

"Nay, you but slept longer than I."

"Where have you been?"

She held out her catch with a proud grin. "There's no need to eat dried fish when the ocean is so near."

Giles sheathed his sword but not the stern look upon his face. "Never do that again."

"What?"

"Leave my side. Don't you realize I'm supposed to protect you?"

She could argue with him. But it would serve no purpose. "Alas, I had forgotten, brave knight. This weak and defenseless maiden will never leave your sight again."

Her sarcasm was not lost on him. His handsome face turned an alarming shade of red and he strode toward the back of the cave, watering the horses while Cecily proceeded to build up the fire and cook her catch. When she judged it done, she broke open the shell with a rock and dug out the sweet white meat.

Boiled and buttered, it could not have tasted better.

The smell drew him back to the fire, as she knew it would, and he took what she offered without a word. He sat and ate, occasionally closing his eyes as he chewed, the irritation on his face slowly fading.

"I love lobster."

"I know." Ah, it felt good to say that back to him. "You are not the only one who is observant."

His brow rose. "Are you saying you spied upon me?"

"Certainly not." She would not admit that her gaze had always been drawn to him. Not ever again. One such humiliation in her lifetime would be sufficient. "Everyone saw the stack of shells you left upon the table at the last harvest gathering. Faith, the men were *wagering* on how high it would get."

He smiled and Cecily's eyes widened. His lips curled in such a boyish manner, his head tilting to the side and a fall of his thick silky hair shadowing his high cheekbone and angled jaw. He looked slightly embarrassed and proud and utterly delicious.

Heaven help her.

"I'm sorry," he murmured. "About raising my voice to you. I forget what you truly are, even though you showed me the proof of your powers—"

"No," she hurriedly protested. She could not bear that smile alongside an apology. It was more temptation than she could defend against. "I apologize for my saucy tongue. Mother always chided me for it."

He captured her with his gaze. Although he had the physique and grace of the elven, his eyes were entirely human. A normal-sized dusky green, like the color of the ocean on a cloudy day.

"Despite what your father kept telling me, I saw nothing but a normal girl for many years." His lips quirked. "A very pretty normal girl, mind you, who could stay submerged beneath the waves for an unusually long time, but who showed very little magical ability. But now I have seen the proof of your powers and I know you can surely defend yourself but I have not adjusted—"

"Do not," she interrupted. "Please do not treat me other than a normal girl. I could not bear the changes that have happened to me otherwise."

Silence lay between them for a moment, until Cecily could finally tear her gaze away from his.

"Well, then," he said, the jauntiness in his voice sounding only a bit forced. "You have now agreed to my full protection and I have yet found a lady who regretted it." He rose and began to gather up his things and pack them back onto the horses.

Cecily rolled her eyes, a grin on her mouth despite herself, and doused the fire and packed her belongings. She allowed herself to enjoy the mosaic on the walls for a last time, but soon they were both mounted and on their way.

Giles took paths that led them farther and farther from her ocean. It made Cecily feel an odd sort of panic, but thankfully the land still held so many lakes and streams and fountains that she comforted herself with the sight of them.

But within a few hours even those bodies of water started to dwindle.

"Where are we?"

"Dorset," he replied, sparing her no glance, for his eyes constantly surveyed their surroundings, and she would swear the tips of his pointed ears perked at every rustle of the brush. They rode through a soft land of rolling hills and yellow gorse, an occasional fiery red tree dotting the landscape. Giles must have taken a route specifically designed to avoid any more villages or towns, for nary a cottage did she see.

The landscape changed as they rode down into

a valley, and soon they were surrounded by rocky mountains and tors.

"There is a spring ahead," breathed Cecily. She could smell the water.

Giles turned in the saddle and looked down at her with a worried frown. "What is wrong?"

She wiped away a trickle of sweat that seeped from beneath her straw hat. "I have discovered that I'm... uncomfortable without the presence of the ocean beside me."

"We are in the sovereignty of Firehame, and will see more flame than water. But by evening we will reach the Hants, and there are many streams within the forest and you should feel better. I should have thought—I have a map memorized in my head, but it lacks much detail. Where is the spring? We will stop there for our midday meal."

Cecily gave a crooked smile of relief and pointed to the right. Giles found it beneath an overhanging boulder, with enough shade for them to sit side by side while they ate another meal of dried fish and journey bread.

When she had finished, Cecily removed her tucker and dunked it in the cool liquid, dousing her face and neck. She did not think about the cleavage she revealed until she felt his gaze upon her.

She turned and he swallowed his last bite. Rather forcefully.

He quickly averted his gaze and Cecily frowned, pushing her soggy tucker back into the *V* of her bodice. She could not figure this man at all. Oh, she well understood that after living in the same village for years—despite the fact that they'd barely exchanged a few words to each other in the past few—it would be natural for them to feel some sort of familiarity with one another. Especially after Giles had revealed his secret.

And she had always felt a certain… light-headedness around him. Most of the village girls did. He could not help his handsome face or fine figure, no more than she could help her large odd eyes. But since that dreadful night when she'd made such a prodigious fool of herself, she had realized he felt no attraction for her person whatsoever.

Yet he looked at her with such hungry eyes…

Pshaw. 'Twas only her way of transferring her own desire to him. He looked at her bosom as he would any woman's. He was but a man, despite the mix of elven blood that flowed through his veins.

And she could not even think that they were friends. Temporary companions forced to journey together.

She had misread his kindness and natural charm before. This time she would not. *She would not*. No matter how many times she had to tell herself—

A muscular arm wrapped about her shoulders and then her mouth, dragging her deeper into the hollow of the boulder. His hand muffled her cry of surprise but she reflexively struggled anyway, gathering her magic to help free her from his hold.

"Stop," he whispered, his mouth against her ear. "Fire demon."

What?

But she didn't have to wait long to understand, for several whirling orbs of flame bounced along the valley floor, no more than a few feet from where they huddled. Following those harbingers walked a creature she could not have imagined.

Red fire shaped a being that had legs like a man but flowed across the ground rather than stepped. A black, dripping mess formed the semblance of a face and an emaciated body.

Cecily froze and Giles angled his body in front of hers, that sword of his appearing to jump from his scabbard into his hand.

The horses had been grazing on a patch of grass in the path of the creature. Their nostrils flared and they suddenly bolted, their flight not hampered a whit by Giles's and Cecily's belongings still strapped to their saddles.

The fire demon laughed, tossing a ball of orange flame at the beasts, hitting poor Belle squarely on her rump. The little mare squealed, her shorter legs pumping to overtake the faster gait of Apollo. Cecily gasped in sympathy, and the demon stopped, glowing eyes studying the rocky walls of the valley.

When those red orbs slowly settled on their hiding place, a flush of weakness made her muscles go limp. When the unnatural creature flowed toward them, Giles let out a curse and leaped at it. Cecily watched, still frozen with fear, as the demon threw another ball of fire straight at Giles.

He dodged, with unnatural elven swiftness, his sword slicing through the fireball and dissolving it into a shower of sparks. It appeared that the blade had enough power to disarm the magic of a fire demon, if not that of an Imperial Lord.

The flaming creature roared, making Cecily jump and finally freeing her from the terror that had held her immobile. Her hands trembled but her fingers followed her commands, coaxing the water from the spring, swirling it into small translucent tornadoes.

Giles danced around the demon, dodging more flaming spheres and occasionally getting in close enough to nick the thing with the tip of his sword. Wherever he touched it, a small hole appeared, but quickly closed up again with a lick of black fire.

The demon roared in frustration and this time gathered a blob of black sludge that dripped down its face, flung it at Giles. It hit the blacksmith on his injured shoulder, setting his coat aflame.

Cecily pelted Giles with a tornado.

It doused the flame but made him stagger in surprise, his gaze flying to hers in fury as he fell. The demon laughed, or at least, a similar imitation of one, and moving as swiftly as fire igniting dry thatch it swooped down upon the blacksmith. Giles rolled with an agility and grace that testified to the amount of elven blood flowing in his veins, but Cecily could not see past the flames to tell if he'd avoided the demon's attack.

"Fie," she breathed, and launched the full force of her swirling water at the monster. But the small spray had little effect on the demon, and the spring quickly ran dry. Cecily reached deeper into the earth, inside the very mountain itself, where an underground river flowed dark and cold. It came to her call through the narrow opening of the spring, cracking the edges of the earth and shaking the mountainside itself.

A deluge of water fell upon the fire demon and the

creature turned its burning red eyes in her direction, screaming defiantly as it slowly withered to a puddle of black.

Cecily shivered from that final glare, slowly coaxing the raging water to calm. Her heart beat a staccato rhythm and her legs shook as she stood. But Giles had not moved, and she soon found herself running to reach his side.

"Giles."

He lay on his back, his eyelids shut, fist still closed about the hilt of his sword. But his chest rose and fell—surely she could see it moving! Black sludge covered him from head to toe, and Cecily called the water again, this time a bit more slowly, easing it over his body in gentle swirls.

"Giles," she whispered again, crouching over him, her shoes sinking into the mud. With an impatient flick of her fingers she sent the remaining liquid back to the spring, her trembling hands smoothing the blacksmith's hair away from his face. His skin had been scorched red, the tips of his thick black lashes and the edges of his brows burnt away. The leather of his breeches and coat had been blackened, yet his blade still shone like newly forged metal.

But she had not been mistaken. He breathed, although it had an odd, wheezing sound to it.

Tears burned the back of her lids. Perhaps she should not have interfered in the battle. Perhaps Giles wouldn't have been harmed if she hadn't distracted him with her magic.

Cecily let out an impatient grunt. Or perhaps he would have died. She would not regret her actions now.

His skin looked ready to blister. She knew as much as the next village maid did about basic healing, and she'd recognized some herbs near the spring...

She suited thought to action and quickly made a poultice of wet leaves and laid it on Giles's face and hands. But she did not know what to do if his lungs had been affected by fire and smoke. She needed to get him to a healer, and for that, she needed the horses.

Cecily stared down the rocky valley, squinting her eyes for sign of any movement. She could not wander off and leave Giles but they needed the horses. She had no idea how far the animals had gone, and she didn't know if they'd kept to the valley or found a route out of it.

She squared her shoulders and began to walk in the direction their mounts had run, every instinct within her screaming against leaving the blacksmith alone and unprotected.

But despite her elven strength, she could not carry him all the way to the nearest village.

She found Apollo just as night fell. The animal had actually been walking toward her, and nickered a greeting when she called his name.

He hung his head when she reached him, pushing his nose against her belly.

Cecily rubbed his neck in relief. "You were returning to your master, weren't you?"

Apollo snorted, a shudder running through his great body.

"Don't be ashamed. I don't blame you for running."

He lifted his head and shook it.

"Well, you will do better next time, that's all."

Cecily picked up the dangling reins and led him over to a rock so she could reach the stirrup, and he stood quite still while she settled herself on his back. Deeper shadows from a full moon danced along the valley floor, the gloom of the evening making the jagged rocks and tors look entirely different... and somehow menacing.

She held the reins loosely. "Find your way back to Giles, Apollo."

He broke into a confident trot, in spite of the uneven ground, and Cecily melted into the saddle with relief. He would find their way back, and she would pray he did not stumble into a hole or over a shadowed rock. For a moment, she allowed herself to tremble with fear and exhaustion. She had expended most of her energy in the use of her magic and she'd never seen such a creature as the fire demon. What other dreadful things existed outside her little village?

She could not wait to find her father and return home... or if not to her old home, they could find a new one. One without monsters and swords and a man who confused her beyond all reason.

Her heart jumped at a sound from behind her, and then settled again when she saw the dark form following them, recognizing the sound of Belle's lighter hoofbeats.

Cecily had walked farther than she'd thought, yet reached the spring sooner than she could have hoped for. She could barely make out the form of the black-smith as he lay in shadow, but he looked to be on his hands and knees, his head bowed to the ground.

Apollo approached his master, head hanging down again, and stopped when Cecily slid from his back.

"You're awake," she cried, happiness making her voice sing the words.

Giles looked up at her through the fall of his pale hair. "What the hell did you do to me?"

She frowned in confusion at his words, but when she reached his side, Cecily understood. His hair had bonded to the mud when she'd dried it and the ends of the strands were still stuck. He'd managed to rip the rest of his body from the mold, but she imagined it would hurt to rip his hair out of it.

"Oh. Just hold still and I'll have you out in a moment." A little water to soak the dirt again, then some more to wash the strands clean when they slipped free, and he sat before her, looking almost as good as new.

"Your skin did not blister."

He frowned. "I imagine it did, and already healed."

"Elven blood."

"Indeed. And where have you been?"

His anger drained the happiness she'd felt on seeing him alive and well. "I went to fetch Apollo, but apparently he'd already decided to return to his master. I didn't have to go far."

Giles nodded and stood, wavering on his feet for a moment. "I have words for both of you, but they shall have to wait until I wet my throat." He slowly made his way back to the spring, gathering dry branches along the way, Cecily collecting her own armful and adding it to the fire that he started.

The horses shied from the flames, and after a few

seconds of her own instinctive fear, Cecily stepped closer, around the fire and back into the hollow of the boulder. The air had grown chill with nightfall.

Giles drank and then washed from the diminished spring by the light of the flickering flames. When he finished, he turned toward the black shapes of Apollo and Belle, removing their bags and saddles. "You should have stayed," he said to the large gelding. Then he turned to Cecily. "You should have run."

She did not answer. It took all of her willpower to still the chattering of her teeth.

Apollo nickered softly in apology and Giles stroked the animal's forelock a moment, transferring his hands to Belle when she sidled up for some of the attention. He left them loose to graze, despite their earlier abandonment, and brought the bags within the small shelter.

"We'll have to sleep here for the night."

Cecily jerked her head in acknowledgement, hugging her arms about her.

"It's not that cold," he added, but wrapped his cloak about her before he settled at her side after laying a blanket on the ground. He rummaged in his sack for a moment and held out a hunk of journey bread. "Eat this. It will help."

She shook her head. She could not control her jaw enough to chew.

"Damn it," muttered Giles. "Don't you know what you've done? By using your magic, you've alerted Breden of Dewhame's men to our location. The shaking of a mountain isn't something he will ignore. What with everything else that has happened, he will be sure to send soldiers to investigate. Have you so little faith in my abilities that you feel impelled to rush to my rescue?"

The inner strength Cecily had relied upon up to this point dwindled to a tiny core. She was tired unto death and could no longer control her shaking. Nor could she stop the tears that welled up in her eyes when she looked at him. "I th-thought you were going to d-d-die."

His eyes widened, the creases smoothing from his brow, the muscles in his jaw relaxing.

"I c-could hide my magic in the village," she continued, "because nothing ever h-happened there. There were no b-b-battles or m-monsters. No one I c-c-cared for had ever been threatened with more than a s-s-splinter!"

He slid a bit closer, his arm creeping around her, the heat of his body such a welcome relief that she did not pull away.

"Hush," he murmured.

But an anger bordering on despair continued to fuel her words. "And now my magic has been l-l-let loose and it comes to my call with a simple thought and your sword may have survived th-that demon thing but you might not have and you were l-l-lucky to come away with naught but singed brows and blackened breeches."

Cecily took a breath. The heat of his fingers touched her chin and she raised her head. "And then I had t-to leave you to find the horses not knowing if you'd be alive when I returned..."

Somehow his mouth lay mere inches from her own. Firelight flickered off the planes of his cheeks, the sweep of his chin, the straight length of his nose. His eyes looked enormous, the green barely visible in the darkness, two large deep wells she could easily drown in. Her senses heightened; she could smell the burnt leather of his coat, the sharp aroma of the herbs from the poultice she'd made him, the underlying spicy scent of his skin. She felt his arm about her now like a hot band of soft steel, felt his breath across her mouth like a gentle caress, the feel of his fingers beneath her chin like rough leather.

"Hush," he whispered again. "All is well."

And then he set his lips on top of hers, a gently soft touch she felt clear to her toes. How many nights had she dreamed that he'd kiss her? Not for a long while now, but for many years she had yearned to know what his lips felt like. Then she had hated him. And now…

And now he touched her with such reverent tenderness that she wondered what feeling lay behind it.

Cecily could never have imagined the circumstances that brought this kiss about.

Her mind spun while his mouth moved hesitantly over hers. This felt nothing like Will's kiss. It did not comfort or soothe. Instead, it set a tingle racing through her body, made her heart beat faster and her breath quicken. It made her feel alive and aware of parts of her body she'd never taken much notice to.

His tongue brushed her lips. Cecily's mouth parted on a sigh, her hands reaching for him, encountering the hard slope of his shoulders, the silky texture of his thick hair. Her head tilted backward as he increased the pressure on her mouth as if he couldn't get close enough to her, couldn't taste her fully.

And then his tongue swept against hers, a lovely tangle of smooth heat that made her breasts throb and peak. Made the place between her legs ache and grow damp.

Merciful heaven. She had not known what a kiss was until this moment.

He groaned. A shudder racked his body and he pulled away from her, panting hard, his face twisted with pain.

"What is it?" asked Cecily. Had his injuries not all healed? "Where does it hurt?"

His mouth quirked at her words. "Not somewhere that my elven blood can heal."

She frowned. "I do not understand."

Giles straightened his spine, turning his face from hers to stare into the fire. "I shouldn't have done that. It seemed but a simple means to silence you. I forgot how you affect me, Cecily. I promise not to let it happen again."

Cecily blinked. A kiss meant so little to him that he used it as a way to silence her? Such a vast gulf of experience yawned between them she feared she might never bridge that gap. Apparently what she'd felt from that kiss was completely one-sided. Her imagination at work again.

She collapsed on the blanket, wiggling to escape a protruding rock, and closed her eyes. She would regard that kiss as casually as he did, and be proud of herself for no longer being childish enough to think it meant a thing.

Perhaps tomorrow she would ask him what he'd meant by saying that he'd forgotten how she affected him, but for the nonce exhaustion overwhelmed her, as if he'd taken what little stamina she'd had left, and she plunged into sleep.

But when she awoke in the morning Giles had already put out the fire and saddled their mounts, and Cecily ate a cold meal while they rode. When she attempted conversation later, the blacksmith shushed her, his gaze warily roaming the gentle hills that had replaced the rocky tors.

Cecily frowned, trying to ignore an itch from her wool coat, and the ache in her bottom from sitting in a saddle so much. It seemed to her that Giles purposely avoided having a conversation with her. He had barely looked at her once this morn, and when he accidentally caught her eye he would flush and look away.

Did he regret that kiss so very much then? Or did he fear that she would misunderstand it, as she had done with his kindness when she was a young girl?

Cecily leaned over and patted Belle's neck. Fiddle, the man probably hadn't given it another thought.

Trees had swallowed the road some time ago, and when it finally cleared a bit, she caught a glimpse of buildings through the branches.

"Stay close," murmured Giles. "This is the town where I'd planned for us to spend the night before we encountered that demon. We'll have to be on the lookout for bluecoats now, but I'm hoping Breden of Dewhame won't risk angering another elven lord by sending his troops into another sovereignty."

Finally, she could speak, and words flowed from her tongue like a dam breaking. "What was that demon-thing? And why are we stopping here now?

Do you really think Breden suspects I'm alive? Or does he think someone else made the mountain shake? Surely there are others that can manage that feat?" And why did you kiss me? Did you feel nothing at all?

But she could not voice those last two questions.

He turned and looked down at her, his green eyes appearing even more vibrant with the shadow of the leaves behind him. His white-blond hair shimmered in the dappled sunlight, his dark brows a startling contrast. The singed tips had already grown back, along with his thick eyelashes.

"I think," he said, with that shuttered look on his face again, which Cecily suspected meant he knew more than he told her, "the fire demon was but a stray from Firehame Palace. Mor'ded used to craft them to do his bidding, and no doubt he would not regret it getting loose and causing a bit of mayhem in the countryside. The elven lords are easily bored, Cecily. Don't ever underestimate that sensibility with them."

She tilted her head up at him. "You said 'used' to craft them. Does he not do so anymore? And why not?"

A half smile curved his sensual lips. Cecily ignored the thought that she now knew they were also firm, warm, and tasted exquisite.

"You are a clever woman," he said. "I should be reminding myself never to underestimate *you*." Giles scanned the empty streets as they rode into the town proper. "There should be more foot traffic. Maybe this wasn't such a good idea. But damn, I'm tired of the stink of burnt leather."

"It's a splendid idea," urged Cecily. "I would give much for a hot meal."

"And I for a new coat. Let's go then; the inn is this way, and they serve a hearty stew—"

His scabbard flapped against his hip and suddenly his sword flew into his hand. Giles looked about, urging Apollo backward, pinning Belle against the back wall of a cottage. Cecily caught a flash of blue before Giles's body and the top of his horse blocked her view.

And then she heard the sound of running feet, the shouts of soldiers, and the oddest keening noise from the blade. Giles and Apollo erupted into a fury of motion, dodging, swinging, and fighting to protect her.

Cecily raised her hands, but the village had only one small well, surely not enough water for her to vanquish the number of soldiers that had appeared from doorways and alleys and roadways. She would have to go deeper again, like she did with the mountain, but the underground stream ran thinly, far underground...

"Do not even think it," shouted Giles while dropping low in his saddle to swing at another soldier.

Cecily lowered her hands into her lap, clasping them about her reins until the whites of her knuckles showed. She would wait. He could not fight them all, for just as in the village, they numbered in the hundreds.

Giles spared no more attention to her, his sword moving so quickly she saw only flashes of the metal. If she didn't feel so terrified, she would have admired his deadly skill.

She wondered why none of the soldiers had discharged their weapons, instead of fighting close quarters with such a dangerous opponent. And then she realized that perhaps they wanted her alive.

Would she even recognize her blood father when she saw him again?

And then Giles angled Apollo so Belle had a clear escape route to an open road.

"Go," he shouted.

Cecily shook her head. She would not leave him.

"I'll follow," he insisted, and then slapped Belle on the rump.

Her poor little mare had withstood the sound of battle for long enough. She took off with a leap, nearly unseating Cecily, and galloped down the unfamiliar road with nary a caution for overhanging branches or potholes. Cecily lay over the horse's neck, praying that the next turn in the road would not take them into another group of soldiers.

She heard another set of hoofbeats behind them. She glanced back and relief replaced her terror. As he promised, Giles did indeed follow. Bloody sword in hand, eyes squinted against the wind of their flight, pale blond hair streaming like a silk banner behind him.

And a smile on his face.

Cecily turned back around, and soon Apollo's greater stride overtook that of Belle. Her little mare snorted at the big gelding, and when he slowed, she quickly followed suit to an easy gallop.

"Redcoats," shouted Giles.

Cecily nodded. The uniforms of the Imperial Lord of Firehame.

"They showed up behind the blue," said Giles,

his eyes sparkling with laughter, "and soon Breden of Dewhame's men turned to face the new threat. It seems Mor'ded of Firehame will not tolerate the presence of another elven lord's soldiers, no matter the reason."

"Will we be followed?"

His expression sobered. "It's possible. But if so, we will lose them in the forest of the Hants."

Giles glanced at his sword, and Cecily followed his gaze. He had not wiped it clean, and yet now the blade shone clear and bright. She suppressed a shiver. Had it truly absorbed the blood of its victims?

She raised questioning eyes to Giles but he just shrugged, and sheathed the sword.

The blacksmith kept their mounts to a hard gallop, occasionally slowing to let the beasts catch their breath. At noon he allowed them to walk, so Cecily could eat her meal. Close to nightfall they encountered the edge of the forest and finally ended their mad flight.

Giles gave one last look behind them before the woods obscured their view. "I don't think we were followed."

Cecily lifted her head. "I smell water."

"The forest is littered with streams and brooks, despite the fire spells of the elven lord. It's as much of a normal wood as can be expected in England, so we have little to fear but a few forest deer and the occasional dormouse." He grinned, that odd euphoria from battle still affecting him. "Now, if we were entering a forest in the sovereignty of Verdanthame, that would be another adventure! The elven lord of the green scepter has twisted and shaped his woods beyond human imagining."

"Have you been there?"

He shook his head. "Nay. But one day I shall."

And Cecily saw him clearly for the first time. Giles Beaumont was a wanderer, craving adventure and new experiences. It filled his soul as much as her affinity for the ocean completed hers. She did not understand it. This joy for battle and excitement. But she recognized it. Thomas had the same sort of restlessness about him.

How it must have chafed at Giles to be stuck in their small village. How he must have resented the task of watching over her.

Yet, he had hidden it so well. She would never have suspected his true nature if they hadn't been forced to make this journey. Indeed, had she ever tried to see beyond his handsome face and perfect body?

His nature contrasted sharply with her desires for a comfortable home, nights by the fireside, pleasant tasks of gardening and sewing.

Cecily's fingers flew to her lips, the memory of that perfect kiss. They would never suit. Perhaps he had known that all along. Perhaps that's why he'd regretted kissing her. And she'd been too caught up in her infatuation to see it.

His innate passion would make it difficult for him to travel with a woman, any woman, without responding to her physically. She could not take it personally, or her heart would never survive a second rejection.

But Cecily couldn't be sure if she had correctly assessed the situation, and fiercely wished she could talk to her mother about it. She missed her dreadfully, and the realization that she would never see Mother again overwhelmed her anew.

"Cecily?"

She glanced up in surprise, hating the way she loved the sound of her name spoken in his deep voice. Then she looked in the direction he pointed, and her sadness faded.

Five

GILES KNEW HOW SHE MUST HAVE BEEN FEELING. CECILY had such a soft heart, a peaceful spirit. The events of the past few days might have been glorious for him, but a trial for her. When he'd stumbled upon this little glade, he had expected to hear her gasp with pleasure.

Instead he found her sight turned inward, a frown on her lovely face, her enormous eyes dark from her thoughts. But when she did glance up, his heart lightened, for her reaction was everything he'd hoped for.

They stood at the edge of a small clearing, a large boulder creating a small pond from the clear stream that ran between the elms. A carpet of emerald grass stretched around the pool of water, dotted with tiny yellow flowers and the occasional red poppy. The sun had fallen but a full moon had risen to replace it, creating a soft glow about the glade.

Off in the distance, a warbler sang a late-night tune.

"Is it safe?"

Giles nodded. "We lost our pursuers. You can swim while I make camp."

Her eyes closed for a moment as if he'd offered her heaven. But she did not move from her horse.

"Cecily?"

She hung her head. "I do not think I can move."

"What do you mean?"

"My legs. They don't appear to want to work."

Giles suppressed a smile, slipping off Apollo's back. "My apologies, my lady. Your muscles are not used to riding as hard as we did today." His words brought forbidden images to his mind. He was a cad. But damn if he couldn't help his base thoughts around this tantalizing woman. She had bedroom eyes and a body meant for hard riding, but more of the loving kind. He didn't know how Will had managed to keep her pure. But he knew she was. Giles would have intervened if the lout had pressed for anything more than a kiss.

He strode over to her horse. Enough of these thoughts. He always felt aroused after a good fight, and the battle today had surpassed any previous heightening of his senses. Any woman would have conjured carnal thoughts in him, and Cecily wasn't just any woman.

He could never bed *her* without serious consequences.

He held up his hand and she clasped his with her much smaller one, a frisson of pleasure at the contact racing through him. He did not know why she affected him like no other woman ever had, but perhaps being forbidden to him fueled his desire.

He was the experienced man, and she an innocent maid. He would have to keep control over their attraction to each other.

Then his gaze flew to her lips and they begged to

be kissed again. *Again*. What had he been thinking last night? Giles could not believe he'd blundered so badly. But it had seemed so natural for him to bend down and cover her mouth with his. As if he had done it all of his life. Or as if he'd wanted to.

Damn it, his thoughts had wandered off again.

"Can you unhook your leg from the support?"

She gritted her teeth, and then shook her head. Giles gently took hold of her thigh and calf and lowered it up and over the support of the sidesaddle. Then he quickly put his hands under her arms and she fell from her perch against him.

Her legs wobbled. Giles curved his arms about her back and held her upright. Her hair smelled of lavender and country air, the fine strands of it tickling the underside of his chin. She felt so small that a wave of fierce possessiveness struck him, an urge to protect her, to keep her safe, despite the dangerous power he knew she could wield. Power that made her more than capable of protecting herself.

If he didn't let her go soon, he might never. "Can you stand now?"

She nodded, her face against the front of his open shirt. Her cheek felt like the softest of rose petals.

Giles abruptly let her go, and she staggered for a moment, but remained upright. He spun and busied himself with removing Apollo's gear, trying to keep his breathing even. This woman muddled his brain with the feelings she aroused in him.

"You will be able to stretch your muscles with a swim," he said. "That should make them feel—"

A splash sounded from the pond. She had wasted

little time in regaining her element. Smallclothes littered the green of the grass in a line to the water— hints of lace and the other finery that always made women so appealing to him. Her sleek wet head rose from the water and he could just see her smile of pleasure from this distance.

Giles turned back to his chores, her happiness making him feel suddenly lighter. He allowed Apollo and Belle to roam free, grazing on the sweet grass around the pond, occasionally sucking up a drink of water and eyeing the strange sprite who playfully splashed their noses.

He placed his hands on his hips as he tried to survey the trees in the fading light. A small hollow carpeted with moss between the roots of a grandfather oak would make a fine sleeping place. He dug a shallow pit for the fire in front of it. With the flames in front and the tree at his back, they should be well protected from any nocturnal visitors of the scavenging kind.

He shook out their blankets and tossed them in the hollow, dug some dried fish and journey bread from his sack and frowned at the thought of eating it again.

He should have known better.

"Giles," shouted Cecily. He turned just as she tossed a small trout onto the grassy bank. The swell of her breasts were exposed to his gaze for a moment but then she dove again, surfacing to toss another fish beside the one still flopping about. He watched as she repeated the process several times, chiding himself for hoping for more than a brief flash of her pale skin, but unable to stop gawking.

Finally she had caught enough that she waved at

him and dove, and he knew she would stay under for a time, so he killed the fish and gutted them, wrapping them in pliable leaves and burying them in the coals. Giles told himself he didn't mind cooking while she hunted, but he set some snares deep in the woods, thinking that on the morrow a few fat hares would be a fine change from fish.

Just because he allowed her to contribute did not mean that he could not provide for both of them on this journey. And he would protect her. He would not fail her as he had failed John, nor would he ever exchange harsh words with her, as he had done with his father. When he parted from Cecily, he would do so without any regrets to plague his conscience.

In an odd sort of way, Cecily and Thomas had been his only family for the past nine years.

When Giles returned to the pond, she still had not surfaced. But he knew she could stay submerged for hours and did not worry. Instead he shed his coat and boots and stockings, thinking that he would welcome a bath himself, if only to cool his blood. But would wait until Cecily went to sleep before he attempted it.

He could not trust himself with more than one of them naked at a time.

At first Giles found himself hanging back from the clearing behind a bush. How easily habit took over. He did not need to spy upon her anymore. Indeed, it would be best if he sat in the open, returning to the fire when she emerged.

He settled on the grassy bank, watching the moonlight shimmer on the water's surface. Even the infamous Sir Robert Walpole, leader of the

Rebellion, would have to agree that Giles had earned his place in the ranks as a true spy after this journey. Another man would never have been able to resist the temptation Cecily offered. He knew he wouldn't have been able to if he had not known her so well. Thomas forbidding him to touch the girl would only fuel a man's temptation. But Giles knew that Thomas had been right.

If he bedded Cecily, he would have to wed her. And they were not meant for each other. Not just because of their disparate natures, but because she was meant for someone more worthy than he.

Cecily Sutton was England's best hope for freedom. He understood that better than any man.

And when would the worrisome woman come up for air?

A bubble broke the surface of the water. Giles rose to his feet, the grass a cold prickle between his toes. The small woodland sounds suddenly ceased, even the rustle of the trees seeming to still in the sudden silence.

His sword trembled at his hip. Damn. Giles dove.

He could see nothing but shadows upon shadows. The water buffeted him like a huge fist, batting him away, sending him tumbling head over heels more than once. Cold tendrils slithered against his skin. Jagged scales tore at his clothing. The weight of his breeches and sword dragged him down and he fought to regain the surface, desperate for a breath of air.

The pond could not be this deep.

With one mighty kick he rose, gasping for air, the water roiling around him.

"Cecily!"

The moonlight now seemed bright by comparison to the depths below. A column of swirling water erupted in front of him and Giles drew his sword, which came swiftly to hand, the blade humming as if it longed for magic just as eagerly as for blood.

For the creature that held Cecily in its jaw was surely made of magic.

A fish too large for such a small pond, with jagged teeth and slimy green scales and fins that resembled the blades of a knife. She fought within the confines of its great jaw, forcing water to keep its mouth open while she tried to push her way past the prison of its teeth.

But the monster kept her trapped, and Giles acted before the thing could submerge again, near leaping across the frothing water to plunge his blade into its side. The fish twisted, slamming him with its tail, making bright spots of light dance in his vision.

And then it was gone.

Giles dove blindly, his body sucked down in the wake of the beast's passage. Again he felt buffeted by some force, and realized it was Cecily's magic commanding the water to push the monster back up to the surface. But this time he held his naked blade in his hand and it dispelled the force of her magic and he plunged down, down…

His feet hit a solid surface. Not the pebbly bottom of the pond but a rubbery slick surface…

Giles spread his feet and plunged his blade downward.

A shudder. A keen from his sword more felt than heard. And then he rose up again, the pressure bringing him to his knees until the beast broke the surface of the water. He managed to suck in a desperate breath of air before the fish rolled. His devil-sword slid easily out of the monster's flesh and Giles leaped, landing in a fury of a wave.

A black slick stained the water, slowly growing as the creature thrashed weakly. When the fish finally stilled, it began to sink.

Giles did not have breath to call her name. He swam to the great head, the jaw still closed but lax now. Cecily lay trapped inside, her eyelids closed, her hair wrapped about her like a shroud. He used his sword as a lever, desperate to get her free before the monster sank below the surface. But he could not force the teeth apart until they slid underwater, weightlessness aiding him. A gap opened, just large enough for her slim body to get through and he grasped at her, fingers slipping off the wet surface of her skin.

Her hair wrapped about his fist and he winced, but used that tether to haul her free.

Not enough hands.

Giles sheathed his sword, and with one arm about Cecily's waist and the other paddling madly, he swam to shore. Collapsed on the grassy surface and just breathed.

The pond gave one last heave and the fins of the beast disappeared beneath the moonlit waves.

"Cecily." Her skin looked so pale against the dark grass. So delicate and vulnerable. He picked her up, cradling her in his arms, smoothing her wet hair out of her face. "Wake up."

She did not stir. But she breathed. In that he placed all of his hope.

Giles held her close, kissing her brow, her nose, her mouth.

"You cannot die," he murmured. "You are England's best hope. You are *my* best hope."

She felt so cold.

Giles rose and brought her to the grassy hollow, laid her gently on the blanket and covered her with his cloak. He built up the fire, never taking his gaze off her. Watching for a sigh. The stir of a lash.

Nothing.

Something tightened in his chest and he frowned at the weight of it while he stripped off his breeches, drew his sword, keeping it close to hand while he crawled beneath the cloak to lie beside her.

His chilled skin soon became warm, but not hers. Giles gathered her closer to him, her head beneath his chin, her bottom against his lower belly. He threw a leg over hers, cradled her arms within his own.

"It is my fault," he whispered. "I did not think Breden of Dewhame would dare trespass this far into Mor'ded's sovereignty. But that beast had to be his."

The fire crackled. Far off through the trees, an owl hooted. Giles could not stop rubbing his hands over her skin, kissing the wet cap of her hair.

"You do not know how long I have wanted to hold you in my arms. How tempted I had been to accept the offer you made me so long ago. But I knew I could not trust myself with you. You are too easy to love, Cecily Sutton. And I have my duty."

She still did not stir. An anger born of desperation made Giles turn her in his arms. "I am your protector, now and always. You cannot leave me."

And he cradled her face with one hand and lowered his mouth to hers, seeking to take some of his own life and breathe it into her. He willed her to respond as he pressed his lips gently against hers, sweeping across her mouth again and again.

A tremble ran through her body. Giles's heart leaped.

"That's it, dearest. Come back to me."

He pressed his mouth harder against hers. Felt her sigh and open her lips. He swept his tongue inside, coaxing her own to do battle with his.

For a time, Giles could feel nothing—could think of nothing more than the sweet response of her mouth moving slowly beneath his own.

And then she began to tremble. Hard. Small convulsions wracking her entire body.

Her eyelids flew open. "G-Giles?"

He tucked her head against his neck.

"W-what h-h-happened?"

"Hush. You are safe. Nothing will harm you now."

Her teeth chattered. He held her closer, but gently, afraid he would crush her in his arms.

"Sleep," he murmured. "I will watch over you. As always."

She did not speak nor open her eyes again, but soon her trembling eased and he felt the gentle rhythm of her breathing. A natural sleep this time. She would be all right. With a smile on his face, he allowed his own exhaustion to overtake him.

When he awoke the next morning, Giles felt sure he now qualified for sainthood. His rod throbbed against the back of Cecily's thighs, so engorged it pained him to move away from her. He gritted his teeth and emerged from beneath his cloak, the morning air chilling his skin and raising prickles of his flesh.

She mumbled in her sleep and rolled over. Giles carefully wrapped the cloak back around her and then took off at a near run, eyeing the still pond for only a moment before diving in.

Egads!

The cold nearly stole his breath but succeeded in cooling his unmanageable rod, so he swam about, looking for any sign of danger. But the monster had disappeared, along with the blood that had tainted the water last night.

Which did not mean that Breden of Dewhame didn't have other nasty creatures hunting for his half-breed.

He climbed out of the pond, sluiced the water off his skin with his hands, checked his breeches to see if they had dried. Already blackened and now stiff from their dunking, he tossed them away with a grimace, returning to camp and digging out another pair of leathers. His blackened coat would have to do, for he had nothing left but a suit of broadcloth to wear when he reached London.

The back of Giles's neck tingled, and he turned to find Cecily watching him with those enormous blue eyes of hers.

"You're awake." He tried for jolliness, but did not quite succeed. Her gaze traveled from the top of his wet head, lingered on his bare chest, and then hovered somewhere about his knees. He felt as if she'd raked him with live coals.

"You must be hungry." He dug through the ashes at the edge of the fire and retrieved the fish he'd buried there last night. She quickly sat up, holding the cloak over her chest, the deep glaze in her eyes fading as he handed her the parcel.

"Eat," he urged, unwrapping his own leaves and pulling out the white meat. It fell off the bones, almost too tender.

She followed his lead, albeit taking smaller bites. He passed her the waterskin, watching her throat move in fascination as she swallowed.

Damn, now he could barely manage to look at her.

She did not eat much. "I don't feel well."

"I'm not surprised. You expended a healthy dose of magic last night and I'm thinking you took quite a blow to the head. It took some time for you to come around."

"I do not... I don't remember much. Except for the shark..."

"Ah, well, I'm not sure if we could call it that."

She sighed. "Another monster. Is the world so full of them, then?"

Giles grinned. "I hope so." But he quickly sobered at the sad expression crossing her face. "Cecily, that was one of your father's—Breden of Dewhame's creations. He never would have trespassed so far into another elven lord's sovereignty unless he felt it worth the risk."

She shivered, holding the cloak more tightly against her. "You think he's looking for me?"

"I do. Although I can't be sure if it's you specifically, or if he's heard of your magic and is just blindly seeking the wielder... but we should avoid contact with any body of water until we reach London."

She nodded, and Giles worried about her listlessness.

Perhaps she needed more time to heal. "Does anything hurt? I mean, in particular?"

Cecily shrugged. "I just don't feel like myself."

"We can stay here and rest a few days…"

She glanced over at the pond and shuddered. "No. No, let's move on. If I cannot be in water until we reach London, I would like to get there as quickly as possible."

Giles nodded. He'd hated to suggest it, for he knew how miserable it would make her to stay out of her element. But he could not risk any more harm to her until he delivered her into the hands of Sir Robert.

He stood to retrieve her clothing, which still lay on the grass near the pond, but her voice stayed him.

"Giles. I seem to recall… you kept me warm. And you said some things…"

He had spoken from his heart in the heat of the moment, and now that his head ruled once more, he felt grateful she had not heard his words.

"I assured you that you were safe with me. That is all."

"I see. I owe you my thanks. For saving my life— even if you value it only for England's sake."

His jaw grew rigid in sudden anger. He could not understand why. "I value you for your own sake, Cecily. And mine. Never doubt it." And he strode away, picking up his shirt that still lay near the pond, the cloth warmed by the sun and feeling heavenly as he shrugged it on. He fetched her clothing, liking the way the soft cloth felt in his hands, and returned it to her, neither one of them meeting the other's gaze.

Giles left their campsite to give her privacy, and

checked his snares, satisfied to see he'd caught two fat hares. He tied them into a bundle and looked forward to roasting them for dinner.

Apollo came swiftly to his call, Belle right behind, and he had them saddled by the time Cecily finished dressing.

He helped her mount, remembering the silky feel of her skin against his as he lifted her into the saddle. Her face looked pale and she swayed a bit in the seat.

"Perhaps you should ride with me."

She shook her head, the long black braid she'd woven in her hair swinging across her back. "I'll manage."

Giles shrugged and mounted Apollo, setting off through the trees at a slow pace, constantly glancing behind to make sure she remained in her seat. It would have been easier if she'd just agreed to ride with him, although he couldn't help but admire her fortitude.

Sunlight filtered through the canopy overhead, mostly giant oaks with a few elms sprinkled throughout. A mist wove its way through the thick trunks and gave the forest an ethereal quality that kept Giles quiet, searching for enemies, magical or human. They stumbled upon some brambles around noon and he called a halt.

Cecily slid from her horse more gracefully than she'd managed yesterday, and began to pluck the juicy berries and pop them into her mouth. Giles joined her, and in companionable silence they fought the bees for their feast.

He passed her the waterskin and studied her face. Although she still looked pale, a rosy blush tinted her cheeks and her lips had been dyed a deep red from the berries. He fought the urge to kiss them to see if they tasted of wine. "How are you feeling, my lady?"

"Better."

"Good. We still have a long ride ahead."

But despite her words, when they reached the end of the Hants and entered into Surrey he turned in his saddle to find her swaying precariously. He leaped and caught her before she hit the ground, thanking his ancestors for his elven speed.

Giles ignored her protests as he lifted her onto Apollo, loosely wrapping Belle's reins around the pommel so the mare could follow unhindered. He swung up behind Cecily and settled on his horse's rump. "I cannot watch you and look for danger at the same time."

She leaned back against his chest and sighed. "I don't know what's wrong with me. Perhaps I hit my head harder than I thought."

Giles breathed in the scent of her, wrapping one arm about her waist and holding the reins with the other. She felt soft and warm and he tried not to think about how natural it seemed to hold her in his arms.

"I think it's more than that," he said, tapping Apollo's sides to get the horse moving again.

"Of course," she grumbled. "You know me better than I know myself."

Giles frowned. Now why should that annoy the little minx? "I just know your affinity to the water. Perhaps because your magic is so tied to it, your body and mind are, as well. I cannot remember a day when you did not swim in the ocean."

She stiffened. "Giles."

"Yes?"

"I cannot hear the waves."

"Cecily, we have not been near the ocean for days."

"I know, I know. Yet I have always heard them in my mind. But I cannot any longer."

A note of panic edged her voice.

Giles searched the countryside for any sign of stream or fountain, for he had only been looking for danger and not comfort. But they rode through the sovereignty of Firehame, and despite the natural greenery of Surrey, the elven lord's magic dotted the landscape. Pockets of fire sprung amongst meadows carpeted with buttercups, alongside the road, between hill and dale. Flame trees crowded against beech and chestnut, their fiery red leaves flickering in the breeze like the flame of a million candles.

It made him feel hot, dry, and parched. He could only imagine how it affected Cecily, who had thrived in the wet land of Dewhame.

Giles reached for his waterskin, passing it to her. "Drink. Every few minutes I want you to take a sip. We will stop at the next stream and you will swim."

She turned her head and looked up at him. "But I thought you said—"

"I have changed my mind. We are far beyond the point where Breden of Dewhame will dare invade with his magic." At least, Giles hoped. But he would rather fight another monster than watch her wither away.

He had avoided farmsteads or villages, often leaving the road to find a path through the woodlands. But they did not stumble upon a body of water large enough for Cecily to bathe in, and toward nightfall he finally woke her.

"Do you smell water?"

She straightened abruptly. "Where are we?"

He smiled. She had dozed against him for most of the day. "Still in Surrey, but close to the Thames, I think. At least, it seems to be wetter and cooler."

She took in a deep breath. "Yes, I feel it. But too far away."

"A runoff then?"

One elegant finger pointed to a rise of land within the forest. Giles urged Apollo forward, frowning as the horse labored up the slope. Odd, he would expect a pool at the base of a hill, not the top, for water ran ever downward. Perhaps on the other side...

But when they reached the crest of the rise a small waterfall tinkled merrily over some fallen stones, a crystal pool forming within a ring of standing stones nearly thrice his height. Cecily slid from the saddle and flew across the thatch of thick grass and clover within that protective circle, bending to scoop up the clear water and bury her face in it.

Giles hesitated. He'd heard about the ancient circles of stone that dotted England. Older than the coming of the elven lords, they were rumored to be places of power erected by England's true ancestors. Some offered protection, while others might open a gateway to... ah, he did not know. But when the elven lords brought magic to England, it changed more than just the landscape.

But Apollo had enough of his dallying and made for the spring, Belle right behind, and Giles placed his hand on the hilt of his sword, waiting for a tremor of anticipation. Despite his blade having an annoying bloody will of its own, it did serve to warn him of any danger.

But it lay quiescent in his scabbard, nary a sound or movement to indicate anticipation of battle, magic or otherwise.

So he dismounted while Apollo slurped rather noisily, washed the dust from his own face, and watched Cecily from the corner of his eyes.

Her hands sifted through the water as if it were gold.

"It's not large enough for you to swim in," he said, "but I imagine it will make a creditable bath."

She turned and smiled, her enormous eyes glowing in the twilight. A funny feeling spread through him at the knowledge that he'd brought that smile to her face.

He swallowed. "I'll just, um, make camp. See to the horses."

She nodded and he scooped up Apollo's reins, making his way back through the circle of stones, the ground beneath him feeling like a spongy cushion. From the vantage of the rise, he would be able to spot anyone or anything creeping up on them. He shrugged off his superstition and decided the place made for a good camp.

He kept his back to Cecily, his imagination filling in the sight of her nude body in the crystal water, the waning moon turning her skin to glowing ivory.

Devil-a-bit, he needed a woman! And soon. Tomorrow they would be in London and he would visit a bawdy house at his first opportunity.

Maybe that would get Cecily out of his blood, if not quite out of his heart.

Giles froze, saddle in hand.

He did not... he could not... Yes, he would admit he had a soft spot for her. How could he not, after being her protector all of these years? He knew her ways, the gentleness of her soul, the habits that he found endearing. Becoming fond of her only allowed him to perform his task better, so why not?

That did not mean that he loved her. He could never love—

"Giles?"

"Yes?" He dropped the saddle, but did not turn.

"Can you bring me my sack? I have washed this dress and would like to change into the other while I let it dry."

Damn.

He untied it from Belle's saddle, which he'd yet to remove, and strode over to the pond, his eyes downcast, placing it on a stone near the water.

"I find it most amusing," she said, "that after years of spying upon me, you can now be so shy."

He flushed. Looked up. She sat on the bottom of the pool, water barely covering her breasts, her hair spread about her, looking like some beautiful naiad who could steal his soul with the curve of her mouth, the crook of her finger.

"I gave you your privacy for your sake, my lady. I have already seen all that you have to offer."

Gads, she looked as if he'd struck her, but he had not said the words harshly, indeed, his voice had held a teasing note. Feeling like a complete dunderhead, he turned on his heel and walked away.

He busied himself with the fire, with the horses, and when she returned fully dressed to sit upon the blanket he'd laid out for her, he went back to the stream, cleaning and gutting the hares. Giles roasted them and they smelled delicious. His stomach rumbled as he turned them on his makeshift spit, and he watched Cecily surreptitiously, for she drew a comb slowly through her hair, a sight he could not resist. Her eyes half-closed with pleasure, her lips parted slightly while she drew the comb through the gleaming black strands. He'd watched her perform the simple task for years and had never witnessed another woman move with such sensual grace at the doing of it.

Like the first night they had spent together, he had laid out their blankets on opposite sides of the fire, and when they finished eating he lay down on his, staring up at the stars. Last night he had held her in his arms, and throughout most of the day. He felt oddly bereft at the moment.

"I did not mean…" He never had difficulty finding the right words with a woman. Except for this one. He sighed. "You have a great deal to offer, Cecily. To any man."

"But not to you."

"No. You are meant for someone better than I. And I… I am meant for a life of danger in service of the Rebellion."

"I see."

But he thought she did not. Nor could he say anything more. 'Twould only make the tension between them worse.

He had given her his cloak again, but she did not need it this night. Indeed, the air felt so warm that he allowed the fire to dwindle to red coals.

The sound of roots tearing from the soil and teeth chomping on the sweet clover reminded him that the horses would alert him to any danger, so he allowed exhaustion to overtake him when he heard Cecily's deep breathing.

Still, he drew his blade before he fell asleep, keeping it in his hand. He did not trust that Breden's soldiers had given up. Or that spies might not be trailing them. Or that the innocent-looking stones that surrounded them might not conjure up some dreaded beast...

His sword woke him.

The vibrations had barely traveled up the length of his arm when he sprang to his feet, knees bent in a fighting crouch as he looked for the danger.

At first he thought morning had come, until he saw the blackness of night still beyond the circle of stones. The horses dozed not far off to his left, heads gently leaning against one another. Insects still chirped; frogs still croaked.

Cecily stood in the middle of the clearing, her hands spread in supplication.

The circle of stones glowed with white fire all about them.

Giles could not see nor sense any danger, yet his sword still vibrated. But intermittently, as if confused.

"Cecily."

She turned, and he saw past her, and in two bounds had leaped to her side.

"Get away from her," he demanded, waving his sword threateningly.

The other man narrowed his eyes.

"Giles, don't you recognize him? It's my father."

Breden of Dew—ah, no, not her birth father. The man before them possessed entirely human features, although he rivaled the lords with a rougher kind of beauty. Thick gold hair framed a handsome face with thickly lashed gray eyes and a strong jaw, although the man looked younger than Giles remembered.

"Thomas?" Where had he come from? Had he been on his way back to the village? Yet the odds of stumbling across him in miles of woodland seemed too remote for Giles to believe.

"Father," said Cecily, her hands out to him again. "Why can't you come to me?"

And Giles realized that Thomas did not look quite... right. The outline of his body shimmered and flickered, while ribbons of hazy color slithered about him like snakes.

Cecily took a step toward her father. Giles gently held her back. "No. Don't you see something is wrong?"

She blinked. "But it's him. We found him! Oh, Father, I am so happy. I thought I might never see you again—Giles, let me go!"

Thomas—if indeed it was Thomas who faced them—opened his mouth to speak. But although his lips moved, no sound came out and he fisted his hands in frustration.

"It's these stones," said Giles. "They have conjured up the image of him. Or his ghost. I don't know. But you must stay back, Cecily. Who knows what evil is intended by this?"

"No. He's not a ghost or an illusion. It's my father, Giles. I can *feel* him."

Thomas's eyes suddenly widened. The shimmer

around the other man's body grew. His golden hair whipped around his head then shot straight backward, as if some force pulled at him. His coat flew open, the flaps drawing back and then somehow vanishing. He held out his hands to his daughter, his mouth moving again, gesturing wildly. Trying to tell her something.

Cecily cried out. She struggled and twisted, taking Giles by surprise. He was used to dealing with those not of elven blood and perforce had gotten into the habit of not using his full strength. Especially around women, fearing he might unknowingly injure them.

But Cecily possessed even more elven blood than he did. Although she still could not surpass his strength, he constantly underestimated her.

She broke free of his hold and flung herself at Thomas. The force that had been drawing him backward, dissolving his coat and hair and the edges of his shape, seemed to suck him away in one mighty burst.

Cecily hit empty air, landing with a grunt amid a patch of clover.

They remained motionless for a moment, as the white fire coming from the stones began to fade.

Giles expected her to turn upon him in fury with tears of anguish or screams of recrimination.

But instead she turned and met his gaze with a calm that shook him. He automatically held out his hand and helped her rise.

"You were right. He was not here."

He breathed a sigh of relief, not releasing his hold on her hand. "These stones are ancient sources of human energies. I should not have trusted you to their safety."

"Thomas once told me that some of these stones run across lines of energy within the earth. A power made greater by the magic that has flooded England. A power that—if harnessed—can allow the crossing of time or distance."

Giles frowned, fully understanding where she was going with this. "You think he used them to reach out to you."

"Yes, I do. And he wants me to find him. It is important."

Giles frowned. That may be, but he still did not trust this place. "I still think it was naught but illusion."

"But who would have sent it? Only the elven lord of Dreamhame, Roden, would have the power to cast such an illusion. Why would he be involved in this? And how would he know where to find me?"

"It could have been a half-breed of his. Those with other elven blood do wander into other sovereignties, dear lady. I come from Bladehame."

She shook her head. "That is still too far-fetched. I agree that Breden might be concerned with me, yes, but I can't see him admitting to the other elven lords that I even exist. It would be... an embarrassment to him."

She made sense, but still... "There is too much here which I do not understand, and I will not put your safety at risk. We will leave at once."

"No!" She placed her other hand against her breast and lowered her voice. "No, Giles. Thomas might be able to contact me again. And this time I will watch his mouth, try to read the words he so desperately wanted me to hear."

He could not withstand the plea in her voice. And he had witnessed her stubbornness too often to doubt it. He'd have to carry her away fighting if he tried to make her leave before morning.

Giles strode over to the fire, dragging her along with him, and picked up her blanket, placing it next to his. "Then you will sleep with me tonight. It's the only way I can be sure you won't wander off."

He pulled her down beside him, wrapping his arm firmly about her waist, his other hand still clutching his sword. She felt warm and soft and smelled of spring water. Giles did not question any ulterior motives he might have for insisting she sleep with him again.

As the glow of the stones finally faded to black, he just allowed contentment to fill him.

Six

THEY REACHED LONDON THE NEXT EVENING, CECILY planted firmly in front of Giles on Apollo's back. Giles insisted she ride with him, that she still looked pale, that the appearance of Thomas had shaken her delicate sensibilities.

Cecily did not argue with him. She had spent the night awake, hoping Thomas would appear to her again, but he had not, and she could no longer feel any lingering presence of him. She felt too tired and disheartened the next morning to put up much of a fight when Giles insisted they leave. Indeed, she would not have managed to keep her seat today without Giles's arm about her when she nodded off. Besides, this would be the last day she spent with Giles, perhaps even the last time she ever saw him. She did not know what might await her in London. But it frightened her that she would be alone, without friends or family.

Giles had been a constant presence in her life for as long as she could remember. Although she did her best to hide it after that dreadful night when he'd rejected her, her heart would always leap at the sight of him. Knowing he was near made her feel more alive, somehow.

Will had been a comfort. Giles an excitement that made her primp a bit longer in the mirror… pay more attention to her clothing… walk with a sway to her hips.

And now. Now he had kissed her. Held her in his arms. Despite his constant attempts to keep his feelings at a distance from her, he sought ways to touch her with but the slightest excuse for it.

The contradictions in his character confused her. And she regretted she might never uncover the mystery of him.

"If I did not have Breden of Dewhame's half-breed with me, I doubt I'd be given instructions to go to Sir Robert himself," muttered Giles sometime later.

Cecily jerked upright. She'd half-dozed off again. They approached the city by a small road that obviously was not the main thoroughfare to London.

"Where would you have gone?"

He shrugged, muscles rippling against her back. "Thomas was my contact. I probably would have had another one much lower in the ranks of the Rebellion, if my task hadn't been so important."

Houses began to multiply around them.

"So you have been privy to the Rebellion's innermost circle. That makes it more dangerous for you."

She could feel his smile, if not see it. "And more important. I don't think even my father would have believed my good fortune."

"Yes, I felt sure that's how you would view it."

They entered the city proper, suddenly battling for passage amongst wagons and coaches and men on foot carrying chair boxes behind them. Flaming lamplights lit the throng in the streets: servants, children in rags, costermongers, and gentlemen distinguishable by their white wigs. Cecily could not help but stare, for most men in her village could not afford a wig, much less such fine ones that mimicked the flowing locks of the elven lords so perfectly. The wigs had been powdered with some glittering dust that gave off sparkles of silver even in the lamplight, eerily duplicating the brilliance of the elven lords' hair as well.

The crowd thinned as the glass-fronted shops dwindled to be replaced by brownstone townhouses, and then suddenly they passed over a bridge, a large stone sign etched with the words: *Charing Cross*. The fishy smell of the Thames tickled her nose as she looked down on boats and ferries, and farther down the river, fine-masted ships with sails gleaming in the dusk.

A glow to her left caught Cecily's attention. "What is that?"

She felt Giles's head turn. "That, my lady, is Firehame Palace. Home to the elven lord Mor'ded, and his lovely mistress, Lady Cassandra Brydges, mother of the new Duke of Chandos."

Yellow fire danced along the walls of the palace, flared to the tops of its soaring towers, and lit the heavens above like a beacon. The flames somehow looked menacing, as if they could suddenly flare forth and destroy the city around them into cinders. She shivered.

They entered a narrow street and turned a corner and cut the ominous flames from their view. Giles stopped Apollo before a well-kept building, a small sign near the entrance proclaiming it to be an inn.

A young lad came out to take care of their horses, and Giles made arrangements for a night's lodging. Cecily did not question or protest the single room until they stood inside.

Giles held up a graceful hand. "I thought you would like to rest and change before you meet Sir Robert. Then I will hire a chair, and follow on Apollo by the alleys—"

"No." The panicked word fell from her lips before she thought. "I will not go without you."

"There is no reason to be afraid."

"I'm not," she lied. "It's just that… there will be no one there whom I trust. Sir Robert will try to use me and the only protection I will have against that is you."

He frowned and Cecily feared she knew his thoughts.

"Do not worry," she continued. "Once I am familiar with the players, I will not hold you to me."

A knock at the door startled them both, and Giles turned to answer it, almost eagerly. A maid stepped in with a bucket of water, filled the washstand in the corner of the room, and quickly left.

Giles nodded his head toward their bags, which he'd placed near the bed. "You will have the room to yourself while I check on the horses. I will send a message to Sir Robert, telling him of your arrival, and leave the arrangements of your meeting up to him." And he left.

Cecily stood still a moment. Giles had not said whether he would accompany her or not. He'd brought her safely back into the arms of the Rebellion and finished his task. She knew he would not be eager to stay with her, but his abandonment hurt all the same. She had thought their journey had brought them a sense of companionship, but apparently she'd been wrong.

She quickly performed her toilette, trying to fluff out her quilted petticoat for more volume, using damp hands to smooth the wrinkles from her favorite calico dress. The gown had a pattern of small roses and a modest neckline, and Cecily thought it would make a suitable presentation, especially with the pearl buttons down the front, and the lace ruffles at sleeve and throat. She twisted up her hair and covered it with a lace cap, the trailing lappets brushing her shoulders and making her feel a bit elegant.

She stepped in front of the cracked mirror, pinching her cheeks to combat the paleness in her face.

Giles knocked and she bade him enter.

He opened the door and stared at her a moment, a slight flush darkening his cheeks. "You look... I have arranged a private dining room for you to sup. A lackey will take you there and I will join you after I change."

He sounded so stiff and formal, as if he spoke to some great lady instead of familiar, ordinary Cecily.

She remarked on the first part of his comment. "I'm sure I look exactly what I am. A village lass still fresh from the farm... but that is good, for then perhaps they will underestimate me."

A grin softened his face. "Your beauty will rival the ladies of London, regardless of the costume you wear. But you are right, they will underestimate you. That has always been *my* fault."

Cecily brushed past him on the way out the door,

his shoulder touching hers as if he'd intended the contact. She refused to acknowledge him with a lingering look. Surely he would at least join her for dinner, as he promised. They would have one last evening together.

The lackey led her into a cozy dining room, the fire banked against the warmth of the evening, but a dozen candles lighting the private area. Giles's funds must be padded by the Rebellion, for surely a mere blacksmith could not afford this well-appointed setting.

She sat at a table laden with linen and crystal, surveying the scenic paintings on the walls. When a serving maid brought the covered dishes into the room, she refused to touch them until Giles joined her, despite the mouthwatering smells wafting up from them.

She did not have to wait long. When he entered the room he seemed to fill it up with his presence. The candles glowed brighter; the crystal sparkled more brilliantly. The pale blond hair near his temples looked slightly damp from his wash, the fall of it glimmering down his back from a thorough brushing. He wore a broadcloth suit with brass buttons. Not the attire of a wealthy man, but one that his broad shoulders filled without benefit of padding or cut. He still wore boots below his stockings, although they'd been buffed to a fine polish.

Cecily's mouth watered.

He took a seat and uncovered a dish, and without further ado, began to eat. She joined him in companionable silence, the only sounds to break their meal the sound of muffled laughter coming from the common room, and an occasional comment from one of them on a particularly tasty bite.

Giles glanced over at her now and again, whatever formality he'd tried to adopt earlier now completely forgotten, for he would smile and nod, just as he had over their campfires. Cecily's heart flipped every time she caught his gaze, but she would hide her reaction beneath a calm smile.

A knock at the door interrupted the serenity of their dinner. A young lad handed a folded bit of paper to Giles, accepted the coin in return, and quickly backed out the door.

Giles opened the missive. "Sir Robert will send a carriage for you at midnight. You'll wear my hood and cloak, and leave the inn as stealthily as you can."

Cecily set down her fork, no longer interested in the rest of the meal. "And so it begins. You never answered, Giles. Will you accompany me?"

He downed the last of his port and pushed his chair away from the table, legs squeaking on the hardwood floor. "He does not say I should accompany you, and I'm not sure if they'll allow me past the grand front door, Cecily. *I* am not the future hope of England."

"Please don't call me that. And if this Sir Robert wishes to speak to me, he will have to welcome you as well."

Giles pulled at the kerchief about his throat as he muttered, "I'm sure that's something they could not have foreseen. I wonder what they'll make of it."

"What do you mean—no, never mind. Just say you will accompany me tonight."

"Yes, I believe I shall." A wicked grin spread across his mouth, and near took her breath away. For a moment she could only stare at him, and he returned the favor with a darkening of his green eyes. He leaned forward in his chair, his hand reaching across the table, past the salt and the china plate of butter and the stem of her goblet, and clasped her hand. She felt his touch thrum up her arm and travel clear to her toes.

"Cecily."

"Yes?" The word left her lips on a soft breath.

"I will miss you."

She closed her eyes for a moment. She would not allow his words to mean more than he intended. "Perhaps. But you will also be glad for another assignment. One with more adventure and intrigue. You must have found my little village so quaint and boring."

"It was not as bad as all that. Do you remember the time when that badger got into Old Man Hugh's cottage?"

"And ate the pie that the widow had made for Hugh? Fie! I think the whole village came out to witness the commotion. I will never forget the sight of him chasing the animal about with his broom. The poor beast."

"Hugh, or the badger?"

Cecily laughed.

Giles squeezed her hand. "It's only a few hours before midnight. Do you want to return to the room to rest a bit, or would you prefer to stay with me here?"

Cecily lowered her lashes. "I could not sleep if I tried."

And so they stayed at table, Giles never once relinquishing her hand, even when the serving girl came in to clear the dishes. They told stories of the village, Cecily with longing and Giles with nostalgia, as if he spoke of memories of a place that he'd already left far behind. And the time flew by faster than she could have imagined.

The clock on the mantel chimed midnight and Giles abruptly stood, jarring Cecily from her contentment.

"It's time," he said. "Let me fetch my cloak—I'll be but a moment."

He fled the room and she tried not to be disappointed by his apparent eagerness. If it had been up to her, she never would have let the evening end.

But she must face her new future, eagerly or no. She stiffened her back and shoulders, determined to be strong. Cecily did not know what this Sir Robert might have planned for her, but she would hold to her own ambitions. She would think only of Thomas, and if this Rebellion would not tell her his whereabouts, then she would find some way to track him down herself.

When Giles returned to the dining room he took one glance at her face and froze in the act of shrouding her with his cloak. "Damn. I would not want to be Sir Robert tonight."

Cecily pulled the cloak over her head, trying not to muss her cap or hair, and followed Giles through the half-empty common room to the waiting carriage outside. She ducked into the plain black coach, surprised by the contrast of the inside. Her hands touched velvet-cushioned seats, the walls had been painted with scenes of playful cherubs, and every bit of trim shone with the luster of gold.

Giles took the seat across from her, watching her face as the conveyance lurched forward. "Although Sir Robert prefers to travel in secrecy, he does appreciate his comforts."

"Yes, I see." Cecily turned and stared out the window, watching the lamplights flit past. "I am not discomfited by grandeur, Giles. For some reason this all seems… commonplace to me."

"I should think it would."

She met his shadowed gaze. "What do you mean?"

He took a deep breath, and then shrugged. "I suppose you'll find out soon enough, and they might use it to unsettle you."

"Use what?"

"You still remember nothing of your past life? Before you settled in the village, that is."

Giles had asked her this once before, and she'd flinched from the memories. But she would need any advantage she could, and he was obviously trying to help. She frowned in concentration. "I remember running and hiding in dark places. I remember the storm. The relief when we settled in the village."

The coach bounced as they hit a pothole. Giles reached forward and placed her hand upon a leather strap bolted to the sidewall. "Hold this, or you might wind up in my lap." He gave her a wicked grin.

Cecily scowled. For a man who couldn't wait to be rid of her, he still could not seem to stop his flirting. She ignored the frisson of excitement that raced through her from his touch, from the nearness of his face.

Giles's eyes widened at her expression, and he

relaxed back into his seat. "They will not know what to do in the face of such determination. Cecily, can you recall anything before the running and hiding?"

"My mother's face. Another woman's… she sang songs to me. A garden, the sting of a bee. Little things that have no meaning. And yet there is obviously more."

He nodded, glanced out the window. "Your mother was a widowed countess. You are, by title, the Lady Cecily Sutton. You were born in a fine mansion, but your mother left it all behind to protect you from the elven lord when your powers became apparent."

Cecily should have felt more surprise than she did. But perhaps somewhere deep inside, she had known it all along. "I am deeply touched by my mother's sacrifice. She never said a word about our past life, although it explains a great deal—I think she detested that little village. But a title hardly matters to me."

"You are a peer of the realm, Cecily. Of course it matters."

She shook her head so hard the lappets on her cap swept against her cheeks. "My mother gave up the title, so as far as I'm concerned, I never held it."

"You can't just dismiss a title. At least, not to those who matter."

"Ah, you mean the esteemed Sir Robert? He will discover soon enough that he cannot bribe me with the trappings of society. I care for nothing more than my sweet cottage by the sea."

Her breath hitched on the last sentence, and Giles fell silent until the carriage slowed. "We are here."

Cecily pressed her nose against the glass. The carriage rolled through a massive square, a fine park in the center of it, which sported those flaming trees and a fountain of yellow fire. When the coach came to a full stop and Giles flung the door open, a golden light spilled into the dim interior. He helped her down the steps, and she drew strength from his strong warm hand as she looked up at the home in front of her.

Giles had been right. Her entire village could surely fit into the massive dwelling.

Despite her brave words, Cecily felt her knees quiver as they approached the front door. Two stone gargoyles sat on either side of the front step, an odd combination of lion and bird, and their eyes seemed to follow her every movement. Before Giles could raise his hand to lift the brass knocker, the door flew open, and a uniformed man bowed and stepped aside, beckoning them in.

"May I take your cloak, madam?" he asked as soon as he closed the door behind them. Giles unwrapped her while Cecily stared about. Pockets of fire littered the massive hall, casting eerie shadows upon the marble floor and a line of statues that paraded down the walls. Frescoes of angels and clouds covered the ceiling high above her head, and crystal chandeliers divided the firelight into sprinkles of starlight.

"I have been given instructions to show you to the library upon your arrival," sniffed the doorman, looking down at her with disapproval. He turned to lead them down the hall.

Cecily snapped her mouth shut and told herself to quit gawking.

"The trappings of society," whispered Giles.

She glared at him and he smiled jauntily back at her.

Thank heavens he had agreed to accompany her, for somehow he made her feel like her normal self in these rather daunting surroundings. Giles took her elbow and prepared to lead her after the doorman, but that stiff-legged gentleman took a glance over his shoulder and said, "Not you, sir."

The smile froze on Giles's face and Cecily felt his sword tremble. He patted the scabbard, another look crossing his handsome features. A sort of acceptance.

"He is with me," said Cecily, watching Giles in confusion. Had any man in the village dismissed him in such a manner, he would have reminded the fool of his skill with a weapon.

The doorman stopped and turned, a polite rise of his bushy brows his only response.

"I will not step one foot farther without him," she insisted.

"Cecily," whispered Giles. "Do not argue. The man is well aware of my place, and it is not among such esteemed personages."

"Your place is at my side, at least for tonight. You promised."

He shrugged. "Aye, so I did." Giles met the stare of the officious steward, his expression quite different than it had been a moment ago. "Majordomo, tell his lordship that the lady refuses an audience unless I am at her side, and until she dismisses me I continue in my duty to protect her in every conceivable way."

The doorman's face did not alter a whit as he turned and proceeded back down the hall.

That sword of his trembled again and Giles patted it with a sigh. "Sir Robert will not like this."

Cecily frowned. "Will he punish you?"

"Me? I'm too low in the grand scheme of things for him to bother with. He might, however, make my next assignment extremely dangerous." And those green eyes glinted with eagerness.

"Then I will go in alone." Cecily strode down the hall, picking up her pace when she heard his footsteps behind her. "Go away, Giles. I will not assist you in your suicidal desires."

"Don't be ridiculous. You don't even know where you're going."

No, she didn't. All the doors along the hall looked exactly alike. But at that moment one of them opened, and the majordomo, as Giles had called him, bowed and swept his arm toward the open door. "His lordship will see… both of you."

When he rose, he gave Giles a look that made the blacksmith shrug, as if he sympathized with the other man's apparent discomfiture.

It irritated Cecily to no end. Fie, of course there were social distinctions in the village, but not so large a gap that one man was forced to feel inferior to another. Although Sir Robert may be Giles's leader, she saw no need for the blacksmith to react as if he did not belong in the same room with such an august personage. Or for the servant to assume the same.

Giles's strength of character certainly gave him every right to escort her into the room.

A man sat near the fireplace in a high wing-backed chair of leather, a blanket over his knees despite the warm evening. A heavy man with an elegant white wig, a rather longish nose, and dark piercing eyes beneath thick brows. He stood, the blanket falling about his ankles, and bowed to her. "Lady Cecily. What a pleasure to finally meet you."

Cecily curtsied a bit awkwardly, being woefully out of practice. Everything about this man, indeed, about the entire room, screamed elegance. From his velvet jacket to the twinkle of rings on his fingers, from the polished oak walls to the thousands of leather-bound books encased in exquisitely carved shelving.

She realized she'd forgotten her gloves.

Cecily didn't often have the opportunity to wear them, and she could picture them perfectly in her mind, wrapped in white paper, nestled snuggly in the bottom of the trunk at the foot of her bed. In her cottage. Hundreds of miles away.

She clasped her hands behind her back.

"Beaumont," said Sir Robert, inclining his head toward the blacksmith. "You have our gratitude for delivering Lady Cecily safely home."

Giles bowed, somewhat stiffly, like a soldier to his commander.

"Lady Cecily," continued Sir Robert, "will you be seated? I fear we have much to discuss."

Cecily took the chair across from him, her gaze flying to Giles. As soon as Sir Robert sat back down, the blacksmith took a standing position next to Cecily's chair, his solid presence allowing her to relax. She removed her hands from where she'd hidden them within the folds of her skirts.

Sir Robert's eyes sparkled as they went from her to his spy. "My dear girl, you must be exhausted from your journey. May I offer you some refreshment? A spot of tea, perhaps?"

"No, thank you. Giles—Mister Beaumont and I have eaten but a few hours ago."

"I see." He did not look up at the blacksmith. "Allow me to be the first to welcome you home, Lady Cecily. I have had reports from Dewhame, but I would like to hear from you what happened, if you're up to it."

Cecily took a breath. It would be best if she took control of the situation from the start. "This is not my home, Sir Robert, and I certainly have no intention of permanently making it so. My home was in Dewhame, in a little cottage by the sea. Now, it will be wherever my father is. And that is why I have come to you. To seek him out."

Sir Robert's heavy brows nearly rose up to his wig. This time he did look up at Giles. "Beaumont. Report."

And Giles began to speak, not only telling his superior about the invasion of the village, but also condensing an account of the last nine years of watching over her. Cecily flushed during certain parts of it, but thankfully Giles's report did not extend to confessing intimate details about her. His omissions reassured her that although his first loyalties lay with the Rebellion, he still held some feelings for her.

When Giles finished some time later, his deep voice hoarse from talking, Sir Robert sat back in his chair, rubbing the sides of his chin with his fingers, his gaze occasionally going from Cecily to the blacksmith.

Or perhaps she should now think of Giles as a spy. The role of blacksmith had always been a ruse, and yet she still had difficulty thinking of him otherwise.

"Do you believe Breden of Dewhame knows that the sorcerer he's been chasing might be his daughter?" Sir Robert finally asked.

She felt Giles's shrug. "I'm not sure, sir. But I don't believe so."

"Then there is still a chance." Sir Robert pinned her with his gaze. "We had hoped you would be loyal to our cause, Lady Cecily. After all, if not for our interference, you would no longer be alive. You do understand that it is the Rebellion that has protected you all of these years?"

"Oh, indeed, sir, I do understand. I understand that you seek to use me as your tool, whether I will it or no. But my father showed me I have a choice, and I will not be used by you or anyone."

"Ah, Thomas," he muttered. "What have you done by claiming this girl as your daughter?" Then Sir Robert leaned forward, his hands clutching the blanket he'd drawn back up around his knees, his dark eyes now fixed upon her with an intensity that was frightening. "Is your loyalty to your *birth* father, then? Do you wish the elven lords to continue their slavery of the English people?"

Cecily blanched. She had not thought of it in that way. And if she continued to let this glib man control the conversation, he would soon have her committing her soul to his cause. "My loyalty is to Thomas, my *true* father, and that is why I have come. I want you to tell me where he is."

Those dark eyes glittered, and Cecily wondered what machinations might be going on behind them. He seemed to come to a sudden decision, for the corner of his mouth quirked and his hands relaxed back onto his lap. "We don't know."

Cecily's heart dropped. "How can you not know? Wasn't he on a mission for you?"

"Yes. But we haven't heard from him for months, and my contacts cannot locate him. It's almost as if he disappeared off the face of the earth."

"But I saw him…"

"So Beaumont said in his report. But he also said he wasn't sure what you had actually seen. And yet, it is the best clue we have had to his whereabouts in some time. I have a proposition for you, Lady Cecily."

Fiddle, she did not like the sound of that. But what other choice did she have? "And that is?"

"I will give you Thomas's last known location. I will provide you with the funds and supplies you need for the journey. In exchange for one small favor."

She suddenly felt Giles's hand on her shoulder, but she did not need the warning. The favor would not be small by any means.

"I want you to accept a mission on behalf of the Rebellion when you return. Whether you have found Thomas or not."

Anger evaporated any lingering nervousness Cecily might have felt. The decanters on the sideboard shuddered, the liquid contained in them responding to her magic. "What sort of mission?"

"If I could be sure of your loyalty to our cause, I might be able to divulge that… but as it is…" He shrugged his velvet-clad shoulders.

"That's blackmail," hissed Cecily. "If you have it within your power to help me find Thomas, then you will, make no mistake of that, sir." And without any conscious volition of her own, the stoppers on the decanters suddenly popped out, hitting the ceiling with enough force to dent the plaster. Port and brandy and gin swirled from the containers, forming tiny cyclones above the sideboard.

But Sir Robert didn't seem to notice, his attention suddenly fixed upon a creaking sound coming from the side of the fireplace. "I don't think this is wise," he muttered.

A portion of the paneled wall suddenly swung into the room, and the most dazzling couple Cecily had ever seen stepped from behind it.

"Ah, Robert. I adore that secret passage from the palace to your library," said the woman, brushing cobwebs from her shoulder. "It makes me feel like one of your spies again."

Sir Robert quickly rose and bowed deeply. "Have you ever stopped, my lady?"

She laughed, a trilling sound that made the man beside her smile tenderly in response, and Cecily could not help but stare at him. He did not need the black scepter in his hand for her to know that the elven lord of Firehame stood before her. Mor'ded's ethereal beauty gave him away. Like Giles, he had pale white hair, but the elven lord possessed the silver sparkles in those thick strands that made it glow with a sterling sheen. His eyes were similar to her own, large and luminous, faceted like crystals, but a midnight black to her blue. His skin was so pale and translucent it nearly glowed with its own light, and his face so exquisitely formed he did not seem quite of this earth.

Cecily preferred Giles's golden tan and green eyes. It made his beauty at least human.

The woman stepped forward, unperturbed by Cecily's gawking, and held out her hand. "It has been too long since I last saw you, Cecily Sutton. You have grown into a beautiful woman."

Cecily frowned, for she could not remember the lady, but she rose and clasped the hand extended to her. "I'm sorry, but I don't—"

"Allow me to introduce you," Sir Robert smoothly interposed. "Lady Cecily, meet Lady Cassandra Brydges, mother to the future Duke of Chandos, and lady to the elven lord of Firehame." He bowed deeply to the elven lord. "Your Most High, allow me to introduce Lady Cecily Sutton, daughter of the widowed Countess of Warwick, and bastard to one of your people, Elven Lord Breden of Dewhame."

Cecily felt grateful for Giles's warning of her mother's status, for surely she would have been flustered by the introduction. Instead, she calmly curtsied, keeping her lowered position until the elven lord bade her rise.

Lady Cassandra still held her hand, and helped her upright. "You remember me, do you not? I am the lady who rode next to you on your escape from Firehame."

Cecily had tried so hard to forget that wild flight. The feel of the rain slapping her face, the laboring beast beneath her, the power as it flooded her veins while she called forth the lightning that blasted their pursuers…

"Oh, my dear," said Cassandra. "Please forgive me. I did not wish to remind you of something painful."

"No." Cecily took a deep breath. "No, it is all right, and best that I acknowledge it now. I owe you my thanks, my lady, and I am grateful I can finally voice it."

Lady Cassandra patted her hand, a puzzled look on her face. "Well, it is good to see you again, safe and well. How is your mother, the Lady Eleanor?"

"My mother... she was killed when Breden of Dewhame's army invaded our village." Cecily tried not to think of how much she still missed her mother, or she would surely start crying in front of everyone.

Cassandra's lovely face fell with even more sympathy. "I am so sorry. It seems you have been through more trials than any young woman should have to face." Then she reached out and enfolded Cecily in a warm embrace, her empathy so genuine Cecily could not help but respond to it. Had Lady Cassandra not already saved her life, she would still adore the other woman. Her anger faded somewhat.

Cassandra guided Cecily back to her chair, while Giles quickly dragged a velvet settee closer to the fireplace, taking up his station by Cecily's side again as soon as the elven lord Mor'ded had seated himself.

Cassandra gave Cecily's hand one last pat before she settled her skirts beside the elven lord. She wore a dress of emerald silk, stiff with embroidery about the hems and sleeves, elbow hoops creating such a wide expanse of cloth that her waist looked miniscule by comparison. Her rich brown hair had been artfully braided with tiny silk roses and pearls and then swept into a high crown upon her head.

Cecily felt dowdy by comparison, her best dress of calico now looking more poorly than it had but a moment ago.

Yet she could not feel jealous of the other lady, merely a sincere admiration. Despite the fact that the other woman sat near the elven lord. Cecily could not imagine getting that close to the powerful man without swooning. His mere name struck terror into the hearts of thousands, yet here he sat, directly across from her, Lady Cassandra's hand gently enclosed within his own. The way he looked at his lady, with a tenderness that belied his reputation, made Cecily frown in confusion.

Mor'ded of Firehame caught her staring, and those black eyes hardened to flinty coal, a mask of indifference falling over his features. His fingers tightened around the black scepter he held, reminding her he commanded more power than she could imagine. With those talismans, the elven lords held the barrier around England, cutting them off from the rest of the world.

With those talismans, they had the power to destroy everything she loved.

For a moment Cecily couldn't breathe. She had feared this meeting with the infamous Sir Robert but had faced it with resolve, intent upon finding her father. But she had never expected to meet with Lady Cassandra, much less the elven lord himself. Surely the elven lord could not know that the king's most trusted advisor, Sir Robert Walpole, led the Rebellion against him? And yet… hadn't Lady Cassandra said she had been one of Sir Robert's spies when she emerged from behind the wall? How could that be?

Had Sir Robert betrayed the Rebellion to Mor'ded

of Firehame? Or did conspiracies exist that she had no means of understanding?

Cecily glanced up at Giles, who stood as still as a statue, his gaze fixed on some point in the wall across from him, like a servant at table. But his hand stole out again to rest upon her shoulder. She felt prodigiously glad she'd insisted he come. Despite his loyalty to the Rebellion, Cecily trusted him. He would not allow any harm to come to her. The past few days had proven that.

"Robert," said Lady Cassandra, "you cannot send her after Thomas without telling her the entire story. Do you think I saved her life all those years ago for you to risk it by sending her out blind?"

Cecily stared in confusion at Lady Cassandra, who smiled at her and said in a loud whisper, "Peephole. Over the fireplace. We heard every word."

Ah. Cecily nodded and tried not to enjoy the sight of Sir Robert squirming in his chair, but she felt secretly glad that he now knew how it felt.

"But we cannot be sure of her loyalties, my lady. How can we trust her with such sensitive information?"

"Because we must. Don't you see that she will go after Thomas whether we help her or not?" She gave Cecily an admiring glance.

"You do not need to question my loyalties," Cecily hastened to assure her, "for they will always be to my father. And *his* loyalties lie with the Rebellion."

"So we have yours by default," said Mor'ded. His voice startled Cecily, so similar to Giles's, yet silkier and more melodious.

She gathered her courage and spoke directly to

him. "I do not understand, Your Most High. Is the Rebellion in some way aligned with you?"

"You might say that." His arm stole around Lady Cassandra. "You see, I am not what I appear to be. You do not need to fear me, Cecily."

"Are you sure?"

Mor'ded smiled, the expression changing his face from merely beautiful to heaven-sent. "I am different from the other elven lords."

"In what way?"

Flames of yellow fire suddenly erupted in his palms. He formed them into orbs and tossed them in the air, like some juggler performing at the fair. "I am half-human. Like you."

Cecily narrowed her eyes, expecting some jest at her expense. But why they would do such a thing...

"Allow me to explain," interjected Cassandra, giving the elven lord a frown. "You see, my dear, Mor'ded of Firehame has been dead for nigh over nine years. The man at my side, the current elven lord of Firehame, is his half-bastard son. And he is as dedicated to freeing England just as much as I am."

Could it be true? She could not see a trace of humanity in the elven lord who sat across from her... except when he gazed at Lady Cassandra. "But how?" Cecily managed to ask.

"That is a long story and can wait for another time," replied Mor'ded—or at least, the man who pretended to be him. "For the moment, let us make an exchange. If I douse my flames, perhaps you will allow your little cyclones to calm? They are rather annoying."

Cecily felt her cheeks redden. She had forgotten

about them, and apparently they had not stilled when her anger had faded. With a wave of her fingers she sent the liquid back into their decanters.

"What a lovely talent," said Lady Cassandra. "Have you explored the full extent of it?"

"I can no longer call the power of a storm, if that's what you mean."

"It isn't, my dear. And I believe I understand why that would be difficult for you to do again. I was there, remember?"

Cecily nodded, feeling a bit ashamed. But why else did Sir Robert suggest a mission for her, unless he sought to use that more formidable power?

"Because I am half-human," continued Mor'ded as if he had never been interrupted, "I age at a normal human rate, unlike the elven lords, who age so slowly it is nearly indiscernible to us. But I am beginning to show signs... a wrinkle here, a gray hair there. Not enough to yet betray my charade, but it is a condition we are forced to address."

Lady Cassandra leaned over and kissed his cheek. "Your human side is what I love most about you."

"Indeed?" He turned and caught a strand of her hair between his elegant fingers. "I thought my *magic* brought you joy, my lady."

Her cheeks reddened, and for the first time Cecily noticed the ring on Cassandra's finger. A rosebud of gold that suddenly bloomed into full flower. "Perhaps. But there will always be magic between us, my lord. Of a human kind."

And then as if he could not resist any longer, the dread lord of Firehame kissed Lady Cassandra, with such passion and longing that Cecily felt her face heat. How she wished for a man to feel such passion for her. She glanced up at Giles without meaning to, and wondered about the look on his face as he watched the two lovers. Did she see an echo of her own longing? Wishful thinking, indeed. He had desire only for adventure and his cause.

And he refused to meet her gaze.

Sir Robert cleared his throat. "Yes, well. Are you familiar with the power of the other elven lords, Lady Cecily?"

"Of course." She fought to keep the flare of annoyance from her voice—she wasn't some ignorant peasant. Lady Cassandra obviously felt affection for the leader of the Rebellion, but she could not profess to the same.

"Although the elven lords constantly war and seek to best one another," he continued, "on rare occasions they play together. Long ago, elven lord Roden of Dreamhame desired the elven lady, La'laylia of Stonehame, and crafted her a ring of gold to hold one of the lady's magical gems. Forged within the black fire by the former lord Mor'ded, the might of three elven lords working together gives the ring the power to fool them all, and would take the power of three to uncover the truth of it. Fortunately, in our time the elven lords rarely make an alliance long enough to work together… nor would they in this case, to uncover the magic of what they would consider a harmless ring."

Cecily felt as if Sir Robert wove a bedtime story, and she had to force herself to consider the very real implications of what he said. "Lord Roden wields the

magic of illusion and glamour, and Lady La'laylia of
Stonehame can enspell her gems for many purposes.
So what does the ring do?"

"Ah," replied Sir Robert, shifting excitedly in his
chair, setting his white wig of imitation elven locks
slightly askew. "This is where it gets interesting. For
you see, the elven lady La'laylia fooled Roden of
Dreamhame. She convinced him that her face had
begun to age, that she wanted to stay beautiful for him
forever, so he cast the ring with the illusion of youth."

"I can understand the desire," murmured Lady
Cassandra, her eyes downcast. Mor'ded of Firehame
took her hand in his and kissed the palm of it.

"But she had no intention of using the ring herself,"
continued Sir Robert, pausing dramatically.

Which Cecily considered completely unnecessary.
"Then what did she want it for?"

"For her human lover," said Mor'ded, his midnight
eyes fixed upon his lady. "It's why she needed the
might of three to cast it, for only then would she be
unable to see through the illusion herself. Despite the
differences between the two races, there are times
when love, or at least lust, conquers all barriers."

"I daresay," agreed Sir Robert, beaming at Lady
Cassandra. "Lady La'laylia of Stonehame had fallen in
lust with her half-breed slave, a man captured in her
recent skirmish with the lord of Bladehame."

Giles dropped his hand from Cecily's shoulder, and
for the first time, neglected his military posture and
shifted where he stood.

"She could not bear to see her half-breed lover turn
into an old man," said Lady Cassandra, with a wealth

of sadness in her voice. "And so her slave stayed young for his lifetime. But even the elven lords cannot hold back death. La'laylia buried him with the ring still upon his finger."

Cecily surmised the Rebellion wanted the ring for Mor'ded of Firehame, so he could continue to fool the other elven lords with his masquerade. But what of the Lady Cassandra? If they managed to find this ring, she would turn into an old woman while her lover never aged.

As if Cecily had spoken her thoughts aloud, Mor'ded leaned toward his lady and whispered, "As you have just said, there will always be magic between us, my lady."

Lady Cassandra glanced up at him, tears in her soft brown eyes, but a brilliant smile blossoming upon her mouth.

"So you sent my father on a mission to rob a grave," said Cecily, turning her attention back to Sir Robert. "Or did Roden discover La'laylia's deception and take the ring back?"

"He tried," answered Sir Robert. "But he could not find where she had buried the slave. And although the ring is unusual in that it can fool even an elven lord, the spell itself is harmless to their rule. The tale soon became lost to time, naught but a recording in the Rebellion's archives, until we realized we might have a use for it."

Cecily expelled a breath, leaning back in the cushioned chair. "Thomas journeyed to La'laylia of Stonehame's sovereignty then, in the land of Stonehame. Did he find the grave?"

"We don't know," said Lady Cassandra. "I asked my maid, who has a talent for finding... things, if she could locate him. But alas, she could not find the light of his magic anywhere within the seven sovereignties. But her gift is not infallible—surely the vision Thomas sent you confirms this. He is the best spy the Rebellion has ever had. I have faith he is still alive."

"We can be sure of nothing but his last known location," warned Sir Robert. "He met with another contact of ours, a professor of archaeology at Oxford University."

Lady Cassandra leaned forward. "So you see, Cecily dear, how important this mission is. Not only for your father, but also for the entire country. Many people have suffered to put a half-breed on Firehame's throne, and Dom—the new Mor'ded has already saved many lives. But it will be dangerous. More dangerous than we might know."

"I understand." Cecily smoothed the folds of her skirts, wiping the moisture off the palms of her hands. How simple life had been in the village, the world of the elven lords and their magic seemingly far removed. But now she had been thrust into the thick of things, and for Thomas's sake, she would not turn back. "But it makes no difference. I must still find my father."

Sir Robert nodded, his face still slightly creased with uncertainty, but Lady Cassandra, and even the dread Lord Mor'ded of Firehame, smiled with complete confidence at her.

"Nay, Cecily," said Giles, suddenly breaking his subservient silence. "You will *not*."

Seven

THE ROOM WENT DEATHLY QUIET AS ALL EYES TURNED to stare at Giles. Sir Robert glared at him for daring to speak; Mor'ded of Firehame's black eyes held no expression, but Lady Cassandra's soft brown gaze glittered with an odd, merry interest.

Cecily looked at him as if he'd suddenly gone mad.

Giles would not allow them to intimidate him, not even the powerful elven lord, who could probably toast Giles to ash where he stood.

Giles had listened to the tale of the ring with growing excitement and foreboding. Excitement for him, who relished the adventure Thomas had become a part of, but foreboding for Cecily. She could not venture into the Lady La'laylia's sovereignty of Stonehame, a land rumored to be as arid and dry as any in England. Cecily could barely withstand the scarcity of water since they left Dewhame.

There might be little water for her magic to call upon, unless she summoned it from a great distance. And how much time would that take if she were in the midst of some danger?

He knew what his leaders intended. They would send Cecily out to test her magic, putting her into danger to see if she could use the power of the storm again. For she could call upon the power of the sky no matter which sovereignty she stood in.

This might be a trial by fire to see how much use she could be to the future of the Rebellion.

But they had not counted on Giles being here. And although he had great respect for Sir Robert's leadership, Giles did not always agree with his methods on how England gained her freedom. But up until now, he'd never had cause to dispute them.

Cecily, of course, recovered first. "Don't be ridiculous, Giles. Of course I will go after my father. That's why you brought me here, remember?"

Giles lowered his voice, ignoring the others in the room and focusing on Cecily. The lady would listen to reason, and right now, her safety negated any other considerations. "I did not realize the enormity of the task. Nor did I think they would truly send a young woman after Thomas."

She blinked those luminous blue eyes at him. "But you must realize I am best suited for it."

"I realize nothing of the sort. You, my dear, are the worst person to be venturing into Stonehame. It is nearly as parched from mining as Bladehame, and you would have to cross the length of it to get near your ocean again. And you would wither before you managed it."

A flash of uncertainty flickered in her elven eyes, and then that luscious little mouth firmed with resolve. "You saw Thomas. He reached out to me, and I will not turn my back upon him."

Giles swiped a hand across his brow. He would not debate that again. But surely Thomas would not have wanted her to risk herself on his behalf. "I forbid you to go."

She rose to her feet and poked a finger against his chest, the little minx. "You have no right to tell me what to do, Giles Beaumont."

"Do you think I spent the last nine years keeping you safe just to let you toss your life away?"

"Ha. You resented every moment of it. And now you're finally free! Why don't you just enjoy it?"

"Because I..." Giles frowned. Cecily was right. He would finally be free to take on more important missions. Missions that involved the travel and adventure he'd always craved. She would soon be nothing but a part of his past, and he should be glad of it. So why couldn't he let her go?

Giles lifted his chin. "Because you are England's best hope."

"She is indeed," interjected Lady Cassandra, in a voice that shook with some suppressed emotion. "And we would not send her on such an important mission without aid. Sir Robert, I believe we have found the perfect man to accompany her."

The heavy man replied in a low voice. "Do you think this is wise, my lady?"

"Indeed I do."

Giles did not look at Sir Robert to see if he would agree or not, for Cecily's eyes had narrowed along with her lips, with a fury he hadn't seen the likes of since Breden's men invaded her village. "You are the last person I would want to go with."

Hadn't Giles heard those very words from her lips before? It hadn't mattered then and it didn't matter now.

Sir Robert harrumphed. "So, Beaumont, I assume you accept this new mission?"

Giles lowered his head, his gaze still fixed upon Cecily's stubborn face, and softly growled the words, "Damn right, I accept."

"Well then." Sir Robert clapped his hands together and rose. "I'll ring for the footman to show you to your rooms. I suggest you both get some rest, for we have much to do in preparation for tomorrow."

Giles glanced up, suddenly becoming aware of the rest of the people in the room. Lord Mor'ded watched him with a face that could have been carved from stone, but Sir Robert's cheeks had turned red and Lady Cassandra looked... amused. Well, he'd surely managed to make a muck of things. "I... I apologize for my behavior. It appears my habit of protecting Lady Cecily has become ingrained in me."

Lady Cassandra nodded elegantly. "So it seems. Which makes you a perfect candidate for this mission. You will bring her back to us safely, Mister Beaumont, and for that confidence, I thank you."

Giles bowed deeply to her.

"Come, love," continued Lady Cassandra, rising and settling her skirts about her ankles, "it is time to return to the game."

Mor'ded of Firehame grimaced but rose in one fluid motion. "It was enjoyable to not have to pretend for a while."

"Fie, it makes our stolen moments all the sweeter."

And she reached up and kissed his cheek, the elven lord's jet black eyes warming at the gesture.

Giles would never have guessed at such passion between the two, had he not been privileged to meet them in such intimate surroundings. He had always thought the Rebellion had fueled their romance, but now he wondered if it hadn't been the other way around.

Lady Cassandra hugged Cecily again, bidding her to be careful on their journey, and then the lady and her elven lord left the room via the wall near the fireplace. Shortly afterward, a footman appeared at the door in response to Sir Robert's summons.

Cecily nearly fled the room.

∼⊱⊰∼

She did not speak to him again until they were halfway to Oxford. They were to meet with a professor of archeology in the university city, following Thomas's last known location.

They rode through Buckinghamshire, a gentle land of rolling hills and peaceful countryside dotted with occasional flame trees. Giles had chosen a course as parallel to the River Thames as possible, hoping to somehow bolster Cecily's magic before they entered the land of Stonehame. He might have exaggerated slightly, for Stonehame had many more rivers left than Bladehame, but La'laylia's magic had indeed drained the waterways to a shadow of what they had been before.

His heart lifted at the thought of what sights awaited him in Stonehame, while at the same time he struggled with fear for Cecily.

"Why did you do it?" she asked.

Giles glanced beside him, where she rode atop Belle. Sir Robert had wanted to provide her a new mount, but Cecily had insisted on the little mare.

He patted Apollo's neck, understanding Cecily's desire for the loyalty of a beast. "Do what?" he replied.

"Demand that you accompany me."

Giles shrugged, for he barely understood it himself. Oh, granted he'd gotten into the habit of protecting her, but he had to admit that he had not been thinking when he'd insisted upon it. Only reacting to what his gut told him. "I have always wanted a dangerous assignment, after life in that little village. Can you think of any other that Sir Robert could have given me that would offer as much danger and adventure?"

Cecily brushed the loose tendrils of hair off her face. She wore a new dress, one that befit her role as daughter to a prosperous merchant, her former wool riding habit now replaced with a blue silk. To avoid attention she wore a black hooded riding cloak, the hood pulled low over her forehead. A matching blue silk lined the inside of the headpiece, and made her eyes appear an even more extraordinary blue.

The guise that Sir Robert had provided them seemed simple enough: a merchant's daughter traveling to Stonehame to purchase gems for her father's girdle factory, the man sick with the gout and unable to make the journey himself, and said old man lacking a son and forced to rely upon the training of his daughter.

Lady La'laylia of Stonehame encouraged the participation of women in business and trade, and the disguise further helped explain the amount of notes they carried, which Giles fully expected to use for bribery. Although he had official documents of entry stating Cecily's nature and business, Giles knew a thing or two about the border patrols. And about getting the information he'd need to discover Thomas's whereabouts.

Giles had been relegated to the part of Cecily's guide and guard, with clothing consisting of a brown frock coat and buckskin breeches, of a finer cut and quality than his blacksmith's garb. He wore new half jackboots, polished to a fine gloss, and a three-cornered black hat, with a new sword belt for his devil-blade.

He looked half-gentleman, half-servant, possibly a retired soldier. Giles approved of Sir Robert's attempts to keep his enemies guessing.

"Giles?"

He started, realizing he had lost himself again in the blue of Cecily's eyes. An annoying habit, that. "What?"

"I said you did not give Sir Robert the opportunity to offer you another mission."

Giles sighed. Why did she keep pestering him for answers when he barely knew the truth of it himself? "I didn't want another one, Cecily. Remember, Thomas is a friend of mine. He's been my guide and mentor for many years. I want to find out what happened to him just as much as you."

"Perhaps."

But she kept searching his face with those crystal eyes of hers, as if trying to see into his very soul.

"Besides," he muttered, hoping to put an end to this conversation, "you need me."

"Not enough to endure your resentment."

Giles brought Apollo to a halt, the smaller mare stopping right alongside. A wagon loaded with hay rumbled by them, but he'd already discarded it as a possible threat, and ignored the driver. He leaned down until his face lay near inches from her own. "What are you talking about?"

A small flush stole across her cheeks. "You made it very clear in every conceivable way how you felt about watching over me all those years. You couldn't wait to be rid of me. And then"—she snapped her tiny fingers—"just like that, you insist on accompanying me to find my father. And now... now I must bear the thought of you forced into my company again."

The little minx made no sense. He reached out and took her chin in his hand. "But I *offered* to go."

"And that's what I cannot figure." She frowned, tiny lines etched across her heart-shaped forehead. "You are a wealth of contradictions, Giles Beaumont. You act as if you cannot bear to be near me, and yet you find every excuse to touch me. You say you cannot wait to be rid of me, but there you sit, still watching over me."

Giles dropped his hand. Damn, and he had thought he'd done such a jolly good job of keeping his distance. Hadn't he lain all night with her, skin-to-skin, and kept her pure? She should give him some credit, at least. "I am not meant for you. Thomas made that very clear. But that doesn't mean I do not want you. There, is that what you wished to hear?"

She gasped. "You want—"

But Giles did not wait for her to finish. He did

not appreciate being forced to admit it so baldly. He heeled Apollo and set off down the road, listening to make sure she followed. She had little choice, after all, since she rode atop Belle. As soon as he heard the little mare's hoofbeats close behind, he took a path toward the river, hoping the water would distract Cecily.

Why did she continue to make him acknowledge the fact that he wasn't good enough for her?

They rode for a time in silence, the soft beat of the horse's hooves in the dirt a harmonic accompaniment to the soothing murmur of the water beside them, punctuated only occasionally with the splash of a fish breaking the surface or the trumpeting of a swan.

He stole a glance at her. Cecily wore a soft smile, making her appear even more beautiful than usual. Giles spun back around, swiping the hair off his face.

The only way he could make sure she survived her mission was to accompany her. But damn if it didn't threaten to kill him.

They reached Oxford toward evening, riding through narrow, cobbled streets until he found an inn. They walked through the common room, nearly filled to bursting with students, and Giles glared them all down when they dared to cast appreciative looks upon Cecily. His devil-blade hummed and pulsed at his hip.

Aye, it would surely kill him.

He made arrangements with the innkeeper for supper in their rooms, and relaxed only when he had Cecily safely within the confines of her own.

"Giles," she murmured, glancing around the small sparse room, "there is but one thing I wish to know, and I promise never to speak of it again."

He tried not to groan, for he'd suspected that their earlier conversation had been on her mind all day. "I'm tired. Can this not wait until the morrow?"

She shook her head, black locks gleaming in the lamplight. "Tomorrow we hunt for Thomas in earnest. And I must have this settled before then."

Giles leaned against the doorpost, crossed his arms, and looked down at her with a sigh. "What?"

She looked into his eyes. Cecily had such a habit of avoiding his gaze most of the time, that a direct look of hers could rattle him. He did not move, but he tensed in his negligent pose.

"All I want to know is"—she took a deep breath—"if Thomas hadn't forbidden you, would you have accepted my offer all those years ago?"

He frowned. "Your offer?"

"Do not pretend you don't know of what I speak."

"Faith, Cecily, you were but an innocent girl. Of course I wouldn't have accepted."

"But now. Now that I am a woman. You said… you said that you wanted me."

She would flay him alive, this one.

"My desire for you would have consequences." He glanced over at the tiny cot, a vision of her bare body tangled in covers coming unbidden to his mind. He pushed away from the doorframe and took a step backward. "There are too many reasons for me, for us… Don't you see that Thomas was right? Now you know who you are—in comparison to who I am."

She actually looked confused for a moment, then she frowned. "I am not England's best hope, or whatever your Rebellion has styled me. I am just Cecily

Sutton, a plain country girl who likes to sew and keep house and swim in the ocean."

"You swim because it draws you. Because you have powerful magic to command. And you are *Lady* Cecily Sutton, an earl's daughter and a peer of the realm. Don't you realize what a tangled web we would create if I allowed myself to give in to temptation? Don't you know how easy it would be for me to do so?"

And because it gave him the flimsy excuse to show her, he stepped forward and took her into his arms. She felt so delicate, and yet within that small frame he could also feel the strength of her magic, the force of her will and personality. Her lips parted, eager and ready, and the devil take him if he hadn't want to do this again—each and every moment—from the first time he'd kissed her.

He covered her mouth and tried to take her very essence into himself. She tasted like fine wine, sweet and burning and heady. He felt her arms snake around his shoulders; her fingers tangle in his hair, his scalp tingling from her soft touch. Giles groaned and gathered her closer, lifting her off her feet, deepening the kiss until their tongues tangled in frenzied passion.

He had to remind himself that she didn't know about passion. That given her sheltered life, she would be completely ignorant of the act. But *his* body knew, and it responded with a tightening of his breeches and a shiver of anticipation.

Giles crushed her against him, smashing her skirts and petticoats, his hand roving down her backside, pushing her body against the part of him that yearned for contact.

Two drunken students chose that moment to stagger up the stairs, their arms around each other, singing snatches of a bawdy tune. Giles released her, his breath labored and his world turned entirely too far upside down for his own comfort.

Cecily stared at him with complete trust in those large gemstone eyes. She stood with arms parted, as if bereft, and he longed to snatch her up again.

She still had no idea how close she had just come to having her life entirely ruined.

Giles turned and stepped back out the door, frowning at the two drunkards, his hand to his hilt, and despite their foxed state, they managed to show some sense and quickly stumbled down the shadowed hall.

Giles glanced back into her room. "Keep the door bolted tonight. I will be right next door, and the walls are so thin that I will hear the slightest noise."

She stayed his hand when he would have closed the door, her fingers covering his, that odd current of excitement that her touch always caused in him making him freeze.

"Who are you, Giles Beaumont?"

It took a moment for him to understand the course of her thoughts. He shook his head. "I am no one of such great importance, Cecily. And I'm more than happy with my lot."

"You are wrong." She dropped her hand. "And you have just proven it again. You are my protector, Giles Beaumont. Now, as always. And none of your protests will change that."

She closed the door, none too gently, and Giles stared at the splintered wood mere inches from his nose. Damn him if the little hoyden didn't have the right of it. But that didn't mean it gave *him* the right to...

He spun and went to his room, slamming the door behind him.

Did it?

⌘

They managed to get to the University of Oxford without referring to the conversation of the night before. For which Giles could only feel incredibly grateful. Cecily had managed to completely confound him, and he now questioned what he had once taken as a surety.

And something had changed between them. A subtle difference in the companionship they'd formed on their previous journey. She radiated some new confidence, and when he grinned at her she returned it easily, her smile bold and promising. Giles sternly refrained from touching her, despite his habit to do so, telling himself that their heightened attraction for one another was entirely his fault.

And then damn if *Cecily* didn't take to touching him at every opportunity. Her hand lingered in his when he helped her mount Belle. Her shoulder brushed his own as they walked across the campus green. She smoothed the hair from his face with fingertips that made his skin burn.

And Giles relished every touch, leaning toward the slightest contact between her skin and his. He could not help it.

She would always be his one and only weakness.

They entered the building and a student directed them to Professor Higley's office. It smelled of dust and mold; the myriad of books lining the walls and floor a perfect background for the tattered old man's bespectacled face. "Yes, yes, what is it?"

Giles escorted Cecily into the room, his hand mere inches from the small of her back. When she abruptly stopped and his fingers met the silky fabric of her coat, he could not pull his hand away from her warmth.

"We have come to see you about my father," she said to the old man. "Lord Thomas Althorp."

"Ah, well," he replied, blinking owlishly, "then you had best shut the door behind you."

Giles complied while Cecily found a chair, removing a stack of books to perch on the edge of it.

Professor Higley set aside his quill and folded his ink-stained hands on top of his desk. "Rebellion business, is it?"

"Yes, and no. You see, Lord Althorp is my father, and he's missing. You are the last man that he spoke to."

"Ah well, I told him the search for the ring would be dangerous." He leaned forward. "We can't even be sure it's a real artifact, but many people *think* it's real, and that's more dangerous than you can imagine."

Giles had taken up position as her guardian behind her chair, and he could feel the concern the other man's words caused in Cecily. Without thinking, his hand covered her shoulder. "We would like to know what you told Thomas about the ring's supposed location."

The professor's gaze switched to his, quickly traveling down to center on the scabbard lying against Giles's hip. "It's in my report." He licked his lips.

"I am a loyal member of the movement and would not shirk from my contributions. I left nothing out of it."

"I'm sure you didn't," assured Cecily. "But it might be helpful to have you recall that conversation to us directly. Would you be so kind?" Her voice sounded as smooth as water running over stone, the entreaty within it a promise and plea, all at the same time.

The professor seemed to lose himself in her gaze, for which Giles felt complete sympathy. Then the old man blinked a few times and stood, removing a key from his coat pocket and opening a glass case. He lifted out a yellowed document with gentle hands, placing it on his desk. "Come closer, my dear. This is an old map of England and the landscape has changed, but this is where we are, you see?"

Cecily rose and bent over the desk, Giles following suit. Lines radiated outward from a center point near the old man's finger, separating England into seven sections with the precision of a sliced pie. Each sovereignty held the traces of faded dye: black for Firehame, green for Verdanthame, brown for Terrahame, silver for Bladehame, violet for Stonehame, gold for Dreamhame, and blue for Dewhame.

"Yes," Cecily replied. "But what is that smudge near your finger?"

"Ah, well. That is a place to be avoided at all costs, and not a topic under discussion at the moment." His gnarled finger moved upward into Stonehame, but not as far into the sovereignty as Giles had feared. "This is where you will need to journey."

"Stafford," said Cecily. "What is there?"

"Shoes," muttered Giles. "Thousands and thousands of shoes. Stafford is well known for the making of them."

"But not as well known," interjected the professor, "for the gravesite of Sebastian Delacourte, former lover of the elven lady La'laylia." His finger shifted to a tiny etching of craggy spires. "The town lies within the shadow of these stones, a mountain of quartz pulled from the very recesses of the land by the magic of La'laylia's violet scepter. Some even say the lady Annanor of Terrahame had a hand in the unearthing of it."

Giles nodded. Annanor of the brown scepter had the power over the very land itself, and he would not doubt the two elven ladies would aid one another in a play against one of the elven lords.

"It is rumored that Sebastian's grave lies within these very stones," continued the professor, "encased in a crystal coffin, the ring that La'laylia of Stonehame gifted him with still upon his finger. His face as youthful as when he lived." He straightened, his back making small popping sounds. "Many have tried to scale these mountains and all have failed. So if the coffin does exist, we will never know."

"My father may have found it."

"Ah, my dear. I hate to dash your hopes. But no man has ever emerged from those mountains alive."

Cecily blanched, and Giles took her arm and gently guided her back into the chair.

"Tell us the story of the lady La'laylia and her slave, this Sebastian Delacourte," said Giles. "We would like to hear your version."

Unfortunately, the old man's story matched the one

they had been told at Sir Robert's, and when he came to the end of it, Giles looked at Cecily. "I suppose you still want to pursue Thomas?"

She tilted her chin. "How can you doubt it?"

He grinned. "I did not. We will leave at once."

"Wait," said Professor Higley. "This place you asked about earlier." His finger moved back to the spot not far from Oxford. "It is a forest of wild magic that no sane Englishman would dare enter. I daresay it would be best if you skirted the area entirely."

"What kind of wild magic?" asked Giles, his attention immediately captivated.

"The locals call it the Seven Corners of Hell."

"I see. It's the exact spot where the boundaries of all seven sovereignties meet. I imagine the mingling of those different powers would cause some chaos."

"Very good." Professor Higley glanced at Giles as if the class dunce had just proven to be the most brilliant. "That is the prevailing theory, at least. That water meeting fire, and earth meeting sky, illusion meeting cold metal, et cetera, has created a confluence of energies that constantly battle one another. Indeed, the entire forest appears to shift before one's eyes, and trees may be replaced with barren desert or a thick mist of clouds or... we have a professor who has studied the phenomenon. And the creatures that occasionally emerge from it."

"Creatures?"

The professor shuddered. "No man who has ever entered that forest has come out alive, but we think the creatures who emerge from it may have once been men... horribly disfigured or altered by the wild magic."

Giles heard Cecily's small gasp of dismay and quickly squelched his curiosity. "We will be sure to avoid the place, although it will add hours to our journey."

"Most wise of you," said the professor.

Giles took Cecily's hand and lifted her to her feet, escorting her to the door. Her fingers felt cold.

"Thank you for the information, Professor."

"Yes," she added. "You have been most helpful."

The old man beamed at her words, but the intelligent eyes behind the spectacles stayed fixed on Giles. "Should you ever weary of adventuring, young man, you should take up the robes. It's a shame to have such a keen mind go to waste."

Giles flushed with pleasure. He had always been proud of his physical prowess, and women had confirmed his good looks with their eyes since he had been a lad. Perhaps he had started believing in his own disguise after spending years pretending to be a thickheaded blacksmith, but he had never considered himself quick-witted. Becoming a scholar had not occurred to him, but he suddenly realized the worlds that books may open for him might be an interesting pursuit.

"Oh," said Cecily, a wealth of sadness in her voice. "He would never give up adventuring, sir. It's as much a part of him as his green eyes."

❧

Later that day, Giles thought Cecily had been more right about him than she knew. For instead of crossing the river and keeping it between them and the forest, he chose the other way around, his curiosity getting the better of him.

"You are incorrigible," she said with a look of annoyed indulgence. "That's the forest Professor Higley told us to avoid, isn't it?"

Giles stared into the thickly wooded forest to his right, hoping to see one of the dread creatures the professor had spoken of. What manner of beast would it be? Clawed, fanged, a complete deformity of human arms and limbs?

"We are keeping well away from it," he assured her. "I just wanted to see it with my own eyes."

Cecily followed his gaze. "It looks perfectly ordinary—"

The trees suddenly disappeared in a blaze of fire, leaving behind a landscape of gray ash. The earth split; Giles could feel the ground beneath their feet shake from the force of it, making Apollo snort and Belle squeal. The ash flowed down into the chasm and a green mist erupted back out of it.

"Damn," blurted Giles in complete admiration.

"I should have known better," muttered Cecily.

The mist swirled and formed columns that flowed like water, snaking about in a mad dance but never crossing the original line where the trees had once stood. Still, Giles guided Apollo farther away from the place.

Black flames erupted from within the mist, creating a wall of midnight that the sun could not penetrate. Twinkles of light appeared within the blackness, sparkling like so many jewels. Giles felt entranced by the display, until he noticed that Cecily appeared even more beguiled.

"Come," he urged. "There is another river up

ahead and it will be safe for you to take a swim before we board the ferry."

"Giles, look." She raised a trembling hand toward one of the spots of light. "See, it's growing larger. And there's a figure within…"

Cecily tried to urge Belle toward the light, but the little mare stoutly refused. With that elven speed that made the outline of her body blur, Cecily leaped from the saddle and took off at a run.

His blade rapped him smartly against the thigh, but he hardly needed the warning.

"My fault," snapped Giles, leaping from Apollo as quickly—if not quite as gracefully. He bounded across the tall grass, catching up with her only because her skirts hampered her legs. He wrapped his arms about her waist and lifted her off her feet, swinging her about from the momentum of their flight. Her petticoats swirled just above the line where the forest had once started.

"Put me down!"

"What is wrong with you? You heard what the professor said."

"But Thomas…"

Giles turned his head toward that ball of light, squinting against the glare. It had grown twice its former size in the short time it had taken him to reach Cecily. And the figure it surrounded looked exactly like a youthful Thomas.

Had he not been holding Cecily within his arms, his devil-blade would have already been in his hand.

Thomas opened his mouth and Giles heard him speak, but so faintly he could make out only the sound of Cecily's name. She struggled against Giles's hold, and from the corner of his eye he could see a wall of blue racing toward them. She had called the river water.

"Cecily," he said, fighting to keep his voice calm. "Stop this."

"But Father wants to tell me something important."

"We cannot hear him. And we cannot venture within that madness. Look!"

Something tore at Thomas's hair and clothes, just like it had done within that circle of stone. A mist curled about his throat, about his mouth, stifling the words he struggled to say. His hair and coat streamed behind him, and despite his efforts to keep his feet planted, they began to slide backward.

Black fire blossomed beneath Thomas's feet and engulfed the ball of light, and within one breath and the next, caused a conflagration that heated Giles's face and hands with sudden pain.

A blanket of water doused his body, pushing him to the ground, Cecily still within his arms.

They both lay still for a moment, breathless and stunned. When Giles finally sat up, a thick tangle of trees met his gaze.

"Good thinking," he said, wiping the dampness from his face. "Although I'm not sure your water would have protected us from the black flame if we had ventured inside of it."

Cecily struggled to her feet, peeling wet cloth from about her legs. "I would have gone to him."

"I know."

"It would have been insane."

"No. It would have been... understandable. But

I don't think that what we saw is truly Thomas. A vision of him, or a sending, yes. How could he be alive in such a place?"

"You are right. But he is trying to tell me something, and obviously using any means he can to do so."

"Yes. The magical properties of the standing stones, and now the wild magic of this forest." Giles glanced through the trees. Things slithered between the enormous trunks in the darkness beneath the thick canopy. He caught a flash of red eyes, a slither of a spiked vine. "I believe you are right, and with luck, we will find another place of magical energy that Thomas can tap into. But in the meantime we must find *him*, and not his sending."

Cecily turned and made a shooing motion. The remaining column of water rolled back upon itself and returned to the river she'd called it from. "Will this alert Breden of Dewhame to my presence?"

Giles frowned. "I don't think you used enough magic for him to sense. And besides, he doesn't know where to look for you now. Lady Cassandra would not have sent you forth unless her lord assured her of that."

Cecily cocked her head, as if considering something for the first time. "But what if I had used the power of the storm? Surely he would sense that, even if we went to the farthest reaches of England."

"Since Breden of Dewhame is the only other to possess that power, it would not be lost amongst all the other magical energy that permeates England. So yes, Cecily. I believe he could find you that way. But since you have vowed not to use it, we don't need to worry about it, do we?"

A dry, soft nose suddenly bumped his head. Giles glanced up and grinned at Apollo. The beast shivered from fear, but he had stayed near his master this time.

"Good boy," he said, his clothes squelching as he rose to his feet. "What say we get the hell out of here, before that forest decides to change its shape again?"

Without waiting for her to answer, Giles swung up into the saddle and held his hand out to Cecily. Apollo might have the training of a warhorse, but Belle had been only a pleasure mount. She stood far off in the distance, her ears cocked toward them, but not coming any closer.

As soon as he felt Cecily settle behind him, Giles urged Apollo into a gallop. The gelding immediately lunged forward, anxious to expend his nervous energy. Soon Giles heard the pounding of Belle's hooves as the mare caught up to them, but he did not suggest that Cecily switch mounts.

Within a few hours they entered the sovereignty of Stonehame, although they wouldn't meet up with the border patrol until they crossed the river. Giles found a private shelter of trees for them to dismount and eat their afternoon meal.

He winced when his boots hit the ground, his feet sloshing within the sodden leather. Their ride had dried his neck cloth and the very front of his waistcoat, but the rest of his clothing still felt uncomfortably damp. He lifted his arms to help Cecily dismount and she fell into them, her riding coat as dry as the rest of her clothing. His brows rose in surprise.

"Shall I dry you, too?" she asked with a hint of mischief in her blue eyes.

"How might you manage that?"

"Oh, 'tis the same as calling the water, only in reverse. I expel it from the fabric."

"Even my boots?"

"Aye. Now close your eyes and hold very still."

He dropped his arms from about her waist but peeked at her from lowered lids, suspicious of her reasoning. And to his infinite joy, discovered he had the right of it.

She started with his hair, which had completely dried from their gallop, but he wouldn't be fool enough to protest when her fingers felt so good against his scalp. He barely felt her touch when she reached his neck, her fingertips nothing but a soft whisper against his skin, like the touch of a dragonfly's wing.

The chill that Giles had taken from his damp clothing burned away from the inside out.

Her palms caressed his coat at the shoulders, slowly traveling down the front of his chest, leaving dry cloth behind. She stepped closer to him to reach his back, and he breathed in the scent of her, fisting his hands against the urge to enfold her in his arms. She stared at him with eyes glassy with desire, and when she licked her lips Giles thought he would go mad.

Her hands reached his hips and his devil-blade tingled. He nearly snorted in surprise.

But she quickly passed over the scabbard and stroked the fabric of his breeches, and the result of that touch did not surprise him in the least.

Giles sucked a breath through his teeth when she reached behind him and caressed his bottom. He looked down upon her head, that lovely face mere inches from the fall of his breeches. He felt certain she had no idea what that intimated. But when she leaned back and stared at the swelling of flesh beneath it he knew her next actions were intentional.

She molded her hand against him, as if trying to seek out his shape beneath the fabric, rounding her hand over the top of his member and stroking the length of it down to his ballocks.

Giles closed his eyes fully and stopped breathing.

Apparently satisfied she had learned all that she could, Cecily swept her arms down his thighs, pushing at the hard muscle, then over this boots. Giles felt his stockings dry right inside of them.

He heard the rustle of her skirts as she stood. "Now I will go take that swim you promised me."

Giles jerked his head in semblance of a nod. When he heard her footsteps behind him he remembered to breathe again.

"You are a fine figure of a man, Mister Giles Beaumont," she said before she disappeared within a rustle of bushes.

The merriment in her voice caused such a fierce emotion to swell within his chest that it overpowered the raging of his body. What an exasperating, tantalizing, absolutely stupendous woman.

❦

They had little difficulty crossing the border, with only a minimal bribe once the patrol discovered that a woman had come to Stonehame to conduct business. The rumors that La'laylia of Stonehame encouraged the authority of women appeared to be true, although the stories that Giles had been told about the land seemed to be exaggerated.

Perhaps if they had gone as far as Westmorland, where Stonehame Palace stood in Appleby, they might have seen more proof of the elven lady's excavations which had altered the landscape. But this far south, rivers still flowed and heather and greenery covered the hills.

Giles could only feel grateful that he would not have to witness Cecily withering from lack of water. And smug satisfaction that the Rebellion's plans to force Cecily to call upon the power of the sky would be foiled. There was enough water to easily come to her call, should she need it.

Although Giles vowed it would not come to that. She would not need her magic for protection. She had his sword.

They passed through Warwick, where he restocked their supplies from the market town, and quickly rode through Birmingham, for it reminded him too much of Bladehame with its iron factories. By the time they reached Wolverhampton the rivers became smaller, mounds of quartz and granite replacing the gently rolling hills, patches of brown earth testament to the mining that had taken place.

But the River Sow still flowed strong in Stafford, and although the marshes that were rumored to once lie hereabouts had completely dried up, Giles felt that could be no bad thing.

They rode through the outskirts of the city, Belle and even Apollo hanging their heads with exhaustion, for he had pressed them during the day and through half of the night. Indeed, since they had crossed into

Stonehame, Giles did not call a halt until he saw that Cecily felt ready to drop from exhaustion. He fell into slumber as quickly as she. It was the only way he could think of to keep his hands off her, after she had given him such a bold invitation by the river.

He could ignore it only because she surely did not realize the consequences of her actions.

Giles quickly found a reputable inn and ordered the stableboy to feed their mounts extra oats and water, then made arrangements for their stay, stressing that a *lady* had come to Stonehame to purchase jewels for her girdle factory.

The merchants came in droves, eager to show their support. Several of them women.

Giles stood behind Cecily in the common room of the inn while she met with the traders, making his presence known, but keeping unobtrusively in the background. At night he visited the taverns, listening for any rumors of a golden-haired man who had come to find the fabled ring of Sebastian Delacourte.

He hated leaving Cecily alone in the inn at night, but it took distance and a good deal of ale to prevent him from entering her room and ravishing her.

For reasons he could not understand, the urge to accept the offers of the women who approached him in the taverns held little appeal.

Giles subtly asked about Thomas, but no one appeared to have seen him. Which was no surprise, since the man had the magical talent to fade into the background when he chose. It was what made him such a good spy. The only thing of interest Giles heard was on the third day when a cobbler deep in his cups insisted that he'd heard the crystal mountain sing a death song about the same time Thomas had been in the city. His companions hushed him with an almost superstitious fear, and they refused to explain no matter how hard Giles coaxed them.

After several days of trading, Giles felt it safe enough to pursue their true goal. He took Cecily to the base of the crystal mountain that shadowed Stafford.

Eight

CECILY HAD NEVER THOUGHT MUCH ABOUT SHOES before. In the village, leather slippers and boots had been more practical, and so she'd always focused on dresses, for she could sew her own. She had not realized shoes could be just as beautiful, or that such a variety existed anywhere in the world.

As she and Giles rode through the cobbled streets of Stafford, her head swiveled from one window display to another. Shoes with feathers, with diamonds, with heels and without. Shoes that buckled or tied. Red shoes, black shoes, lavender, and blue...

Cecily pulled up on Belle's reins, transfixed on a window display. In the very center, perched upon a slip of lace, gleamed a lovely pair of gem-studded shoes. Made of pale blue silk damask printed with starfish, they sported a crystal-studded buckle that winked in the sunlight, and on closer inspection, tiny silver stones outlining Scallop seashells.

The clear stones looked to be topaz, and the yellow ones most likely a shiny stone called pyrite. Cecily had learned much while she'd traded, and fortunately the merchants had been eager to teach her, but she couldn't be sure if it had been because of Giles standing behind her, or Lady La'laylia's support of women in trade.

She sighed with sheer longing at the glorious shoes.

"You could have them, if you want," said Giles.

"They are too dear."

He lowered his voice. "I'm sure your mother has funds set aside for you. You need but take up your position in society again."

She turned and studied his beautiful face. Ah, he still sang that same tune, insisting on pointing out the vast differences in their social positions—despite her avowals that she didn't care a fig about it. "It is natural for women to admire pretty things, Giles. That does not mean they are willing to give up their happiness for them."

He frowned, that sculpted mouth turning down at the corners, but some inner emotion lit his eyes. He wore his black hat pulled low over his brow, his blond hair appearing even whiter in contrast, his pointed ears tucked under the brim. A white neckerchief about his throat made his skin look a deeper golden brown, the coloring enhanced by their journey. His eyes shone a vivid green in the sunlight, those dark brows and lashes drawing attention to their brilliance. In his buckskin breeches and wide-sleeved coat, sword belt at his hip, he made such a dashing figure that Cecily did not fault the maids on the walkway for turning to stare.

Her eyes must have given away her admiration, for he shot her a grin of supreme arrogance, and tapped Apollo's sides with his heels, leading them through the crowded streets again.

Ah, how much she admired... and loved him. It

almost hurt at times, twisting at her heart and fluttering in her stomach. So easy now, to admit she had always loved him, since she discovered that he wanted her in turn. But he showed it in a different way, and that realization had confused her at first.

Will had been a simple man, with simple needs. A house, a home, a wife who could cook and sew and raise his children.

Giles Beaumont was much more complicated.

She stared at his back, the elegant posture, the long, flowing white hair. People made way for him through the streets, parting like the sea for Apollo to step through. Giles exuded a confidence—with enough of a hint of danger—for strangers to sense.

And yet, when a young apple-seller held up her basket for him to peruse, she did not show any sign of fear. On the contrary, the child's eyes shone with innocent trust that he would not brush her aside like so many others had already done.

Giles bought two apples and slowed to hand one to Cecily, his gaze lingering on hers for a few precious moments.

She bit into the tart fruit, a rush of sweetness countering the sharpness, licking the juice from her lips. Giles swallowed and took the lead again.

Cecily smiled. She thought she now knew Giles better than he knew himself. He'd had so many women throwing themselves at him that he could not separate love from the physical act. So she had made sure he connected the two with her. That one had been easy enough for her to rectify, although she still flushed at the way she had fondled him so boldly.

Still, just because she drove him mad with physical desire did not mean he could admit to loving her. She didn't know how long it might take for him to realize his need to protect her stemmed from that emotion.

Or did it?

Cecily shook her head, the hood of her cloak slipping down off her mobcap. No, she would not doubt herself anymore. Hadn't she held back her feelings for years because of the mistaken idea that he would reject her again? She had thought she was not attractive enough for him. What an illuminating experience to discover that he felt he wasn't good enough for *her*. She had only to fully convince him she cared little about the social positions that separated them.

Cecily pocketed the core of her apple to give to Belle later, and smiled at her own confidence. She was no longer that woman who had once hid in her little village. She had become someone who could endure the hardships of the real world to find her father.

The crowds thinned as they reached the edge of the city, stately mansions replacing the brownstone shops. Gems glittered in the very bricks of the homes, winking in a myriad of colors. Statues carved of crystal into the shapes of animals and birds glowed softly from cornices above, and beside the stairs of grand entrances below. Lions roared, dragons spread their wings, and gargoyles leered.

It seemed that the cities had grown more brilliant the farther they rode into the interior of Stonehame, their construction enhanced by the local crystal called from the depths by La'laylia of Stonehame, the crystal itself often colored and striated with vibrant hues.

Cecily could not imagine what Stonehame Palace might look like, for Giles had told her it had been crafted entirely of amethyst.

At first it felt odd to see a crystal spire jutting from the middle of a swath of grassland, but Cecily had become accustomed to it the farther they had traveled into the sovereignty. But the mountain of stone that came into view once they'd cleared the buildings of the city astonished her.

Gray clouds moved over the skies, covering the brief morning sunshine, but even in that dimness the mountain of crystal blazed, as if it possessed some inner light. It sat in the middle of a field of tall grass, the enormous base of it a cluster of square-shaped stones angling inward toward the top into four-sided capped spires.

"Oh, dear," muttered Cecily.

A river ran straight to the base of it, and they rode parallel alongside. Belle snorted at the tall grass that swished against her belly, the much taller Apollo eyeing her with a merry gleam as he stepped lightly over the growth.

"Do you hear that?" asked Giles.

Cecily cocked her head. The river gurgled beside them, the grass rustled in the rising wind of the coming storm, the leather of their saddles creaked, and from far away, she could hear the faint sounds of the city. And between and betwixt those soft noises shivered a song that she couldn't quite catch the tune of.

"It's the mountain," she replied. "The crystal is singing."

Giles nodded, pressing on a bit faster, the song becoming louder the closer they came to the mountain, until it nearly set Cecily's teeth on edge when they reached the base of it.

She soon became accustomed to it though as Giles made his way round the big pile of rock. They came to the river again on the other side of it, for the water seemed to flow directly under the mountain. They searched for a shallow place to cross, then continued their journey back to the river across from where they started.

Giles dismounted and placed his hand against the smooth wall, snatching it away in surprise before holding it up again. Cecily dismounted and followed his lead, but when she felt the vibration of the stone beneath her palm she did not start, for his reaction had prepared her.

"It shivers with its song."

"Aye." Giles stepped back and craned his neck upward. "But it can't be alive, despite appearances to the contrary."

Cecily wasn't so sure, but Giles had proven to be extraordinarily intelligent as well as beautiful, and she trusted his judgment. She stroked the smooth, cold stone, trying to peer into it, for it had a cloudy translucence to it that made her think if she looked hard enough, she could make out the shapes beneath the surface.

"It's going to be hell trying to climb this," said Giles. "I don't see any hand- or footholds, but I suppose the stone may be soft enough to chip my own."

"I don't think this is ordinary quartz. I don't think it will be possible for you to break it."

As if she'd challenged him to do it, Giles tossed her a cocky grin and pulled his sword from his scabbard, whipping it about his head in a completely joyful show of bravado, and jabbed it point-first at the stone.

The mountain shuddered, its song turning into a discordant whine, and they both covered their pointed ears until the sound stopped.

"What the devil," growled Giles.

Cecily lowered her hands. "I wonder how Thomas managed it?"

"There has to be a way—stop it, you stupid hunk of iron." Giles wrestled with his blade, which appeared to be intent on plunging itself back into his scabbard.

"I think your sword agrees with me that it cannot break the stone. Let it be, Giles, before it lops your leg off."

"Coward," he accused, allowing it to slam back into its sheath.

"It didn't appear frightened. More like… indignant."

Giles frowned. "It's an enchanted blade. I have seen it turn stone to rubble."

"But this mountain may be enspelled by Lady La'laylia to protect Sebastian's grave." Cecily's heart soared. "Which means Thomas may have found it."

"If he managed to find a way in. I don't think any sort of tool will dent this thing." He slapped the wall.

Cecily took a few paces and then turned, craning her neck upward. Nothing but a bare expanse of smooth rock until near the top, where one crystal formation met another. "I do not see how Thomas could climb this. And we saw no cave or opening." She refused to believe that her father had given up or had died trying.

"It makes me wonder about the death song," said Giles.

"What death song?"

Giles leaped to her side. "A cobbler said he heard the crystal sing a death song, but the townspeople wouldn't explain what it means. I gather they live in fear of something within the mountain."

"This happened at the time my father was here?"

"You are quick, Cecily. Yes. But we can't assume that there is a connection to Thomas."

"Can't we?"

Giles shook his white-blond hair. "No."

"But it could mean that he found a way inside."

"I don't see how."

They stared in awe at the height of the massive stone. Then Giles reached out and smoothed the hair away from her cheek, for the wind had risen and tossed it about. Cecily suppressed a smile of triumph. For days now, she had been the one to bridge the physical distance between them.

"You do think Thomas found a way inside," she accused. "You just don't want me to worry."

His hand strayed to her shoulder and rested there. "It is impossible that Thomas managed to scale this mountain, and we can't even be sure he tried. Perhaps he came across some new clue that led him in another direction. I just think we need more information. Perhaps the Rebellion has some documents in their library about this mountain—or perhaps we should go back and speak to Professor Higley again."

"That would take too long," she protested, trying to think despite the distraction of his nearness. "I do not know where Father is sending me those messages from but it cannot be a good place."

A raindrop pelted her on the cheek, and they both glanced skyward. The gray clouds had turned a smoky black, and they would be drenched before they made it back to the city.

Water.

Cecily strode to the river, leaned forward in a crouch, and trickled her fingers in the shallows, scattering tiny minnows. Her gaze followed the current to the base of the crystal, where it seemed to flow into the very stone itself. But surely it discharged into some fissure or cavern, perhaps far beneath the rock. "If we cannot find a way in from above, perhaps we can from below."

Giles had trailed her, his green eyes narrowing as his gaze followed hers. He quickly discerned her thoughts. "No man can survive that long under water."

"But I can."

"No. No, Cecily, I forbid it."

"You forbid... Giles, I think you are taking this protection thing a wee bit too far."

He folded his arms across his chest and scowled. "I cannot follow you in there. Therefore, you cannot go. It seems logical enough to me."

The rain started to come down in earnest now, plastering Cecily's cap atop her head, streaming down the corners of Giles's hat. She rose and tore off her cloak. "There is no danger to me. If the water does not resurface somewhere under the mountain, I will just swim through to the other side. You know I cannot drown and the water will aid me in whatever way I desire."

"On the contrary. You do not have gills. I admit you can stay under for hours, but you have your limits."

Cecily yanked off her mobcap, quickly shed the pins from her hair, placing them in the ruffled cloth for safekeeping. "Giles, you know good and well it's near impossible for me to drown. What is the real reason for your stubbornness? Afraid you might miss out on some adventure?"

His lip crooked, a devilishly handsome expression that made her insides flutter. "That's only a *small* part of it."

Cecily grinned back at him, unbuttoning her riding coat. "Most likely there will be no way in from beneath. But I promise to give you all of the details should I indeed find Sebastian's grave." She untied her skirt and petticoat, and they dropped with a heavy squish. She discarded her shoes and rolled off her hose, but the look on Giles's face made her leave on her stays and chemise.

Hungry, she decided. He looked very hungry.

He licked rainwater from his lips and muttered, "I still think this is a bad idea."

"Lady Cassandra would not have sent me after my father unless she felt my magic would help find him. I *need* to do this."

And before he could say another word she ran into the water, and with a final leap, reached the center of the river and dove.

The storm had robbed the river of enough sunshine to light the murky depths, and Cecily swam in near darkness. Slick scales brushed her arms and legs more than once, and her toes brushed the top of river grass, but when the current increased she swam in a dark void of nothingness. And then fell over some precipice and tumbled down, down, into the very deepest recesses of the earth.

Cecily used her fear to bolster her magic, gathering a shield of water to encapsulate her body, giving it strength by swirling the outer edges to protect herself from jagged walls or rocky outcroppings.

And still she dropped, the current tossing her around until her head swam with dizziness.

Then she thought she leveled out for a moment before the current pushed her upward, her shield springing against the force of one obstruction after another, unable to fatally injure her, but battering her about nonetheless.

Perhaps Giles had been right. Perhaps this had been a bad idea.

But she allowed the water to take her where it would, keeping her eyes open for the least glimmer of light.

It came in the form of a murky sort of grayness.

At the same time, she felt her stomach fly up into her throat as the upward motion suddenly ceased and she dropped down again, and then spun in a circle. Cecily swam upward, dropping her shield as she broke the surface of the water with a gasp of relief. She swam out of the small whirlpool and wrapped her arms about a jutting rock, looking up at the crystal spires of a large cavern.

She closed her eyelids to steady her vision for a moment, for she felt as if she still spun in circles. Then opened them again.

To her right lay the floor of the cavern, more spires creating a sort of maze across the surface, in places meeting the spires that grew downward from the ceiling above.

The cavern glowed with an eerie sort of light, and when she hauled herself out of the water and rested a moment against one of those crystal pillars, she felt the vibrations of the stone mountain.

Cecily sighed with relief. That wild journey could have brought her anywhere, into some subterranean depth of tunnels and caverns, instead of her hoped-for destination. Or she could have bypassed the interior of the mountain completely, appearing on the other side.

Her gaze went to the pool in the floor, to the whirlwind of water that gushed a fountain in the middle of it. She'd been spat out like a cork from a champagne bottle.

The outer edges of the whirlpool broke away, flowing to the other side of the cavern before disappearing beneath a rocky outcropping, presumably continuing on to form the river on the other side of the mountain. She hoped the journey would not be as difficult going out as it had been coming in.

But enough. Cecily ran her hands down her clothing and hair, shedding the water. She must hurry, or no telling what Giles would do. He might attempt to follow her, and he would never survive that journey. She would trust his good sense only so far, especially when it came to protecting her.

Her lips curved upward as she wove a way through the crystal spires.

To her surprise she quickly came to an opening,

and when she ducked through it, a flat expanse of crystal spread out before her, open to the sky above.

Cecily would give much to see this place in the sunlight. Even with the gray skies the floor glowed like some ethereal hall of a mythical god, catching what meager light it could and tossing it from one crystal surface to another, lighting the soaring columns that surrounded the open space.

Cecily squinted. Something stood in the middle of this great expanse. A small building, like a garden pavilion, but made of the same stone as the mountain. And beneath it a square shape…

She stepped out onto that smooth surface and soon became drenched yet again, but this time from the rain. It fell in sheets, obscuring her vision, so she could not quite make out what lay beneath that pavilion until she reached it.

A box of stone. No, a coffin.

Cecily dried herself yet again, staring in wonder about the pavilion, which was decidedly larger than it had looked at a distance. Statues had been carved to form the pillars that supported the roof. A gryphon with beak opened in a scream of rage stood next to a hydra with multiple heads that sported needle-sharp teeth. An ogre with eyes of amethyst stood sentinel on the other side. A demon crouched, a centaur reared, a hellhound snarled… all of them in protective stances as guardians of the coffin.

And they had failed.

Cecily stepped closer to the coffin, watching her footing, for shards of crystal lay scattered about. Several cracks marked the top of the coffin's surface, and on the other side it had been shattered asunder, revealing a skeleton draped in cloth of gold.

The carvings of the guardians sported cracks as well, and the entire back side of them had been shattered as thoroughly as the coffin. Oddly enough, the inside of those pillars held a hollow shape of the creature that had been carved on the outside of it.

Someone had found Sebastian's coffin… or someone's coffin, since the appearance of the corpse certainly did not look youthful, as the professor had described. But perhaps Sebastian had aged to normal when his ring had been removed?

With a shudder that carried to the soles of her feet, she searched within the cloth of gold, which crumbled at her touch, and around the skeleton, which she feared would sit up at any moment and strangle her.

But she could not find a ring. And her certainty that it had been her father who had found this grave, and had somehow managed to shatter the crystal that Giles's sword could not, steadily grew within her.

"Father," she finally said, "you took it, didn't you?"

As if in reply, the rain abruptly ceased.

Cecily could not stop trembling. She must get away from this place. The ogre kept staring at her with accusing eyes, and the hydra looked as if it would slither forward and rip her apart with those sharp teeth. She turned and hurried back across the crystal hall toward the entrance to the cavern, heedless to use her magic to clear a path, her feet splashing through the puddles, her steps purposeful to avoid slipping on the wet surface.

The rain had stopped but the wind had not, for it

took the song of the mountain and amplified it, until it almost sounded like words now accompanied the tune.

"Cecily."

She came to an abrupt stop, her feet slipping out from under her, and went sliding across the smooth crystal, bumping up against one of those soaring columns. She sat up slowly, her backside aching, and used the column for support to rise.

That voice. It had sung her name. And it had sounded like—

"Cecily."

She felt the song, too, this time, within the vibrations of the stone beneath her palm. "Father?"

"Yes."

Could he be using the crystal as a voice? Didn't one of the traders tell her it was a natural conductor of sound and vibration?

"Where are you?" she cried.

Cecily felt the answer vibrate against her hand, but could not make out the words. She set her ear against the column.

"You were with me. Why did you not stay?"

"When? Where? What do you mean?"

"…not long."

She slapped the stone in frustration. "I cannot hear you."

"…weak."

"Just tell me how to find you!"

"…Hell."

No. She could not have heard right. Her father wasn't dead; she knew it in her heart. And he certainly would not be in hell. He was the bravest, kindest, most heroic man she would ever have the privilege to know.

Cecily closed her eyes, but still the tears leaked from beneath her lids. "Father," she moaned.

And then faintly. So faintly that at first she couldn't be sure that she'd made out the words of the tune.

"Seven Corners."

Cecily angrily dashed the tears from her face. Hell. And seven corners. The last place Thomas's vision had appeared to her had been in that forest of wild magic. Could he have actually been within that chaotic place?

Merciful heaven.

"Father, do you mean the Seven Corners of Hell? Is that where you've been imprisoned all this time?"

"Yesss."

"How is that possible?"

She waited with bated breath, her ear smashed as hard against the stone as she could manage. But she heard no more words within the mountain's song, just the rhythmic tune of the gentle breeze that now swirled about her.

Cecily tarried as long as she could, hoping he would speak to her again. But she could not forget Giles. If she took too long, he would come after her, even if it meant he would drown.

The thought of his lifeless body spurred her to action, and she retraced her path through the cavern, getting lost only once, with the sound of the water leading her back to the whirlpool. She dove beneath the overhang, letting the current carry her on a wild journey yet again. She hoped Giles had thought to wait for her on the other side of the mountain, where the water emerged. For if not, she would have to trudge around the crystal, and exhaustion overwhelmed her by the time she reached the gently flowing river.

She should not have doubted him.

Cecily's head broke the surface of the water; she blinked, and saw him standing on the riverbank beneath the gray skies, the rain having let up. She had never been so glad to see him, despite the anger that tightened his mouth. But when she trudged through the shallows, weariness dogging her steps, his expression changed.

She stumbled over a loose stone and he leaped across the distance separating them, catching her in his arms. Giles dragged her up his body and stared into her eyes. "Don't you ever leave me like that again."

And then his warm mouth met hers, and she threw her arms about him and returned his kiss with all the newfound confidence she possessed. He kissed her with a desire that warmed her blood, his lips so smooth and firm, his arms like a gentle band of steel about her. He smelled of rain and damp wool, tasted like water fresh from a spring.

He set her down reluctantly, staring again into her eyes. Cecily saw something within those depths. Something different that reached out to her very soul and made whatever barriers standing between them seem trifling.

"Come," he said, swooping her up in his arms and carrying her back to land.

He had found a tree to shelter the horses, far off to her left, but had apparently sought no such covering for himself. She saw the muddy path he had worn along the edge of the river from his pacing.

Cecily touched his sodden hair. Had he stood in the rain the entire time while he waited for her? "But don't you want to know what happened?"

"No. Not now."

He helped her into her clothing and Cecily accepted his assistance, used her magic to dry the material, doing the same for him with a sweep of her hand. Giles crooked a brow at her, his look telling her he realized she did not need to fondle his clothing to dry it, but when he would have smiled at the innocent look she gave him in return, he did not. The intensity of the emotion that had taken hold of him would not allow it.

His strength had always impressed her, but never more so than at this moment, when he leaped into Apollo's saddle, still holding her in his arms. He ignored her protests that she felt perfectly capable of riding her own horse.

They rode silently back to town, Giles cradling her against him. After all the distances they had traveled, the short trip back to the inn felt the longest of them all. For his determination lay in his eyes, in his gentle but firm arms, in the stubborn set of his jaw.

Cecily shivered, but not with the cold. Anticipation thrummed through her veins, banishing any lingering tiredness and making her acutely aware of his every move.

Giles had come to a decision.

When they reached the inn, he slid from their mount and set her on her feet, his warm hand firmly grasping hers. He bowed. "My lady, may I escort you inside?"

An undercurrent of meaning lay in his words. Cecily nodded, as a lady would to her servant, and Giles's mouth quirked, but the expression in his eyes did not change. He led her through the rather empty common room, up the stairs to her very door, and turned the handle.

For a moment, Cecily's feet stayed rooted to the floor. Her guise as a prosperous merchant had provided her with lodgings vastly superior than any she had stayed in before. A large bed with feather-stuffed mattress sat in the corner of the room near an ornate gem-studded fireplace. Colorful rugs softened the hardwood floors, chintz drapery flowed across every window, and fresh flowers brightened the carved quartz tables scattered throughout the room.

She stepped inside and turned, unable to meet his gaze. For days now, she had sent him invitations with a glance, the touch of her hand. The last time he'd come to her room, Giles had kissed her and walked away.

This time he would not.

She had wanted him for years and now that the moment was upon her, a small kernel of fear raced through her, a thousand questions plaguing her mind. What if she disappointed him? What if he disappointed her? And what would the future hold for her once she gave her body to him? Their dreams and goals were so very different...

"Cecily."

She looked up at him. The storm had abated but the clouds still hung over the sun, darkening her room with a dreamy sort of light, casting his cheekbones with soft shadows, turning his green eyes to that velvety dusky shade.

His intent had not changed. He had made his decision. But she would have the final say.

Cecily knew the importance of this moment even more so than Giles realized. She feared they would not survive the journey into that place of wild magic. This might be the last opportunity for them to be together. She held out her hand in invitation. In one graceful movement, he closed and bolted the door behind him and gathered her in his arms.

She sighed into his mouth as his lips covered hers. Oh, she could get used to kissing him. She placed her hands on his shoulders, his coat warmed by his body heat, exploring the breadth of his shoulders. How many times had she wished to touch him without reservation? To feel herself in his arms?

His palm went to her cheek and he gently guided her head to match his own movements, sweeping his lips across hers several times before pressing a bit harder, parting her lips beneath his guidance. His tongue swept into her mouth for but a moment, but a promise. And then she felt her cloak fall from her shoulders, felt his fingers briefly at her buttons before her coat parted and met the same fate.

He did not fumble at the ties of her skirt or petticoat or the laces of her stays. She slipped off her shoes when he picked her up and carried her to the bed, and he sat her down on the edge of it in nothing but her chemise and stockings. She looked up at him as he backed up and shed his own coat, but he stepped forward and kissed her again as if he could not resist the offering of her parted mouth.

When he broke away she shivered and he frowned. "Are you cold?"

She shook her head.

He went on one knee before her and slowly lifted the hem of her chemise, untying the garter around her right stocking before gently rolling it down her leg. He took twice as long at the task than when he'd dressed her by the river, his open palms sweeping across her skin with a brand of heat.

Cecily laid a shaking hand upon his bent head. She had forgotten to dry his hair. The dampness quickly fled beneath her touch, allowing her to stroke her fingers through the thick, fine strands. Although it lacked the silver sparkles that lit an elven lord's hair, it had a sheen all of its very own, a vibrancy that made it gleam even in the dim room.

Her stocking fell to the floor with a whisper and Giles started rolling the fabric off her other leg. He lowered his head and Cecily gazed in stunned surprise as his mouth followed the movement of his hands, leaving a trail of kisses atop her thigh. His lips felt soft, his breath so warm, a hint of moisture following every touch. She had not even imagined his mouth across other parts of her body, and it lay so close to...

A flush of wetness between her thighs made her squirm.

Giles looked up at her, his eyes glassy with desire, his face taut and soft all at the same time. "You are not afraid."

All thought had fled, and she could not remember the questions that had unsettled her but a moment ago. Indeed, all of her attention had centered upon his touch. "No."

He grasped her beneath the knees and pulled her toward him, her chemise lifting up over her thighs and hips, exposing the dark mound of hair between her legs. She glanced down and flushed, but his gaze stayed firmly fixed upon hers.

"You are still not afraid?"

Fie, she had trusted him with her life more than once. She surely trusted him in this.

He nodded. "Lie back."

Cecily relaxed on the coverlet, her gazed fixed upon the ceiling, wondering why he thought she needed to rest. But he continued to remove her remaining stocking, continued to cover her skin with kisses, and she closed her eyes as she focused on nothing but his touch.

He kept kissing her even after he'd removed her stocking, trailing a fiery path up her calf to her thigh with the heat of his lips. She remembered what she'd witnessed on the beach all those years ago and assumed that would be all there was to it. She had obviously missed the kissing part.

She felt his hands clasp her knees and gently but firmly push them apart, and she did not resist, for which he rewarded her by kissing her inner thighs.

Fiddle, she had apparently missed the *best* part.

And then she felt the wet heat of his tongue, and an urge to buck, which she firmly resisted, considering it a very unladylike impulse. But Giles knew her body better than she, for his hands quickly slid up to her hips, caressing her for a moment before he spread his hands across the length of her, his fingers meeting just over the curl of hair between her legs.

He ran his fingers through it the same way that she'd run her own through the hair atop his head.

After her first start of surprise, she realized it felt delicious, and allowed him to pet her to his heart's content. His touch slowly dropped even lower, until he stroked the part of her that had become sensitive enough for her to become aware of it. A part of her body that throbbed with a sudden life of its own.

"Ah," she sighed, and it seemed to be all the invitation Giles needed. His hands spread her thighs even wider, his warm strong grip holding her open, and she flushed at the thought of the view he had of her. But only for a moment, for she felt a wet warmth on that nugget of flesh that had suddenly demanded all of her attention, and a pressure that nearly elevated her off the bed.

Apparently a man could kiss a woman *anywhere*.

But he did more than just kiss her. She felt his tongue stroking, and then a suckling... ah, the man did wicked things with his mouth. Cecily began to pant, grabbed the coverlet beneath her palms and caught it up in her fists, pulling against the cloth as her body strove toward something. Just. Beyond. Her grasp...

She tossed her head. She squirmed. She bucked. What was he doing to her? She wanted to ask him but had no thought for speech, for her entire body and soul concentrated on this sudden new feeling.

A shiver ran through her. Cecily's body fragmented into a thousand scintillating parts as a rush of indescribable pleasure ripped through her body, making her cry out Giles's name in wonder and delight. She rode that wave for a long while before her body settled back to earth again.

He left her. It took Cecily a few minutes before she finally had the sense to sit up to see where he had gone. She blinked.

He stood across the room, having discarded most of his clothing—including his drawers, for he wore nothing but his white cotton shirt, which he had already unbuttoned and was in the process of pulling down his arms. Cecily had seen parts of him, his backside on the beach, his naked torso as he worked the bellows at the forge, flashes of his body while they had journeyed. But the entirety of him standing before her... All that golden naked flesh stunned her.

Cecily had felt the shape of him through his breeches on that day she'd boldly fondled him. But it had not prepared her for the sight of it now.

He let his shirt fall and tossed the hair off his shoulders.

She would not say it. He was too arrogant by half already. She would not... "You are beautiful."

He grinned and strode to the bed, lifting her wrinkled chemise over her head, and pulled her into his arms.

"If you had any idea," he murmured, "how delightful you look right now, with your lips swollen from my kisses and your glorious eyes bright with remembered pleasure..." He kissed her, his lips sweeping across hers. "A day hasn't gone by that I have not been struck by your beauty, Cecily. Not a single day."

Her heart turned in her chest. She stroked the muscles of his arms, reveled in the feel of his strong shoulders. "What did you do to me?"

He kissed her cheek, traveled a path to her ear, making her shiver when he spoke. "That was but one pleasure. To prepare you for the greater one."

She raised her brows in disbelief and he laughed, scooping her up in one graceful move and laying her on the bed. His gaze traveled from the tips of her toes to the top of her head, and she realized she lay before him wantonly naked.

She sighed.

He leaned down and caught it with a kiss. His hair tumbled over his shoulders, tickling her throat, her breasts. She curled her hands in the length of it and held on as he ravished her mouth, a slow burn starting inside of her again. She tried to stop him when he pulled away but he did not allow her any control. His mouth moved to the base of her throat, down to her breasts, and she wondered. She hoped.

Ah. He kissed the bud of one nipple, then the other. He stroked them with his tongue until she groaned, and then he suckled.

He had an extraordinarily talented mouth.

Within moments he had her squirming again, but this time she felt a longing for something entirely different. She wanted to be a part of him. For him to make himself a part of her.

"Giles..."

He slid into the bed beside her, the full length of his hot skin touching hers. And it felt so right. As if she'd felt him against her before and would forever more.

He gathered her close, his hands stroking her back, the curve of her bottom. And then he rolled until she lay beneath him, his chest propped above hers, his pale hair hanging wildly about his face, the muscles in his arms and shoulders rippling as he maneuvered his legs between her own.

Cecily watched him. She still remembered the look on his face when she had seen him with that other woman. She wanted to make sure she caused that same exalted expression when he lay with her. No, she wanted to surpass it. She wanted to bring him more pleasure than any other woman ever had before.

Cecily trembled.

"Are you afraid now?" he whispered.

"No."

"Lift your legs."

She immediately complied, her thighs rubbing against his hips. Giles shifted. Something soft and hard touched her wet opening.

"Now?"

"No. And no and no—"

He kissed her again, much to her delight. Cecily put her hands against his broad chest, traveling the breadth of it with curiosity. How could a man be so soft and firm all at the same time? His skin felt like satin, the muscles beneath like the hardest stone. Her fingers stroked the thin layer of hair on his upper chest, tickled the path of it down to his abdomen, where his skin pressed against hers. She swept her palms upward again, across the two large muscles and over the small peaks of his brown nipples.

He shuddered and deepened the kiss, his tongue moving in and out of her mouth.

So, Giles's nipples were sensitive as well. Ah, how she would love to see if her kisses could be as wicked as his. But that would have to wait for another time, for Cecily felt his urgency, his need to claim her. And she wanted it as dearly as he did.

He shifted again. She felt the stretch of her muscles and wondered how she would manage to fit all of him inside of her. But determination made her grasp his bottom... oh, fiddle. More satiny skin, more taut muscle beneath. She explored this new part of him, staring wonderingly up into his eyes.

Giles gritted his teeth.

Cecily pushed him down against her, her strength equal to his when she applied her full elven vigor, which he'd apparently forgotten, judging by the look of surprise that crossed his features. A brief stinging pain accompanied her gesture and she gasped.

Giles frowned and studied her face. "You must let me continue to lead in this."

She nodded.

He locked his arms and waited until she squirmed a bit. Then he penetrated her more deeply, this time only a slight ache accompanying the gesture. Giles then pulled slowly out of her, and slowly back in again.

This time it didn't hurt at all. Cecily smiled.

He repeated the movement, but went a bit deeper the second time. And even deeper the third, until she wondered when she would reach the end of him. But his movements became faster and she got caught up in the rhythm, in the sensation that again he stoked some fire as he had earlier. One that would result in another blazing inferno sundering her body.

Cecily had always imagined *his* pleasure when she fantasized about making love to him. She had never thought of her own.

Giles threw back his head, a moan low in his throat as he continued to rock faster and faster. No.

She wanted to see his face. She grabbed his hair and yanked his head back down and their gazes met as the fire built between them.

Cecily pulled her legs nearly beside her ears as she fought to take him into her deeper. But Giles held back. Instead he increased his tempo, his muscles bulging, his eyes intense as he stared into her own. And then he shuddered, an expression of pure rapture delineating his handsome features, making him nearly glow with a matching inner beauty.

Cecily's body responded to his pleasure, the feeling that spread through her this time not a sundering, but rather a deeper flare that enfolded him inside of her and throbbed in time with him.

Giles watched her until she stilled. "I have dreamed of your face beneath me for so very long."

Her heart swelled. He could not have made any other declaration that sounded as sweet to her ears as that one.

She expected him to roll over and hold her for a time, but he left the bed and she heard the splash of water from the washstand, then he returned with a wet cloth and carefully wiped her. Despite his even more intimate ministrations but a few moments ago, his attention made her blush.

"Are you tender?" he asked.

"A bit."

"It will fade." Giles tossed aside the cloth and knelt by the edge of the bed in all his dazzling nudity, clasping one of her hands within his own and rolling her over to meet his gaze.

"I love you," he whispered. "Will you marry me?"

Nine

THE DARLING GIRL LOOKED UP AT HIM WITH THOSE faceted blue eyes and said, "Yes."

His heart soared. She had spoken truly, then, when she said she didn't care about the differences in their circumstances. He did not know how he would deal with her social set without being forced to knock a few heads together, but he would try.

"But," she continued, "we shall have to wait."

He dropped her hand and rose, sat on the edge of the bed next to her, raking up the bedding and gently covering her body. The sight of her rosy skin proved too much of a distraction for him to focus on their conversation. And it appeared it would require his full attention.

"Why?" Giles dragged his fingers through his hair. When she had disappeared under that mountain, he had come to terms with himself. Even if it meant giving up his dreams of becoming a true spy for the Rebellion, even if he must go live among the gentry or in a hovel by the ocean, he could not live without the lady. "My dear Cecily, I have been waiting nigh onto ten years now, and the past few weeks have been a sheer torture of indecision."

"I know." For a moment, he thought he saw tears glistening in her eyes. "But we do not have time to wed. We must leave as soon as we are able."

"You found something in that mountain. What is it?"

"I saw Thomas."

"Wait." He held up his hand, sat back on the edge of the bed. "Start from the beginning."

She nodded and sat up, hugging the covers to her chest, thank the devil. He had never seen such a beautiful pair of—

"The river did provide a way into the interior of the crystal. I surfaced within a cavern and found my way out to a hallway, of sorts. Open to the sky and flanked by crystal columns. Such a beautiful place—"

"Please, Cecily, just get to the important parts."

"I found Sebastian's tomb—at least, I think it was his. The coffin had been cracked open, along with several statues of rather fierce-looking guardians. But I couldn't find a ring. And then I heard... do you know how the crystal sings? I thought I heard my name in that song. I thought I heard my father's voice."

Giles reached out and touched her cheek. He did not doubt that Thomas had found a way to reach her again. "What did he say?"

"He told me where to find him. He's... Giles, he's trapped... or imprisoned... in the last place we saw a vision of him. That place of wild magic."

"Seven Corners?"

"Aye. And I must go find him."

Giles glanced over at his sword belt, close to hand

on a side table, the plain hilt of his devil-blade winking at him from the scabbard. He had feared an attachment to Cecily would end his ambitions, and yet she brought him more excitement and adventure than he could ever have hoped for. "*We* will go find him."

She huffed. "Giles, you heard what the professor said. No human has ever come out of that forest alive… or unchanged."

"No one with your level of magic has ever ventured within before, either. And I have my blade, Cecily." He could not dampen the excitement from his voice. "I will protect you."

"Me? I do not want to see *you* turned into a monster."

He laughed. "I will not allow it." She gave him such a look of disgruntlement that he could not resist leaning forward and wrapping his arms about her. "My dear, Thomas must have something very important to tell you if he's asked you to follow him there."

"That's what I'm afraid of." His chest muffled her voice. "I will not feel guilty for stealing this time with you. It might be the very last—"

"Cecily, quit this foolishness. We will have our whole lives to spend together. But you are right—our marriage must wait. We must leave for Seven Corners at once."

She sighed, her breath hot against his naked chest. He lifted her chin and kissed her, loving the way she tasted, the way she responded to his touch with no artifice whatsoever. He would never allow anything to harm her. Marriage or no, he *would* be her protector, now and for always.

For the first time since losing his brother and father,

Giles felt whole. He had not realized he missed having a family, but now that he knew Cecily had become a part of him, the emptiness he had carried inside of him suddenly eased. Perhaps he hadn't been looking for vengeance after all. Perhaps he had only been looking for someone to love again.

❧

Giles pressed their mounts hard on the journey back to Oxfordshire, again waiting until Cecily looked to be falling from her saddle before he called a halt for the night. She did not complain, and despite her words, he thought she might carry some guilt for not coming to Thomas at once. Giles assured her that an hour would not have made any difference to Thomas's situation when he had been missing for months.

For his part, Giles would not feel guilty for those stolen hours. Indeed, he thought it would always remain in his memory as the happiest moment of his life.

Although he ached for her even more fiercely than he had before. He'd had a taste of heaven and he longed for more, but could only comfort himself with their closer relationship. He did not need to concoct any reason to sleep with her in his arms.

When they reached that strange forest, it looked exactly the same, much to Giles's wonder and Cecily's obvious dismay.

"We still do not have a plan," she said.

Giles shrugged. "How can we make a proper plan when we do not know what we will be facing?" He leaped from the saddle and patted Apollo's neck to calm him. Cecily always liked to map things out, for it gave her the illusion she was in control. "We will improvise as we go along."

"That doesn't sound very reassuring." She dismounted as well, then hugged the little mare. "Belle will not go in there."

Giles nodded at both their shivering horses. "I didn't expect she would." He started removing Apollo's saddle. "We will leave them in the meadow. Apollo will wait for me and Belle will not leave his side."

Cecily nodded and began removing her own tack. She had learned to be quite proficient at it. "I can call the water from the nearby river to place a shield around us."

Giles placed his saddle under a leafy bush, the only shelter outside of those woods. "Then how will we see where we are going?" He placed Belle's tack beside Apollo's and covered it up with a blanket. Giles handed Cecily the smaller bag of their supplies and tied the heaver sack to his belt.

"You have a point," she replied, tying her own sack to her girdle. "But I will not go in there unprotected—no offense to your devil-blade."

Giles stared into the woods, trying to penetrate the shadows and the darkness. "I wonder how often it erupts into black flame? Or was that caused by Thomas's appearance?"

She waved a trembling hand at the woods. "Who knows? There's nothing within but chaos!"

Giles reached out and dragged her into his arms. "Wait for me here."

She felt as stiff as steel. "We have already discussed this."

He grinned. "I had to try."

Giles bent down and kissed her until she stopped trembling.

"I've been thinking," he murmured against her hair. "All of the powers of the elven lords meet at this place, which means Breden of Dewhame's magic is a part of it."

"So there will be water within?"

"Just so. You will have a weapon to command."

"If we don't get roasted to ash, first."

Giles glanced up and kissed the top of Cecily's head. "You have already called to it."

River water flowed toward her, translucent bands of pale blue curling and twining with the movement of her fingers. "Just a bit. Enough to protect us from that black flame, if we need it."

"Then we are as prepared as we can possibly be."

He set her behind him and strode toward the towering forest. His sword began to tremble, but he did not need the warning. When Giles reached the first line of trees he unclenched his fists with relief. They hadn't disappeared into a flame of black fire. Yet.

Cecily touched his shoulder. "Look, Giles, to the left."

"Keep behind me," he ordered before looking in the direction she pointed. A small orb of light danced a merry jig above a path bordered with craggy roots. "It could be a trap."

"But Thomas appeared in a ball of light, remember? Perhaps he's only strong enough to send this smaller one."

"You truly want to follow it?" A sliver of water slipped around his neck and tapped his cheek, as Cecily used her magic as easily as she used a finger.

"Which other path would you choose?"

She was right. Giles stepped into the woods, ignoring the water that trickled down the front of his shirt. He'd become used to Cecily's magic, just as she had become accustomed to his sword. What an unlikely pair they made. No, what a *likely* pair they made.

"You're right," he agreed. "None of them look very promising—are those vines slithering across the ground, or snakes?"

She stood so close to him he felt her shudder. "Do you see those red eyes staring at us?"

"Follow the ball of light, then." And he turned and headed down that path, making sure he stayed in front of Cecily to meet any danger first.

They circled around trees whose girth easily measured the height of three men, the canopy so far above them that it seemed as if it would take hours for a single leaf to hit the ground. An eerie silence haunted the forest and Giles stepped lightly, avoiding the crackle of leaves or the pop of a dry branch. His ears pricked at the slightest sound from within the twilight of the woods: a low growl, a shuffling footstep, the shriek of some small dying creature. His gaze searched between bush and bramble for enemies but he could not see farther than a few yards. Vines swayed from above, curious blue growths attached to them that spread from one vine to another like the sails of a ship. A green mist swirled about the bushes that fought for space between the trees, and each time the mist shifted the plants appeared to change shape.

A limb reached out to touch him and he squinted to discern its shape, for it looked for all the world like some desiccated arm with tattered clothing for leaves and a hand of twiggy fingers. It tried to touch his hair, and his devil-blade jumped into his hand and he swung. A shriek filled the silence and the severed limb fell at his feet.

"Giles?"

"Yes?" he panted.

"Where are you going?"

He turned, suddenly realizing he could no longer feel Cecily holding on to the back of his coat. She stood on the path, the ball of light impatiently bounding up and down.

Giles stood between two scraggly bushes. "I swear I saw the path veer in this direction."

Cecily clutched her shoulders and hugged herself. "This is such a strange place, Giles. I do not know how Thomas has lived in here for months."

He sheathed his blade and leaped to her side, enfolding her small body in his arms. "Do not worry, we will rescue him. But I think this wood is purposely trying to make me lose my way. I will keep my eyes on our guide instead of the path, and we will not be separated again. You stay by my side from now on."

She nodded and he let her go, but caught up her hand and kept it securely within his own.

The orb had waited for them, pulsing with a soft glow, but quickly shot ahead as soon as they started to follow again. They walked in silence for a time, until Cecily began to lag behind him.

Something cold tickled the back of Giles's neck and dripped down his back. "How much is it tiring you to trail half the river in our wake?"

"It is not a great use of my power and I should not feel this tired. I have gotten used to being away from the ocean and the wealth of water in Dewhame. I think… I think it is this place fighting my magic, for I have to struggle to keep the water in its shape."

Giles glanced behind them. The clusters of liquid lacked their usual sleek form, distorted about the edges and leaking in their wake. Perhaps a third of the water she had called from the river still swirled behind them.

And then his blade trembled on his hip and Giles turned, pushing Cecily behind him. Something approached them from down the path, in the shape of a human but not walking with the stride of one. Giles drew his sword and waited, for they would not turn back.

"Could it be Thomas?" Cecily asked, stepping to his side but keeping at least a bit behind him.

"I do not know. But do not rush forward, and let me handle this." He remembered his battle with the fire demon. "Do not use your magic unless you have to. Agreed?"

"I do not make the same mistakes, Giles."

He could not help but grin at the offended tone in her voice, but the expression soon faded as the… creature neared them. Giles smelled it first. The stench of rotting meat hit his nose like a solid wall and he swallowed against the urge to retch, like Cecily began to do beside him.

Giles took a step forward. "Stop."

The thing grinned at him. Green blotches covered a misshapen face and its teeth looked more like an animal's than a man's. A tattered black uniform hung on a massive frame, fur springing between the tears.

The creature held up its hands as if to strike, claws sprouting from the tips of stunted fingers.

Its eyes looked human. But they held the gleam of madness and Giles did not hesitate.

He leaped forward and swung, his devil-blade singing as it whipped through the air. The creature swiped at Giles but he easily dodged it, dancing away from its longer reach. A look of confusion crossed that monstrous face and it clutched its gut, looking down at the blood that spouted between its claws. It grunted and lunged forward, one long arm taking a last swipe at Giles before it fell.

A claw scratched Giles's cheek.

As soon as his blade absorbed the blood, Giles sheathed it and strode back to Cecily.

"Do not look at it," he said, holding out a hand to her. "It is no longer human."

"Did he... did it have gray eyes?"

"No, Cecily. It was not Thomas."

Her breath hitched with relief, and then her eyes widened. "It hurt you."

"'Tis but a scratch. I did not expect that it could move as fast as an elven, and it got lucky."

She lifted a hand, those delicate fingers moving gracefully as she called a tendril of water. He stood still and allowed her to wash the scratch, even though he knew his elven blood would probably heal it by the time she finished.

She cared for him. He remembered that Cecily had been the one to help him when he had fallen from battle in the village. If only he had realized sooner how much time he had wasted with other women. None of them seemed to satisfy, and he now knew it was because only one woman had been meant for him.

"Cecily." He had breathed her name out loud.

She smiled, the brilliant one that made her blue eyes dance and her cheeks apple.

"I... damn." A black wall shivered behind her. "The black flame; it's coming."

Cecily gasped.

He grabbed her hand and they ran, both of them clearing the fallen creature with one leap. The glowing orb barely stayed ahead of them as fear prompted them to use their full elven strength to run faster than they ever had before.

Giles heard it coming, hissing and screaming behind them. He felt the heat of it, unlike any other ordinary fire, his back burning like the devil, and wondered how long it would be before his coat burst into flames.

Cecily's puny drops of water would be like trying to douse a campfire with spit.

But at the thought, he abruptly felt the heat on his back ease a bit. Giles dared a glance and realized the clever girl had devised a liquid wall behind them, protecting their backs for as long as they could stay slightly ahead of the flame.

"Water," she gasped.

He grinned. "Well done."

"No. Ahead."

The trees before them thinned, and he could just spy the gleam of a lake. They leaped over a fallen log, Cecily's skirts flying upward, staying plastered above her knees from the wind of their flight. That small advantage allowed her to run faster, her legs no longer hampered by her dress.

Giles had no idea she could run like the very wind. He pressed himself to stay ahead of her, admiring her strength, awed by the amount of elven blood that must flow through her veins to give her such abilities.

But they still would not reach the lake in time.

They burst into open ground, sunlight blinding them for an instant. The trees behind them roared as they went up in flame. The heat robbed Giles of breath. The earth shook beneath his boots.

He squeezed Cecily's hand in farewell.

And then the lake rose up to meet them. An enormous swell curled over their heads and beneath their feet, sending Giles head over heels, Cecily's hand his only anchor.

Her power continually surprised him. She had called this wave, protecting them from the fire.

But what matter? He would now drown instead of burn. But Cecily would live, and that's all he truly cared about.

Giles held his breath for as long as he could, until he quit spinning and slowly floated in calm water. Then his lungs demanded a breath and he knew it would be liquid flowing in that would hurt like hell but he opened his mouth...

And then his eyes.

A bubble of air surrounded his head, the sound of his breathing oddly magnified in the small space. Beyond the clear barrier he could see Cecily's face, her black hair floating around her like some silken cloak, her blue eyes gleaming and more lustrous than he could ever imagine. She smiled, completely at home in her element, chest rising and falling as if the very water itself provided all the nourishment she needed.

Perhaps she did have gills.

Giles pulled her toward him, amazed that they had managed to keep their hands clasped through all of the chaos. Her face penetrated the bubble, a sheen of water over her lovely features, and she kissed him: cold, wet, and utterly delicious.

They floated toward the surface, Cecily twirling around him in some aquatic dance, silver fish weaving around her skirts and nibbling on his coat.

His air grew stale and Giles frowned, but Cecily pointed up and he saw another bubble descend from the surface, and she led him from one to another, the new one settling about him with only a brief plunge into wetness.

"You are…" He could not think of a superlative strong enough. "Astounding."

She smiled again, almost shyly, and then pointed upward, releasing his hand and kicking away from him.

"Not without me," he whispered, quickly catching up with her.

The water roiled at the surface, tossing them to and fro, and they both quickly went back down. And waited for the maelstrom to pass. Cecily guided him to the floor of the lake, through grasses that flowed gently back and forth, into schools of fish that parted before them and tickled him with smooth scales and feathery fins. He could barely see in the dim light, more shadows than anything else, but Cecily apparently did not suffer from the same problem, for she guided him with confidence.

The lake had calmed the second time they floated to the surface, and they risked a look above water, Giles's bubble merging with the open air.

Nothing but ominous forest surrounded the lake.

"We had best hurry," he said, his voice so much quieter to his ears in the open air. "Who knows how long this will last?"

"But we don't know where to go."

"Look." Giles nodded to a small spot of light on the shore. "Apparently we haven't lost our guide."

He had the devil of a time swimming in his clothes. He shed his coat and waistcoat on the way, finally removed his boots and tucked them in his belt before Cecily noticed his struggle. She twisted a hand and propelled both of them to the shore on the back of a wave.

"Thank you, lady," he said as the water receded. "But you should conserve your strength. We have no idea what this place may do next."

"I'll do what's necessary." She flicked her fingers at his clothing, shedding the water, making it possible for him to pull on his boots without grimacing. He admired her confidence and worried she would overextend herself, all at the same time. Confounding woman.

She had already turned to follow the orb. Giles caught up with her with a leap, his gaze trying to penetrate the surrounding forest, wondering what sort of other creatures might lie in wait within. How did they survive the inferno? Was it but an illusion that would not harm if one knew the trick of disbelieving it? Did everything reappear after that cleansing?

Giles shook his head, noting that Cecily had dried his hair as well. He should not try and question the chaos of seven conflicting streams of elven magic. He could only try and survive it.

Fortunately the orb did not take them back into the forest. Just beyond the shore of the lake stood an open meadow thick with clover and poppy. A crystal spire sat in the center of it, reminding him of the scenery predominant in Stonehame.

The orb shot across the meadow and disappeared inside the crystal.

Cecily ran after, Giles following a bit slower, watching for the return of black fire and heaven only knew what else. But nothing emerged from the trees and the clover did not change shape and try to swallow them.

"Thomas," screamed Cecily as she stood before the crystal.

And then she collapsed in a heap of skirt and petticoats.

He crossed the distance still separating them and knelt, pulling her into his arms. "Cecily?"

She breathed, but her lids stayed closed, eyelashes fluttering. After all they had been through, why would she suddenly succumb to shock?

Giles looked over at the crystal. It was more translucent than the quartz that had made up the mountain in Stafford, and instead of shadowy clouds within it he could clearly see… a pair of boots. And above that, a fashionable pair of breeches, a coat threaded with silver. A frilled shirt and a cravat of ruffled lace. And

Thomas's face, his gray eyes wide, his golden hair frozen in a halo about his head.

"Damn," muttered Giles. And then louder. "Damn you, Thomas! Why did you call her here when you're already dead?"

That orb of light that had led them here appeared again, flowing out of the crystal and growing to a man's height. Thomas appeared inside it. "Because this is important."

Giles glanced from the body frozen in crystal, and to the animated vision of the man in the ball of light. And then back down to Cecily as her eyelashes fluttered open.

"Thomas?" Her gaze skittered over to the crystal, and Giles quickly turned her toward the vision. She sat up, a smile of relief lighting her face. "Father! You frightened me. I thought you were—"

"I am. No, Cecily, don't you dare faint again. I can't ever remember you doing such a thing before." His face creased. "What you must have gone through... I'm sorry to have put you through all of this. But I know you're strong enough, my girl. I have counted on that."

Cecily rose very purposely to her feet, brushing at her skirts and adjusting the sleeves of her coat. Giles rose with her, standing by her side, his arm ready for support if she should need it.

"But why?" she demanded. "What could possibly be so important that you've brought me half across England and to this—this dreadful place?"

"Information, my dear. And the ring, of course. Our leader needs it."

Cecily narrowed her eyes, a good healthy dose of

anger replacing her sadness. Giles nodded in satisfaction. She would not break.

"You have always put this Rebellion before me," she snapped. "Why did I think this would be any different?"

Thomas shook his head, his brow crinkling. "That is not true. I protected you from them until the day I died. I could do no more after that. And you were the only one I could reach with my sending."

"Because I love you." Cecily clasped her hands together. "Because we share a bond that nothing can sunder. Not even your—"

"Death? You can say it, my dear. I've gotten quite used to the idea."

"But—but how? What happened?"

Thomas swept back his golden hair, and perhaps because he was looking for it, Giles saw the ring upon his finger. A square lavender stone inset in a thick band of gold. No wonder Thomas appeared more youthful than Giles remembered. It looked as if he clutched something else in his other hand, but Giles could not quite make out what it might be.

"I have much to tell you," Thomas replied. "And although I can send you this illusion much stronger standing next to my body, I do not know how long my strength will last. This place… is quite unpredictable."

"We know," muttered Giles.

Thomas glanced at him. "Beaumont. Thank you for keeping her safe."

Giles nodded.

Thomas's attention quickly swung back to Cecily. "I need you to take the ring back to our new

Mor'ded. You know of his alliance with us? His new... situation?"

Cecily nodded. "He needs it to hide his human age—"

"Precisely. But you must tell him to take to wearing gloves when he speaks with the other elven. La'laylia of Stonehame is aware of the theft, and may recognize the ring and remember a human she once loved long ago."

"So it *was* Sebastian's grave. How did you get inside the mountain?"

Thomas smiled, flashing even white teeth. "With music."

"I should have guessed," muttered Giles.

"Indeed." Thomas held up a hollow crystal tube with three finger-holes in the top of it. "It took me some time to discover the whereabouts of the key to the door in the mountain, for I never dreamed it to be in the shape of a flute. The crystal instrument is enchanted with a resonance that responds to the pattern carved on the side of it. I found it in a temple dedicated to La'laylia and had a devil of a time stealing it, and only by sheer chance did I think to play the tune backward to break open the coffin. Unfortunately, the guardians' tombs opened as well."

"The creatures surrounding the pavilion," breathed Cecily.

"Just so. Magical creatures that I had no hope of vanquishing. So I fled."

Giles could not help the stupefaction in his voice. "To *this* place?"

Thomas shrugged. "It's amazing what one will do when being pursued by a four-headed snake, a snarling hellhound, a roaring demon... ah, I knew I but traded one danger for another, but I hoped such enchanted creatures would be affected by the wild magic within these woods. And I was right. They... fractured."

"But it didn't matter," huffed Cecily. "You lost your life all the same."

"But to a much greater purpose, my dear."

Giles had been studying the small crystal instrument. "*It* protected you through the maelstrom. You played the flute again, didn't you?"

Thomas grinned. "Well done, lad. A final act of desperation... yet it did create an opening within the spire, and I stepped through. But this stone lacked an open space, forming around me and cutting off my air, and yet... it has somehow kept my consciousness alive." He raised his arms. "And it allowed me to uncover the secret of the Seven Corners of Hell."

"But Professor Higley told us all about it." Cecily stepped forward, as if she longed to throw herself into his arms, and pulled back only at the last moment.

Thomas lowered his hands and looked at his daughter with just as much longing in his gaze. "We humans know only that this is the place where the border of every sovereignty meets. We could only guess the convergence of the different magics is what created the chaos. But my dear, this place is more than that. It is the doorway to Elfhame."

Giles sucked a breath between his teeth. "What do you mean?"

Thomas answered, although he kept his attention riveted on his daughter. As if this was the last time he would ever see her, and he must drink his fill. "When the elven lords created the doorway between our worlds, they did not close it all the way. There is a small opening, and indeed, this is the source of their magic. Through that opening flows the magic of Elfhame, like a river flows and spreads into a lake. This is why the elven do not press beyond England's borders, for the magic can puddle only so far. And the scepters are useless without the magic."

"Have you seen this opening?" asked Giles.

Thomas pointed to a group of stones between the meadow and the woods. Giles could just discern the glimmer of a small spring that bubbled up from within the shelter of the crystal rocks, creating streams flowing away from it. "It is there."

Cecily frowned. "I see nothing unusual about it."

"When the black fire comes, it changes. We do not see it truly, but that is the center. I can't imagine a way to close this opening to stop the flow of magic, nor do I know if a true doorway between the worlds can be opened, or how. But if you bring this information to the Rebellion, perhaps those who follow me will figure out a way."

Giles scratched his face. Damn if the little scrape from that monster's claw hadn't healed yet. "How do you know this for a fact?"

Thomas nodded. "Good question, Beaumont. I trained you well." His gray eyes suddenly gleamed with some inner wonder. "I saw Elfhame. When this place erupted again, I could actually see the flow of magic from that stream with unshielded eyes. And I caught a glimpse before…"

Cecily's breath caught.

"Before all hell broke loose."

Cecily dashed the tears from her eyes. "But why did you take on such a dangerous mission in the first place? Breden's soldiers raided our village and they killed Mother. And now you are… and I have no one."

Thomas flinched when he heard of Eleanor's death, but he didn't appear to be surprised. Giles wondered how long Thomas had been trying to contact Cecily, and if he'd managed to be with her before she could see his actual vision. Thomas would know then, how hard Giles had tried to keep his distance from his daughter. Did he also know that, in the end, Giles had failed?

Odd, how it no longer seemed to matter.

"Cecily, my love." Thomas floated forward, as if he would embrace her if he could. "What have I always told you? The good of the many outweigh the needs of the few. I think I did you more harm than I knew, by loving you as a father should. I allowed you to become selfish."

She opened her mouth to protest. Giles put a hand on her shoulder.

"I know you want nothing more than to stay in that little cottage by the sea," continued Thomas. "But don't you see the world has need of your gifts?" His gaze flicked to Giles. "Don't you see that others need your help?"

"I did not think…"

"I know, my dear. But now it is time for you to think about it. Will you promise me?"

Cecily bowed her head, tears freely flowing down her face. She did not sob or wail, just cried those thick drops of moisture.

"You are the only one I know of who has the level

of power to survive the magic within this place. Will you at least take the ring, and the information I have given you, and bring it back to Sir Robert?"

She nodded.

Giles felt this odd squeezing in his chest, an overwhelming sympathy for her. He rolled his shoulders to loosen the tension in his muscles that the feeling had created. "I foresee only one slight problem, sir. The ring"—and he nodded at the crystal capsule—"is in there with you."

Thomas frowned, his gaze still fixed upon his daughter. "You need to break it open with that sword of yours."

"I tried that before, with that mountain of crystal in Stafford. Didn't work."

"And your sword showed good sense. Had you broken it, the elven lady would have been upon you in a blink."

Giles glanced down at the hilt. It could show good sense? He had come to treat his sword as if it were alive in some way, but the fact that Thomas shared similar thoughts shook him. "It is naught but an enchanted blade."

"But more powerful than we know, I think." Thomas held out a trembling hand to his daughter. "Cecily. Dearest."

She looked up.

"The crystal has kept my soul bound to this life. When it is broken… I may not be able to come to you again."

She shook her head, but stayed silent.

"I love you, child. More than if you had been my

very own. Remember what I said, and remember what value I placed on my life—do it now, Beaumont. You may not have much time left."

Giles quickly glanced at the trees for a sign of black fire, sighed with relief when he didn't see it, and drew his devil-blade, swinging it at the pillar in one smooth movement.

Ten

"No!" screamed Cecily, and she lunged forward at the ball of light, falling through it as the crystal spire cracked, Thomas's vision fading as his physical body tumbled to the ground.

The ground beneath Giles's feet trembled.

She spun, threw him a furious glare, and dug through the shards of crystal until she reached her father. She picked out the pieces of stone that had lodged in his face, swept his coat clean of debris. Her hands left behind smudges of her own blood. "Now I will have nothing left of you," she said. "Nothing left at all."

Another odd emotion swelled in Giles's chest, something akin to envy this time, and he scratched at his face yet again. Cecily made him feel the damndest things. He recognized the emotion as unworthy but could not suppress it fully. He hoped that someday, Cecily would love him as much as she did her father. He had no family left to mourn him when he passed, but it had never bothered him before now.

The ground shook again. The faint scent of black fire reached his nose. Giles bent down and removed the ring from Thomas's finger. The other man's golden hair quickly turned gray at the sides, and a few wrinkles seamed his face, the corners of his eyes. Giles pocketed the ring, hesitant to put it on his own finger, despite the fact that the elven lords deemed it harmless—or perhaps because of it. Thomas still clutched an object within his other hand, and when Giles drew it forth he realized it was the small crystal flute the man had spoken of. He tucked it in his pocket next to the ring, and the ground shook again.

"Cecily, we must flee."

She turned to look at him with blind eyes, the rims red from her tears. Then she blinked and focused her gaze, her eyes widening with fear as she studied his face.

"Yes, the fire is coming." He held out a hand, she clasped it, and he helped her to her feet. "I'm not sure if we can outrun it this time."

"We… we don't need to. Just hold my hand tightly, Giles."

He nodded, trusting her as he had never trusted anyone before in his life. Giles glanced over his shoulder, the acrid stench of the fire even stronger now, and spied the black flame dancing over the treetops. But the sight of it did not make his heart race as much as what Cecily did with her magic. The lake they'd sheltered in before erupted, an arm of it reaching out to them, forming into the rough shape of a hand.

Giles looked down at Cecily.

"Take a deep breath," she warned with a grim smile.

And then the hand of water reached them, lifting them both off their feet, curling over their heads like some giant fist. Giles could no longer see past his nose, for white spray and bubbles churned in front of his face. He closed his eyes, spun head over heels, Cecily's hand his only anchor as the wave propelled them forward with a speed he could barely comprehend.

His lungs had just begun to ache for want of another breath when he rolled one last time and came to an abrupt stop, the water receding about him.

Giles sat in a wet meadow, muddy grass beneath his bottom, still holding Cecily's hand. He glanced over his shoulder, saw the chasm open in Seven Corners to swallow the maelstrom, and did not wait for the eruption that would follow. He lifted Cecily to her feet and dragged her as far away as he could before he collapsed in exhaustion, dragging her atop him to cushion her body.

The thrill of survival raced through Giles. "That was amazing," he said.

She looked down at him, sadness still in her eyes. He wished he could make it disappear. He wished he could bring back Thomas for her.

Giles smiled his most radiant smile, the one that he knew brought women to their knees. "Had I known how exciting it would be with you, I would have taken you up on your offer long ago. Little girl or not."

"No, you wouldn't," she replied. "You may be a rake, but you have always been an honorable one."

He laughed, bouncing her on his chest. "Well, my wandering days are over. There is only one woman I will be taking to my bed from now on, and no other could compare to her."

A tremulous smile curved her mouth. "Do you mean it, Giles?"

"Aye, my lady, I do. Did you think I asked you to marry me out of some sense of honor?"

"Perhaps."

He laughed again, curled his arms about her waist, lowering her face closer to his. "Mayhap that had a little bit to do with it. But the truth is… I want to spend the rest of my life with you, Cecily. I can't imagine living it without you." His grin faded as he looked deeply into those crystal blue eyes. "I'm sorry about Thomas. But you are not alone. You will never be alone, as long as I draw breath."

She lowered her head and kissed him then, a kiss he never wanted to end, for he had never been kissed like that before. Such tenderness. Such love and longing and a need for him that spoke to his very soul. And in that moment, he knew their hearts met as one, melding together with a finality nothing could ever sunder.

When Cecily finally came up for air, Giles released a breathless gasp. "If we continue this, my dear, we shall be making love in mud, and although the idea has its merits…"

She swatted him gently and stood. "We must save our energy to find Apollo and Belle. I have no idea where my wave dumped us."

Giles sat up and glanced around, muddy hair sticking to his cheeks. "I think that way."

And so they walked for a time, the mud drying on his clothes until he felt as if he strode in armor, his boots as stiff as wooden clogs. They found their horses and rode away from that hellish forest toward Oxford, stopping at the edge of a river as the sun lowered from the sky, beneath a copse of willows that offered a bit of privacy and shelter.

Cecily slid from Belle and immediately discarded her clothing, Giles watching her with a longing gaze. Their mission had been too urgent for them to indulge in love-play on their journey to the Seven Corners of Hell, but now that they had survived the dire task and the excitement of true peril still flooded his veins, he could not help the direction his thoughts wandered.

He needed to possess her with an urgency that surprised him. But after what she had just gone through, he did not want to push her.

She dove into the water and sighed as if it brought her comfort she sorely needed, and he dismounted and made camp to the sounds of her splashing. But once he'd finished he could not deny the need to clean his prickly clothes, and after removing his sword belt, walked straight into the river himself, washing the mud from the fabric. Trying not to glance her way when the flash of pale skin caught his attention.

"Giles."

He turned. Moonlight shimmered across the waves, danced in her enormous blue eyes, played along the soft curve of her shoulders. It seemed that being in her element had revived her strength, for the exhaustion that had dogged her steps throughout the day had faded to be replaced by...

He had not mistaken the invitation in her voice.

Giles leaped from the river, and with a speed that surely surpassed an elven's natural abilities, he undressed and tossed the soggy garments over the root of a tree. He flung his boots next to his breeches and strode back into the water. It licked at his naked skin, the chill of it unable to douse the fire that burned in his blood as he watched Cecily swim closer to him.

She stood, water sluicing down her breasts, down her taut belly. And held out her arms to him.

Giles caught her up in an embrace, his mouth seeking hers with a need that frightened him. She wrapped her arms about his neck as he nearly devoured her, the darling woman opening her mouth beneath the onslaught, taking all he offered without hesitation.

At last he released her, holding her face close to his pounding heart. "I love you."

She pulled slightly away from him, looked up into his eyes, studying his face with a frown that confused him. "And I have always loved you. No matter what happens, Giles, I will never stop loving you."

Ah. She worried about their future. About her dream for a cottage by the sea, and his desire for adventure. "As long as we are together, we will work it out."

She nodded, stepped away from him with a sudden wicked gleam in her eyes. "I see the cold water doesn't bother you."

Giles glanced down at the obvious proof of it, looked back up with a grin on his lips. "Apparently not."

She took his hand. "Then come." And led him deeper into the river, until it enfolded over both of their heads, shafts of moonlight penetrating the depths.

Giles did not start when the bubble appeared around his head this time, just eagerly awaited her kiss to pierce it. But it did surprise him for a moment when he felt the water seem to thicken around him, slither against his body in undulating ribbons. Ah, he'd never felt anything like it before. A soft caress twirling about his chest, around his legs. Silky pressure along the skin of his thighs, between his legs, beneath his hair and along the back of his neck.

Cecily made the water come alive. And it sought to touch him with an erotic slide across every inch of his skin.

When it curled and tightened about his shaft, he gasped, the bubble making the sound loud to his ears, and reached out for her.

Cecily led him a merry dance. He would grasp her slick skin to have her slip away from his fingers. Giles would feel her breasts slide across his back, turn to grasp nothing but swirling water. Her hair tickled his feet and he reached down, only to tumble over in vain, his feet toward the surface and his own ghostly looking hair swirling around the bubble that surrounded his face.

Her magic astounded him yet again. For the bubble continued to surround his head.

He would die of frustration sooner than he would by drowning.

And then he felt her warm palms against his cheeks, the smooth glide of her hands as she penetrated the bubble, a sheen of water sliding up her face. When her lips met his he no longer knew which way was up, a thrill coursing through him that he'd never known before.

He clasped her in his arms, triumphant he'd caught his flirtatious mermaid.

Cecily's hands replaced the teasing of the current, roaming the contours of his back, smoothing over the rounds of his bottom. He could not help pressing his shaft tightly against the warmth of her legs.

Cecily drew her mouth away from his, trailing kisses across his cheek, down his chin. She lightly bit his neck and Giles growled, soft and low.

"Release me, Giles. I promise I will not go far."

It took every ounce of willpower he possessed to loosen his hold.

She slid down his body, until the crisp hair at the junction of her legs stroked his engorged shaft.

Giles panted. Another bubble replaced the air he'd managed to use up so quickly, and he wondered how she knew he needed it. For her own head had withdrawn back into the water, her dark hair swirling around that lovely face, rays of moonlight highlighting a soft cheek, the curve of her full lips.

He felt the blood leave his head as they slowly drifted upright again, Cecily curling around his body akin to the mermaid he'd likened her to. She twirled about him as she'd done with her water, but the heat of her skin brushing his brought another dimension to the pleasure. When he felt her hair tickle between his legs, and looked down to see her face rising upward, trailing kisses along his shaft, he could bear no more.

He caught her arms and dragged her up. Saw the gleam of her teeth as she smiled and drew up her legs, wrapping them around him, slowly floating toward the tip of his erection, until her moist warmth kissed it with a softness that made him groan.

Giles resisted the impulse to buck against her. He ruled on dry land, but here and now she had control of this game, and he did not wish to argue the point. It felt too damn good.

She pressed forward so slowly he had to grit his teeth. She encased only the tip of him with her warmth, her water-magic still circling his shaft in ever-tightening spirals. He became aware again of the strokes still circling the rest of his body, curving around his arms and chest. Smoothing around his legs and pushing up between them, creating a pressure that made him throb even harder.

The silky water pushed and prodded in places that he hadn't known could feel so tantalizing.

When Cecily tightened the grip of her legs, her heels digging into his backside, and fully encased him inside her, the contrast of her hot sheath from the cold water nearly made him come undone.

Thank heaven for experience. Otherwise he might have lost his control.

Cecily relaxed her legs and pulled slightly away from him. The pressure of the water that had circled his shaft now roiled between them, a vibration that surely touched her nub.

Ah, clever woman. She had learned so quickly.

Cecily abruptly clenched her legs and pushed against him again. Clutched his shoulders and repeated the movement. Giles placed his big hands under the smooth mounds of her bottom, but only to caress, not to guide. He threw back his head and allowed her to control the rhythm, allowed himself to become lost in the myriad sensations this lady and her magic created for him.

The world tilted upside down.

Blood flowed to his head again.

Giles climaxed with a furious pleasure he'd never, ever experienced before. Felt the tremors of Cecily's own pleasure course through her warm body.

And they both held on to one another as if they could never let go while they slowly drifted upright, back to the surface of the lake.

Giles watched as her head slowly broke the surface, now some beautiful naiad brought to earth for his private pleasure. Water dripped down the curve of her nose, saturated her eyelashes to form a dark circle around her eyes, making them appear even larger and more crystalline. Her hair curved about her face like ribbons of midnight, and her lips captured droplets in the curve of her smile.

The urge to say something meaningful enough to bring tears to his eyes made him take refuge in a cocky smile. "Where have you been all my life?"

"Right under your nose."

"Aye, and me too stupid to do anything about it."

She laughed, as he'd hoped she would, and swam back to shore. Giles did not have a prayer of meeting her stride in her element, and truth be told, his muscles felt like jelly, so he lazily swam after her, admiring the sight of her wiggling bottom as she emerged from the water and walked across the riverbank.

They shared their meal that night with laughter and old memories of the village. And if Giles noticed a hint of sadness creep back into her eyes, he quickly teased her until wicked merriment replaced it. And when they both crawled beneath the blankets to sleep, nothing could stop the both of them from falling into complete oblivion.

~

Giles awoke with his hand on his sword and her hair against his lips. He breathed in the faintly floral scent of it, kissed the black strands for good measure, and rose.

He felt as if he ruled the world.

With a self-mocking smile, he stoked up the fire, spitted the fish they'd caught last night after they'd made love, remembering the laughter as Cecily tossed him one squiggling catch after another. She could be a wicked wanton one moment and a funny companion the next, with a healthy dose of proper lady betwixt and between.

Giles never thought to marry. Because he'd never thought to fall in love with a woman like Cecily. And now he could not wait for her to wake, to find the nearest village and make their bond legal. It would be done before they returned to London, and even the fire lord himself could not gainsay it. Giles would give the elven lord the ring, and Sir Robert the secret of the Seven Corners of Hell and a crystal flute containing an enchanted tune.

And Giles would take Cecily. A prize worth all the rest, and then some.

He sat near the blankets and watched her sleep, feeling like a fool but unable to help himself. The birds twittered so loudly amongst the trees that he couldn't believe she slept through the racket. A soft breeze blew off the river, tickling the hair tumbling across her cheeks until he could resist the impulse no longer, and carefully smoothed back the errant strands.

Her eyes fluttered open to stare at his face, and she sat up with a start.

"I'm sorry," he murmured, an unfamiliar heat rushing to his face. "I didn't mean to startle you."

Cecily gave him a hesitant smile, her gaze wandering across his features for a time, until her smile slowly firmed and warmth flooded those faceted blue irises. She reached up and placed her hand over his left cheek, and he turned his face and kissed her palm.

Her sigh was all the invitation Giles needed.

In one lithe movement he threw back the blanket and crouched over her, his hands flat on the ground beside her head, his knees next to her thighs. His hair flowed over his shoulders to surround her face, her black locks a strong contrast against his white.

She had worn nothing but her chemise to sleep in, her nipples outlined clearly beneath the thin fabric. He let his gaze wander over them for a moment before he lowered his head and kissed each peak.

Cecily arched toward him.

Giles drew back and smiled at her. "Last night I allowed you control, but now we are on dry land and it is my turn."

Before she could reply, he dipped his head and kissed her lips, a long lingering caress that stole her breath. He trailed a path along her cheek to the tips of her pointed ears, whispering what he planned to do to her, until she started to pant and squirm.

"I have no magic but my love for you, lady."

She wound her fingers in his hair, making his scalp tingle. "That is all I need, Giles. More than I had ever thought to have."

He kissed her again, long and slow, while he gently tugged up her chemise, exposing her breasts. She shivered, and he did not think the gentle breeze caused her reaction. He trailed kisses down to her neck this time, suckled gently at the skin there, smiling at her startled gasp.

Apollo snorted off in the distance, an answering wicker from Belle, comforting sounds that told Giles they would have no interruptions.

His mouth lazily wandered to her breasts. They were beautiful, firm and full, with rosy peaks that begged his attention. He licked first one, and then the other, circling them with his tongue for good measure. She tasted divine.

"Giles," she whispered, her hands wandering over his bare back, making his flesh tingle in response.

He lowered his body, leaning on one elbow, leaving one hand free to explore while his tongue continued to play with her now-taut pink buds. When he trailed his fingers over her thighs she opened her legs without a single prompt from him.

Giles hid his wicked smile against her bare flesh.

He explored her moist folds, ran his fingers through her silky stiff hair, lifting his head for a moment to gaze at the sheer perfection of her body. Flawless, luminescent elven skin, pale as milk without a single blemish to interrupt the smooth expanse of it.

He had never seen a more beautiful woman. The thought that she was truly his, after so many years of wanting her and knowing he could never have her, made his heart leap inside his chest.

Giles glanced into her face and those blue faceted eyes drew him in.

"You are mine," he said, surprised at the huskiness of his voice. "I will always be your protector."

She did not answer. They stared at each other for a timeless moment, until the earth seemed to pause, and the birds ceased their raucous calls, and the very wind hushed to witness the love between them.

Giles slipped a finger inside her moist heat.

"You are mine," he repeated.

She arched her back.

Fie, she felt tight and wet and utterly magnificent. He slipped in another finger. She trembled. He hesitated to slip in another; she felt so small. How had she managed to take him all in?

But she had, and was a virgin no longer.

With one quick movement he pushed his fingers deep inside her and smiled when she gasped, bucking against his hand.

"Tell me," he growled, penetrating her deeply again.

"I… I am yours. I have always been… Giles, I need more."

He mounted her in one smooth movement, gritting his teeth for control. She felt so right. So perfect. He kept one hand between her legs to stroke her nub while he copied the rhythm with slow, deep thrusts, watching as her lids drifted closed, her lips parting on a sigh.

He'd had sex with many women. He'd made love to none but her. His heart and soul gave her as much as his body offered, if not more.

Cecily dug her nails into his back, grasped his bottom in urgent demand.

But he would not hurry toward that peak. He continued his gentle movements, loving her with each stroke, making her pant and cry out his name. Time and again she neared the precipice and he froze inside of her, arms trembling with the willpower it required.

And then he would resume his loving, her desire more easily stroked, building to an even greater height than before.

Until finally, with a groan of sheer delight, she fell.

Giles quickly followed, gathering her close against him until he could feel the pounding of her heart echo the throbbing of his own release.

When the world managed to right itself he kissed her tenderly, smoothed the silky hair off her moist forehead.

"I love you," he whispered.

"I know," she replied. "I felt it. I did not know it could be so... wondrous."

He could not help but smile. Precious lady.

Cecily took a deep breath, released it on a sigh, and took another. "I smell roasted fish." Her stomach grumbled.

Giles laughed. "Indeed, my lady. Let me fetch you some... although I fear it may be burnt by now."

He quickly put words to action and handed her the fish. She took the stick from his hand and carefully peeled away the charred outer part, picking off pieces of white meat and popping them in her mouth, watching him break camp as she chewed.

"We will find the nearest village," said Giles as he rolled their dingy clothing from yesterday into a tight ball, "and find the parsonage straight away. I won't wait for you to change costume, mind you, so you'll have to be married in whatever clean gown you have left." He turned and threw her a wink to soften the command in his words, but he meant every bit of it.

"I think… I think it would be best if we made straightway to Oxford, Giles."

Her softly spoken words staggered him for a moment, and he jerked the ties of their baggage in place with a bit too much force. "Why?"

Giles heard her soft footsteps as she neared him, felt the warmth of her hand against the back of his shoulder, but he did not turn around. He could not. He spoke his deepest fear. "Have you changed your mind?"

"No. No, of course not."

He breathed a sigh of relief. For a moment there, his old insecurities of the gulf between their social stations had risen to threaten him again. His worry that Cecily would not wish to wed against Thomas's wishes. Just because he had managed to overcome those obstacles, did not mean that she…

He turned. "Again I ask you. Why?"

She looked at him with her heart still in her eyes, and it puzzled him even more. "Oxford had such lovely churches. Wouldn't it be grand to marry in one of them?"

Giles frowned. He knew her well enough to know she would prefer a quiet marriage in a small town, a setting similar to the village they had left behind. He had believed her wholeheartedly when she'd professed her rejection of the title and the grandeur that it could provide her.

"Cecily," he said, his voice tinged with exasperation, "tell me the real reason you want to hie off to Oxford."

She lifted her small hand and placed it against his

cheek. Then she leaned up on her toes and kissed him. He could not help it when his arms pulled her close, when he responded to the touch of her mouth. But he would not allow her to distract him. At least, not until after he finished thoroughly kissing her.

Despite their prolonged loving just moments ago, his body responded to the feel of her warm body against his, and only the thought that she had to ride today stopped him from carrying her back to their bedding.

Which he just might do if he didn't stop this now. He pulled away and tossed the hair away from his face. "Tell me."

Cecily placed her hand against his left cheek yet again. "The Seven Corners of Hell… marked you with its magic."

He blinked at her stupidly for a moment, then reached up and pushed her hand away, scratching at his cheek. It still itched. Where that monster had clawed him. His elven blood should have healed that small scratch by now.

Giles stalked to the river, trying to see his reflection in the water. But it rippled too much, and he could make out only a darkish image of his face. An even darker splotch covering the left side of it.

"How long have I looked like this?"

"Since… since the Seven Corners of Hell… just before we escaped the black flame."

"What is it?"

"I don't know. But Professor Higley said a colleague of his was studying the creatures that emerged from that wild forest. Perhaps he could tell us."

Giles spun. Had the creature he'd fought passed on

some disease with that small scratch? "Tell us, what, exactly? Whether I'm going to turn into a monster or not?"

She blinked, her eyes suddenly filling with tears. "No, Giles. You assured me that would not happen."

He closed the distance between them, her sorrow outweighing his fear. "Yes, yes of course, hush, and do not cry. All will be well, I promise. We will go see Professor Higley and his friend. I'm sure it is nothing."

And so they rode for Oxford, Giles assuring Cecily the entire way that it was but a scratch and nothing to worry about, until he half-believed it himself.

Until they reached Oxford toward evening.

The university streets thronged with students returning home from their studies, costermongers trying to sell the last of their wares, and box chairs bringing home the gentry… or perhaps taking them out for the evening. As usual, the crowd parted before Giles, more than one glance cast warily toward the sword at his side. But unlike the last time they'd ridden through these same streets, the reactions of people when they glanced at his face were entirely different.

Giles had been aware of his good looks since he'd reached puberty. He'd never questioned his ability to attract others, especially those of the opposite sex. He hadn't considered himself vain. It was but a fact from constant observation.

But today when people looked at him, it was if they were repulsed. They glanced quickly away or stared rudely in disgust.

His hand stole to his cheek. How badly had he been marked?

Giles shook back his hair and lifted his chin, pulled up on the reins. "You there, girl. An apple for the lady and me."

The street urchin skipped toward him, a smile forming on her narrow face, the apples in her basket a bit brown and her delight in selling them obvious. But when she reached his side and looked up at his face, her eyes widened and she took a step back.

Giles fished a few coins from his pocket. "Come here, girl. I won't bite." And he punctuated his words with a smile. The smile that had always managed to make women of any age swoon.

The child winced, but did manage to fish out two apples from her basket and hand them up to him with shaking fingers. Giles tried to hide his dismay by giving her an extra half pence. The child snatched it and ran.

He pulled Apollo alongside Belle and handed Cecily the brownish fruit.

"I could not see my reflection very well in the water. Has the mark altered me so very much?"

Cecily took a bite of the apple and chewed while she stared at him thoughtfully. "Your features are still as handsome as they have ever been, Giles Beaumont. Shall we find a room before we meet with the professor, or visit him straight away?"

He frowned at the odd way she'd answered his question. "We see the professor now."

❧

Giles escorted Cecily into the room that Higley had directed them to. The old professor had been astounded by their foolishness in entering the Seven

Corners of Hell, had been equally revolted by whatever had been done to Giles's face, and had told him again that he would welcome Giles into the ranks of the academia.

As if Giles's adventuring days had come to an end.

Cecily did not like going so far down into the depths of the old building, for the laboratories were all located beneath the ground floor, and she continued to shiver even when they entered the warmth of Professor Quinby's lab.

Various… things floated in bottles of cloudy liquid, and an acrid stench permeated the air. Tubes and jars littered the tables the same way that books had overtaken Professor Higley's private office. But the man who greeted them looked nothing like his colleague. Quinby looked to be quite a young man for his position, with a shock of red hair and a cherubic face that belied his grisly work in progress.

A cadaver lay on a table before him, a twisted figure of what might have once been a human being. The professor took one look at Cecily's face and quickly set aside his bloodied tools and pulled a sheet over the lump he'd been carving.

"May I help you?" he asked, his face turning almost as red as his hair, his gaze fixed in stupefied adoration on Cecily's face.

Giles tried not to bristle while he made introductions, ending with, "Professor Higley sent us."

Quinby's eyes flew to Giles's face and widened until they threatened to pop out. "I don't need to ask why. Good God, man, don't you know you shouldn't be alive?"

Cecily gasped and Giles took a step in front of her. "What do you mean by that, sir?"

The other man shook in his shoes, although whether from fear or excitement, Giles could not tell.

"I'm dreadfully sorry," the professor replied. "It's just that I never expected someone with the green plague to walk in through my door. They usually have to be carried."

"It's green?" Giles fingered his left cheek. "Give me a mirror."

Cecily shook her head. "No, it's not necessary, because you will heal him, won't you, Professor Quinby?"

The redhead stepped forward, his features suddenly intent with interest, studying Giles's face. "I daresay, I have yet to meet someone from Seven Corners who remained sane. That is where you picked up the… disease, is it not? For I pray there is no other place of such disastrous magic."

"I fought a monster within that forest," replied Giles. "The creature managed to nick me with one of its claws."

"Claws, you say? I've seen several specimens like that, almost as if an animal had somehow merged with the man. But the plague is rarely contagious, even when injected directly into the bloodstream. Of course, my experiments were outside of the magical confluence itself, and perhaps the powers within are responsible for the actual contagion."

"You purposely injected yourself?" whispered Cecily.

Giles glanced down at her horror-stricken face. "Mirror. Surely you have some type of looking glass, man!"

The professor started, quickly turned and rummaged through a cabinet. He pulled forth a shiny disc of silver and handed it to Giles.

Although not as clear a reflection as a mirror, it still showed Giles a much sharper image than what he had seen in the stream or the glass windows on the street.

He could not speak. A dark patch covered the left side of his face, as he had noticed before. But what he had not been able to tell was the putrid green color of it. A vivid color that reminded him of gangrene… and the hideous decomposition of the creature he'd fought. He could not see past the revolting color of the blemish covering the side of his face to his own even features, for the mark demanded attention.

Giles had never thought of himself as particularly vain. Until this moment.

How had Cecily hidden her revulsion?

And how could he ever continue to spy for the Rebellion, when he carried such a distinguishing mark? Thomas had taught him how to blend with a crowd, how to use his good looks to glean information from even the most reluctant maid.

Something broke within Giles. Perhaps his dreams. Perhaps his self-esteem. But he knew he might never heal unless he rid himself of this mark. Giles mentally shook himself and picked up the thread of conversation between Cecily and the professor.

"—but it will not turn him into a monster, will it?" she asked.

"Are you sure it hasn't spread since this morning?"

"I am sure. It ceased to grow the moment we left the forest."

"And yet you said nothing," interrupted Giles.

Cecily clasped her hands together. "There was naught to do about it. Until now."

Giles turned on Quinby. "So? Is there indeed something you can do?"

The other man shrank backward. "I can only offer you some assurances, sir. Have you felt the impulse to… kill anyone?"

Giles shrugged. "I leave that up to my sword."

"I see." Although clearly, he did not. "You speak quite rationally, so I can deduce that the plague has not spread to your brain and infected it with madness. And based on my own observations of the cycle of this disease, and confirmed by Lady Cecily, I do not imagine it will progress any further."

"But you can't be sure?"

"Alas, no, I'm afraid not. The truth is, you are the first sane creature—er, man I have met who carries such a mark. Lady Cecily says you possess a healthy amount of elven blood within your veins, and I believe this, along with the removal from the vicinity of the influencing magic so soon after initial infection, has halted its normal growth. However"—he paused, glancing at Cecily—"I would suggest you pay attention to any signs of unusual rage. This may be an indication that the plague touched your brain, however lightly."

Giles felt furious at the moment, but nothing beyond his usual limits. "You do not need to fear for her," he said, sensing the direction of the other man's thoughts. "The moment I suspect madness, I will fall upon my blade."

Cecily made a strangled sound within her throat, and Giles placed a hand on her shoulder to help steady her. He must take her from this place—its smells and green body parts floating in jars—before she collapsed.

"But you cannot remove this... disfiguring mark from my face?"

"I'm afraid I cannot, sir. I have not found a cure for the plague, and cannot venture into the forest where I can study the growth of it. But I will promise to renew my experiments with more vigor on your behalf, and will contact you through Professor Higley, should I achieve any success. I'm afraid that's the best I can do."

"It is more than I would have expected, Professor Quinby. And I thank you."

Giles led Cecily from the room, out into the night, absently noting that it had started to rain. He pulled out his cloak and hid within the folds of the hood all the way to the inn they had stayed at previously, leaving it on and allowing it to pool water on the common room's floor while he made arrangements for two rooms.

Cecily hissed a protest in his ear, but he did not acknowledge it until they entered her room upstairs.

"Why do we need two?" she demanded as soon as he'd shut the door behind them.

Giles set the lantern the innkeeper had provided him and busied himself at the fire, building it up to a bright glow. He then flung back his hood, catching a glimpse of his disfigured face within the looking glass across the room. "How could you have made love to me this morning? When I look like... this?"

She looked confused, and then angry. "Do you

think me so shallow, Giles Beaumont, that a little mark could alter my love for you?"

Giles tore off his sodden cloak. She did not understand that everything had changed. But in time, she would. To avoid prolonging the inevitable, he spoke as truthfully as he could. "We shall not marry."

"I beg your pardon."

"I can no longer marry you, Cecily. I will not subject you to such danger."

"This is complete nonsense, Giles Beaumont. You heard the professor; you will not turn into a monster. And you promised me you wouldn't. So there." And she stomped her tiny foot.

The gesture would have made him smile. But an hour ago. "I promise you I will kill myself before I allow that to happen. But there is more to consider than you know, and once you've had time to think on it, you will realize this."

"What can there possibly be to consider but our love for each other? I have waited my entire life for you, and damn if I will allow anything to destroy that."

Giles closed the distance between them, caught her small hands up in his. He resisted the urge to kiss her mouth, and instead, kissed her fingers.

"And I love you, my dear. Which is why it is impossible for me to marry you. Perhaps you can overcome my… disfigurement, but others will not. If we marry, you face a life of exile and uncertainty. I cannot do that to you."

"Stop this, Giles." Her breath hitched, and her eyes welled with tears.

Damn, he could not take much more of this. "Don't

you see that my life… my happiness, ended when that creature marked me? I will no longer be able to pursue any of my dreams. Including the glorious fantasy that has been my last few days with you."

"You are just feeling sorry for yourself. It ill becomes you, Giles."

"Perhaps. But it is my sorrow to bear… alone." And he dropped her hands and walked out the door, no longer able to look at her.

No longer wanting her to look at the ugly thing he'd become.

Eleven

It rained throughout their entire journey back to London. Cecily gloried in the feel of water covering her body, felt her skin drink it up until she felt stronger than she had since leaving Dewhame. At least in body. Her mind, on the other hand, spun in frantic circles of argument, which she subjected Giles to whenever she thought of a new way to refute his stubborn insistence that he'd ruin her life by marrying her.

She tried every one of them on Giles, to little affect.

He was determined to sink into a misery of silence and self-pity, and she could find no way around that barrier. Not even by enticing him with her body, which she tried as a last resort.

Although he trembled with need, although his body quickly responded to her invitations, the stubborn man managed to rebuff all of her advances.

And now she had run out of time, for even through the downpour, she could see the glow of the fiery walls of Firehame Palace in the distance. Their return journey seemed much shorter. Panic curled in her breast and threatened to rob her of the ability to think clearly. She might never see him again.

"Giles, I can go on no farther. I must rest."

He gave her a measured look, as if he could see into her mind and knew what she planned to do. "You will manage."

"But I can't go to Sir Robert's looking like this. Can we not stop at an inn so I can tidy my appearance?"

He sighed. "Cecily. You cannot change my mind. You cannot weaken my resolve."

Had he read her mind? "Even if I were to fling myself at you bodily without a stitch of clothing on?"

He would have smiled at that, but a day ago. But this new Giles did not smile. Instead he reached up and pulled the hood of his cloak farther down his head until shadow covered his features.

"You do not love me enough," snapped Cecily, suddenly furious at his stubborn resolve. His self-pity. His inability to understand she loved him for more than his beautiful face. "If you did, you would not let something so small come between us."

He did not answer for a long time. She heard nothing but the sound of the rain pelting their cloaks, the squelch of the horses' hooves through mud, and then the clack of them across the cobblestones as they entered the city.

When he finally spoke his voice sounded deep and sorrowful. "It is because my love for you is so strong that I will not allow you to marry a monster."

"You are not..."

But he hunched his shoulders and she knew—like so many times in the past hours—he would not listen to her reply. The understanding that she had truly lost him, after barely having gained his love, struck Cecily like a blow, and she stared at the city around them with blind eyes.

They rode past hovels and then tall brownstone buildings, down a wide street lined with elegant shops, clubs, and coffeehouses. Finally turning down a narrow lane that backed grand mansions, until Giles pulled up the reins next to a stable. He swung down from Apollo and fetched a boy to care for the horses, and then escorted her through the back entrance of Sir Robert's manse.

The grandeur of the home no longer made her feel small and insignificant. Cecily had been through too much to ever feel that way again. But she couldn't bear soiling the plush carpets, so dispersed the rainwater from their clothing and hair with a quick wave of her hand. Giles did not acknowledge the gesture.

When they entered the library and Sir Robert rose to greet them, he studied Cecily with a frown and then nodded, his gaze quickly traveling to Giles. "Report," he demanded.

Giles threw back his hood and the older man gasped.

"Egads, man, what happened to you? No, no wait. I have specific instructions that I am to call them first before I hear of your journey." Sir Robert strode over to the fireplace, the skirts of his coat swishing with his steps, and pulled upon a sconce set within the stone.

Cecily removed her cloak and took a seat next to the fireplace, allowing the warmth to erase some of the chill from her bones. If not her heart.

The fire lord and his lover must have been eagerly

awaiting word of Cecily's arrival, because the hidden panel soon swung open, and they stepped into the room.

Lady Cassandra quickly made her way to Cecily's side and crouched, the lace of her skirts piling one atop the other as she looked up into Cecily's face. "Thomas?"

Cecily shook her head, refusing to allow the tears to come to her eyes.

Lady Cassandra made a choking sound and rose, crossing the room to stare out the window. Rain streaked the panes and hid the view, but Cecily knew the lady had blind eyes at the moment. Mor'ded of Firehame followed his lady, placing an arm gently around her waist.

Cecily glanced over at Giles. He stood near the doorway where they had entered the room, his gaze fixed upon the crackling flames of the fire. She missed his habit of standing at her side. Missed the warmth of his hand upon her shoulder.

"Report," Sir Robert demanded again, and Giles began to speak. He told every detail of their journey with remarkable accuracy, although he left out the most important parts. How he had discovered his love for Cecily. How they had planned to marry. How Giles had ultimately broken her heart.

By the time he had finished speaking, Lady Cassandra had returned to the fireplace, taking a seat upon the velvet settee as she had at their last meeting, the pretend Imperial Lord Mor'ded of Firehame settling close beside her.

When Cecily met her gaze, a moment of shared grief passed between them, and then Lady Cassandra sighed. "I am so sorry, Lady Cecily. Had I suspected what awaited you at the end of this mission, I would never have allowed you to go."

Cecily swept the hair back from her face. "On the contrary, Lady Cassandra. I do not think you could have stopped me." And then she glanced across the room at Giles. "Nor do I regret the journey, for I have learned many things about myself."

Lady Cassandra and Lord Mor'ded followed her gaze, both of them squinting their eyes at the gloomy shadow Giles stood within. He stepped forward into the light cast by the candles and fire, revealing the full impact of his mark, turning his face so the light caught the green color of it and made it glow hideously, overshadowing his perfect features.

Giles took a breath, strode over to the elven lord, and withdrew the ring from his pocket. "I believe this is yours."

Mor'ded of Firehame stared at the jewel as if it were a snake. "I regret the price you had to pay for it, Mister Beaumont. England will never know the debt it owes you. But I shall never forget."

Giles placed the ring in the elven lord's hand and gave him a sweeping bow. The graceful movement of his body as he performed the gesture made Cecily's heart ache.

Sir Robert cleared his throat. "This new development... dare I say, Beaumont, that it will alter the missions I had in mind for you. I'd hoped to send you to several sovereignties to rescue children before their testing. But if a child vanishes every time a man with a green mark on his face appears..."

Giles did not shake the hair back from his face, as was his habit, but instead allowed those white-blond strands to lie across his cheeks, partially obscuring that blemish of wild magic. "I understand my life is forever changed, Sir Robert."

And Cecily lowered her gaze in empathy, knowing how devastating it would be for Giles to give up his plans. If the Rebellion had aided Giles's brother, perhaps John would never have been sent to Elfhame—which truly meant murdered. Cecily understood Giles would see every child he saved as his younger brother.

"But the Rebellion will surely find other missions for him," she said.

"But of course," interjected Mor'ded. "A man of Mister Beaumont's loyalty and skills is invaluable to us."

"Indeed," agreed Lady Cassandra. "Nothing is ever irreparable, Cecily. We are only challenged to find new ways of adapting to change."

Cecily glanced up to find everyone staring at her.

Yet she cared for the attention of only one man. She gave him a hopeful look of entreaty, but Giles only scowled and stalked across the room back into the shadows.

"Still," said Sir Robert, "that mark of his makes him easily distinguishable. We shall have to plan carefully, Beaumont, so your next mission will not be your last."

Silence from the shadows Giles stood within.

Although," continued Sir Robert, ignoring the silence and centering his attention on the rest of them, "I would not blame Mister Beaumont if he wanted to retire as a reward for the information he has brought us." The man rubbed his dry hands together, a sound that made Cecily want to grit her teeth.

Lady Cassandra frowned. "I believe that is the last thing he would wish for, Robert."

"Fie, Cass, I wished only to remark on the incredible findings of Lord Althorp. Thomas outdid himself this time."

"At the cost of his life," snapped Cecily.

"And we must focus on that which we have gained," replied Sir Robert. "Who would have known the Seven Corners of Hell harbored a doorway to Elfhame?"

"The black dragon of Firehame would have," said Mor'ded. "But apparently Ador thinks this is another piece of the puzzle that we humans must solve to be worthy of our freedom."

His voice held a curious mix of fondness and resentment that baffled Cecily. "I do not understand whose side the dragons are on."

"Ah." The pretend Lord Mor'ded of Firehame leaned back against the cushions of the settee, his black velvet coat falling open at the unbuttoned waist, exposing an embroidered waistcoat and the frills of his white cambric shirt. "I don't believe they are on anyone's side, other than the scepters they are bonded to. The dragon-steeds cannot act directly against the elven lords, but aid us however much they can in their quest to return home. But perhaps I speak too broadly, for I can vouch only for Ador. I do not know how much the other dragons would stir themselves to aid us. They may want to return to Elfhame but I think they have found our world quite… comfortable."

"Your Most High," said Sir Robert, "do you think it is wise to reveal so much to this girl?"

"Are you blind where she is concerned, Sir Robert? Do you not see that the girl before us is not the same one that left us but weeks ago?"

Cecily heard the shuffle of Giles's feet, but she did not turn her head in his direction. When she had not been thinking of ways to bring Giles back to his old arrogant self, she had been thinking about what Father had told her in Seven Corners. And with Giles's newfound gift for silence, she'd had perhaps too much time to think about it. And she realized Thomas had been right.

She had wanted only to be safe. And happy. She had considered only her own feelings.

Perhaps in much the same way Giles now thought only of his.

So and so. If she had the power to help the Rebellion free England, she could not deny the gift. And right now would be the time to test her newly found resolve. "Does the new information my father provided change the mission you had in mind for me, Sir Robert?"

His jowls wiggled with the force of his head swing. "I daresay…"

Imperial Lord Mor'ded leaned forward, his black eyes glittering like the faceted jewels they so resembled. "It makes it all the more important. We had always thought the scepters were the source of the elven lords' magic, but now that we know they are but a tool, we have the ability to weaken them even more."

Lady Cassandra plucked at the lace of her sleeves.

"I'm not sure, love, if it would be wise to wrest the scepter away from an elven lord. Imagine the consequences when they tear England apart to hunt for it."

Mor'ded patted her hand. "I doubt we will ever agree on this matter, but I say again—what other choice do we have? We must make a bold move and I can see no other way to cause such a significant weakening of their hold upon England."

Cecily glanced between the two, sensing an old argument, swallowing at the import of their words. She would be diving headfirst into more dangerous waters than she had ever thought. "You want me to steal a scepter?" she whispered in disbelief.

"I'm afraid," said Sir Robert, his attention still focused on Lady Cassandra, "that recent events have only enforced Lord Mor'ded's argument. Without the scepters, the elven lords will not be able to tap into the greater magic—although their own powers would still be formidable, of course. But imagine, my lady, what would happen if we could—"

Cecily raised her voice, perhaps a bit too loudly, but she could only blame the sheer incredulity she felt as the reason. "You want me to *steal* a scepter?"

They all turned to her in surprise, but only Lord Mor'ded of Firehame reacted, pulling out the black rod from the sheath hooked to his waist. He held it up to the light, where Cecily could see the runes written across the surface. "As you can see, it is not impossible."

"Yes, yes, of course." Cecily's mind spun. "But it is said that only an elven pureblood can wield the scepter... that it would destroy any human foolish enough to touch it."

"I believe in most cases that may be true." Mor'ded's fingers tightened on the scepter until black smoke curled around the top of it. "But for a half-breed... we have discovered those with *enough* elven blood can wield it."

Cecily shivered.

"Cease, love," said Cassandra.

The elven lord blinked, and the smoke faded, and he slammed the thing back in its sheath.

"But how do you know I have enough?"

"Remember, Cecily. I was with you the night we fled Firehame Palace." Lady Cassandra gave her a gentle smile. "I saw the strength of your gifts. Only the Imperial Lord of Dewhame has the power of sea *and* sky... even his champion, General Owen Fletcher, can command only the waters of earth."

"Besides," interjected Sir Robert, "we aren't asking you to actually use the thing. Only to bring it to us."

Cecily stared at him in astonishment. Ah, well, *that* makes it so much better. She glanced over to the shadows, hoping that Giles would interfere, as he had before. That he would insist the task was too dangerous for her. His silence only made it clear he had severed any ties to her. Emotionally as well as physically.

And Cecily had vowed to make her father proud of her. Had decided to help England in whatever way she could. Just because she discovered she didn't like the manner in which she would serve, was no reason for her to go back into hiding. She quickly dispersed a brief vision of a little cottage on a hill by the sea.

She lifted her chin. "Let me make sure I understand. I assume you want me to steal my birth father's scepter, since each one is attuned to the elven lord's magic, and perhaps I will have a chance of touching Breden's scepter without it completely annihilating me. But you forget that I can't use the power of the sky."

"Won't. Not can't," grumbled Sir Robert.

Lady Cassandra shot him a quelling look. "Just the fact that you possess so much of the elven lord's magic may allow you to hold it."

Despite Lady Cassandra's initial reluctance for this mission, she appeared to now be supporting it. Cecily looked deep into those soft brown eyes and realized Cassandra looked a bit wistful. As if she wished she could be the one to go on this mission. "You would like to, wouldn't you?" murmured Cecily.

A quick nod of that elegantly coiffed head.

Of course the lady would not give her a task she wouldn't be willing to do herself. That realization brought Cecily more comfort than it should. "But Breden of Dewhame has been looking for me."

"Not you," said Sir Robert, "just a hint of the power you used when he invaded your village. Our sources tell us he has given it up for some vestige of one of his own spells. He can't be sure you even exist. And since he hasn't seen you since you were a babe, he would not recognize you either. Are you committed to this enough for me to give you the rest of the details?"

Cecily took a breath, glanced at the lord and lady, the hopeful looks on their faces. Cecily quaked at the thought she might have the power to make such a difference in the fight for England's freedom. What if she failed? But she wanted nothing more at that moment than to wipe the smug look of doubt off Sir Robert's face. "Yes. Yes, I am."

A choking sound from the shadows. Astonishment from the faces of those surrounding her. Lady Cassandra appeared proud and worried all at the same time.

Sir Robert leaned forward, the curls of his white wig falling over his shoulders. "You will go to Dewhame Palace as the servant of Lord Longhurst, a loyal spy of the Rebellion. This way you will avoid appearing in court and will have access to all the gossip of the servants… who know everything first anyway. You can be almost invisible in that role. We have also gained a map of many of the secret passages within Dewhame Palace, so you can move about even more freely."

Cecily nodded. The man made it sound so easy. "And what is the plan for stealing it?"

"Err, I daresay that will be up to you. You must move when you have enough information and feel that the time is right."

Her amazement must have shown on her face, for Lord Mor'ded quickly interceded. "Breden of Dewhame will have no reason to suspect anyone would dare touch his scepter. Indeed, the elven lords' arrogance is the Rebellion's most powerful weapon. Within each of their chambers is a crystal stone that they use to communicate with one another. There is a cavity within the top of it that holds the scepter, and if Breden is anything like my fath—me, he will often leave it within the stone. Find a way into his chambers when he is not about and you may be able to take it without him even knowing."

For some reason Cecily doubted that, but when Mor'ded of Firehame gifted her with a smile, changing his beauty to nearly ethereal, she could only nod dreamily in agreement with him.

Lady Cassandra stood, a wondrous swirl of lace and ribbons, and faced the shadows where Giles silently listened. "There is still the matter of what to do *after* she gains the scepter."

Cecily appreciated that Lady Cassandra did not say *if*.

"The elven lords don't often work together," continued the lady. "But in this matter, I believe they will. They will combine their powers to hunt down the scepter and there is no place in England where Cecily will be safe."

"Assuming," said Mor'ded, "that Breden of Dewhame will admit to having it stolen. The elven lords will sense something amiss and try to contact him, but I'm counting on his arrogance to hide the matter."

"Still," replied Cassandra, "Breden himself will scour the countryside until he finds her."

Silence fell over the room for a moment. Cecily could hear the rain spattering against the windows, the crackle of the fire. Sir Robert's heavy breathing.

But not a sound from the shadows.

"Breden of Dewhame cannot find her if she's no longer here."

Lady Cassandra collapsed back down onto the settee. "What do you mean, Robert?"

"I had an epiphany, my dear. What about Wales?"

Mor'ded's black eyes sparkled and he sat forward. "Indeed. I should have thought of that myself. It's the perfect place to hide the scepter and Lady Cecily. If the scepters are not the source of magic, as we had always assumed, that means they can be taken past the barrier. And it has yet managed to proceed beyond the mountains of Wales."

"*If* they can be brought past the barrier secretly," said Lady Cassandra, her forehead still puckered with doubt.

Cecily latched on to the implications in their words. "I will have to leave England?"

"We have always thought of Wales as a part of England," said Mor'ded, "despite the stubbornness of the Welsh and their freedom beyond the barrier." At her raised brow, he shrugged and continued, "Not indefinitely. I hope one day we shall have need of you—and the scepter—once again."

Cecily tried very hard not to bristle at his words. Of course they had little concern for how their plans would affect her life. They had more important issues to consider. And she had already decided to sacrifice herself for England. Thomas had given his life. She should be able to face banishment. But it would mean she would never see Giles again, and therefore could never win him back. And despite everything, she had still harbored hope of that.

But as they continued to discuss plans for delivering her safely out of England, Giles's silence on the matter proved he had abandoned her. Cecily did not believe for a second that he had stopped loving her. She would never believe it. But he had obviously given up all hope of a future with her. So what did it matter if she left England? Without his love, it held nothing for her anymore.

"How would I get past the barrier?" Cecily finally asked.

"You must really learn to pay attention, my dear," said Sir Robert. "That's what we've been discussing for the past few minutes. We have established an underground system, of sorts, for saving the children whom we rescue from the trials. The elven lords have allowed only a few openings through the barrier which permits trade with the outside world, but the Rebellion has managed to gain the allegiance of a few ships."

"There are several things you should know," interrupted Lady Cassandra. "You will no longer have your magic once you're beyond the magical barrier surrounding England. You will still possess your physical elven traits: beauty, grace, and speed. And we can't be sure what will happen to the scepter; for this is the first time we have ever attempted such a thing. The trade goods of the elven do not possess any magic once beyond the barrier, but they still retain the attributes that the use of magic created them with: cloth exceptionally fine, or jewelry exquisitely crafted, or wine rich beyond imagining. We cannot even guess what properties the scepter might retain past the influence of elven magic."

"It will be fascinating," mused Sir Robert, "to find out, though. After all, the human world is not entirely devoid of magic."

Cecily recalled the ring of stones through which Thomas had first contacted her. They were an ancient source of humankind's own power, and had nothing to do with elven magic, so she agreed with Sir Robert. But what might the scepter still be able to do? And she would have no magic to counter it with.

No magic.

For years she'd tried to hide her powers, to pretend they did not exist. And now she would be facing a future where she would truly be able to live like an ordinary human. Sir Robert and Mor'ded and Lady Cassandra watched Cecily as if they expected some outcry from her. A refusal based on the final injustice of having her magic taken from her.

They did not know her at all.

Cecily smiled. "Wales, you say? I've heard it's a beautiful land."

A collective sigh of relief. Then Lady Cassandra rose and held out her hand to Cecily. "We have much to do to prepare you for this mission. Robert, will you be so kind as to ring for your man to escort us to Lady Cecily's room?"

Within moments the outer door opened, and a liveried footman bowed to them. Cecily followed the lady to the door, passing so close to the shadows Giles hid within that she fancied she could feel the heat of his body.

Cecily slowed her steps. Surely he would step forward and stop her. Would insist he accompany her. Would demand that she allow him his protection.

But he did not stir. Indeed, he appeared to be holding his breath.

And at that moment, she knew. Knew she could never break past the distance that the mark had brought between them. He would no longer be her protector.

Whatever small hope she'd been holding onto died. She would never win him back. He would not give her the opportunity.

Cecily hurried after Lady Cassandra, a sudden anger building within her. Damn Giles Beaumont for making her love him. Damn him for giving up on their love so easily.

She would focus on her mission and try to forget him. He had broken her heart once before, and she had managed to survive. It would be harder this time, but she would do it.

The footman closed the door to the library behind them, and Cecily thought she heard a sudden clamor of raised voices behind it. But she refused to allow herself to care about any discussion that Giles may be having with Sir Robert and the elven lord.

She had her own perilous task to focus on.

❧

Cecily traveled in a coach to the city of Bath, and after the first day she missed Belle with a severity that made her eyes water. Instead of the mare's smooth, even gait, she was subjected to a constant bouncing and tossing about within the closed box of the carriage.

And when they finally stopped for the evening, she faced a dirty inn with watery stew and the constant chatter of other travelers.

Cecily longed for the times when she'd traveled with Giles. The evenings spent beneath a star-speckled sky, the scent of a fresh stream to bathe in. The quiet talks and the comforting sound of the horses grazing. The heat of Giles's strong body as he crawled into the blankets beside her—

No. She would not torture herself with such musings. Especially not now, on the last day of her journey.

Cecily stuck her nose out the window, grateful for the fresh air. And the scent of water. It had grown quite strong the moment they entered Dewhame and her entire being had quivered in delight at the abundance of it. But as they neared Bath, she realized the small fountains and streams of the country were nothing when compared to the wealth that awaited her up ahead in her father's—Breden of Dewhame's capital city.

"Lord Pennington, the wretch is sitting upon my skirts again."

Cecily turned to glance at the lady sitting next to her and sighed. The large woman wore a wealth of skirts suited to her frame, which meant Cecily had but a sliver of the seat to sit on already. But still, she somehow managed to scrunch even closer to the window when the lady's husband glared at her over his periodical.

Lady Cassandra had dressed Cecily for her role as servant only too well. Despite the fact that she did not work for these people, they treated her on the trip as their *own* personal servant. When they weren't ignoring her, of course. Cecily had come to understand Giles's meaning of the social gulf that existed between the classes. That line appeared to be significant beyond the borders of her little village, and she had yet to see anyone cross it. It made her understand some of her mother's behavior at times, and suddenly made her miss her even more.

Cecily sighed and tucked that hurt alongside the others and buried it deep within her heart.

"Mortimer, dear," said Lady Pennington to her

little brat, a boy about one-and-ten years of age. "Fetch my box from beneath the seat, will you?"

Mortimer screwed up his face at Cecily. "You heard her. Fetch it."

Cecily glared at him but he responded only by sticking out his tongue. She sighed and levered herself up to reach beneath the seat, withdrawing a pasteboard box filled with pastries and sweetmeats. She'd found it more peaceful to comply with their requests, rather than dispute her employment to them.

Lady Pennington took the box with a sniff, offering everyone a treat but Cecily. Her stomach grumbled, and she hoped Lord and Lady Longhurst would be more kind to her. After all, Lord Longhurst knew her part as servant was nothing but a ruse. And yet...

Cecily sighed and poked her nose out the window again. It appeared the gentry preferred to bathe in perfume rather than wash the smells from their body, and the strong scent made her head swim. She took a deep breath and realized she would have to get accustomed to these new people and her role among them. She could not afford a slip, and she should be grateful to the Penningtons for allowing her to adjust to it before she reached Dewhame Palace.

If only she could manage to stop missing Giles. Not his protection—despite what he would have her believe. She could take care of herself quite handily, thank you. But his company. The sheer presence of the man. Cecily had felt dead inside the moment she'd left him behind in London.

She sighed again. Best to get accustomed to that feeling as well.

Cecily's nose suddenly twitched. Water. A wealth of water. She did not know so much could exist on top of dry land. But as the city came into view, she realized that Bath wasn't truly dry.

Fountains decorated the front stoop of every single dwelling. Spilled to overflowing inside every square. Burst into a cloudy mist atop the very roofs, to trickle slowly down the walls of the buildings. And the buildings themselves...

Cecily stuck her entire head out the window, ignoring Lady Pennington's outcry at the sheer impropriety of it.

The buildings had all been painted in soft tones of blue and green, and not a one of them had been constructed with a straight line. Corners had been softened with a slight curve, even the windows sporting rounded panes instead of square. Water flowed down the gutters of the street, carrying refuse out of the city. They passed a large building with a statue of Zeus in the front and a sign that read, *The Royal Bath*. And then another, with a smaller statue of Poseidon, and a sign that read, *The Queen's Bath*.

But the city itself could not compare to Dewhame Palace.

Their carriage passed through the walls surrounding it, walls that had been constructed to look like the swell of multiple ocean waves. Cecily blinked. The waves actually appeared to flow with movement.

And then a flood of water doused her head and she ducked back inside, sputtering, Lady Pennington shouting at the droplets of water that Cecily pelted her with.

But when the carriage finally rolled to a halt and they emerged from it to stand in an inch of swirling water, the lady quit complaining, for her rich clothing was soon dampened along with the rest of theirs.

Cecily craned her neck up at the palace walls. Water streamed down the sides of the blue-tinted stones, picked up the meager sunlight and transformed the curtain of water into glimmering translucence. Within the courtyard itself, stone carvings spouted waterfalls that sprayed white mist into the air, speckling Cecily's cheeks and arms.

She wanted to hold out her hands and twirl in the abundance that surrounded her.

"Girl," snapped Lady Pennington, who had managed to find an umbrella and stood within the slight shelter of it. "Don't stand there gawking. Help with the baggage."

Cecily replied without thinking. "But I'm supposed to find my employers—"

The lady slapped Cecily's face as offhandedly as she'd slapped her son's more than once on their journey. "I'll hear no guff from you, girl, while I stand here and ruin my best set of shoes."

Cecily blamed the wealth of water surrounding her. She had never felt her magic so strongly on land before. It had built within her like the swelling of the tide, energizing and powerful and yes, even deadly. She feared the strength it had given her, and cursed herself when her fingers lifted of their own accord and called just a bit of it to her.

So easily.

It swirled around Lady Pennington's shoes and

lifted her slightly off the flagstone, the lady tumbling over in a heap of sodden skirts and hoops. She shrieked and Cecily winced, ashamed of herself.

Then fear skittered through her. She had vowed not to use her magic until she needed it to accomplish her task. Lady Cassandra had told her that she risked exposure if she used too much of her powers too soon. That her fath—the elven lord, Breden of Dewhame, might question such a strong gift.

Cecily reached up to take her small bag from the coachman, and guiltily accepted a small trunk of Lady Pennington's to carry as well.

When she turned, the lord had helped his wife to her feet, Mortimer still stifling his laughter behind his hand. Lady Pennington had gone from soggy to utterly drenched, her hoops askew and the feathers decorating her cap and bodice hanging sadly down and plastered to her skin.

Cecily looked around beneath lowered lids. But blue-uniformed soldiers did not pour forth from the palace door to arrest her and she trembled with relief. She had used only a bit of magic. Surely Breden of Dewhame's nobles commanded that every day and it would be lost amongst the other powers.

Still, she vowed to learn from this lesson. She must not let her control slip. She must accustom herself to being treated as less than an equal.

When Lord Pennington ushered his wife into the palace, Cecily meekly followed, accepting another trunk from the coachman to lug along.

The inside walls of the palace had been painted with murals of flowing waves, and although they moved as magically as the ones outside, they lacked real water. Even the floors were finally dry, although they sported rugs of soft hues that appeared to ripple beneath their feet.

Lady Pennington staggered. "La! I always forget how dreadful this place is," she muttered.

"Hush," commanded her husband, his small eyes searching the rounded corners of the hall. "We love it here, don't we, Mortimer?"

"Yes, Father," the boy dutifully answered. Then turned and stuck out his tongue out at Cecily just for the pleasure of it.

The palace steward met them at the end of the long hall, directing two footmen to relieve Cecily of the lady's trunks. She flexed her fingers, which had gone rigid from the weight of the handles.

When she did not follow the lord and lady when they started down the main hall, the steward turned to her with a raised brow.

"I... um." She should not allow the man to rattle her. "I am here in service to the Lord and Lady Longhurst. Can you direct me to their chambers?"

The steward consulted a damp set of papers within his hand. "Ah, yes. I have instructions for your arrival. It is quite kind of you to assist the Lord and Lady Pennington on their journey here."

This time Cecily raised a brow. As if she'd had any choice.

And the man gave her a knowing smile, and she suddenly didn't feel quite so lost. Apparently a camaraderie of sorts existed among servants. Not enough to cross the boundaries of their proper place, but enough to make her realize that Sir Robert had been right to send her here in the role of a servant. She could learn much in very little time.

Cecily smiled back at him, forgetting to keep her lids half-lowered over her large eyes.

The man started, and the two other lackeys who stood at his side awaiting his instructions both gasped in unison.

Oh, dear. What had she done?

"You there," said a voice from across the hall.

Cecily cringed and dropped her gaze to the steward's pointed shoes, refusing to look at the speaker. For the voice had the richness of an elven lord, velvety and musical like Lord Mor'ded of Firehame's.

She heard the sound of heavy boots approaching and told herself to run, but her feet stayed firmly planted to the floor. She had been in the palace only for a few minutes, and already she had betrayed herself to Imperial Lord Breden.

A fine spy she turned out to be.

Twelve

"LOOK AT ME, GIRL," DEMANDED THE STRANGER.

Cecily swallowed and slowly raised her head, then felt her legs turn to jelly in relief. The man who stood before her could not be a pureblooded elf. Although he sported faceted blue eyes and pointed ears, his white-blond hair lacked the silver sparkle that Breden of Dewhame would surely have in his hair.

The man reached out a graceful hand and tilted her face to the light. "You carry a good deal of elven blood within your veins for a servant. Who are you?"

Cecily opened her mouth, but could not find words. This man wore the clothing of a soldier, although his coat had been crafted of blue velvet and not wool, and the gold buttons at hem and sleeve had been inset with small diamonds. The hat he carried under his arm had some type of insignia upon it, but designation of rank had not been something Lady Cassandra had deemed Cecily had time to study.

The steward consulted his papers again and cleared his throat. "Her name is Lucy Stratton, my lord general. She is servant to Lord and Lady Longhurst."

Cecily started. Ah, *that* military designation required no study. General Owen Fletcher, champion to the elven lord, with enough magical power to call upon a wave from the Bristol Channel to win a battle. Rumors also had it that the man used his magic in perverted ways that even the elven lord had not devised. And that he enjoyed the doing of it.

With the way the general now stared at her, she could well believe the rumors.

General Fletcher stroked her cheek. "Egads, those eyes." Then he ran a callused thumb over her lower lip. "So, you received all the beauty of the elven but none of the magic, eh? Pity. You're far too lovely to be a servant of naught but a man's desire."

Cecily stepped away from the general's touch. She could feel his lust as a palpable thing and it made her stomach roil. She could not imagine anyone's hands upon her but Giles's. The thought that her role as servant would not protect her from the general's advances...

"I am not a slave, sir."

The steward raised his rather bushy brows. "Indeed, she is not."

The general turned on the smaller man. "But I have taken a fancy to her, Hastings." He called the water from a nearby fountain; Cecily could feel the tingle of his magic. Fletcher crafted the liquid into thin translucent strands, wrapped them warningly around Hastings's throat, somehow managing to strengthen the water without creating swirls of force.

Cecily frowned. She could feel the slight brush of a chill. Ah, Fletcher had half-frozen the water to make it more solid. Something she had never thought to try.

The steward answered in a strangled breath. "Then you will have to take up the matter with Lord Longhurst. Assuming Lucy will accept you as her employer."

Which she had no intention of doing. Fletcher glanced at her and she glared. Perhaps the general was used to women falling all over him—he certainly was handsome enough. And perhaps some women were foolish enough to think bedding the man would give them some type of power beyond their current positions. Or perhaps they just feared him.

But Cecily did not. He might have thought of ways to use his powers beyond her scope of knowledge, but her magic surpassed his by leaps and bounds.

She wondered if he had sensed that in her. If that's what had caught his attention enough to interest him in a mere servant.

Hastings's face had turned an alarming shade of red. But the smaller man stood firm, staring down the general in what appeared to be a long-standing battle of wills. Cecily imagined the steward answered only to the elven lord, and none other. And that the man must be exceptionally good at his post to have value enough to thwart Breden of Dewhame's champion.

The noose of water about the steward's throat suddenly froze to solid crystals, then shattered upon the floor like so many diamonds.

"Devil take you, Hastings," growled the general. "You're always trying to spoil my fun."

The steward rubbed his red throat. "But who else will curb your appetites, General?"

And Fletcher threw back his head and laughed, his white hair reaching past his waist. "That's famous!

Who indeed?" He lowered his head, brought his face close to Cecily's, and softened his voice to an intimate whisper. "Life is sweetened by a challenge, is it not? Fie, the bravery in those blue eyes. Whence does it come, I wonder? And can it be broken?"

Cecily stuck her nose in the air and the general laughed again.

He slapped Hastings on the back. "My thanks, as usual, lord steward. What an excellent game you have begun." And then strode away.

Cecily released a breath of relief.

Hastings nodded at her in sympathy. "General Fletcher loves a game as much as the elven lord himself. It is bad luck that you have caught his eye, my dear. Stay out of his way, and mayhap he will forget you."

"Thank you."

He shrugged. "Follow me."

Cecily complied, wondering if the steward could be a member of the Rebellion. She felt sure Sir Robert would not reveal all of his players to her. But she did not ask, for Hastings likely wouldn't tell her anyway. She decided that he might just be a good man among many evil ones, and accepted his attempts to rescue her with silent gratitude.

Water flowed down the walls of the main hall just as it did on the outside of the palace, but fell into a marble trough running below and flowed to a large pond at the end of the walkway. Swans and ducks floated on the glassy surface, shaded by the weeping fronds of some trees that Cecily could not identify.

They passed a staircase that resembled the interior rings of a needle shell, curving round to the upper levels of the palace, with the speckled brown spots on the ivory surface. But her guide continued on to the servants' stairs, stone treads worn to shiny smoothness, dark and dank all the way to the basement floor.

"You will come here to take your meals if you are not bidden to take them with your employers," said Hastings. "You will also fetch dinner from here if they wish to dine in their rooms."

Cecily stared around the enormous stone chamber. The cook and several other servants stared back. Only the slaves kept their eyes averted, intent on their tasks, their ragged clothing and bare feet making their status obvious. Several servants sat at a massive table of driftwood, frozen in the act of talking and chewing at the same time, studying Cecily with avid curiosity.

No fountains flowed here to relieve the heat of the massive fireplace and many ovens, but the humidity coiled about the very floors, swirled along the walls. Cecily sucked in a deep breath, but the upper lip of the steward began to sweat, and with a grimace, he quickly led her back up the stairs.

Cecily went over the map she'd memorized in her head, coordinating it with the actual layout of the palace, trying to match the secret passages with the public rooms.

It would take her days of exploring to gain her bearings.

Hastings took her up another flight of servants' stairs. "I caution you to avoid the ground floor where the court assembles, and the second floor, where the elven lord and the permanent members of the court reside."

"General Fletcher's rooms are there as well?"

"Just so." The steward stopped and opened the door at the top of the stairs. "Stay here on the first floor if at all possible. These are the guest chambers, where Lord and Lady Longhurst reside for the nonce."

Cecily hurried her steps to keep up with the spry man, passing door after door—and fountain after fountain—until they came upon a set that looked identical to the others. "Thirteenth door on the right," she panted.

Hastings gave her a smile of approval, then knocked.

A lad opened the door, his freckled face scrunched up with authority, his small uniform smartly tailored to resemble an adult's. "Whom may I say is calling?"

Only the slight crack in his voice belied his formality.

"Hastings. And Miss Lucy Stratton, reporting for service."

The lad nodded, shut the door, and then promptly reappeared. "His lordship is waiting for ye."

Cecily smiled at the village accent in his voice, and the lad returned it hesitantly as she stepped past him into the apartments.

Lord Longhurst possessed a nose reminiscent of his name, and a set of intelligent hazel eyes that flashed with alarm and anger when Hastings recounted the scene in the hall with General Fletcher.

"Lucy is my cousin's daughter," replied Longhurst. "I promised to keep her safe while she was in my employ."

"I understand, my lord," replied Hastings. "It's why I thought to bring her to you myself, and warn you of the general's interest."

Cecily glanced between the two men. Her suspicions that both of them played a part in the Rebellion solidified.

Lady Longhurst, on the other hand, appeared oblivious to all but her own self-interests. "Can you set hair, Lucy?"

The lady had a sweet voice, reminding Cecily of her own mother's gentle tone. "Not very well, I'm afraid."

"Never mind, then. I just hoped to have a bit of variety. Ellen knows only one or two styles."

Cecily glanced at Ellen, a sweet-faced, rather vapid-looking girl. Better and better. She did not need clever people watching her. "I can, however, sew a fine stitch. And I have designed my moth—a fine lady's clothing."

Lady Longhurst clapped her hands. "Oh, how divine!" She leaned over and gave her husband a kiss on the cheek. "You dear man, to send me a girl who can redesign my wardrobe! It's sadly in need of it— the damp and mold, don't you know? And we just can't afford the palace mantua-maker. My goodness, you'd think she spun gold instead of cloth to make her dresses."

Lord Longhurst patted his wife's hand, and exchanged a look with Hastings and Cecily. And then cleared his throat. "Well, I'm glad you are happy, dearest. And you see, Hastings, that Lucy will be kept busy enough to avoid the general's interest, so we need worry about it no longer."

Hastings bowed his way out of the room.

"Ellen," said Lady Longhurst, "why don't you show Lucy her room? She must settle in, and gain her rest tonight. For tomorrow we shall go shopping for new fabric!"

Lord Longhurst emitted a soft groan at his wife's

words as Cecily followed the other girl from the withdrawing room, which boasted a small pond surrounded by rose trees, through a plain door into her new quarters.

Ellen pointed at the bed that sat across from her own. "I suppose yer not used to such finery, coming from the country and all."

Cecily eyed the small room with a raised brow. Perhaps the linens on her bed at home lacked the fineness of these, and her wardrobe lacked the intricate carving on the wood, but she would give much to be back in her humble cottage.

Ellen blinked. "Ach, don't mind me. Trying to put on airs, I am. And ye so homesick and all. I'm Ellen." And she thrust out her hand. Cecily clasped it gently. "The lad is my younger brother, Jimson. He has a bit of magic, ye know." She lowered her voice conspiratorially. "He can hide in a mist. I'm warning ye, so yer careful when ye change yer clothing. He's a bit of a scamp."

Cecily smiled. "Thank you, Ellen."

"Oh, my. Ye talk fine fer a country girl. Do ye have any magic?"

"Do you?"

"Ach, no. Not enough elven blood in my family line. Jimson and I have different fathers. But ye—ye have the elven eyes. And such perfect skin and teeth."

Cecily shrugged, set down her bag, and tested the bed. Hard as a rock. "I inherited only the looks. I have no magic to speak of." And apparently that mattered a great deal within the palace, for the girl gave her a pitying look.

"We shall get along splendidly, then. For we must make ourselves useful with nothing but our own two hands. Our kind must stick together, don't ye know."

❧

Cecily spent the next several days shopping for clothing material during the day. And sneaking about the secret passages at night. And missing Giles so strongly that she muffled her cries in her pillow.

Ellen had decided to trust her, and mistook her misery for homesickness, and tried to be even kinder. She slept like a stone, so Cecily need not worry about the girl becoming suspicious of her activities. Jimson, however, liked to spy on her.

Late one evening, Cecily had decided to explore a new tunnel in the passages, discovering a peephole into General Fletcher's private rooms, when she felt the shiver of mist upon her back. She spun and squinted against the darkness, her small candle illuminating the dank corridor only so far.

A spot of humidity looked a bit... thicker than normal.

"Jimson," she whispered. "I know you're there."

The spot wavered, but did not dissipate.

Fie. She would have to make the lad show himself. She wiggled her fingers unobtrusively, and the mist evaporated to reveal the freckle-faced boy.

"Why are you spying on me?" she snapped.

"Why are ye sneaking about the palace? How did ye know about this passage? I thought I was the only one who knew about it—and how did ye uncover me anyway? Only one of the nobles can do that, and not too many of 'em, either."

Cecily tried to look bewildered. "What do you mean, uncover you? You just appeared out of the mist."

The lad lowered his head and scowled. "Ye know, Lucy. We can stand about all night pretendin' to be stupid. Or ye can just decide to trust me."

"Why should I?"

He twisted his foot in a crack on the stone floor. "Why do ye think Lord Longhurst employs me? Because of me sister? Lud, 'tis the other way around. I keep me ears open and tell him what I hear, and he keeps me sister happy."

"I see."

"No, ye don't. If the elven lord knew of me spying—if Owen Fletcher realized what I know of him—ha, if Lord Longhurst hisself knew what I suspect him to be a part of..."

Cecily frowned. Did Lord Longhurst realize how much the child had discovered? Should she tell him? But obviously the lord trusted the lad, or he wouldn't allow Jimson to become so privy to his life.

A sound behind her made her turn, place her eye to the peephole in the wall of the passage, to behold a room decorated with thousands of seashells. They created mosaics on the walls, the floors, around several fountains. General Fletcher entered his bedchamber, swaying with drunkenness, the slave girl within his arms appearing just as foxed. He staggered to his bed, pulling the girl down with him, smothering her with kisses while she giggled.

A movement at the far end of the room drew Cecily's gaze, and she watched the water from a large decorative pond surrounded by statues of sharks displaying their teeth. The water suddenly rose into the air and swirled to form a sphere of translucent liquid. The slave girl's gaze snapped back to the general, who had lifted her in his arms and approached his magical creation.

"I will bring you pleasure like none you have ever experienced before," he boasted.

The girl smiled at him coyly, pressed her hand against the bulge of his breeches. "I have no doubts, my dear general. I can feel—"

Her screech cut off the rest of her sentence as the general tossed her into the ball of water. It swallowed her with a thick, sucking sound.

Cecily shivered at the similarity between the way Fletcher used his magic on the girl, and the way she had used it to love Giles. And the complete utter perversion of it. Whereas she had used the currents and flow to bring Giles pleasure, Fletcher used it for his own twisted satisfaction.

The water was so clear she could see every detail of the girl's struggle. Invisible currents tore at her clothing, ripping it from her body until she floated within the ball surrounded by naught but her thick white hair. She struggled to gain the surface, to break through the barrier of the water, but it thwarted her every effort with mad whorls of movement. Her eyes grew wild with the need to breathe, the effort to prevent herself from taking the breath that would drown her.

General Fletcher smiled as he watched her struggles, slowly removing his own clothing until he stood as naked as the girl. He had a wickedly beautiful body.

He strode toward the suspended sphere of water. "They never last long enough," he murmured.

His hands moved with elegant precision, and the girl rocked in time with his forceful motions, her legs spreading, her mouth open in a scream of pain...

Fletcher dove in with her.

Small hands covered Cecily's eyes. A low voice whispered in her ear. "'Tis not something a lady should see. Come away, Lucy."

And Cecily allowed the boy to lead her down the passageway, until he turned and looked up at her. "Hush, now," he murmured.

She stifled the odd sound that she had not realized she'd been making. Wiped away the tears she had not known she'd been crying.

And decided to trust the boy.

They had reached a branching of the passageway, and a small beam of weak sunlight and a slow trickle of water through a crack in the outer wall slanted across their path. Morning already. And she had to fit Lady Longhurst today, and start on the sacque dress designed for such a delicate silk she feared it would take hours to stitch the pleats evenly.

Cecily collapsed on the floor, suppressing a sneeze as her petticoat and skirts puffed up dust despite the humidity in the air. Jimson crouched closely beside her.

"I have a map of the palace's secret passages," she said.

The boy nodded, eyes wide.

"But I can't seem to find one leading to my fath— the elven lord's private chamber."

"Ye don't want to find it, lady."

"Do you know if there is one?"

He shook his head. "I'm not barmy enough to go near his rooms. No one does, 'cept mebbe that dragon of his."

"Kalah? Is the chamber that large, then? How would the beast manage it?"

Jimson scratched his head. "Big doors?"

Despite herself, Cecily smiled. She had yet to see the blue dragon. Should she approach the beast for help? But Mor'ded of Firehame had said he couldn't be sure Kalah would aid her, and the thought of approaching the monster and actually speaking to it…

Ah, how she wished she'd never left her little village. To tread such dangerous paths… to see such evil that existed in the world. To have her heart broken…

But then, she would never have known Giles's love.

And the image of a small cottage near the sea suddenly seemed like an isolated place. A lonely life.

Cecily straightened her spine. "Then I will have to find the passage myself, Jimson. Or devise another way into the Imperial Lord's chamber. It's very important that I find one."

"I know I shall regret asking ye this, but, lady, why the hell do ye want to sneak into his rooms?"

Cecily swallowed a reprimand at the lad's choice of words. The wisdom in his blue-green eyes bespoke a knowledge of the world beyond his years. She couldn't imagine what he'd seen and heard, living in this foul place. She thought of the poor slave girl and shuddered.

"I'm going to steal…" Cecily paused. She might be making a mistake. But it would take her years to explore all of the passages within the palace walls and she could not bear the thought of living here that long.

She needed his help. She would trust her instincts. "The scepter."

He snorted a laugh. Not quite the reaction she had expected. "Ah, fiddle, yer as mad as Fletcher."

"The general? What do you mean?"

"He talks about it to his water demons all the time."

"Water demons?"

"The nymphs who visit him in his pool. The Imperial Lord created them with his magic, and now they pop up everywhere throughout the palace. 'Tis all the water, ye see."

Cecily nodded, pretending that she did, although she had never spoken to one before, despite her affinity to water. Perhaps they preferred the company of men. "What does Fletcher tell them?"

"Oh, fer a time he blathered that he could wrest the scepter from the Imperial Lord and rule the world." Jimson gave her a wry smile. "Then I'm guessin' he tried to touch the thing, cause he quit talkin' about it fer a time and twitched whenever he saw the scepter."

Cecily frowned. That did not bode well for her. But she knew she held more power than General Fletcher, she *sensed* it somehow. And at least the scepter had not annihilated the general for touching it. Perhaps she might be able to try to accomplish her task without losing her life.

But either way, she had resigned herself to the consequences.

"But lately…" started Jimson.

Cecily leaned forward. Obviously the lad wasn't used to divulging his information to anyone other than

Lord Longhurst. Despite her own leap of faith in the boy, he still didn't quite seem to trust her. "Yes?"

Jimson scrunched up his face. "Does Lord Longhurst know what yer planning?"

Cecily had yet to find a time when she could speak with the lord alone, and besides, she had doubted the wisdom of a frank discussion with him. "I'm not sure. Sometimes it's best not to know everything. That way, if something should go wrong —"

"Ah, don't fret yerself over his lordship. Should he or his lady be in danger, I'll hide us all with me mist and spirit them outta the palace without anyone being the wiser."

"Except the elven lord."

He shrugged. "I 'spect he'll be too busy to pay us much mind."

"You shall help me, then?"

"I didn't say…" Jimson rocked back on his heels. "I'll have to ask his lordship if it will be all right for me to help ye. If he thinks it's best, aye, I'll find ye a way into the monster's den."

The boy rose to his feet and Cecily quickly did the same, placing a gentle hand on his shoulder when he started to walk away. "Jimson, please. What had Fletcher started talking about lately?"

The boy trembled beneath her touch. Surely he wasn't frightened of her? But no, he turned and gave her a crooked grin, allowing her hand to stay on his shoulder.

"The general started down a different path of mad talk a few months ago. He said as how the Imperial Lord sensed someone with strong magic… someone

who shoulda' been sent to Elfhame years ago. And
then that someone disappeared."

Cecily held her breath. The blood in her veins
actually seemed to stop flowing. "Did they know who
that person might be?"

"Nay. The Imperial Lord decided it was only a
bit of wild magic. But the general, he went on about
finding the half-breed as if he really existed, and using
him to defeat the elven lord. Stupid, eh? For why
would anyone who holds the scepter need Fletcher
anyway? He may have the magic of a champion but he
sure don't have the good sense to go with it."

Cecily dropped her hand from his shoulder. Jimson
sighed and started down the passageway and she
followed a bit blindly, wondering if she could turn this
new information to her advantage… or if she should
flee the palace immediately.

When they entered the dressing room and closed
the wooden panel behind them, Cecily could hear
Lady Longhurst's sweet voice calling out for Ellen.
Cecily glanced down at Jimson, but he'd already
disappeared in a cloud of mist, and so she went to
answer the lady's summons.

"Oh, Lucy," said Lady Longhurst. "There you are!
I don't know where everyone has gone off to this
morning." Then she lowered her voice. "Although
I have my suspicions."

Cecily's stomach flipped. She did not want this
kind, vacuous soul involved with the business of the
Rebellion. "I'm sure I don't know what you mean,"
she murmured.

"That Ellen. She's in love, don't you know?"

Cecily shook her head.

Lady Longhurst placed a hand over her heart. "I told her that handsome stableboy would just use her then cast her aside, but it appears she did not listen to me."

"It is… difficult to deny one's heart, my lady. Despite the risk of being hurt."

"La, I suppose you are right. There was once this soldier—well now, never mind that. You shall just have to go and fetch her, Lucy, despite the impropriety of it. I shan't be able to leave the room until she fixes my hair, and I have a most urgent meeting with Lady Sherwood."

Cecily frowned. She had taken the steward's advice and avoided the public rooms and castle grounds. She had ventured into the realm of the nobility only once, when the lady had forgotten her fan and Cecily knew that Lady Longhurst—being Lady Longhurst—would be distraught without it, and Ellen was nowhere to be found.

The girl had probably snuck off to be with her lover. Cecily tried not to be envious.

Cecily had managed to catch the lady just before she entered the blue withdrawing room off the main hall, and handed her the fan without Lady Longhurst even quite realizing it. She'd quickly retraced her steps but had felt the gaze of someone upon her, and turned to face the lascivious blue eyes of General Owen Fletcher.

Cecily had picked up her skirts and fled, resolving never to go beyond the bounds of the servants' areas again.

"Perhaps you should send Jimson to fetch her," suggested Cecily.

"Good heavens, and let the young man know of his sister's wantonness?" Lady Longhurst shook her rather tousled-looking head. "No, my dear. This calls for the delicate touch of another woman. Go to the eastern stables, the smaller one, mind. I daresay you will find Ellen in the hayloft, sleeping off a night of passion." She tittered. "It's not the first time she's been late. Let's hope it shall not be the last."

Lady Longhurst was a romantic. Cecily should have known.

The mirror near the door of their chambers reflected a few cobwebs in her hair, so Cecily quickly tidied herself before she left the rooms, then snatched up a hooded cloak despite the warm day. She used the servants' entrance to reach the palace grounds, and stood for a moment within the herb garden, trying to visualize the mental map she had memorized.

Straight ahead would be the main stables. To the right, the smaller one.

Cecily pulled the hood of the cloak farther down her head to hide within the shadows, painfully reminding her of Giles. Her breath hitched but she started to walk confidently forward, choosing a path that took her a bit closer to the practice grounds, where the soldiers displayed their sword work, and gave a wider berth to the pavilions that had been spread on the lawn for an outdoor gathering of the nobility.

A strong breeze blew across the land, and Cecily clutched her hood to prevent it from flying off her head, peeking around the edges of it to stare at the wonder about her. Clusters of crystal boulders littered the grounds, waterfalls tumbling and frothing over them to pool in flower-sheltered glades. Mud hampered the fighters in the practice arena; a layer of water glistened just beneath the grass where the nobles gathered, a makeshift platform protecting silk skirts and damask shoes from damage.

Even the gravel path that Cecily walked squished wetly, and time and again she trod over small bridges where streams bubbled along underneath. Off in the distance, geysers of white water split the air and enormous fountains sprayed sparkling mist with the glitter of tiny jewels.

Power flowed through Cecily. She breathed in the humid air and reveled in the feel of it. If her father hadn't hated her, she might have felt as if she'd come home.

She caught a whiff of the rank odor of the stables, then the breeze shifted and brought the perfume of the nobles along with it. And then the scent of honest sweat as the wind shifted yet again.

If the breeze hadn't also brought the song of his devil-blade to her ears, she might never have known he was here.

She could not mistake the sound of that sword.

Cecily turned. And froze. Neither could she mistake the grace of the man as he fought. He had stripped to his breeches and boots, and his tanned chest gleamed in the morning light, shining with a layer of moisture from his exertions. He slashed and parried while his blade hummed, against several other men as the rest watched with mingled looks of disbelief and fascination.

Only Cecily suspected that he fought more to keep his blade from delivering a killing blow than he did against the pathetic maneuvers of the other fighters.

"Giles," she breathed.

The wind tore off her hood and set her cape to billowing about her, but she barely noticed. The sound of clashing steel rang in her ears. The distant laughter of the nobles sprang up now and again.

Why was he here? Surely it could not be a coincidence. Or had he joined Breden of Dewhame's army with the rest of the villagers, then? Hoping to make a new life amongst old friends?

No. He had come to protect her. She knew it as surely as she knew the feel of water within her hands. He would deny their love, deny the right to marry her, but he could not stop himself from keeping his vow to protect her.

Perhaps it had become a habit he could not break.

Cecily smiled. For the first time since leaving London she felt fully alive, the sight of Giles's flowing white hair, the muscles in his forearms bunching as he swung his sword... she could suddenly see with a clarity of vision that she thought she had lost. Every fiber of her being tingled with newfound awareness—

"Does the sight make you long for a man, Lucy?"

Her pulse jumped. She turned to face the general, his faceted blue eyes—so like her own except for their coldness—fixed upon her face.

"It's why the ladies like to break their fast so close to the practice yard." He stepped closer and leaned down until she could feel the heat of his breath on her cheeks. "They enjoy the sight of half-naked, powerful men. What a delight to discover the prudish little Lucy does as well."

"I do not—"

"Oh, come now. Your secret is safe with me. Indeed, I long to share many secrets with you."

Cecily could hear the calls and whistles of his friends within the shelter of the pavilion. Had she become a challenge? Were his advances so rarely refused that she'd become an embarrassment to him?

He grabbed her roughly up in his arms and kissed her.

Cecily tried not to retch. She fought against his hold, but despite her elven strength, he appeared to match hers and she could not free herself.

Giles. If he had recognized her... If he saw this bastard assaulting her...

Cecily gathered the power to her fingertips and called to the water swirling along the path. She snaked tendrils up the general's legs, beneath his coat and around his neck. She gave the liquid more strength by chilling it to near-ice.

She learned quickly.

Owen Fletcher suddenly realized he couldn't breathe.

He released her and Cecily staggered a bit, horribly aware that she could no longer hear the sound of clashing blades. She turned and saw Giles come to an abrupt halt at the edge of the muddy yard.

She met his gaze for a timeless moment, those delightfully human green eyes speaking to her more clearly than words ever could.

Giles wanted to run Fletcher through with his sword. He controlled himself only because the general had shown enough good sense to let her go. But he barely kept the urge under control, for his devil-sword hummed for Fletcher's blood.

Cecily knew the power of Giles's blade, suspected the strength of the general's power, and did not want to find out if Giles would survive the battle.

She spun, and fled. Catcalls rang out from the pavilion, but she did not spare a glance for the nobles. Instead she turned once to look for Giles. He had returned to the yard, to the center of another mock-battle. Cecily nearly shook with relief as she slid behind the garden wall.

Thank heavens she'd had the presence of mind to keep her magical defense against Fletcher unobtrusive. She doubted that anyone else besides Giles knew how she'd escaped from the general's embrace. Except the general, himself. She shivered at the look of shock, and then cold calculation, that had been on his face. She must avoid him now more than ever.

She did not remember Ellen until she returned to Longhurst's rooms and found the girl already there, collapsed upon the velvet settee.

"Lady Longhurst?" panted Cecily.

The girl waved a weary hand. "Gone to meet with the court gossip."

"His lordship?"

"Off to his own business, whatever that may be."

"Capital." Cecily collapsed on the sofa beside her. "You have a piece of hay in your hair."

Ellen giggled. "That's not the only place, I'm sure. Why are ye breathing so hard?"

"I was running."

"From what?"

"The champion. General Fletcher."

Ellen sat up, her face becoming serious. "Ach, that's a man to avoid, Lucy."

"I know. But Ellen…"

The girl's reddish brows rose.

"There's someone else."

Ellen snorted.

"What I mean to say is… where would a girl meet a man? Privately. With a guarantee that no one else might… overhear them?"

"That's the way of it, then?" Ellen sighed. "Ye have to be careful, Lucy. A man can be slippery when ye are tryin' to catch him."

She was one to talk. Cecily waited.

"Are ye sure?"

Cecily nodded. Enthusiastically.

"Well, unless he works in the stables, I don't recommend it for a tryst. That straw pokes ye in places ye don't want poked."

Cecily frowned. "Where, then?"

"I know of several places where the nobles go. There's always some love affair or another going on. 'Tis like a game to them, methinks."

"I don't want to risk being seen by anyone at court."

"Not if Fletcher is after ye." Ellen firmed her mouth. "All right then, best to get ye another man and the general might leave ye alone. I'm only telling this to protect ye, mind." With her conscience apparently clear, Ellen brightened again. "We servants have our own trysting places. There's a cave behind the big waterfall— the one near the north gardens. Do ye know where it is?"

Cecily nodded. She would find it.

"Climb up to the second boulder, and then under the falls. It's dry near the back of the cave and yer fellow servants have probably left a blanket or two in there. Oh, and there's a black rock near the entrance. Don't forget to put it on the top of the boulder if ye don't want to be disturbed."

Cecily admired the efficiency of the method. "Thank you, Ellen. Truly." And she clasped the other girl's hands within hers and gave them a squeeze, then went to Lady Longhurst's writing desk and withdrew a piece of paper, dipping the quill in the inkpot only a few times to scratch out her message.

She sealed the note with a drop of wax and turned and held it out. "Here, Jimson."

Ellen started and glanced around the room suspiciously.

The lad materialized from his mist. "How do ye *do* that? Most of the nobles can't even tell when I'm around."

Cecily ignored his question. "Can you deliver this message for me?"

Jimson scowled, glaring at the missive. "To the man with the ugly mark on his face?"

Heavens. He'd been following her for longer than she'd thought. And saw much more than the average person. Lord Longhurst had done well in hiring the lad. "Indeed."

He gazed up at her with questions in his eyes, and she glanced warningly at Ellen, then shook her head.

"All right, then," he finally said. "But I'm tellin' his lordship about it."

"You certainly will not," snapped Ellen. "This is a private matter, Jimson."

He looked mutinous until Cecily nodded. "Do what you think his lordship would wish."

He smiled in relief and dashed off, and Cecily went to start her sewing, and then prepare for her midnight rendezvous.

Thirteen

CECILY CREPT OUT OF THE PALACE USING A PASSAGE SHE hadn't explored before. It branched several times. One way presumably led to the great hall, and the other to a conservatory, but since neither room was remotely close to the elven lord's, she hadn't bothered with the tunnel.

Until now.

She doused her lantern before she slipped through the hidden door in the palace wall. The moonlight provided adequate light for her elven sight, and so she left her lantern outside to mark the location of the entrance and pushed the door closed, the opening disappearing beneath the continuous fall of water that slithered down the outer walls. With her hood now plastered wetly atop her head, she made her way across the palace grounds and through the gardens, the rest of her cloak soon becoming equally damp.

Cecily kept to the shadows cast by the full moon, using Jimson's trick of hiding within a mist to avoid the notice of the palace guards. She'd never thought to use her magic in that way, and after the dreadful

knowledge she'd learned of how her gift could be
perverted, she felt grateful to Jimson for showing her
such a benign new skill.

As she neared the waterfall, she wondered how
Giles might manage to sneak away to meet her. Jimson
had said he'd delivered her missive, but the man had
taken it with nary a word in reply.

Her heart sank as she gazed around the enormous
fall of water. Surely Giles would come. He would
have questions for her about her mission, for he would
need to know what she'd discovered in order to plan
on how to protect her.

Although Cecily had no intention of talking to him
right away. She had already tried words and they had
not worked.

She made her way to the side of the falls, near a tree
that surely could not be native to England, for it sported
massive fan-like branches that fell to the ground like the
fall of the back of Lady Longhurst's new sacque dress.
Cecily stepped across the leaves, staring up at the large
boulder Ellen had spoken of. With her elven sight, she
could see quite clearly by the moonlight, but she doubted
Giles would have such an advantage with his human eyes.

A hand closed over her arm and pulled her backward beneath the fans of the tree, Cecily stifling her
yelp of surprise.

Familiar warm arms enfolded her. "Do you think
this was wise?"

Cecily placed her hand over his mouth. "It's not
safe here. Come."

He hesitated but a moment before he released her
and then followed, up to the second boulder, raising

one dark brow as she placed the black rock behind them. But he took her hand when she held it out to him and followed her as she plunged through the thin cascade of water at the sides of the main waterfall.

The stone shook beneath her shoes, the massive torrent tumbling down in a roar that pounded at her ears and sprayed a chill mist within the cavern behind it. Cecily could see that the cave extended far back into the mountain of crystal, probably deadening the sound of the falls and ending in a cozy chamber as Ellen had promised. But she did not head in that direction.

Cecily stopped near a smooth boulder and turned to face Giles, the stone at her back and the water pounding at her front, just behind him. The moonlight penetrated the chamber enough to outline his full lips, to allow her to see that he shaped words. But she could hear nothing against the crashing might of the falls.

Cecily smiled. Used her elven speed to undress faster than she had ever managed to accomplish that feat in the past, her sodden cloak falling heavily at her feet, her girdle unbuckling with nary a touch, her loose gown flying from her shoulders, the purposely loose ties of her stays leaping out of their holes, her petticoat dropping down her hips with ease, her chemise following. Until she stood in nothing but her stockings and shoes.

She stepped lightly out of the shoes.

His eyes stared at her blindly, and he probably assumed that she could see little as well. That his blemish was hidden to her sight.

Cecily reached up and stroked the shadow on his

face, which glowed an eerie green even in the darkness. Giles jerked backward toward the fall of water, his mouth moving in some muted protest.

Cecily continued to smile as she called her magic, creating tendrils from the water and using the strength already existing in the falls to gently nudge him back toward her. She had him at a disadvantage and intended to make full use of it. How long had it been since he'd last touched her? Surely he must long for her as much as she did for him.

She reached up again and stroked his cheek, his jaw. He responded by fisting his hands at his sides, by locking his muscles. Cecily brushed the hair away from his face, gloried in the feel of the thick silkiness of it. She rose to her tiptoes and put her mouth against his, trembling as that touch raced an excitement through her veins.

He did not try to push her away. But he did not relax his defenses, his muscles now clenched to shivering tautness.

"So strong," she breathed, her words as easily muffled by the roar as his own had been. Her fingers slid down his neck to his hard shoulder. She reached out her other hand and slid off his soldier's coat, the cheap wool scratchy against her palms. "You have taught me well, Giles. I am no longer the hesitant innocent who traveled with you to Firehame. I have learned your desires and I know that you love me."

She shed his plain waistcoat just as easily, despite his refusal to help her, his arms still fisted at his sides. The buttons of his shirt proved difficult, slippery with the spray that surrounded them, but unlike her own clothing, she took her time, and managed to strip his chest bare. "Will tonight make you see how foolish you're being?"

His bare flesh prickled as she slid her hands over the curve of his muscles, down the ridges of his belly. Sleek skin. Hard muscle beneath. Cecily's breath quickened.

She unbuttoned the flap of his breeches. Felt his sword tremble in its sheath. But the stubborn man refused to respond.

"So that's to be the way of it, then?" Cecily rather enjoyed speaking without him able to hear. She reached up and untied the handkerchief knotted around his throat. "I must play dirty?"

He swallowed. She grinned.

"The skin at the side of your neck is sensitive, is it not?" Cecily leaned forward and kissed him just beneath his ear, traced a path with her tongue slightly toward the back of his neck until she reached the spot that she knew would drive him mad. She opened her mouth and sucked, the salty-sweet taste of his skin so very delectable.

Giles broke.

A shudder ran through him and his arms closed around her. His hands swept down her back and quickly to her bottom when he felt nothing but bare skin. She could not hear his groan but she felt it, from his chest to hers as he flattened her body against his.

His large hand grasped the back of her head and pulled her mouth away from his skin with a tug, his lips finding hers unerringly, his mouth hot and demanding, his tongue a tender weapon against her own. Cecily wrapped her arms around his neck for support. Her feet had left the stone floor. "Giles."

He must have felt the vibration of her voice for she felt his answering growl. Cecily's legs rose seemingly of their own accord, wrapped around his waist, until she could feel the soft heat of his skin, the hard muscles of his belly, against the most private part of her.

A distant part of Cecily's awareness knew he held on to her with one hand, while the other yanked down his breeches. But she could focus on nothing but the feel of his mouth so demanding against hers, the glorious rise of joy that blossomed with the knowledge that, try as he might, he could not resist loving her.

Words had not worked with Giles. But surely he understood what she told him with her body?

She loosened her legs slightly and slid down atop the hard length of him.

She focused on that heat, rubbed back and forward across the base of it until his tongue began to mimic the rhythm.

He blindly took a step forward, then another, until the curve of the boulder against her back brought him up short. His arm cushioned her from the chill of it. Giles trapped her between his hard heat and the unyielding stone, braced his arm against that solid surface and cradled her bottom with the other.

He tore his mouth from hers and buried his face in her breasts, feasting on them like a man who had been denied sustenance for far too long.

Cecily moaned. Arched against him. Buried her fingers in his hair, every touch conveying her love for him. Her want of him.

Shivering heat raced from her breasts to her core, making her squirm atop his large hand.

Giles did not hesitate. In one smooth movement he pulled her up and lowered her onto his shaft, entering her with a swiftness that stole her breath. That filled her until she thought she might die from the sheer pleasure of it. He slid out, then penetrated her again and again, until she felt a scream well up in the back of her throat.

"More!"

Surely he could not hear her cry, but he understood the sense of it, his thrusts more powerful, slamming into her until she clutched his shoulders with a fierceness that almost frightened her.

Almost.

Cecily lifted her face up to the water that flowed over them, the sweet liquid flowing into her open mouth and crashing over Giles's bent head. Lud, when had she called up her magic? For a portion of the waterfall now curved in an unnatural angle into the chamber, to tumble down their joined bodies, to cover them with a slick layer that allowed their skin to slide easily across the other's.

Giles raised his head, staring blindly at her, a sudden smile lifting his lips. He said something, and then his mouth descended on hers, sucking at the water on her lips, pulling away to let the water flow across them before repeating the pleasure.

And pushed himself even more deeply inside of her. Until the rhythm he set seemed to echo the pounding rush of the falls. Until the water that had come to Cecily's call spun about their entwined bodies with a motion that tugged her hair from her coiffure and swirled it around her head, raced across her skin with a cool heat that made her body tingle.

Giles flung back his head, shouting something as his entire body shook with pleasure. And then Cecily succumbed as well, her eyes closing as wave after wave of sheer delight controlled her body.

They clung to each other for a long moment, joined as one being. Until Cecily's magic faded away, the water flowing down their bodies to pool on the stone floor, to slowly join the larger rush of the falls.

Giles gently lowered her to the ground, his arm still about her, kissing her softly on the top of her head. Cecily hesitated to end this moment, but he did not have her affinity for the water, and already she could feel the chill of his skin.

She loosed him and gathered up their clothing while he stood blindly, trusting her to take the lead. Cecily caught up his hand, shed the water from their bodies and their clothing, and led him into the cave at the back of the falls. The passage curved, blanketing the sound of the waterfall, and they entered a small chamber that held not only the blankets Ellen had predicted but a small chest besides.

Cecily could barely make out the simple shapes in the gloom of this chamber. When her hand explored the top of the chest and found a flint box and several candles, she quickly used them.

Giles blinked in the sudden brilliance, those heavenly eyes gazing about the mossy stone walls of the chamber before returning to her face, a smile spreading across his full lips. The old smile that Cecily had missed for so long.

And then his eyes hardened and he lowered his

head, his thick hair falling to hide the mark on his face, and busied himself with buttoning up his breeches, checking his belt, which had gone wildly askew during their lovemaking.

Cecily's heart fell. She pulled on her chemise, suddenly feeling a bit vulnerable. She held up her stays. "Will you help me with this?"

Giles glanced up and that grin returned. Although not as easily as it once had. He closed the distance between them and wrapped the garment around her, lacing it up with deft fingers. "This damn thing is the bane of any man's existence."

"I have missed you."

He ignored her words. "Tell me, *Lucy*. How goes your mission?"

She smiled at the use of the name. "You know the details, then?"

Giles frowned. "As much as you were told before you left. I followed you at a safe distance, but I don't know everything that has happened to you since you entered the palace." He tied the ends of her laces. "Although I have learned enough to know how you fare."

Cecily backed away from him, stepped into her petticoats, and wrapped her gown about her, taking a seat upon one of the blankets. Being clothed allowed her to feel a bit more confident. A bit more protected against his pretended indifference.

Giles remained standing in the shadows.

She carefully arranged her skirts about her. "So you did not come to Dewhame to join Breden's army and find glory on the battlefield?"

He shifted his feet, boots swooshing on the stone

floor. "Of course not, as much as my devil-blade might like the idea."

"Then… I cannot believe Sir Robert allowed you to follow me. Or does he know where you are?"

"He knows. Although he's not happy about it."

"So you have the Rebellion's blessing to help me? How did you manage it?"

He picked up his shirt and shrugged into it. "Did you not hear Mor'ded of Firehame say they owed me a great service? I called in the favor… although truth be told, I would have followed you anyway. I think Lady Cassandra knew that. She looked oddly… happy about it."

Cecily tried not to allow the leap of hope in her breast to flare too brightly. "You have reconsidered, then?"

He stiffened, and then let out a breath, stepping into the light. "I told you I would always protect you. But this… this shouldn't have happened. I'm sorry."

Cecily raised her chin. Dunderheaded man! When would he realize the physical act of their love reflected only what lay in their hearts? His vow of protection was but a ruse to satisfy his head as he followed his heart.

She allowed her irritation to flow out of her as quickly as it had come. He had followed her to Dewhame, and that was the important part. It would just take him some time to realize he would follow her to the ends of the earth. She just chafed at the delay. It had felt so wonderful being in his arms again, having him inside of her, that she despised the thought of having to wait another week or month for it to happen again.

A month? Oh, surely not!

Cecily huffed out a breath. "So, Mor'ded allowed you to complicate my mission." She felt a wicked sort of satisfaction at the way her words made his eyes narrow. "I would have enjoyed being there to see his face. Or did Sir Robert actually agree to it?"

Giles picked up his waistcoat and crouched next to her. "Not until I showed him this." And he pulled a small tube of crystal from the pocket, a series of small circles engraved upon the side of it.

Some of the circles had been filled with a black stone, while the others were hollow. It took a moment for Cecily to understand the symbols. "It shows you where to place your fingers."

He nodded. "Indeed. It is the very flute that Thomas used to gain entrance to the crystal mountain. I... I took it from him when I recovered the ring."

Cecily ignored the pain her father's name evoked in her and focused on Giles's handsome face. He had used the object to bribe Sir Robert into allowing him on this mission. "But what possible use could he have for it?"

"It does not matter. It's an artifact of power, and Sir Robert hoards them as a miser hoards his gold. I believe he thinks that one day the Rebellion will amass enough artifacts to conquer the elven lords."

Cecily snorted and Giles nodded in agreement before tucking the crystal flute back into his pocket. "I promised to give it to Sir Robert after I helped you. So now you know how I managed to 'complicate' things. I take it you have formed a plan, then? Other than gaining the attention of General Fletcher?"

She felt her cheeks flush. "That was not my

intention. I met him on my first day in the palace and for some reason he has singled me out."

"For some reason… dammit, Cecily. He's dangerous. And perverted. I will kill him if I see him touching you again, mission or no."

She shuddered. "I know what he is. And he disgusts me. I have done my best to avoid his further notice, and will continue to do so. I assure you I did nothing to encourage him."

He humphed. "One look into your beautiful eyes is enough encouragement for any man… no, do not look at me like that. I believe the last thing you wanted to happen was to gain his notice."

"It frightens me to think of what would happen if you challenged him, Giles. Promise me you will not risk it."

He did not answer. "Tell me your plan."

"I don't exactly have one yet. But I have acquainted myself with many of the secret passages riddled throughout the palace, and I hope one of them will lead me to Breden's private chamber."

His dark brows rose. "That could take years."

"Precisely. So I have enlisted the aid of Lord Longhurst's spy—"

"The lad who gave me your message?"

"Just so. I am hoping he will have more success, since he's apparently familiar with the tunnels."

"It's risky."

Cecily shrugged. "There is little about this mission that is not risky."

"And then?"

"Why, I wait for Breden to leave the palace and sneak into his rooms."

"And then?"

Faith, he was starting to annoy her. "I have no idea. I touch the scepter and dissolve into a thousand bits?"

His face turned white. "Listen to me, Cecily. You have not been trained for something like this. If the lad does find a way into the Imperial Lord's chamber, I want you to send me a message before you attempt to touch the scepter. Perhaps there is another way…"

She shook her head. "There is not, or the Rebellion would have tried it already."

"That is not the point." He leaned forward on his knees, brushed the hair back from her face. "Have you thought of how you might reach the ship once you have the scepter?"

So, Sir Robert had told him of the ship awaiting her in Bristol that would take her to Wales… if she managed to steal the scepter. But she hadn't really thought she'd accomplish the task, so hadn't given much thought to how she would reach the seaport.

And the touch of his fingers made her thoughts spin, so she said the first thing that popped into her mind. "Ellen has a boyfriend in the stables. Perhaps he will lend me a horse."

He made some kind of strangled sound and sat back. "I get the impression that you do not believe you will accomplish this task. That you are intent on becoming a martyr for the cause. Like Thomas, perhaps?"

Cecily dropped her gaze.

"I will not allow it," he continued, his voice so fierce that his sword hummed in response. "You must have a plan of escape before you attempt to take the scepter. You must not go into Breden of Dewhame's chamber alone. I must be at your side—Cecily, are you listening to me?"

She looked up at him then, at his lovely human green eyes, with those dark brows and lashes such a contrast to his elven-white hair. At his generous mouth and elegant nose and high cheekbones. The candlelight made his skin glow a honeyed gold, the mark on his face only emphasizing the perfection of the rest of him.

"And then what?" she whispered, her words almost lost in the darker recesses of the cavern. "Will you then put me on the ship and bid me farewell?"

He blinked, his mouth parting slightly. "I will keep you safe, no matter what it takes."

"I see."

"Cecily." He took her shoulders in his hands, his palms hot against her skin. "Just promise me that you will tell me the moment you find a way into the elven lord's chamber."

She set her mouth in a stubborn line. He wasn't the only one who could pretend indifference.

"Dammit, woman," he growled, and then hauled her up against him, his mouth covering hers with a fierceness that made her heart pound. Cecily melted like snow in the sun, leaning into his kiss and wrapping her arms about his neck. She buried her fingers in the wealth of his silken hair, opened her mouth to grant him inside. He did not disappoint, his tongue sweeping against hers, tangling in a silent battle. His hands pressed her body closer, arching her back and neck.

Could heaven be any more sublime than this man's kiss?

Giles broke away, his breath releasing in harsh pants. "Promise me."

She would give him the moon, if she had the power to do so. "Yes, Giles. I promise."

Again his mouth swept over hers, nibbling and sucking at her lips. He trailed a path of wet heat across her cheek to her ear, his hot breath sending shivers through her. "Thank you."

And then he set her from him and stood, pulling on his waistcoat, his coat, avoiding her gaze. "Have you spoken to the dragon?"

Cecily tried to collect herself. Blasted man. "What? I… no."

"Kalah might consent to help us, if we approach him right. Otherwise, he may be inclined to do the elven lord's bidding."

She dragged the hair back from her face and tried to calmly finger-comb some of the tangles from it. As if he hadn't twisted her emotions one way and then the other. "I'm not going near the dragon."

"He scares you, eh?" A hint of his old familiar grin touched his mouth. "That's a healthy attitude, my dear. But do not worry; I will seek him out while you're exploring those tunnels. We would have no problem escaping on the back of a dragon."

Cecily grimaced. Perhaps not, but she doubted she'd ever find the courage to climb up on a dragon's back in the first place. Not that she'd ever admit it. "He is our enemy, just as much as the elven lord is."

"The dragons are a mystery to us, limited by some enchantment set upon them by the scepters, but they have helped more than hindered the Rebellion in the past. I will try to seek Kalah out in his tower tomorrow night."

Cecily smoothed her hair, divided it for plaiting, but it proved difficult without a mirror.

"Allow me." Giles dropped down behind her and took the black strands from her, his gentle touch making her scalp tingle. She closed her eyes while he took his time fixing her hair, remembering all the times he'd helped her with the chore when they had journeyed together.

"Then will you meet me here again tomorrow night," she asked, "after you speak with the dragon?"

His fingers stilled a moment. "That might be too dangerous."

Cecily wiggled until he began to plait again. "I think not. I have already told Ellen I have taken a lover, and if we are seen, I doubt anyone will suspect anything other than a tryst."

"Ellen is another servant to Longhurst? What about the boy? What is he called?"

"Jimson. He is Ellen's brother."

"Aye, Jimson. Since you have already taken the lad into your confidence, we can send messages to each other through him. Send him to me tomorrow evening, and I will return him to you with a message about Kalah, and a plan for our escape if the dragon cannot be persuaded to help us."

"But why? It would be so much easier—"

He gave a final tug to her braid and stood. "When I spoke of danger, I did not mean…" And then he put some distance between them again, back into the shadows. He lowered his head, hiding beneath the thick fall of his hair. "It is dangerous for me to be near you, Cecily. It is obvious that I cannot keep from touching you whenever we are together, and I do not want to give you false hope. It is my weakness, not yours, and I'm sorry for it. But I see no other way."

"You are being ridiculous." She tried to keep the irritation from her voice, but he tried her patience, he truly did.

"You will not think so when your neighbors shun you because of the man you married. When women whisper behind your back and children taunt you because you married a monster. And then you will start to blame me. And pity will turn to hatred. I do not want that."

Cecily rose, smoothing her skirts. "Not all people are so concerned with appearances, Giles. Just you."

He glanced up, his mouth twisted. "You think so? I had to fight over a dozen men just to get accepted into an army that drafts young boys. I sleep in the weapons shed, because not a single man will allow me in their barracks. Even my old friends from the village will not speak to me now."

"You have seen them? They are here?"

"Aye, including your Will, if that's what you're wondering."

Cecily hadn't thought of Will in so long. It felt as if she hadn't seen him in years. She had changed so much from the girl who had once thought to marry him. Who had thought she'd be content with a life devoid of passion and excitement. "It is good to know they are safe, and still alive, that is all."

Giles gave her a skeptical look and shrugged. "If you would like to meet with Will, I can arrange it."

"I can't imagine that we would have anything to say to one another."

Some of the tension drained from his shoulders. Cecily stepped toward him, laid a hand on his chest. "I am sorry for the way you are being treated. The world is full of the blind, Giles. Yet I truly believe somewhere there is a place for us to be happy together."

"Then you have more faith than I do, Cecily." He stepped away from her hand, picked up the candle, and without another word started back toward the sound of the falls.

Cecily pulled her cloak back over her shoulders and followed, cursing herself for the futile conversation. For a moment, she had felt as if they had resumed some of their previous closeness, but she had forgotten that words did not work with Giles. She could not argue him into a future with her. Seduce him, perhaps. But that would be difficult if they could not meet.

Her mind schemed with ways in which she might allow that to happen while they made their way out of the falls. The water doused the candle as they ducked outside, and Giles disappeared beneath the fanlike tree with nary a good-bye, leaving Cecily to make her way alone to the palace.

But she did not doubt for a moment that Giles followed her somewhere in the shadows, making sure she made it back inside safely.

❧

Cecily put the last stitch in Lady Longhurst's elaborate new gown. She had spent the entire day sewing the dress, for the lady insisted she be allowed to wear it tonight. And truly, it had turned out quite lovely, with layers of lace cascading down the full skirt, down the pleated back. Pearls decorated the hem of each layer, and completely covered the stomacher that would be worn with it.

Cecily vowed to wear a dress just like this one when she married Giles. She had only to figure out how she might make that marriage come about.

"But I have not given up," she whispered.

Ellen poked her head around the doorway of the small parlor. "Merciful heavens, Lucy, is it done yet? I've finished with her ladyship's hair and she's demanding the gown."

Cecily gathered up the yards of fabric and handed it to Ellen. "Do you need my help in dressing her?"

"Oh, Lud, ye are such an angel! Yes, she's in such a tizzy over the ball that she can barely hold still. I never seen her ladyship so excited."

Cecily followed the girl into Lady Longhurst's dressing room, surprised to see his lordship within. Jimson stood at his side, helping the older gentleman tie his cravat.

"Ah, there you are, Lucy," said Lord Longhurst. "It seems we are in a bit of a muddle tonight, eh? My valet took a fever and it seems that her ladyship cannot decide on a choice of fans. Quite the quandary, is it not?"

Cecily returned his smile and immediately began the task of getting Lady Longhurst into the voluminous gown.

"What on earth is a quandary?" asked her ladyship, wiggling into the lace.

"A dilemma, my dear."

"Then why on earth didn't you just say so? Gracious, as if I don't have enough to task my mind without trying to decipher what you're saying. Lucy, dear, the feathers or the lacquer?" And she held up two fans, one with white swan feathers, and the other with an ocean scene painted upon it.

Cecily made a show of serious consideration. "The feathers will make the lace appear harsh in comparison, and the painting will complement the pearls in the gown. Isn't the lace rather like the spray of the ocean?"

Lady Longhurst clapped her hands. "At last! Someone who makes complete sense. You are a gift from heaven, my dear Lucy." She slipped the looped string of the fan over her lace gloves. "I shall have to wave it about frequently, so those less inspired can perceive the meaning of the costume. If only Imperial Lord Breden had not left the palace so unexpectedly this evening! Surely he would appreciate the fineness of my new gown."

Cecily shot a look to Lord Longhurst, who gave a slight nod of his bewigged head without taking his attention off his wife. "We are all saddened by the elven lord's sudden departure, dearest. But I pray you will not allow it to dampen the evening."

Her ladyship looked horrified. "I should certainly think not. Why, the expression on Lady Sherwood's face alone will make the evening a success." She lowered her voice conspiratorially. "You see, Lucy, I have kept you a bit of a secret. My dearest friend has no idea I have such a skilled mantua-maker in my service. When she sees this new gown—la! The envy!"

Cecily knotted the last tie of the stomacher. "I am pleased you are happy with the dress, my lady. But I hope your friend does not solicit my services. I rather prefer the solitude of your chambers."

Lady Longhurst patted her hand and rose. "You are such a timid thing, aren't you, dear? But do not worry, I shall allow no one to steal you away from me. Are you ready, Lord Longhurst?"

"In just a moment, my dear. I cannot seem to find my pearl stickpin. Wouldn't that complement your gown quite well?"

She gave a laugh, a spin of her lace skirts, and left the room, Ellen in tow.

Cecily started to follow when Jimson's hand on her sleeve made her turn.

His lordship studied her through his quizzing glass. "I understand that you may have some… errands to run. And because of your shy nature…" He coughed. "You have solicited my lackey to help you in that regard?"

Cecily dipped a quick curtsy. "If your lordship has no objection, I would be most obliged."

"Indeed, I have suggested to Jimson that he aid you just as faithfully as he has always served me. Is that satisfactory?"

"It is more than I could have asked for, my lord. I thank you."

"Tut, tut, none of that. The pleasure you have brought to my wife this evening deserves reward. Now then, Jimson, have you found that blasted pin?"

Jimson produced the jewelry from his pocket with

a grin, and his lordship leaned down to allow the boy
to affix it to the center of his lace cravat.

"Now, then," continued his lordship after he'd
risen, "I should not keep my lady waiting any longer.
Have a productive evening, my dears."

And he left the room in a swish of magenta silk and
a clatter of diamond-buckled shoes.

Jimson collapsed on the padded bench near the
standing mirror. "Lor'. I don't suppose yer going to
tell me who ye really are."

Cecily tried to look innocent and then settled for
a smile. "No one of great importance, I assure you."

Ellen popped her head around the door. "They've
finally gone. And I'm famished. Do ye want to go
with me to the kitchens, Lucy? Cook made extras of
all the fancy dishes the gentry will be served at the
ball tonight. We servants will have a bit of a party of
our own."

Cecily's stomach growled and she considered the
offer for a moment. Surely General Fletcher would be
at the ball with the rest of the beau monde. But the
thought that he might be lurking about the servants'
quarters in wait for her made her shake her head. She
had seen the look in the man's eyes when she'd used
her magic. "I think I'll remain in our rooms. There's a
bit of bread and cheese still on the sideboard."

Ellen grimaced. "Ye will have to get over this
shyness of yers, sometime. But I won't push ye. How
about if I bring ye up some supper?"

Jimson sprang to his feet. "I'll fetch her some, Ellen.
Ye run along now, and don't worry none about Lucy.
I'll see to her."

"Will ye now?" Ellen studied her brother with a grin. "Lucy, I think the little scamp is sweet on ye."

"Mind yer tongue," snapped Jimson, lunging for her.

Ellen giggled and taunted him all the way to the main withdrawing room.

Cecily sensed a family spat, which they appeared to enjoy and constantly indulged in whenever the lord and lady left the apartments. She followed them with a sigh, hoping to cut it short, for she wanted to take every opportunity this evening to search the passages. With Imperial Lord Breden absent, she felt it safe to explore the tunnels closer to his rooms, for surely they would find one that would lead to an apartment close to his own, if not his very chambers—

A cry. Followed by a splash.

Cecily entered the withdrawing room just as Ellen's head disappeared beneath the surface of the small pond. Jimson stood next to a rose tree, the freckles on his face standing out against his pale face.

"What happened?" she asked, running to his side.

He looked up at her, shock and terror in his blue eyes. "Water demons."

"Here?"

"Aye. But they've never come to our pond before. Why would they? And what do they want with—"

"Ellen," breathed Cecily. "Fletcher's demons." And she dove into the pond, feeling about the sides and bottom for an opening, for the water stayed fresh, so there must be some type of filtration system, and didn't Jimson say the demons appeared all throughout the palace—

Ah. The bottom sloped in the middle of the pond

and her palms found an opening just large enough for her skirts to smash through. Cecily pushed her way inside, fighting the fear of such a confined space, but it opened up a bit, and a stronger current caught her up and plunged her through the watery tunnels until she lost all sense of direction. She prayed that the water system flowed in the same direction the demon nymphs had taken Ellen, for she could do little but allow the current to sweep her along in hopes of finding the girl.

A light above.

Cecily fought her way toward it, breaking the surface of another small pond, within another noble-man's room. Empty. She dove again. And repeated the process another three times before she found Ellen.

The girl looked half-drowned, her cap plastered to her dark hair, the two water demons clutching her arms with a grip that would leave bruises.

"Let her go."

The nymphs smiled at Cecily's words, an unpleasant sight, for their pointed teeth held a shade of green, like moss over stone, and their scaled faces did not crinkle like human skin. It cracked, fissures running across the glossy surface.

"Now, now," said a male voice, with the silken tone of an elven lord, "you can't deprive me of your friend's company so soon, my dear Lucy. She will be so very useful."

The bulging eyes of the demons sparkled mali-ciously at the man's words, and Cecily slowly turned her head toward the handsome face of General Owen Fletcher.

She recognized this room. Glanced once across the

length of it, adjusting for the view she had seen from the peephole. She stood in the same pond where he had tortured the slave girl.

Cecily gathered her magic, creating waves across the surface as it responded to her fear and anger. The nymphs grinned even wider, and one of them held up a knife carved from a seashell—strong and as wickedly sharp as steel, and laid it across Ellen's throat.

"You see, my dear," said Fletcher, striding over to the pond, his green silk coat whispering with his movements, his bright yellow shoes clicking on the mosaic floor. "I rather suspect that your magic might be greater than mine, and I'm not in a mood to discover the truth of it. Don't quite have the time, you see."

Ellen whimpered as the sharp blade pierced her skin, a trickle of scarlet blood looking dreadfully brilliant against her pale neck.

Cecily gritted her teeth as she tamped her magic down. "What do you want?"

"Ah, capital. You have abandoned any pretense as to what you are. Now as to who… I rather think your name isn't Lucy, is it?"

He held out his hand to her as if he were a beau asking her to dance, and Cecily rose from the water on her own, refusing to touch his fingers like one would refuse the touch of a snake. She needed to find out what he wanted from her, for she suspected she now had but a small chance of completing her task for the Rebellion. She hoped only to save Ellen's life. Fletcher would never have bothered with the plain girl if not for Cecily.

Fletcher had changed all of her plans so quickly that her mind still reeled from the suddenness of his attack.

"What do you want with me?"

Fletcher stretched his full lips in a wide grin, his brilliant blue eyes sparkling like sapphires. "You are making quite a puddle, moppet. Allow me." And with a wave of his fingers, water sprayed from her clothing back into the pond. "You know, I've been looking for you for months now. We've had reports of a half-breed with enough power to call a storm, but the Imperial Lord dismissed it as nothing more than ignorant soldiers in awe of magic." He took a step toward her, caught her hands up within his, and smiled as she struggled against his hold. "The arrogance of the elven lords will be their downfall. But not mine, for I have enough humanity within me to be wary."

Cecily gave up trying to escape from his hold and settled for glaring up at him. "I don't know what you're talking about."

"Oh, my dear. Many a noble can call upon the water, make it snake around my neck the way that you did. But not a one of them has the power to alter it to near solid form, except for me. And Breden of Dewhame. And perhaps his daughter."

Cecily stilled. The bastard had taught her that trick himself. And she had fallen for it, using the new skill so quickly. So easily.

He lowered his head, that perfect mouth so close to her own. "Who would have ever thought that you would come to my very door? That I would find you in the last place you should ever be?"

His breath felt hot against her lips. Heaven help her

if he tried to kiss her again, for Cecily did not know what her magic might do.

"Since you're a woman," he continued, "I suppose you could not help but return to your home. That you thought your dear father would welcome you back to the fold after all these years? Poor thing. Don't you know he will kill you?" He lifted one hand and stroked the side of her cheek. "No wonder I was instantly attracted to you. All that elven beauty wrapped in equal parts magic. I could drown in those eyes... so very like your father's."

Cecily could stand his touch no longer. "I won't be your mistress, you... you libertine."

"My...?" The general froze for a moment, then threw his head back, blond hair flying over his shoulders, loosening his other hand so Cecily could gain some distance between his body and hers. He laughed, and as much as she despised him, she could not help but compare his laughter to some glorious song. Damn his elven blood.

Behind them, Cecily could hear the echoing laughter of the demons.

He wiped his eyes with the ruffle of his sleeve. "My mistress? And... and... libertine? Is that the best you could do?" He turned to a cupboard shaped like a curled shark and poured dark liquor into a glass, swirling it about while he studied her. "Devil take it, you are most amusing, Lady Cecily Sutton. For that is your name, is it not? And poor Breden thinks you were tested and destroyed by the fire lord himself."

Fletcher planned to kill her, then. But hadn't she known this the moment he'd taken Ellen? She glanced over her shoulder at the young woman, who sat very still between the two demon nymphs, her eyes wide with shock and terror.

She turned back to Fletcher, grateful that her voice did not shake with the pounding of her heart when she spoke again. "Let Ellen go. And I promise... you can do with me what you will."

"Ah, don't tempt me. You have no idea of my passion for the gentler sex. And you—I believe you would last so much longer than the others." He threw the liquor down his throat in one fluid movement and then cocked his head at her. "But I do not think that's what you were referring to, was it? Egads, don't make me laugh again. We haven't the time for such jocularity. I am not Breden of Dewhame. I do not seek your death. Indeed, if you but do what I ask, I will not reveal your existence to anyone. Including your dear father."

Cecily took a deep breath. "What do you want from me?"

His handsome face twisted in a mocking grin. "The scepter, my dear. I want you to steal Breden's scepter for me."

Fourteen

GILES LAY ON THE MAKESHIFT BED HE'D TUCKED INTO a corner of the weapons shed, his hands beneath his head as he stared up at the beams of the ceiling, remembering every detail from last night. The way Cecily had felt within his arms, the way his body had felt inside of hers, the feel of her water magic as it swirled around them. The ethereal beauty of her face by candlelight.

He muttered a curse and sat up, rubbing his cheeks with his hands. If he continued on like this, he would not be able to resist her invitation, should her messenger boy send one. And he had to protect her. Even if it meant protecting her from himself.

She could not see it now, past the first blush of passion, but he knew people better than she. Cecily would come to hate him for making her an outcast. And although the disease had spread no farther, he had no assurance that it would not overtake him some day, turning him into a complete monster.

He should never have allowed last night to happen. Giles had always been in control with women, but

Cecily had the ability to shatter him with only a touch. Faith, ever since that first day on the beach when she had come within touching distance of him, he hadn't been able to resist reaching out to her.

If he didn't think it would imperil their mission, he would tell Will that Cecily was here. Will would still be in love with her, and perhaps he could manage to gain her heart again. Then Cecily would quit pursuing Giles and leave him to suffer in peace.

Anger flared at the thought of Cecily with another man, but it did not stop him from wallowing in self-pity. And he knew he wallowed. It infuriated him… but sometimes he thought that it might be the only comfort he had left.

Giles had never thought much about his appearance, but he had apparently taken it for granted. Women falling at his feet. Little girls staring at him with large puppy eyes. Men casting him glances of admiration and envy. He had gotten used to it, had taken it for granted. And perhaps it wouldn't be so bad if he had suddenly lost his elven beauty and turned into a plain-looking human. But the contrast of his new life to his old was too great. Women looked at him with disgust. Little girls ran screaming from him. And his easy camaraderie with other men had completely vanished.

Ah, enough of this. He had best put his mind to better purpose, and try to figure out a way to meet the dragon this evening. He would not be able to meet Kalah in his tower; that would raise too many questions. But he'd asked around today, and discovered that the dragon sometimes went to his feeding grounds at night. The fenced pasture of cattle was located a fair distance from the palace, and he hoped the dragon would not mistake Apollo for a midnight treat. He had naught to do but wait until—

The sound of the door banging open roused him from his misery, and he called out, only partly grateful for the interruption. Few of the men would seek him out and he wasn't scheduled for patrol for several more hours, so Giles figured it would be Cecily's messenger boy, even before he saw him come barreling around the stack of swords.

Giles took one look at the lad's face and started to pull on his boots. Jimson had not come to deliver a message for some lover's tryst. He looked scared out of his wits.

"Catch your breath," he told the boy. "Then tell me what has happened."

One gulp. Two. "Fletcher's water nymphs. They took my sister. And Lucy went after them."

Giles cursed and stood, adjusting his sword belt. "Where? Take me to them."

The boy must have had a hefty amount of elven blood, because he spun and ran fast enough that Giles pushed to keep up. They sprinted over bridges and past fountains, around pavilions set up for the overflow of guests at tonight's ball. But the grounds were not yet crowded, and Jimson managed to keep to the shadows. Until they neared the palace walls.

Giles brought the lad up short with a hiss, ducking behind a small fountain, nodding at the two soldiers on patrol. The cheeky lad gave him a wink and did something with his hands, and disappeared into a sparkling mist. When Giles looked down at his body, all he could see was the outline of his sword.

"Bugger it," whispered Jimson. "It won't work on your blade."

"My sword has magic of its own."

"And it's stronger than mine. Can ye drag it along the ground so the soldiers won't notice it?"

Giles shrugged, but removed his belt and did as the boy suggested, scowling when the devil-blade emitted a whine of indignation at the ignoble idea of being dragged through the mud. The sound must have caught the guards' attention, for Jimson passed them with nary a glance, but when Giles followed the thick mist that had become the boy, one of the guards elbowed his fellow and nodded at the movement on the ground.

Giles froze as the two men came over to investigate. Despite the worn appearance of his sword, he knew one of them would try to take it, for sturdy weapons did not come cheap. So the moment they both stood over it, Giles drew it from the sheath and whacked one upside the head with the flat of the blade.

If Giles had not been so anxious for Cecily, he might have laughed at the look on the other soldier's face as the sword swung by itself in the air and smacked him as well.

"Jimson," he whispered over the men's prone bodies, for he could no longer see the mist now that he'd taken his gaze from it.

The lad materialized beside him and motioned him forward to the palace wall. Giles leaped to Jimson's side, watched as the boy placed one foot on a brick near the ground, pressed another high up over his head, and a portion of the wall slid open. They quickly ducked through the stream of water that constantly slid down the palace exterior and were plunged into darkness when the opening closed behind them.

"Now what?" asked Giles, who couldn't see two feet in front of his face.

"Forgot a lantern," huffed the boy. "Take the back of me shirt and hold on."

Giles strapped his sword belt back on and did as Jimson asked, hoping that the ceiling of the tunnels would be higher than his head. When he managed several feet without running into anything, he picked up his stride, urging the boy to go faster. The dank mustiness of the passages made it difficult to breathe, and Giles wondered that Cecily had managed so many nights of exploring these stifling corridors.

They passed several small round openings of light, the beams seeming brilliant in the darkness, but Jimson ignored them all until the passage angled upward and turned. The boy stopped and pressed his eyeball over the hole. He softly cursed, a phrase so colorful that it made even Giles's eyebrows rise up.

"Let me see."

The boy stood aside and Giles peered into a room decorated with enough seashells to blanket the shore of his old village. Mosaics of shells tiled the floor and walls in colorful patterns, but his attention quickly shifted to a pond surrounded by lifelike statues of sharks with open jaws and pointed teeth. Within the water sat two nymphs who appeared to be torturing a servant girl with one lethal-looking knife and both of their jagged claws.

Giles had never seen a water demon so closely before. They reminded him a bit too much of monstrous frogs, and he wondered if that's what the elven lord had used as a source to create them.

"Your sister?" whispered Giles, his attention back on the servant girl.

Jimson strangled out a "Yes."

"Where's Cecily?"

"Who?"

"Lucy. Where's Lucy?"

He felt the boy tremble. "The nymphs serve Fletcher. He might have taken her somewhere else. The demons will know."

"Right." Giles pulled his eye away from the peep-hole. "Is there a way to get into the room from here?"

Jimson's face floated like a white ghost in the darkness. "Never tried. These are *Fletcher's* rooms."

His tone indicated the madness of the thought. Giles smiled, and it didn't feel like a nice one. "Look for one. Now."

Jimson plastered his hands on the dirty wall, franti-cally pressing and poking. Giles joined in, although he hadn't the slightest idea what he might be looking for. Something that gave way beneath his touch?

"Water demons are nasty beasts," whispered the boy. "Beware those teeth, for their bite is venomous. Ahh." Something clicked in the stone, and Jimson kept his hand pressed on it while he continued to search with the other. "Claws are so filthy, I seen a man die from a scratch."

Giles's devil-blade started to hum and lift from his scabbard. He pressed his hand down on the pommel to keep it in place. His cheek burned, reminding him of the consequences of allowing a monster too close. "Do not worry, boy. They won't get near enough to touch you. Didn't you also push a brick at your feet to open the outer wall?"

A high-pitched scream came from within the room.

"Ellen," cried Jimson, kicking at the bricks of the wall. Giles couldn't tell which one opened the door, but with a rattle and a groan a crack appeared before them, spilling light onto the dirty floor. Giles shoved it open far enough to squeeze his body through and leaped across the room, landing in the pool with a burst of sprayed water, his blade flying to his hand.

He spitted the first demon like a fish on a stick and turned to the other who held the knife at Ellen's throat. Damn, the water demon had carved Jimson's sister into a bloody mess.

"Let her go and you live."

The nymph cracked him a malicious smile, those buggy eyes straying to the mark on his face. "Where did you come from, gorgeous?" Her gaze flicked to her companion who still dangled upon his sword. "I never liked her much." And then those buggy eyes widened as Giles's devil-blade began to feast, sucking the fluid from the body until nothing but a shell remained.

Giles flicked the thing off his sword with a grimace. "Where's the other woman?"

The demon carved another circle from Ellen's flesh, but Jimson's sister did not cry out, her mouth slack, her eyes glazed with shock. "As pretty as you are, I do not think I'm inclined to tell you anything."

Giles's sword absorbed the last few drops from the

other demon and twisted in his hand to point at the nymph, quivering in anticipation. "Touch her again, and I will let it fly."

Her eyes studied the blade. "Dark magic, that thing in your hand." She heaved a sigh and released Ellen, who would have slid beneath the water if Jimson had not appeared to drag her away.

"'Twas naught but a bit of fun, warrior. We do not concern ourselves with human ambition overly much."

"Then you won't mind telling me where the other woman is."

She licked her lips with a black tongue, displaying sharp green teeth. "You need more than a human female to properly appreciate such a handsome face." She slid her hands down her chest, over her scaled bosom.

"My palm grows slippery," warned Giles.

She shrugged. "La, you do not know what you are missing... no, do not release that thing! You humans have no idea of the powers that you fiddle with. The other girl is with mad Fletcher. Who else would take his next conquest to the Imperial Lord's chambers?" And she slipped beneath the water with a hiss.

Giles fought the pull of his sword and let her go, for he had given his word. His devil-blade drooped sadly in his hand and emitted a ring of disgust when he sheathed it.

Jimson had dragged his sister from the water and sat on the mosaic floor next to her, washing her throat and crooning words of comfort.

"What is the quickest way to Breden's chambers?" demanded Giles. The time for stealth had passed.

When the boy looked up at him, Giles noted with

relief that those blue-green eyes held steady. "Down the hall. Gold double doors."

Giles had already started toward the exit. "Use that disappearing trick of yours and get your sister far away from Dewhame." He stopped and pulled a sack of coins from his pocket, half of what Sir Robert had grudgingly provided him, and tossed it to Jimson. "Take her to Firehame. You will both be safe there."

The boy picked it up and weighed it in his hand. "What about Lucy?"

Giles drew his sword. "I will protect her. I have *always* protected her."

And Jimson saw something in Giles's face that made him swallow and nod.

Giles reached the door and stepped into the hallway. Silence. The guests would all be at the ball, but he had expected a few guards, especially outside the elven lord's chamber. He sprinted past a fountain of dolphins spraying water from their snouts, a statue of selkies tipping buckets over the heads of marble humans, and crystal-wrought mermaids combing their long hair beneath sparkling waterfalls. But not one living soul. The back of his neck itched as he approached the golden doors. They had been etched with a relief of a map of the realm, seven sovereignties dividing the land of England, looking like slices of a pie the elven lords had carved up at their whim.

Giles reached for the handle with his left hand while his sword jerked away from the doors within his right. He wanted nothing more than to throw the doors open and charge into the room, but the reaction of his sword made him cautious and so he slowly cracked open the heavy door, slipping silently into the Imperial Lord's chambers.

He only hoped his cursed blade would prove as powerful as Thomas seemed to think. It had not protected Giles's father from an Imperial Lord's wrath, nor his brother, John. But it would protect Cecily.

It must.

At first Giles could see little of the room—damn his human eyes. A low fire burned in the hearth of a stone fireplace to his left, a few candles lit a tall pedestal on his right, but the main source of illumination came from across the long room, from massive doors opening onto a balcony flooded with moonlight.

As his eyes adjusted, he regretted the sight. The walls of the room shifted in iridescent patterns that made him look quickly away in dizziness. Hairy plants surrounded a pond decorated with statues of giant squid, arms spread out to reveal the sharp teeth within the carved, round suckers. Water flowed down a wall behind a bed shaped of a clamshell and circled it by means of a trough carved into the very floor.

Moss grew on every stone surface, glowing a sickly blue with a luminescence of its very own. Giles watched his footing as he crept forward, sword aloft and breath shallow in his lungs. A mosaic of seashells covered the floor like Fletcher's room, but the moss hid whatever pattern it had been designed to represent. Giles glanced behind him. A pattern of his bootprints lay behind him, the glow of the moss extinguished by his weight.

Creepy place for an elven lord to live in. It made Breden of Dewhame seem even more alien to Giles.

How could he defeat an opponent he could not hope to understand?

But as he rounded a pillar of moss he realized that he would not have to fight the elven lord. Only his champion. For the room lay empty except for Fletcher and Cecily, who stood near the balcony doors, next to a slab of striated crystal. Cecily appeared to be trying to remove something from within the stone, the tip of it as vivid a blue as her eyes.

"Hurry up," hissed Fletcher. "He could return at any moment."

"It's stuck," she replied, giving another tug. "You should just be grateful that it allows me to even touch it."

"Fie, I can do as much. And once it's within my hands I know it will respond to me."

Cecily turned and gave him a withering look. Good girl. "You do not have the power of the storm."

"You do and deny it. I daresay that makes you a coward, Cecily Sutton. And if you want to see your friend again, I suggest you try har—"

"Get away from her," growled Giles.

The coxcomb turned and arched one white eyebrow at Giles, then made a show of adjusting the lace at his sleeves while those faceted eyes studied Giles from head to toe, finally centering on the green blotch marking his face.

Cecily breathed his name but Giles did not take his gaze off his enemy.

"And what have we here?" said Fletcher. "The barbarian from the soldier's barracks, if I recall. It would be difficult to forget such ugliness. Don't tell me you have some sort of designs on the chit?"

Giles took a step forward.

"Because I doubt any act of heroics will overcome that ugly face, soldier. And I would think that mark would have taught you to leave powerful magic to your betters."

"He's calling his magic," warned Cecily. "Giles, do not—"

With a curse, Fletcher backhanded her with as little regard as he would have given a mosquito buzzing about his ear. Cecily spun and smacked her head against the crystal, making Giles fear for her very life.

Giles roared and leaped, swinging his too-quiet blade. Indeed, his sword had seemed to balk at even entering the room. But the moment Giles struck, slicing open Fletcher's silken waistcoat and drawing the other man's thickly laced elven blood, his sword rang with delight and eagerness.

Giles had the satisfaction of seeing shock replace the arrogance on the general's face. Then a wet noose wrapped around Giles's throat and lifted him off the floor, holding him suspended in midair.

"A magic blade," muttered Fletcher as he clutched his bloody chest with one hand, the other wielding a whip of half-frozen liquid. "You've brought me a prize, you bastard."

Giles cut through the tendril of water, gasping for breath as he fell to the floor with a roll to break his fall. He flipped to his feet. "You'll have to take it from me, first."

Fletcher's mouth dropped open and he released his torn waistcoat, calling another tendril of water from the stone troughs, weaving his magical weapons before him like some mad street performer. "It can cut through my magic? Egads, I wonder if it could kill Breden? The possibilities boggle the mind!" And he laughed a laugh that made Giles wonder if the other man had lost a portion of his sanity.

Giles's sword followed the movements of the whips with a speed that surpassed even his own natural ability. The translucent tips did not venture past the point of his blade, but Fletcher pressed Giles backward, and he allowed it so enough space stood between their battle and Cecily's fallen body.

Fletcher stood next to the pond, draining the water from it as he continued to make his weapons thicker and heavier. He stood close to one of those hairy trees, and damn if their tentacle-like arms didn't appear to tremble just like his blade.

"I regret that I can't play with you longer," continued the general, apparently oblivious to the reaction of the plants. "But you see, Breden may return at any moment. And I really *must* have that sword."

Fletcher spread his fingers and those two thick bands suddenly fractured into thousands of curling, twisting coils. Giles's blade whipped into a fury of action, the like of which he'd never witnessed before. But too many slithered past his guard, twining around his ankles and creeping around his neck.

Giles waited, struggling to breathe. But he would have only one chance. He must close with Fletcher, allowing him little room to maneuver those magical whips. And if those trees were anything like his devil-blade…

He gambled on the depravity of the elven lords' creations.

Giles sliced through his watery bindings and made one prodigious leap. Straight at Fletcher. It took the general by surprise and he staggered backward, his gaze only for the devil-blade, the ropes of his magic mingling to form confused tornadoes above their heads.

But Giles had no intention of using his sword. He lunged sideways and pushed Fletcher into the grasping branches of the tree.

It did not take long for Giles to find out if he had guessed aright. Like the tentacles carved into the squid statues that surrounded the pond, the branches greedily wrapped around Fletcher and squeezed.

A deluge of water fell around them as the general lost control of his magic.

Giles blinked the water from his lashes, watching as Fletcher shriveled before his very gaze, until nothing lay within the branches but the husk of the man.

His devil-blade whined jealously at its stolen feast.

Giles ignored it as he staggered to Cecily's side. He feared to touch her. She looked as still as death. Faith, he could not lose her. She had become a part of him...

He knelt and placed a shaking hand against her neck.

Her pulse fluttered and Giles felt his eyes burn. He laid his mouth atop Cecily's head and breathed in the sweet scent of her. "My love... my love... please wake up."

As if his words held some very magic of their own, her eyelids flew open. "Ellen."

"Hush," soothed Giles, staring into those brilliant eyes, his heart nearly soaring with relief. "Ellen is safe. Fletcher is dead."

Cecily blinked. "What happened?"

"I rescued Ellen from the water demons and Jimson will take her to Firehame where they will be safe. As for Fletcher... I helped him stumble into one of the trees."

"Trees... around the pond... Jimson told me about them. He said they were squid trees and have suckers on their branches, and that Breden of Dewhame boasts of how they can drain a man's blood dry in a few heartbeats." Cecily sat up, wavered a moment, pressing a hand to the side of her head. "Jimson also swore that Fletcher did not have a lick of sense."

His mouth twitched. "The lad was right." Then he pulled her hand down. "Let me see." And leaned forward, feeling her scalp through the mass of her silken hair. "No blood, but quite a good-sized lump. Can you stand, or should I carry you?"

"Yes. I mean, no. I'm perfectly all right."

Despite her protests, he helped Cecily to her feet, and she leaned against him for a moment.

"You have saved me once again," she murmured into his chest. "I fear it has become a habit with you."

His chest tightened at the contrary thought that Fletcher had indeed managed to lay a hand upon her. That Giles *had* allowed her to come to harm, and that he'd been lucky it was only a bump on her head. And he could not speak for a moment.

Cecily pushed away from him with a frown.

"Now," she said, taking a deep breath, "the scepter."

"No," commanded Giles. "You're leaving this place."

"Not without the scepter. Isn't that what we came

for?" And without another word she strode to the crystal and began to tug at the thing.

Giles grumbled a curse, stepped past her to the balcony, and scanned the night skies. A dark, winged shape passed in front of the moon. He returned to her side. "We don't have enough time, Cecily."

"I don't know who is worse," she panted as she tried to wiggle the scepter free. "Fletcher, who enjoys the torture he inflicts upon people, or Breden of Dewhame, who views humans as little more than animals and dismisses their suffering. We cannot turn our backs if we have a chance to strike a blow for the Rebellion, Giles."

He could not help but smile. It appeared that Cecily Sutton had become as much a part of the Rebellion as Thomas had been. As Giles would always be.

"Then get out of the way," he muttered, hefting his sword in both hands.

Cecily quickly stepped aside and put her hands upon her hips. "We tried that once before…"

Giles swung his blade at the crystal. His sword skimmed off the stone with an indignant squeal.

"Damn," he muttered. Cecily was right. They had tried this before. Stupid sword had a will of its own. It had managed to shatter Thomas's tomb, but it had refused to touch the mountain of crystal… but Thomas had said the sword showed some sense, so perhaps harm would come to the blade as well if it cracked this stone…

But Thomas *had* managed to open a portal to the mountain with…

Giles reached into his pocket and pulled out the

crystal flute etched with music that he had taken from Thomas.

Cecily's eyes widened in understanding and a healthy dose of admiration. "Do you think it will work?"

Giles shrugged and sheathed his sword. "If I try and it doesn't, will you leave off? I thought I saw a dragon's shadow pass in front of the moon."

Cecily glanced out the open doors and trembled. It seemed she feared the dragon more than the elven lord himself. "Yes. Hurry."

Giles nodded and tried to memorize the pattern of circles on the side of the flute before lifting it to his lips. He had played a similar sort of instrument as a young lad, but had never been very good at producing music from it.

He blew one cautious note. He had not dared to play the thing until this very moment, for it reeked of magical power. And he had been right, for the one note that he blew had such force—such a haunting other-worldly sound—that the hair on the back of his neck rose. As he moved his fingers in the rest of the pattern, he wondered if the tune had come from Elfhame itself, for it resembled no musical composition that man had ever devised, filling the large chamber with a resonance that bounced off the walls and trembled the very air.

But the slab of crystal did not respond.

Then he remembered that Thomas had played it backward to shatter Sebastian's coffin and studied the pattern again. What issued from the flute when he played it once more grated upon his nerves, lacking any sort of harmony.

But a crack appeared in the side of the crystal.

As fissures spread out, Giles blew harder into the instrument, this time with confidence behind the discordant notes.

The crystal shattered into a hundred shards, the blue scepter coming to rest upon the top of the remains. Cecily reached for it without hesitation before Giles could issue a word of warning.

Touching it, and holding it within one's hands, might be an entirely different matter.

But the scepter seemed to sigh and settle more securely within Cecily's grasp.

"It feels so strange," she whispered. "As if it knows me somehow... No! You cannot make me!"

"What is it?"

For a moment, the top of the scepter crackled. Tiny flashes of jagged light danced about the triangular head. But then it faded and Cecily let loose a sigh of relief.

"It tried to call up all of my magic. The power of the storm. Oh, Giles, get me out of here so I can get rid of this thing. I... I do not want it."

He nodded, casting one last glance over her shoulder before grabbing her arm. This time he *knew* he saw a dragon's shadow cross the moon.

"This way." And he ran, Cecily keeping stride with him.

When they reached Fletcher's chambers, the dead body of the nymph still floated in the pool, but Cecily gave it only a brief glance. Her eyes glittered with satisfaction.

Giles made his way to the passage door. "Do you wonder if you could create one?"

"What? A water demon?" Cecily shivered. "It

never occurred to me to use my magic in such a way. Nor would I want to."

Giles closed the door to the passage behind them, in case the elven lord did not know of it. He prayed he could sneak her out of the castle before the dragon landed and Breden discovered what they had done. He had tasted the champion's magic. Cleverness and a gamble had won. His sword would surely be no match against the Imperial Lord himself.

Cecily took the lead through the passages. Giles offered no protest, for her familiarity with the route and her superior elven sight allowed them to travel quickly.

But she came to an abrupt halt when they reached the outer wall and he gently pushed in front of her. "I hope this opens the same way from inside." He placed his foot against the bottom brick and his hand atop another.

"No, this one," said Cecily, moving his hand to a different brick.

Giles closed his eyes against the feel of her small, warm hand atop his. He had thought he'd lost her this night. For the second time, he had been brutally reminded that he could not live in a world without her.

And then he turned and caught her up in his arms, unable to resist stealing a moment. He bent and kissed her, with all of the desire that lay within his heart, wishing he could make love to her one last time, for he did not know if they might live to see another day.

"I thought Fletcher had killed you," he murmured as he swept his mouth across her cheek.

Cecily sighed, her head falling back, allowing him

to nuzzle the sweet warmth of her neck. "I love you, Giles Beaumont. Nothing can ever change that."

He loved her too. More than she could possibly love him. But she would misunderstand if he spoke his feelings. She would think he was promising her a future together. And so he set her gently away from him and turned back to the wall.

She huffed. "We need a plan before you open that door."

"I'm open to suggestions."

"Jimson taught me this trick with mist…"

He shook his head. "Didn't work on my sword. I lay odds that it will not work on that scepter, either."

"Give me a moment, then."

Giles felt his clothes change from sopping wet to slightly damp, assumed she dried hers as well, for he heard the fabric of her dress whisper as she muttered something about her hair.

"That's the tidiest I can manage without a mirror," she said. "Now then, when you open the door, we shall casually walk across the grounds. Two lovers out for a stroll."

Giles rubbed his cheek. "No one will believe it."

"Nonsense. Open the door."

Giles pressed and it swung open, and they quickly ducked through the fall of water on the outer castle walls. He shut the door behind them, only their shoulders slightly wet again from the dunking.

He buttoned up his coat at the waist, allowing his hair to fall about his face, slightly obscuring the ugly mark. Then he crooked his arm and Cecily hooked hers through his. They casually strolled down the gravel path, avoiding the lighted pavilions, occasionally stopping to embrace whenever anyone else happened upon them.

Half of the guard and the majority of the soldiers would be attending their own revel tonight. Giles saw more than one uniformed man taking advantage of the moonlight for a private stroll with his sweetheart.

"Apollo and Belle are housed in the smaller stables," he murmured, guiding Cecily in the proper direction.

She turned her head and smiled up at him. "You brought Belle?"

He looked down, losing himself in the faceted depths of her eyes. "I thought you'd be happy to see her."

"I am. She's a fast little thing, and so very loyal..."

Something shivered between them. Perhaps the danger of their situation heightened Giles's senses—but he didn't think so. For a timeless moment his entire being focused on nothing but her, nothing but the joy of her arm within his, the beauty of her face, the wonder in his heart that she stood beside him, alive and well. He could not fathom that this may be their last time together. They had grown up so close and yet apart, and now—

"There you are!" interrupted a shrill voice. Giles glanced up to find a rather stout woman bearing down upon them. Damn—he should have never allowed himself to become distracted.

"Lady Pennington," breathed Cecily.

"Who?"

"I accompanied her family on the carriage ride to the palace."

Giles did not need to ask how that journey had

passed. He could hear the vexation in the tone of Cecily's voice.

Lady Pennington reminded him of nothing more than an overburdened cargo ship, lumbering from side to side, using her wide hoops for ballast, her peaked coiffure a mast with the feather atop it flapping like a flag.

"You naughty girl," said the lady, gasping for breath. "I have been searching the palace for you since we arrived."

"Whatever for?" blurted Cecily.

Lady Pennington smiled charmingly and clasped Cecily's hands. "Why, my dear, we had just begun to know each other and I wished to continue the acquaintance."

Cecily appeared thunderstruck, so Giles interjected. "I am sad to say, madam, that your reunion must wait a bit longer. We are on an errand of importance—"

"Pshaw!" she responded, tightening her hold on Cecily's hands. "There can be nothing more important than my friendship with dear Lucy."

Cecily narrowed her eyes. "What exactly is it that you wish, my lady?"

She smiled. "Good girl. Let there be no pretense between us. I have been admiring Lady Longhurst's new gown—why, it is the talk of the ball! But she has been extremely coy about her new mantua-maker, and insists her seamstress will sew for no one but her. Then *I* recalled that you recently came into the lady's employ, and easily put two and two together."

"How clever of you," muttered Cecily.

Giles shifted, glancing around impatiently. They

stood just beyond the pavilion and too far from the stables, but had attracted little notice as of yet.

"Indeed," replied Lady Pennington, missing the sarcasm in Cecily's voice. "That gown will set the latest mode and I vow to have one of my own. You simply must agree to sew some gowns for me, my dear. In honor of our shared journey?"

Cecily scowled, as if it would be the last reason for her to accommodate the lady, but she answered quickly in a valiant attempt at escape. "Yes, yes, of course I shall. But we really must be on our way." She tried to twist her hands from the lady's grasp.

But Lady Pennington only held on tighter, apparently possessing a degree of elven strength, if not magic nor beauty.

Giles resisted the urge to pick the lady up by her ruffled shoulders and toss her out of their way. Cecily, on the other hand, already appeared to have lost her temper. Giles caught the faint whiff of something burning and glanced about again.

"This shall take only a moment," insisted the lady.

"What?" snapped Cecily.

Lady Pennington lost her veil of charm. "Don't use that tone of voice with me, young lady. Why, after everything I did for you on our journey—"

Cecily choked.

"—I should think you could show a little gratitude. Lud! All I need you to do is come with me for but a moment, and tell Lady Longhurst that you have agreed to make me a gown. She keeps insisting her mantua-maker will work for no one but her—merciful heavens! Whatever is happening to your dress?"

Giles glanced down and realized the burning smell came from Cecily's skirts. Worse, a sparkling glow shone through the folds of the cloth, a crackling sound coming from the depths of her hip pocket.

Cecily impolitely cursed and withdrew the scepter; the tip of it shot jagged darts of lightning.

"Lud!" said Lady Pennington. "That looks like— what are you doing with—?"

Cecily mumbled something about her temper and called her magic, drawing a wave from a nearby fountain and dousing her burning gown and consequently, Lady Pennington as well, who gathered a breath and opened her mouth to astonishing proportions.

Giles drew his sword. Cecily's face whitened. "You cannot possibly—"

No, it would make him as bad as Fletcher. But if he just whacked the lady over the head, Giles would not feel too badly about it.

Lady Pennington released the scream that she had called from the depths of her bosom.

"Too late," snapped Giles, slamming the blade back into his scabbard. "Run."

Cecily lifted her skirts and sprinted after him, the scepter within the folds in her fist. Giles watched their backs, but it appeared the revelers were making such a loud noise of their own that they had yet to react to Lady Pennington's screams. This appeared only to infuriate her, because she began to scream louder.

The stables muffled the lady's cries and the dark solitude of the building seemed to give them a measure of safety. But Giles knew guards would be sent to investigate and he quickly went to Apollo's stall, pointing out Belle's for Cecily's sake. Gratitude for their journeys together filled him as Cecily saddled her mount as efficiently and silently as he did.

They led their horses to the open door. Cecily did not hold the scepter in her hand, and Giles hoped she had not tucked it away in her skirts again. A brief flash of light from a sopping wet bag dangling from Belle's saddle reassured him.

"I'm trying to control my anger and fear," said Cecily as she noticed his gaze. "I hoped it would stop reacting to me if I wasn't touching it. I don't understand why—"

"They went this way," shouted a voice.

"I'll check in here," said another.

Giles cursed as a young guard entered the stables, a lantern in one hand and his sword in the other. Cecily started, staring in surprise at William the shepherd, the man she had once intended to marry, now a loyal soldier of Breden of Dewhame's army.

Could anything else go wrong tonight?

Fifteen

GILES TRIED TO CONTROL THE JEALOUSY THAT FLARED IN his chest when the shock faded from William's face and turned into an adoring gaze.

"Cecily? What are ye doing here?"

"Will," she breathed in reply, "I thought I would never see you again."

His face flushed so deeply that Giles could see the color creep over his features even in the dim lamplight.

"I wrote ye," he said, "but ye never answered. This place… it is not what I expected."

"I… I left the village shortly after you did, Will. I did not get your letters."

Giles could not stand it anymore. "We have to go, Cecily."

Will appeared to become aware of Giles for the first time, breaking his gaze from Cecily and turning it toward the taller man. "So that's why ye came. I thought it was 'cause of the mark upon yer face. But it's because of her, isn't it? Ye have always mooned after her."

Giles narrowed his eyes, his hand shifting toward his sword, resisting the impulse to run the man through, but not because they needed to escape. No, it was burning jealousy that prompted his actions. Faith, hadn't he thought about bringing Cecily and Will together? And now that fate had brought about the meeting, Giles realized what a fool he had been to even consider allowing another man to touch Cecily. Will might hurt her.

Cecily stepped between them, placing a hand upon William's shoulder. "*You* left me, Will. And because you did not find what you were expecting is no reason to be angry with me, or with Giles."

He had the grace to look a bit ashamed. "Aye, but ye know I still loved ye."

Apollo nudged Giles in the back and he turned to stroke the horse's broad forehead, resigned to listening to this nonsense.

"But not enough," Cecily told him. "Not enough to stay with me—no, do not look that way, Will. I understand and bear you no ill feeling. Truthfully, it would have been a mistake for us to marry. I am not what you need and you are not... you are not the right man for me."

Giles hid a smug smile.

"I am even more different than I thought," she continued. "And it has made my life... complicated. We are on an important mission, Will. One that may help to free England from the slavery of the elven lords."

Giles turned. Grief etched William's features. But perhaps a bit of relief too. The man knew he could never have managed a woman like Cecily.

Will gave Giles a measuring look. "The guards are looking for a man with a green mark on his face. And a woman who some daft matron swears has stolen the elven lord's scepter."

"Indeed," said Giles.

Will's mouth dropped open and his gaze flicked back to Cecily. "Ye are right. Ye are more different than I would have ever—"

A shout from outside the stables made Will turn. He took one last glance at the two of them before he strode out the door. Giles mounted Apollo in one smooth movement while Cecily did the same with Belle.

"Ready?" he whispered, drawing his sword, regretting having to fight their way out.

She held up a hand. "Wait."

Giles could hear the soldiers shouting to one another. If they waited they would be outnumbered. And then he heard Will's voice rising above the others.

"There's no one in here, lads. But I seen two riders making for the southern gate!"

More shouts and a sudden flurry of pounding hooves followed his words.

Cecily grinned. "That means we'll take the northern gate, then."

Giles shook his head. "How did you know he wouldn't betray us?"

"Will has always been my friend before anything else."

Giles sheathed his sword and tapped Apollo's flanks with his heels. He suddenly felt sorry for Will, having to settle for naught but friendship.

They rode out into the empty paddock and around to the back of the stables, keeping the horses to a sedate walk until they cleared the grounds and reached the gate.

Water flowed along the walls, enhancing the illusion that the wave-shaped structure swelled like the ocean. Two solitary soldiers stood at the gate, both of them looking toward the lights of the palace and the revelry they were missing.

"What's your business?" asked the tallest, his gaze still fixed beyond them.

"My mother is ill," replied Cecily before Giles had even thought of what to tell them. "This kind soldier is escorting me to the city to tend her."

"Pity," said the other guard, giving Giles a brief glance. "I heard there's food and wine aplenty tonight."

Giles shrugged as he rode past them. "A soldier's lot, eh, boys?"

"Ah, damn," the guard continued, ignoring Giles's words. "Henry, the Imperial Lord has returned. I don't suppose we'll have as much merriment after our shift, now."

Cecily caught her breath and turned to look over her shoulder. Giles glanced back as well, his gaze drifting upward to the tallest tower in Dewhame Palace. Despite the distance, no one could mistake the silhouette of dragon wings as they landed.

They had run out of time.

Giles urged Apollo into a gallop once they left the guards' sight, splashing through the watery roadways of the city. The taverns were full—which fortunately left the streets empty, and they encountered only a few chairs and one carriage. Moonlight danced along the wet walls of the rounded buildings, played in the spray from the numerous fountains, and lit their way brightly enough that Giles did not fear for the horses' footing.

He headed for Bristol, one of the few ports with an opening through the magical barrier for trading with the outside world. Even though the Rebellion had the loyalty of a few captains and their ships, the port was so heavily guarded that Giles had worried about getting Cecily safely aboard the *Argonaut*, the small sloop that Sir Robert had arranged for her escape.

If the elven lord flew ahead of them and alerted the authorities, they didn't have a prayer.

He soon discovered he would not have to worry about it.

Breden of Dewhame would not allow them to get that far.

They had ridden for barely an hour when Cecily shouted and pointed above. "Those are not natural storm clouds."

He looked up. Where had they come from? A dark gray mass cut off the glow of starlight, gathering with unnatural speed. Soon, the storm clouds would block the moonlight and the horses would be at risk on this rutted road.

Breden had called a storm to hinder them until he caught up with his daughter himself.

A sudden glow lit the darkening night, and Giles turned to see Cecily holding the scepter within her hand, the top of it ablaze with those small flashes of lightning. She held it forward, illuminating their way.

Giles urged Apollo to a faster gait.

Thunder rumbled within those ominous clouds and a deluge of rain showered down upon them.

Giles cursed and slowed his mount yet again, glancing over at Cecily. Flashes from her scepter echoed in her eyes, wide with fear as they gazed into his own. Water plastered her hair to her head, poured down her face in a translucent sheen. He could see the outline of her legs within her sodden skirts.

The only woman he had ever known who looked even lovelier soaking wet.

"We cannot outrun them," she cried.

His chest squeezed at the terror in her voice. "The hell we can't! Keep the water from our heads, dry the road before us."

A glimmer of hope shone in her eyes and she nodded, waving the scepter before her. The rain abruptly stopped stinging Giles's head and shoulders. The horses' hooves no longer made squelching sounds in the muddy road, but pounded dry earth instead.

"That was so easy," she called. "The scepter—"

Thunder drowned her words and before them, just beyond the invisible dry barrier she'd created, the ground exploded with a burst of jagged light. Belle squealed and Apollo's legs abruptly tried to go in the opposite direction, his rump nearly lowering to the ground. Both horses then spun in circles for a moment, and Giles saw Cecily staring upward.

He followed her gaze and saw Breden and his dragon, Kalah, fly through the storm clouds just above their heads. Despite his dismay, Giles could not help but admire the beauty of the dragon. Kalah's gleaming scales rippled with blues of a thousand shades. Enormous wings battled the winds, the scalloped edges fluttering, the heavy tendons with a tracery of black outlining the rippling muscles. Like the head of the scepter, jagged light streaked from his open jaw.

Giles turned and met Cecily's gaze. She did not appear to notice the beauty of the beast in her terror.

"Giles, your sword!"

He drew his blade, surprised that it resisted his hand. It actually appeared reluctant to engage in battle—

Another streak of light crackled down from the sky from the maw of the dragon. Apollo reared. Giles held up his sword in defense. His blade reflected the lightning and sent it sparking back up to the dragon, who snorted as it unerringly hit his snout.

Breden of Dewhame screamed something, the dragon shook its head, and the elven lord held up his hands, which began to glow brighter and brighter.

Apollo and Belle finally stilled, their sides heaving with the exhaustion of fright. They did not know which way to run.

Cecily stared at him with terrified eyes. "He's gathering the power of the storm within his hands."

"I know. At least the dragon won't help him."

"Nor stop him. Giles, I don't know if I can do this. Breden… he is my father, after all. And I don't want to use this thing." She shook the scepter, the tip of it now ablaze. "The power of it is like a drug, one that I may lose myself in."

He could not bear the agony in her voice. On her beautiful face. He leaned over and stole a kiss, wishing he had the time to do it properly. "I am your protector, now and always. You know that means I love you?"

She nodded without hesitation, the wind whipping midnight hair across her face, her eyes filling with sudden tears. Perhaps she had realized it before he had managed to discover it himself.

Giles turned Apollo back in the direction they had come. "Ride on to Bristol," he commanded. "Don't let Breden have the scepter."

"I won't leave you."

Giles could feel the power the elven lord called. It shivered in the clouds above them, crackled in the air around them. He fancied he could even smell it, sharp and pungent like the stuff used to bleach wool. Even without the scepter, the Imperial Lord held formidable strength.

"Now or later, what's the difference?" he shouted back. Her face fell but he hardened his heart. Giles could think of no other way to keep her safe.

He smacked Belle on the rump. Now with a direction to run, the horse did not hesitate, blindly galloping forward. Apollo started, fighting the reins to turn and run after Belle. But Giles fought his head and kicked his flanks, lowering his upper body over the horse's neck.

And Apollo ran through the curtain of rain in the opposite direction, leaving Belle far behind.

Giles squinted upward. Breden's hands now appeared to be on fire with jagged streaks of lightning. Kalah flew back and forth, trying to decide which horse to follow. Giles wished he'd had a chance to talk with the dragon, to enlist the beast's aid. But perhaps Kalah had decided which path to follow, for the dragon did not pursue Cecily and the scepter.

Breden cursed and railed as the dragon swept downward after Giles. They now flew close enough for Giles to hear the elven lord's words. "The scepter, you stupid beast! Follow the girl!"

Kalah ignored the elven lord and spat a stream of lightning, the bolts bouncing harmlessly on the road behind Giles. Apollo ran faster.

Either Kalah had bad aim, or he was purposefully missing his target. But it looked like Breden of Dewhame would not.

Giles held his sword aloft, while his devil-blade fought to return to its scabbard. "Coward," he yelled at it. "Just because we can't win this fight is no reason—"

And then the world exploded around him.

His sword flew from his hand with the impact. He could see naught but white light. The hair on his head and arms stood up as a shaft of energy surged through his body. Giles's ears rang as he fell. And fell. In such dizzying slow motion that it was a relief to hit the ground.

He struggled to stay conscious, crawling to his knees. He had to put up a better fight than this. Cecily needed more time to get away.

Giles staggered to his feet, blinking his eyelids to banish the whiteness. He could not find Apollo. Better that the loyal beast had kept running.

His ears kept ringing. It took him a moment to realize the sound came from his sword, which lay in a patch of grass near the side of the road. He tried to leap toward it, and fell, mud splashing his face, covering his knees. By the time he held his sword in his hands again, he felt the buffet of wind from the dragon's landing.

Giles turned and faced Cecily's father.

Breden stayed atop his mount, his hands still glowing, but not as strongly as they had before he'd loosed that blast upon Giles. "It seems I have to kill *you* before Kalah will fetch my scepter. I'd be amused to know what you did to annoy him."

Giles stared into unearthly blue eyes, as brilliant as Cecily's but so cold they glittered like ice. The elven lord wore an embroidered coat of blue, with a scarlet waistcoat beneath, as if he entertained at some lavish ball. Lace tumbled down his throat and danced in the wind about his sleeves. His white hair sparkled with tiny silver flashes, as if stardust had been sprinkled within it. He looked almost as beautiful as his daughter.

Giles needed to keep him talking. It would give Cecily more time to get away. "Why don't you ask Kalah?"

One white brow rose. "The beast is oddly reticent tonight. But I daresay I have a more pressing question than that. What happened to my champion? Or did his human blood finally prove what an oaf he is?"

"Didn't your demon tell you?"

"I'm afraid that once my pet told me my scepter had been stolen, I lost my temper. It felt… glorious."

Sweat popped out in Giles's hand and he clutched his sword tighter. The coldness of the elven lord rivaled Mor'ded of Firehame, who at least had some humanity within his soul.

"*I* defeated Fletcher," said Giles. "Just as I shall defeat you."

Breden threw back his head and laughed, the sound like some musical notes of a dirge. "Ah, I wish I had more time to play with you, human. But I must retrieve that which is mine. Although, yes, let us see about this sword of yours."

And without warning, a bolt of lightning flew from his fingers at Giles—the full force of the charge that had unseated him within that single beam. His devil-blade managed to deflect a portion of it back at the elven lord, but the dragon lifted a wing and shielded the elf.

Giles wished Kalah would make up his mind about whom he was helping, here.

Pain shot down Giles's arm and it dropped to his side, his sword falling from numb fingers onto the muddy road. His devil-blade hissed as it fell, steam rising from it as the rain doused the metal. He almost felt sorry for it.

"You animals," said Breden, shaking his elegant head in mock sympathy. "When will you learn that the talismans you craft for protection will never stand up to an elven lord's power? I find it most amusing though. Rather like one of your monkeys trying to defend itself with a branch."

Giles fisted his left hand, for he wanted nothing more than to clutch his right and howl with pain just like the animal Breden accused him of being. The skin of his palm had blackened and the raindrops that fell upon it lanced him like shards of ice.

He had to keep the elven lord talking. Had to buy Cecily more time. But his brain felt addled and his ears kept ringing.

"What difference is there between my sword and your scepter? Talk about waving around a stick…"

Thunder cracked above and shook the very air. Giles thought he heard the pounding of hooves in the aftermath. Had Apollo returned to his master? But he could not look around. He dare not take his gaze away from the elven lord's cruel blue eyes.

"I can see why Kalah wants you dead," said Breden. Lightning zigged from one black cloud to another. The elf lifted his hand toward it as if gathering flowers for a posy and it flew to him, dancing about his hands. "Despite how amusing it is to find a human foolish enough to spar with me, I grow bored. 'Tis our ever-present burden, you see. After centuries of existence, life lacks any sort of challenge." He tossed the swirling ball of lightning straight at Giles.

Someone screamed.

Not Giles, for he'd been ready for the attack. Indeed, he leaped up and forward using all of the elven strength he possessed. As a result, the fireball barely grazed him, setting the tails of his coat ablaze but not altering his course a whit. He flew over the dragon's great head and hit Breden bodily, both of them grunting as they tumbled in a heap down Kalah's tail.

Breden's body burned hotter than an open forge. Giles rolled away from him, dousing the flames of his coat on the flooded road in the process.

A delicate hand touched his shoulder, and he looked up into familiar blue eyes.

"Dammit."

"Are you hurt?"

"What are you doing here? You're supposed to be far away... safe."

Cecily held the scepter in her other hand, the thing glowing an unearthly blue, crackles of light at its tip. "When will you understand that we can never be—?"

"So, it is you," said Breden of Dewhame.

The elven lord had regained his feet. Giles struggled upright as well, although he could not stand so steadily.

Cecily jerked as if his words had the weight to strike her down. Then she lifted her chin and glared at him. "Hello, Father."

"Of course it had to be you," continued Breden. "Only a human who sprang from my very loins would have the audacity—or the power—to steal my scepter."

Giles did not mention that Fletcher had managed to touch the thing. That knowledge might be to the Rebellion's advantage.

"You've led me a merry chase, girl." Breden's eyes glittered with—had he been human, Giles would have said that a bit of pride shone in those blue depths.

"Hiding your power of the sky," continued the elven lord, "has been a clever move. I'm sure I would have sensed a false storm and found you years ago. But alas, it seems you have found me, have you not? 'Tis a pity that I will have to destroy you. This is the most fun I've had in ages."

Cecily blinked at this little speech and Giles's heart ached for her. He knew she had harbored some small hope that her father would welcome her with open arms. That he would not be the monster everyone made him out to be.

"She can use it," said Giles. "The scepter accepts her. I suggest you let her go."

The rain ceased. Only its sudden absence reminded Giles of it.

Something flickered within Breden's eyes. Doubt? Or could it possibly be fear?

"Kalah," he commanded. "Get it for me."

The dragon shifted, scale sliding along scale with a grating slither. Those enormous eyes looked oddly similar to the elven lord's, but the color had been sliced into sections with jagged silver lines, like some badly cut pie. He shook out his great wings with a spray of moonlit water, and then folded them neatly against his sides.

Cecily, who had faced her father with a brave face, blanched as the great beast settled his gaze upon her.

"I think not," said Kalah, his voice sounding like boulders tumbling down a hillside. "You must prove it is your right to wield it, mad elfling." And he picked up his foreleg, studying his talons like a human would inspect his nails, dismissing the three of them with arrogant disdain.

Surprise crossed Breden's handsome features. And then anger. And then anticipation.

Giles stepped in front of Cecily. "I won't let you touch her."

The elven lord laughed, a melodic evil sound, and raised his hands up to the sky. The boom of thunder and the resulting lightning shot straight into his hands, making them glow.

"No," cried Cecily, ducking under Giles's arm and facing her father, avoiding Giles's attempts to shove her back behind his body. "I do not want this thing. I... I hate it!"

White brows rose.

"I shall give it to you. Just let him go. Let the man go."

"Perfect," barked the elven lord. "True love! Time and again I have seen it weaken you humans, and yet you still allow it to control your actions. Come now, Daughter, do not make this too easy for me." And with a flick of his wrist, a bolt hit Giles in the gut, knocking the air from his lungs and sending him flying backward.

Giles lost his vision yet again, but this time he saw nothing but blackness. Cecily's touch upon his forehead felt far away, and the sound of her voice seemed to echo in his head.

"Don't do this, Father. Don't force me to acknowledge my true powers. You will not like the results."

"You can't," spat Breden. "You might have elven blood running through your veins, but you're too human, my girl. Nothing but a sniveling coward of an animal, too frightened of that which you don't understand. It will be humankind's downfall."

Giles's vision started to clear. He raised his head. Cecily had stepped in front of his feet, physically blocking Giles with her body. He wanted to protest. It was his job to protect *her*. But his tongue would not work. Neither would his legs.

"In the same way that love will make us weak?"

Giles blinked. Cecily seemed to glow with her words, the scepter in her hand spitting forth streaks of liquid fire. Devil take it, the foolish woman would embrace the power she had rejected for so long. A power that she feared and loathed and thought would turn her into just as much of a monster as her father. All just to protect Giles.

He could not let her do it. Somehow he struggled to his feet. But the world spun and tilted at a crazy angle.

Breden of Dewhame did not hesitate. The sky rumbled again; Giles could actually feel the earth shake beneath his boots, and myriad lightning bolts flashed in the sky. The elven lord raised his arms to call them to him.

But Cecily had raised the scepter as well.

The lightning split. Half to Breden. Half to Cecily. They would destroy each other.

"No," shouted Giles. But the word issued from his throat as a gravelly whisper.

The world exploded yet again. Again, Giles was lifted off his feet and thrown backward, far beyond the road into a hedge of bushes that broke his fall.

Giles heard a man scream. In anger and sheer agony. Then silence.

A huff of wind warmed his body. He looked up into the luminous gaze of... the dragon.

"This is bound to happen when you fall in love with someone strong enough to wield a scepter," said the beast. "Can you stand?"

Giles nodded, although truly he didn't know until he managed it. He looked over at the road. Two bodies lay still within mud that steamed around them.

Something tightened his chest, his throat. He thought he might scream from the pain within his heart, if he could only manage it.

"She is alive," said Kalah. "So is the mad elf. But it remains to be seen if they are... undamaged."

Giles did not wait to ask what the dragon meant. He staggered over to Cecily, fell at her side.

Black smudged her nose. The front of her dress. She looked lovely, as if for all the world she did naught but sleep. Her chest rose and fell, but so faintly. She still clutched the scepter within her fist.

Giles leaned down and kissed her. Within that touch he put all the love he felt within his heart. All the apology he could manage for the way he had doubted her. Had he truly thought her love would not be strong enough to overcome something as small as a green mark upon his face?

When she would embrace a power she despised to save him?

"Cecily," he murmured. "Wake up, love. It is time to go now."

She did not stir. Neither did the elven lord.

"What's wrong with them?"

The beast's footsteps shivered the mud. He prodded Breden gently with his talon. "They have fried each other. The elven lord has always been mad, but managed to retain his faculties. It will be interesting to see how much of them remain."

Giles looked at Cecily in horror. "She will be insane?"

"Only time will tell. Why do you humans insist that we dragons have all the answers?" Kalah snorted a stream of lightning bolts and Giles flinched. He would never manage to sleep through a storm again. The beast curled his talons around the body of the elven lord and lifted him from the mud with a sucking sound. Those glowing eyes looked up at the sky. "The storm has cleared. Imagine that." And his wings spread to glorious proportions. A beat, and then another, making Giles hunch against the force of the wind he created.

And without another word, the dragon disappeared into the dark night.

❧

Cecily did not wake until they were in the cabin of the *Argonaut*.

It had taken Giles some time to gather the horses and recover his sword, and another few hours to reach Bristol and find the ship. He did not know how much time they might have. But Breden of Dewhame had looked even worse than Cecily, and he thought the elven lord might have suffered the worst from the encounter.

They might manage to escape after all.

The captain did not ask any questions about their haggard appearance, nor inquire as to Cecily's unconscious condition, apparently used to his missions for the Rebellion. He just quickly directed them to a small cabin below decks and went about the business of raising sail.

When a seaman brought two buckets of water, a bundle of cloth, and a little jar of ointment that smelled like herbs, Giles bade him thank the captain. The grizzly sailor nodded, staring at the mark on Giles's face, and then crossed himself in fear.

To his surprise, Giles found that he did not care. Cecily did not bother with such a thing, and only her opinion mattered. He just wished he'd realized it sooner. What if she did not wake? What if her eyes held nothing but madness when she did?

He tried not to think of it as he gently undressed her, frowning at the burn marks here and there upon her smooth skin. He gently washed her, rubbed in the ointment where needed, and spoke to her the whole while.

"I have been a fool. But you know that, don't you? I just hope you will forgive me. Wake up, dearest, so I can tell you what a dolt I've been. You would enjoy that, wouldn't you?"

Her eyelashes did not flutter. Her face looked serene and peaceful. Giles kissed her, but apparently he did not have the magic of a prince, for it did not wake her.

She still held on to the scepter as if it had been welded to her skin.

"I will not allow you to suffer because of me. You will wake and you will be whole. But... but if you are not..." His throat closed and he could not continue. But Giles knew he would not abandon her, as she had not abandoned him when he'd been touched by that wild magic. He would not allow her to push him away. He would feed her if she could not do it herself. He would dress her, care for her. Nothing would come between them ever again.

He would love her unconditionally. As Cecily had always loved him.

Giles gently covered her with a rough blanket, and began the task of assessing his own injuries, stripping off his clothing and tossing them in a corner atop Cecily's. Their cabin was small, containing little more than a bed and a cabinet that latched, and a lantern hanging from the beam in a ceiling so low that Giles had to keep his head ducked. He did not have much room to maneuver, and it became worse when the ship began to sway even more as the captain left the dock in the dead of night.

But he managed to get washed, and it appeared his hand had suffered the worst. He bound it with a clean cloth and glanced at the clothing the captain had provided them. Seamen's clothes that would be too small for him, and would manage to swallow Cecily whole.

Giles sat on the edge of the bed and brushed the hair away from her cheek.

"I love you," he said.

Her eyelids flew open. Panic and fright. He could not tell if madness lay in them.

He brushed his fingers against her hair with a gentle but firm touch, as he had soothed Apollo when he'd forced the horse into the ship's hold. "It's all right, Cecily."

"Where am I?"

"You are on the *Argonaut*. You are safe."

Her eyes grew enormous as she gazed around the tiny cabin. "The elven lord?"

Giles breathed a sigh of relief. She remembered. "He is alive. But Kalah said... Do you know who I am?"

"Don't be a goose. Of course I know who you are."

"Can you release the scepter?"

Cecily looked at her hand in surprise. Her fingers twitched. "They're cramped."

"Indeed." Giles stood and gathered her stays, the only piece of clothing that had managed to survive their battle relatively unscathed. "Can you drop it in here?"

Cecily shuddered. "Gladly." But it took her several minutes to unlock her fingers enough to drop it in the garment. Giles used the laces to tie it into a bundle and stored it in the cabinet, giving the latch a firm tug to close it.

Cecily sat up, holding the blanket over her chest, shaking her hand back to life. "Why did you ask if I knew you?"

Giles resumed his seat. "The dragon said that you and your father had injured each other, in a way that might have... addled your mind. Thank God you seem unaffected. But Breden of Dewhame. It appeared that he got the worst of it."

Cecily slumped. "I did not want... do you see why I have rejected that power all these years?"

"You did it to save my life," murmured Giles.

"I remember," she whispered. For a moment, madness flickered in her eyes and Giles feared for her. Until he realized he but saw the power of the storm. "I called the lightning. I felt it course through my body, my soul. It filled me with a might that compelled me to set it free. To destroy, to burn..." She shuddered. "I felt it when my father attacked me with his own power, but the scepter protected me. It wants to go home..."

"What do you mean?"

She shook her head, tears filling her eyes. "I don't know. I didn't want to know. I did not want the thing whispering its secrets to me."

Giles leaned forward and folded her in his arms, placed his mouth against her hair. "Hush. It is all over now. You have done a great service for the Rebellion. When we pass the barrier, the scepter will no longer have any power over you. Indeed, you shall have no power at all."

She pulled away from him, looked up into his face. "I have tried to deny it all my life, so it will be no great hardship for me. But you... you have always wanted to serve the Rebellion. I suppose you shall return to England after the ship leaves me in Wales?"

The thought of ever being parted from her again made him crush her to his chest. "I think I shall enjoy a good fight without the interference of the curse on my sword." His devil-blade hummed an angry protest from beneath the pile of their ragged clothing. "I imagine that I can still serve the Rebellion in Wales. They will need me to protect you and the scepter, at the very least. And our children will need a father to teach them of our enslaved land. I want you to marry me, Cecily. That is… if you can forgive me."

She tried to say something, but her words were muffled against his chest.

"I vowed to tell you what a fool I've been. I owe you that, and more. I should never have doubted your love for me. I was a fool to think a woman's love could be weaker than a man's. I took my own insecurities out on you, and I shall happily spend the rest of my life making atonement for it."

Giles relaxed his hold, placed his finger beneath her chin and tilted her head up to look at him, gazing into those faceted eyes, knowing that she held his soul within their depths. "I love you more than life itself. Can you forgive me?"

"Yes. I forgive you for all the nights we've wasted apart from one another. But you shall have to start making up for them. Now."

Giles lowered his head. "Your wish is my command," he breathed against her lips. And then covered them with his own. Cecily's arms flew around his shoulders, pressing them even closer together, if that were possible. He uncovered the rest of her glorious body, tossing the blanket on the floor and lowering her down to the bed. He had only one hand to touch her with, although he managed to use the fingers of his right to good purpose.

Cecily moaned and arched her back. Magnificent lady.

Giles covered her body with his, maneuvering on the small bed with all the elven skill he had. He stroked her breasts with his tongue while his hand stroked the nub between her legs, until he felt she was wet and ready enough to join with him.

And then he did not hesitate.

With one smooth movement he thrust inside of her and gasped while she moaned. Slick, tight heat. She dug her fingers into his back, pushing him against her, giving him the permission he badly desired.

Giles possessed her with a fury of need that had him pounding into her faster than the rocking of the ship. That had her calling out his name, thrashing her head and straining against him.

Giles strove to get inside of her as deeply as he could. Until he could not tell where he began and she ended. Until they became one in body as they were in mind, heart, and soul.

His pleasure washed over him as furiously as their lovemaking, Cecily crying out as her climax peaked with his. They drifted down to earth together, two beings as one.

Giles lowered his head and kissed her open mouth. "We became one long ago, didn't we? I was just too dunderheaded to know it."

Cecily smoothed the hair back from his face, coaxing it to lie over his shoulders. Giles did not flinch from her stare. She did not think him ugly. She never would.

"Hush, love," she whispered. "We have both been

wrong about many things. But now… now we have it right."

Giles slid beside her, tucking her body half over his so they would both fit on the small bunk. He felt the smile upon his face and knew Cecily spoke the truth.

Their love might be the only right thing about their world.

But nothing else truly mattered.

❦

A few hours later Giles awoke to early morning sunlight streaming through the open porthole, Cecily standing divinely naked in the middle of the cabin, small globes of water dancing through the window to twirl about her.

Giles crossed his arms behind his head and watched her play, a grin curving his mouth.

"You know," she said, after giving him a coy glance. "Now that I have discovered the joys of my magic, I think I will miss it."

The spheres reflected bits of sunlight within their depths, scintillating colors of the rainbow. They rollicked about the cabin, along the beamed ceiling, about Cecily's head and shoulders. Tiny dots of sparkling diamonds in swirling patterns, expressing her joy and happiness with a cluster here, bursting into a ray of stars, and a pattern there, twirling in a cyclone.

"We can always return to England."

She made a face. "I shan't miss it *that* much."

He laughed. "Come here, my little sorceress. I don't think I've finished making up for all the nights we missed together."

She made a pattern around his head, tickled his nose with a drop of moisture. "There, I have made a crown for you. Such a handsome face deserves to be crowned."

And she meant it. Giles saw the admiration in her eyes, the draw of his physical beauty. She did not see, did not care about—

Suddenly her small spheres of water fell about them like rain, spattering the wooden planks and thoroughly soaking them both.

"What happened?" sputtered Cecily.

"We have crossed the barrier." Giles kneeled on the bed and looked out the porthole, as if he could see a difference. But the magical boundary the elven lords used to keep England cut off from the rest of the world was invisible, and it did not look any different on this side of it.

He turned around and studied his love. "Do you feel any different?"

She shrugged. "I can't... feel the ocean anymore. It has always seemed to pulse in my veins."

Cecily looked bewildered. A bit lost. And entirely liberated.

Giles slid off the bed and crouched, felt for his sword beneath the pile of clothing. It did not jump into his hand. It did not whine for blood.

"It's just a hunk of metal," he murmured, looking down at his blade, his hair falling over his shoulders and hiding his expression from Cecily. His sword had always aided him in his quest for revenge... and yet had always been a burden. "I am free."

He heard Cecily rise and open the cabinet, the rustle of cloth as she removed the scepter from its bindings. "It still hums," she said, "but so weakly I can barely feel it. It cannot overpower my will, but simply lure it. Still, I think I would rather not touch it." She wrapped it back up. "I wonder what Sir Robert will say when we write and tell him we have stolen the scepter and removed it from England?"

Giles set down his lifeless sword. "Even more interesting is that Fletcher managed to touch it without harm. I'm sure Sir Robert will realize that *any* of the scepters can now be stolen, and the thief does not need the power to wield it to do so." He looked up at Cecily. "I predict the theft of many more scepters over the next few years."

She closed the cabinet and turned to look at him. Her mouth dropped opened, and she staggered back against the bed, falling atop the rumpled linens.

"Giles," she gasped.

He frowned. She stared at him now in the same way that strangers gaped at his blemished face.

"What?" he demanded.

"The mark. It's… it's gone."

He held up a hand to his cheek, even knowing he would feel nothing. He did not need a mirror. Cecily's face told it all.

"It wasn't a physical deformity," she continued. "It was created with naught but wild magic—"

"And we are beyond the bounds of magic," he finished.

Giles did not feel particularly altered by the sudden change. He no longer cared about the mark on his face. Cecily had taught him that love lay within the heart, and he would never forget it again. He tossed the hair back from his face and advanced toward her on hands and knees, a low growl of pleasure deep in his throat. "So I am back to my old handsome self. But the question is: will you still love me?"

She held out her arms to him. "Come and see."

About the Author

Kathryne Kennedy is an award-winning author acclaimed for her world building and known for blending genres to create groundbreaking stories. *The Lady of the Storm* is the second book in her magical new series, The Elven Lords, following *The Fire Lord's Lover*. Look for book three, *The Lord of Illusion*, coming to bookstores soon. She's lived in Guam, Okinawa, and several states in the United States, and currently lives in Arizona with her wonderful family—which includes two very tiny Chihuahuas. She loves to hear from readers, and welcomes you to visit her website where she has ongoing contests at: www.KathryneKennedy.com.

An excerpt from

The Lord of Illusion

Available from Sourcebooks Casablanca
February 2012

England, 1774

DRYSTAN HAWKES WOKE IN A COLD SWEAT, STILL seeing visions of fire and blood and death. He blinked his eyes to dismiss them, but as usual, he had also been sent another image and he could never banish this last one so easily. A young woman, beautiful beyond his wildest imaginings, with the most startling multi-colored eyes. Elven eyes.

Drystan untangled himself from his bed linens and raked back his pale hair, knowing he could not ignore the summons, for it was more than a dream or nightmare.

The three stolen scepters of the elven lords called to him.

His bare feet touched the cold flagstone floor and he suppressed a shiver, reaching for his stockings and boots, his own elven eyes quickly adjusting to the gloom of midnight.

"I would like to sleep through just one night," he muttered as he finished dressing, crossing the room of his bedchamber with nary a whisper from the soles of his boots. He had learned to be quiet on his nightly excursions. His fellow orphans already thought him strange enough.

Drystan carefully opened his chamber door, causing only a slight squeak from the old hinges, and peered down the long hall of Carreg Cennen castle. One lone candle shone near the privy, but the rest of the passage lay shrouded in shadow, not even a mouse astir this late. He had taken this same route every night since he had ceased fighting the summons, so he strode confidently to the stairs, thinking he could now manage it with his eyes closed.

He had found it easier to answer the call of the scepters at night, than to suffer the fits brought on by their visions during the day. He only wished he had conceded sooner. Perhaps then the other half-breed children would not have come to treat him like an outcast. Because of the fits brought on by the visions, Drystan had gained the reputation of being cursed, or mad, or at the very least, physically abnormal. And any offspring of the elven lords rarely suffered from lack of physical perfection.

Drystan never knew when the scepters would send him a vision but he would fight it until the world went black, and he would awake in the middle of the schoolroom—a meal—the play yard—surrounded by horrified faces and children crossing themselves against evil.

Yes, when the scepters sent him a vision, it was better to answer the call and find out what they wanted. And as a man, he had gained some control. But the damage had already been done, and Drystan lived his adult life almost as isolated as he had as a child.

Drystan shrugged, discarding his loneliness the same way he removed his greatcoat. He had learned to be content with his own company, had even turned it to an advantage. And he had his books.

His stories transported him beyond the walls of this old castle. Novels where he became a hero who rescued the fair maid. Where he sailed the high seas, fought against the armies of the elven lords. Became a secret spy for the Rebellion.

And inside his stories, he had many friends who did not fear him. Indeed, they admired his strength and cunning and bravery...

Drystan reached the last flight of the circular stairs and entered the kitchens at the bottom of it, slipping past the cook whose bed nestled up amongst the brick ovens, and silently made his way into the cellars. Past the barrels of corn and turnips, behind the wine racks, to the enormous oak door. He fished out his key from his left pocket and unlocked the chains, careful to keep them from rattling.

Not many of the castle residents knew about this chamber, and Drystan had only become privy to it because of his... connection with the scepters. An old prime minister for the king, Sir Robert Walpole, created this storage place for the Rebellion years ago, when he began to smuggle the children that had escaped from the trials of the elven lords to this old castle in Wales. The once-leader of the Rebellion thought it safer to store records and enchanted artifacts beyond the barrier of magic that surrounded England.

He thought they could be kept more safely here, where their magic would be inactive.

Sir Robert had been wrong, at least where the scepters of the elven lords were concerned. They may not have the power they would possess within England to enhance each elven lord's magic, but they still retained a certain amount of dangerous awareness.

Drystan made his way down the earthen stairs into the castle dungeon—which had thankfully been cleared of torture devices and heaped instead with crates and barrels holding artifacts and the private journals of spies, historical accounts of England, and secret correspondences between the leader of the Rebellion and his allies.

He strode past it all without a glance, straight for the small cell in the back of the room. Drystan withdrew another key and opened the door. Bare earthen walls, stone floor. Nothing to indicate the malignant treasure it harbored within.

Drystan collapsed on a square of stone in the center of the room and pounded it with his fist. "All right. I'm here. What the hell do you want?"

The air shivered. The hair rose on the back of his neck. When he had been a lad and the scepters had first called to him, he thought it was God sending him a vision. How very wrong he had been.

Drystan pounded the ground again. Buried beneath the stone lay the stolen scepters of three of the elven lords. The blue of the elven lord of Dewhame, Breden. The lavender of the elven lady La'laylia of Stonehame. The silver of Lan'dor, the elven lord of Bladehame. Drystan knew the story of the theft of the blue scepter, for the two who had stolen it, Giles Beaumont and his lady Cecily, lived in the castle of Wales. They had taken over the running of the sanctuary and the children who sheltered here.

The two half-breed elven who had stolen the lavender scepter, General Samson Cavendish and Lady Joscelyn, had returned to Firehame to continue to aid the Rebellion. And the Duke of Chandos and his warrior-lady Wilhelmina had returned to Firehame as well, after they had delivered the silver scepter into the keeping of Carreg Cennen castle.

Drystan did not know all of the details about their adventures in stealing the scepters, but he had read about them, and more importantly, had seen glimpses of them in his dreams. Dreams he did not welcome.

Except for the lady in his visions. He could still see those rainbow-colored eyes staring at him with such loneliness, and hidden fury. Large faceted elven eyes that seemed to echo the very feelings within his own soul. Those haunting eyes possessed all the colors of the scepters within them: lavender, silver, blue and green, with flecks of brown and black and gold. As if her elven blood held a mix of all seven of the elven lords and their sovereignties. And perhaps each of those powers?

Drystan spread his fingers over the cold stone. "Where is she?" he whispered. "I have searched and searched to find any record of her…"

The ground shivered. Another vision sprang into his head with enough force to make it pound in fury and Drystan clutched at his temples. Seven dragons flew in a maelstrom of color above the swirling blonde hair of a black-clothed woman. The air sundered with a violence that tore apart the very fabric of the universe and the lady watched it all with mouth agape in horror. Then blackness, and another scene. The same woman casting her hands over the head of a child, a flash of a symbol that Drystan could not quite make out branded onto the child's skin. And then a vision of another child, and another, each of them passing along the birthmark.

"I have looked for any reference to the descendants of the white witch of Ashton house," he said to the empty cell. "The records of the family disappear with the elven wars of the fifteenth century. The family was captured and enslaved…"

Another vision assailed him. This time of an ivory-haired child that grew into the beautiful woman with the multicolored eyes. Her delicate face so pale. So vulnerable. She wore a dress of white that billowed around her thin frame and she ran from something hidden in shadow. Something that threatened her. And he knew he must save her. He held her only hope and salvation.

Her eyes kept him spellbound until the vision finally faded.

And then the scepters spoke to him in words he could comprehend.

The descendant of Ashton House holds the key to the doorway to Elfhame. Find her.

Drystan jerked at the unholy voices in his head. Fire screamed through his every nerve, like knives shearing open each vein and filling it with acid. The agony grew until spasms racked his body, until anguish beat at his mind and misery filled his heart. Whatever awareness the scepters held, those alien thoughts were not meant for mankind to endure.

But they had spoken this message to him before, and Drystan managed to hold onto consciousness. A grown man of five-and-twenty years now, he did not collapse into convulsions as he had done as a lad.

It took him some time to find his voice.

"I have tried."

Although it had not been for their sake. Not just because they tortured him night after night. Not just because they would not let him sleep until he answered their summons. But for his own sake. For the lady who spoke to his heart with those unusual eyes. For the sheer desire he had to protect her. To hold her in his arms.

He had barely looked at another woman since she began to haunt his visions.

"I will not stop trying until I find her."

Seemingly satisfied, the tug on Drystan eased, as if the compulsion that the scepters used upon him to draw him into this chamber relaxed enough to allow him his own free will.

He rose, a bit unsteadily, but with purpose. As he did every night, he locked the cell behind him and made his way across the dungeon to the heavy oak table that served him as a desk. He lit the candles, throwing a halo of light around him, casting eerie shadows beyond that circle. He opened the journal that recorded the contents of the storage room and noticed a new entry, written in Giles's sweeping hand. A shipment from Dreamhame, procured with the loss of life of one of the Rebellion's most precious spies.

Drystan felt a shiver of anticipation from the direction of the barred cell, but he hardly needed the inducement. He blinked his own golden elven eyes, a testament to his ancestry from the elven lord Roden of the gold scepter, who ruled the sovereignty of Dreamhame with his magical gift of glamour and illusion. Outside of the barrier of magic, Drystan could not know the strength of his own powers within England, but he often wondered. He held the looks of the elven lord in abundance, from his white blond hair to the extraordinary strength and grace in his limbs. Despite the disdain of the other orphans, Drystan fancied that his own powers would put the rest of them to shame.

And he often wondered how he managed to blend into the background at will. How he could charm someone when he set his mind to it. These were instinctive gifts, surely, remnants of the power that awaited him in England.

Not that he would ever know. Unless...

He stood and searched the room for the new shipment. There, next to the stack of journals from Terrahame. A wooden crate that Giles had yet to open and catalogue. The master of Carreg Cennen castle would not mind that his curator opened and recorded the contents. Indeed, only Giles and his lady Cecily knew of Drystan's connection to the scepters, and his search for the lost key to Elfhame. They kept his secrets and shielded him from the curiosity of the other castle residents.

Like most of the other orphans, Drystan considered them his adoptive parents.

He dragged the crate over to his desk and pried off the lid. A small box sat on the top of mounds of loose papers and books, and when Drystan opened it, a flash of gold winked in the candlelight. A slip of paper described the enchantment of the coin within: it would appear as several coins, fooling any merchant who possessed less than a healthy share of elven blood that he'd received full payment for his goods. Drystan duly recorded it in the catalog, despite the hum of anticipation he felt from the scepters.

This crate contained something important.

Something that would finally help him discover the whereabouts of the descendant of the white witch. Drystan knew it as surely as he knew that snow fell beyond the thick walls of the castle.

He had felt the scepters' compulsion grow stronger over the years. Drystan was dismayed to think that it meant he'd succumbed to their combined will. But perhaps it had only been because he was close to solving the mystery of the whereabouts of the white witch?

He slowly removed the first stack of documents from the crate. He would not rush. He would not give *them* the satisfaction.

But the thought of finding the lady in his dreams made his hands tremble.

He read the first packet of papers. Reports from a man named Mandeville to Lord North—the current prime minister and leader of the Rebellion. North had come to the position as a member of the King's Friends, George the Third's attempt to gather control of his government. A government which held little actual power. The elven lords must be laughing at such antics.

They considered humans as little more than animals. Playthings to use in their elven war games, a pastime that cost the lives of thousands of Englishmen. Just to keep them entertained.

Drystan set aside the packet, recorded the contents, shrugging off the impotent rage that accompanied his thoughts. Despite all of the Rebellion's efforts, they still had not come any closer to freeing England from its slavery to the elven lords.

Although they had managed to save countless children. This was not the only castle in Wales that harbored orphaned fugitives. Lady Cassandra of Firehame discovered that the trials—the magical tests of power the elven lords put their half-breed children through—were a subterfuge for certain death. That the lords did not really send the children who showed exceptional magic to the fabled land of Elfhame. The tests were but a ruse to weed out those who might possibly grow into enough power to threaten an elven lord's rule.

Most of the children weren't truly orphans, for most had families in England, but they all felt and referred to each other that way.

Drystan had parents in Herefordshire County, but he could no longer remember what they looked like. He occasionally received letters from them, and knew he had a brother that strongly resembled Drystan, but apparently Duncan did not possess enough elven magic to be a threat to the elven lords.

Would he ever be united with them?

Drystan rubbed at his eyes.

If this key truly existed… if this brand the white

witch had emblazoned on all of her offspring held a clue to opening the door to Elfhame… Would they be able to send the elven lords back where they came from? Perhaps humans did not have the power, but by all accounts the elven lords were considered mad by their very own people. If they opened the door, would their kinsman come through and take the lords back home? Drystan did not know, but he knew the scepters wanted to return to Elfhame, and they thought that this key might accomplish that.

It might be England's only hope.

Drystan squared his shoulders, feeling the weight of his task, wondering why he had been chosen for it. And then remembered the girl and knew.

He felt he was the only man who could save her. Because he was the only man who knew her torture as his own.

Drystan picked up another sheath of papers and began to read. And then another, and another. Like every night for the past decade, he read until he exhausted even the strength of his elven eyes, until they burned and drooped and he could barely see the words on the page.

It lay at the bottom of the crate, of course.

He opened the leather journal, sighed when he realized it was just a household inventory of Dreamhame Palace from years ago. But the quiver he felt from the direction of the cell made him squint to focus his eyes on the entries. Linens, silver, candles. Gold plate, crystal glasses, silk cloth. And then in the kitchens: caskets of gin, bottled wine, sacks of wheat, cooking pans.

And a scribbled note at the bottom of the entries: three scullery slaves: M. Shreves, A. Cobb, C. Ashton. Ashton.

Drystan's eyes watered and he closed them, felt them throb in time to his heartbeat. How many times had he come across this name in various records? Hundreds. And each time it had failed to lead him to the line of the white witch. His dreams of blood and death would become more violent, as if the scepters punished him for that failure.

Such an impossible task, since Ashton House had fallen in an elven war game between Dreamhame and Terrahame centuries ago, its inhabitants scattered across the seven realms when their ransom was not met.

Had some of them have become enslaved in Dreamhame Palace?

He opened his eyes, stared at the entry. Blinked. *Witch* had been messily scrawled near the edge of the paper.

Had he indeed found the white witch of Ashton House?

Yes! Screamed the scepters in his head, rocking Drystan backward in his chair, the journal falling with a thump upon his battered desk.

And then he gracefully slumped forward, blackness overwhelming him from that final blow to a mind exhausted by years of sleep deprivation.

THE FIRE LORD'S LOVER

BY KATHRYNE KENNEDY

IF HIS POWERS ARE DISCOVERED, HIS FATHER
WILL DESTROY HIM...

In a magical land ruled by ruthless Elven lords, the Fire
Lord's son Dominic Raikes plays a deadly game to conceal
his growing might from his malevolent father—until his
arranged bride awakens in him passions he thought he had
buried forever...

UNLESS HIS FIANCÉE KILLS HIM FIRST...

Lady Cassandra has been raised in outward purity and
innocence, while secretly being trained as an assassin. Her
mission is to bring down the Elven Lord and his champion
son. But when she gets to court she discovers that nothing is
what it seems, least of all the man she married...

---

*"As darkly imaginative as Tolkien, as richly romantic as Heyer,
Kennedy carves a new genre in romantic fiction."*
—Erin Quinn, author of *Haunting Warrior*

"Deliciously dark and enticing." —Angie Fox, *New York
Times* bestselling author of *A Tale of Two Demon Slayers*

978-1-4022-3652-5 • $7.99 U.S. / £4.99 UK

It Happened ONE BITE

BY LYDIA DARE

✿

HE'S LOST, TRAPPED, DOOMED FOR ALL ETERNITY…

Rich, titled, and undead, gentleman vampyre James Maitland, Lord Kettering, fears himself doomed to a cold and lonely existence—trapped for decades in an abandoned castle. Then, beautiful Scottish witch Blaire Lindsay arrives, and things begin to heat up considerably…

UNLESS HE CAN PERSUADE HER TO SET HIM FREE…

Feisty Blaire Lindsay laughs off the local gossip surrounding her mother's ancestral home—stories of haunting cannot scare off this battle-born witch. But when she discovers the handsome prisoner in the bowels of the castle, Blaire has no idea that she has unleashed anything more than a man who sets her heart on fire…

978-1-4022-4510-7 • $7.99 U.S./£4.99 UK

SEIZE THE FIRE

BY LAURA KINSALE
New York Times bestselling author

"Magic and beauty flow from
Laura Kinsale's pen." —*Romantic Times*

AN UNLIKELY PRINCESS SHIPWRECKED
WITH A WAR HERO WHO'S GOT HELL TO PAY

Her Serene Highness Olympia of Oriens—plump, demure,
and idealistic—longs to return to her tiny, embattled land
and lead her people to justice and freedom. Famous hero
Captain Sheridan Drake, destitute and tormented by night-
mares of the carnage he's seen, means only to rob and abandon her. What is Olympia to do with the tortured man
behind the hero's façade? And how will they cope when
their very survival depends on each other?

"One of the best writers in the history of the
romance genre." —*All About Romance*

978-1-4022-4683-8 • $9.99 U.S./$11.99 CAN

Uncertain Magic

BY LAURA KINSALE
New York Times bestselling author

> "Laura Kinsale creates magic."
> —Lisa Kleypas, *New York Times* bestselling
> author of *Seduce me at Sunrise*

A MAN DAMNED BY SUSPICION AND INNUENDO

Dreadful rumors swirl around the impoverished Irish lord known as "The Devil Earl." But Faelan Savigar hides a dark secret, for even he doesn't know what dark deeds he may be capable of. Roderica Delamore, cursed by the gift of "sight," fears no man will ever want a wife who can read his every thought and emotion, until she encounters Faelan. Roddy becomes determined to save Faelan from his terrifying and mysterious ailment, but will their love end up saving him… or destroying her?

> "Laura Kinsale has managed to break
> all the rules…and come away shining."
> —*San Diego Union-Tribune*

> "Magic and beauty flow from Laura
> Kinsale's pen." —*Romantic Times*

978-1-4022-3702-7 • $9.99 U.S./$11.99 CAN